COMBUSTIBLE

ALSO BY HUNTER SHEA

We Are Always Watching

COMBUSTIBLE

A POST-APOCALYPTIC ROAD TRIP

HUNTER SHEA

Edited by My Brother's Editor

COMBUSTIBLE

So, this is how the world ended...

STAR CROSSED

YEKATERINBURG, RUSSIA, ON A WEDNESDAY, SIX MONTHS AGO

Maxim Lebedev was in love with Galina Aslanov.

He'd woken up early on a Saturday with a song on his lips. This alarmed his parents who were accustomed to their sullen teen who slept until the early afternoon.

"What has you so happy today?" his mother asked while she prepared breakfast.

"I must have had good dreams," Maxim replied, even though he knew why his heart felt so full.

Galina had told him last night that she loved him. The words, "I love you, too," had run out of his mouth in an unbridled torrent. The revelation left them breathless, but not so much that they couldn't make out for a while more.

"When will you two get a room?" his best friend Alex had said.

Maxim and Galina had been meeting at Alex's house for the better part of two months on account of Maxim's father despising Galina's father and vice-versa. The two men had grown up neighbors and friends, attending university together and working for the same engineering company.

Their friendship ended, naturally, over a woman.

That woman was Maxim's mother. She'd dated Galina's

father first and he had designs to make her his wife. But she'd fallen in love with his best friend and the two of them had been at odds ever since.

Of all the girls in Yekaterinburg to lose his heart to, Maxim had to fall for Galina. Maybe it was because she was forbidden fruit. Or maybe it was the way her raven, wavy hair framed her angelic face with its full lips and large aqua eyes that dropped him to his knees every time she looked his way.

No matter, it was too late now. They were in love and that was that.

"Can you believe how in love we are?" Galina said to Alex.

His face had scrunched up. "If you're going to start quoting poetry or something, you can both get out and take your chances with your fathers. You're not Romeo and Juliet."

"And why do you say that?" Maxim asked.

"She's too old and you're too ugly," Alex said, smirking.

The couple went into the small basement bathroom and clung to one another as if their lives depended on it. Should they separate, the laws of gravity would be revoked and life on planet earth would end.

"It should be tomorrow," Galina said.

Maxim's heart raced.

"Tomorrow. Are you sure?"

"If you didn't say you loved me back, then no, I wouldn't have been. But..."

"But where would we go?"

"Here."

"Alex has been great, but even he has his limits."

"I'll tell him I'll introduce him to Anna. He likes her, doesn't he?"

"Yes, I do!" Alex said from the adjoining room. "And it's a deal. But I have to meet Anna first. Maybe at the river walk."

So much for privacy.

Time moved with interminable slowness that next morning. Maxim grew restless, pitching in to help his mother clean the house just to burn up some excess energy. She grew more and more wary about her son's disposition, but appreciated the help.

After lunch, he practically leaped from the table, kissed her goodbye and slammed the door.

Outside was cold, which was nothing new, but the young lover didn't feel the bite of the wind.

Galina, Anna, and Alex were at the Iset River. It didn't look like Alex and Anna were hitting things off. They were the very definition of awkward.

That was not Maxim or Galina's concern.

After half an hour of forced conversation, Maxim gave his friend the eye.

"Keys," he whispered in Alex's ear.

"Oh, yeah. The keys. My parents are visiting my aunt and uncle and won't be home until late. But don't press your luck. Be out of there by five."

Maxim and Galina practically ran to Alex's house, hand-in-hand, bursting with their secret love and the anticipation of what was to come.

Alex heard Maxim's scream from a block away. He knew it was Maxim because they liked to scare each other at inopportune times and he'd heard his friend's distinctive screech more times than he could count.

"Something's wrong," he said to Anna, who was about as exciting as a bowl of borscht. He took off after his friend, turned the corner and went into shock.

Black smoke rose from the top of Maxim's head as if he were a chimney. Flames licked out from under his sleeves and the collar of his coat.

Galina, her mouth wide open but devoid of sound, tugged and tugged to get away from Maxim. Despite the fact that he was on fire, he wouldn't let go of her hand.

How could such a thing be?

Alex hopped from foot to foot, unsure what to do.

Galina's eyes met his, pleading him to help her.

He watched in horror as a line of flame ran from Maxim's

arm to Galina's, stopping just short of her shoulder. Her hair caught fire, and then her hat.

Alex whipped off his coat and charged the burning couple. Opening it so it was like a thick blanket, he tackled Maxim to the ground and smacked the coat, hoping to smother the flames.

Galina had finally broken free, but now she was running away from them, the fire consuming her from her waist to the top of her head.

"Galina!" Alex shouted.

She never saw the truck coming.

When it slammed into her, Galina's body hit the ground and skidded twenty yards down the street, leaving a zigzag conflagration that connected the point of impact with the girl's smoldering, broken corpse.

Alex resumed patting down his friend. Maxim groaned piteously.

"Hang in there, Max. We'll get you to a hospital."

No sooner had Alex stood to wave someone over from the accident scene than Maxim sparked to life once more.

This time, no matter what he did, Alex couldn't save his friend.

In the end, the case was labeled unsolved. The prevailing theory was that someone from a gang, or perhaps a deranged person, had set Maxim on fire and fled the scene. Unfortunately, neither Maxim nor Galina were alive to tell their story.

While he grieved, Alex kept thinking, *they were right, they were Romeo and Juliet.*

SHEPHERD'S PYRO
LIMERICK, IRELAND, FIVE MONTHS AGO

Kenny Culhane had one hellacious week.

On Monday, his supervisor at Shannon Airport had called him for a meeting before he'd had a chance to put his briefcase down.

It wasn't a termination so much as a layoff on account of the dip in arses in airplane seats. No matter what you called it, he was out of work.

On Tuesday, his lovely daughter Claire, the apple of his eye and pep in his step, had announced at the dinner table that she was pregnant. Sixteen and dating a lad who had the mental acuity of a stillborn donkey, she proudly told them they were keeping the baby. Said idiot baby daddy, who had plans to be Ireland's rap answer to Bono but could barely string three words together in conversation, was going to be "the best father in the whole world." That stung Kenny. The news nearly broke his wife, Margaret. She'd cried until she passed out hours later. Kenny fell asleep not soon after, embraced by dreams of sending the great white rapper dope to the bottom of the Atlantic.

On Wednesday, no longer able to handle the tension in the house, he'd stepped out to Nan's Pub for a swift half that turned out to be not so swift, not by half. When he returned, Margaret was in a state, having fallen off that rickety footstool and banging her leg up badly. There was blood and bruising and tears and guilt for his not having been there to get the serving bowls off the top shelf.

On Thursday, his car broke down a mile from his house. It sounded as if the transmission had given up the ghost. He pushed it all the way home in thirty-degree centigrade heat, all the while wondering just when his heart would burst.

On Friday, he and Margaret both went to Nan's and had a grand old time. Both were in need of a barrel of libation to ease the pain. It had been going quite well until Noel Smythe got too cheeky and went for one of Margaret's cheeks. Kenny, fully in his cups, took umbrage followed by an awkward swipe. In his state of inebriation, he'd forgotten Noel had been a right good boxer in his day. Kenny's clock was cleaned with cruel and swift efficiency. Claire had a conniption when she saw the state of him, letting him know loudly and in no uncertain terms that he was an embarrassment of a father and thank the heavens her baby daddy would never do such a thing. Never mind that baby daddy was high as a kite and smelled of weed and looked as if he'd pissed his pants just a wee bit.

So it was in a state of pain and disquiet and despair that Kenny Culhane found himself waking up early Saturday morning with a powerful thirst and a throbbing head.

But that wasn't what had awakened him.

The house was redolent with cooked meat. Not just any meat. This smelled as if it had turned. What in blue hell was Margaret cooking at such an ungodly hour? By the stench of it, he wasn't going to be fooled into eating it. Not on your life, Barney Fife.

He stumbled out of bed and rumbled to the bathroom, pulled his pants up and staggered to the kitchen. Thin, gray smoke wavered in an undulating layer a few inches from the ceiling.

He reached out to flip on the light switch. His hand came away coated with a greasy film.

"Jesus, Mary and Joseph!"

Half of Margaret's face sat atop a pile of ash on the seat of a kitchen chair. The wood of the chair had minor scorch marks, though the legs were free from any burn marks. On the floor were the remains of her left leg from the knee down and her right foot, encased in a slipper.

It looked as if the trio of parts left of his dear wife had been surgically removed and taken someplace else, then placed back in place where they belonged after the fire that had consumed her body died down.

To his horror and dismay, Kenny Culhane vomited a bucket's worth of lager on his wife's remains.

Once his stomach was empty, he promptly went to his bedroom, retrieved the small handgun he kept in his side drawer, staggered back to the kitchen and put a tidy hole in his head. His body was found by his pregnant teen daughter an hour later.

The scene was ruled murder/suicide.

History would tell a different story.

OUT OF FOCUS GROUP
SAO PAULO, BRAZIL, FOUR MONTHS AGO

Cristina Lima woke up feeling funny.

She couldn't describe it. Before leaving for work, she'd simply said to her husband, Silvio, "I feel funny."

Silvio, ever the corny jokester, glibly replied, "Better to feel funny than look funny."

A focus group moderator for over a decade, Cristina loved her job, even with all of the travel and long stretches away from home. She joked to her friends that those periods of absence were what made her marriage stronger.

On this day, she had the good fortune of having to conduct a full day of one-on-one interviews at a facility just a few miles from her house. The study was on erectile dysfunction, a tough recruit because Brazilian men were the most virile in all of South America, if not the world. At least according to them. Their wives and lovers knew better.

"*Ola*, Cristina." Raquel, the pretty young project assistant, greeted her at the door. Her too-white smile turned to a frown. "Are you feeling okay?"

Cristina blotted her face with some tissues. She felt fresh beads of sweat replace the ones she wiped away.

"I'm fine, thanks. Must be having a hot flash."

"I'll get you some cold water."

"Thank you. Which room today?"

"You'll be in A Praia for the morning interviews, then after lunch, I'll set everything up for you in A Cidade for the rest of the day." Raquel hustled off to get her water.

The interview room to A Praia had a pair of plush leather chairs with small side tables. The walls had been painted sandstone with light-blue accents. It was small but snug, a far cry from the old days of stuffy conference rooms with long tables and uncomfortable seating.

Cristina poked her head out of the room. "Raquel, can you please turn up the air conditioning?"

"Sure thing."

The first interview arrived fifteen minutes late and was escorted into the focus group room by Raquel. Cristina had unbuttoned the top three buttons on her blouse, revealing some cleavage and a bit of her lacy white bra. This was completely out of character for the moderator, who preferred to dress to 'blend in with the wallpaper' as she would say, so as not to distract the people she interviewed.

Beads of sweat dappled her breasts, neck, and face. The participant, a middle-aged man named Paco, couldn't take his eyes off the view offered to him. Raquel settled him into a chair and stood between the gawking man and Cristina, blocking his view.

"Would you like another water? I can turn the temperature down even more if you want."

Cristina smiled unevenly. "That would be nice. You can start the recording now, too. Thank you."

All focus groups were recorded, if not live-streamed to some market research department around the globe. Raquel hustled to the audio-video room and hit record on the digital system. She turned the thermostat down five more degrees and brought a cold water bottle to the moderator.

As soon as she closed the door, she heard Cristina's muffled voice as she explained to the respondent what would happen next.

Normally, Raquel would man the front desk and wait to check in the next respondent, answer the phone and respond to emails.

On this day, her overriding concern about Cristina had her standing before the video monitor in the back room.

"Can you please." There was a long pause while Cristina took a sip of water and pulled her blouse from her skin. The man leaned forward, unashamedly staring at her chest. He may have come in with erectile dysfunction, but Raquel was pretty sure it wasn't an issue at the moment. "Sorry, can you please tell me how often you...you...are you hot?"

The man shook his head. "No. It's actually kind of chilly."

Raquel saw sweat fall from Cristina's brow onto her legal pad.

"Okay, let's get back on track," Cristina said. "When were you first diagnosed with...with..."

A wisp of smoke curled up and out from the V in Cristina's blouse. Raquel squinted at the monitor. How could that be? Neither Cristina nor the leering respondent had lit a cigarette.

Cristina tried to gather herself, but it looked like she was going to pass out.

The man, his lascivious eyes finally growing concerned, asked her, "Hey, are you all right?"

Smoke was now coming out from under Cristina's skirt and the top of her head.

Raquel ran to the focus group room. Her shoe caught on a slight tear in the hallway rug and she fell face down, momentarily stunned. By the time she'd recovered and was on her feet, the door to A Praia burst open. The man rushed out, shouting, "Fire!"

The scene inside took Raquel's breath away. Cristina was engulfed in flame, her still body sitting upright in the chair. Pulse pounding and tears stinging her eyes, Raquel ran to the kitchen and snatched the fire extinguisher.

Blasts of foam extinguished the flames, but it was too late. The charred flesh of Cristina's blackened corpse popped and hissed.

The smoke alarm finally activated, dousing the room with fetid water.

Five hours later, the man who had been in the room with Cristina was picked up by police in his cousin's house. He was charged with murder, even though there was no evidence that he had set fire to the moderator. Simply put, she was alive when he entered the room, and burned to death when he left. He must have killed her.

Open and shut.

At least for a while.

PREHEAT AND BAKE
PRESENT DAY, WEEHAWKEN, NEW JERSEY

The human body burns at 1,800 degrees Fahrenheit in a crematory.

It seems a bit of useless trivia, and it was, at least until people starting flaming on six months ago. Now it's common knowledge, though there are no game shows to flex our mental muscles with such scientific minutia.

What caught my attention more was that another name for a cremation oven is a *retort*. All my life, I thought retorts were the weapon of choice for snarky assholes. I had no idea that Aunt Cecilia had gone all ashes to ashes, dust to dust in one.

Out of morbid curiosity, I watched a few videos of corpses being cremated. I read blog posts and industry papers. It was weird, I admit. Kind of like being obsessed with the mechanics of drowning while the continents sank into the oceans. Even the end of the world can't stop my natural inquisitiveness. I don't really feel any wiser having gained such insight, but a small part of me, the part that always needs to know, was at least satisfied.

In one of the videos, I watched a couple of guys dressed in what looked like homemade hazmat suits drop shrink-wrapped corpses into cheap boxes (hard to tell if it was pressed wood or a durable cardboard) and wheel them into these raging ovens. The camera lingered for a moment as the flames licked the top of the boxes before the thick steel shutter slowly came down, sparing me from further horror, and maybe allowing the poor, unnamed corpses in said box a shred of dignity.

Cut to a few hours later—I've since learned it takes one to three hours to cremate a body—and the flames are still roaring, but now the box is gone and all that remains is a jumble of bones and, worst of all, a skull. The crematorium tech used what looked like a regular garden rake to smash the skull to tiny pieces, along with bigger bones that I assumed to be femurs and the like.

What shocked me most was that even despite almost 2,000 degrees of punishing heat and flame, there was anything left. I honestly thought that fire, like love, was all you need.

Not so.

After the fire dims and the heat abates, they scrape out the ash and bone bits out with a broom or something that looks scarily like a pizza peel. Watching it the first time, I thought, rather morbidly, *hold the anchovies.*

All of those bits are then dumped into a processor until they are ground into a gray, gritty powder. The bereaved can them pick that powder up in either the equivalent of a glorified coffee can (for the smart and thrifty) or an overpriced urn.

It's illegal to just scatter ashes willy nilly anywhere you please, but that doesn't stop most people. I remember getting a cupful of my grandfather's remains at the racetrack when I was ten and surreptitiously dumping the sandy contents in the winner's circle. My father used to say it was the only time Grandpa had ever seen the winner's circle. Everyone laughed, breaking the uneasy tension. I had no idea what they were guffawing about until I learned later that the old man was one of the worst gamblers to ever place a bet. He'd died leaving behind a mountain of debt and a slew of red Solo cups filled with urine throughout his apartment. True story. And not a point of amusement or pride.

Cremation and dead bodies and pizza peels were never on my radar. I mean, why would they be?

But when people started bursting into flame, it became an obsession.

Or maybe better, an avid interest.

I mean, if your friends and family and neighbors suddenly turned into burned matchsticks, you kind of want to find out the why and how a body crumbles to its barest essence.

Maybe I was hoping to find an answer, despite knowing that thousands of people infinitely smarter than me were working on the, um, problem, and coming up with bupkus. It might have been arrogance or hopeful delusion on my part. It beat sitting around waiting to feel my skin get hot.

I'd never even heard of spontaneous human combustion—SHC for those in the know, and we all are now, whether we like it or not—until everything went to hell. Of all the things I thought would destroy the world, asteroids to nuclear war or a pandemic, people of all races, creeds, colors or status burning up like kindling had never been in the mix.

Spontaneous. Human. Combustion.

I mean, what the fuck?

No one saw that coming, except maybe a few crazies who liked to call into overnight paranormal radio shows. I like to think they were the first to burn. It has a kind of romantic appeal.

The entire world was ablaze and there weren't enough firemen to put it out.

It wasn't the meek that would inherit the earth.

Turns out, it would be the flame retardant.

HOT COPY

"You're stupid show is on."

That was the cue from my wife—at least for the foreseeable future—that I could come out of the bedroom and watch TV on the big screen in the living room. I had been reading an old sci-fi novel to pass the time and hadn't a clue it was so late.

When I entered the living room, I saw her back as she retreated to the bathroom on wobbly legs. An empty bottle of wine was on the coffee table along with a glass with just a dollop of red resting on the bottom. At least she'd had the courtesy to set the channel to CNN for me.

The intro music to The Kenny Silva Honesty Hour drew me like a siren's call. I plopped down on the couch and leaned forward with my forearms on my knees, hands fidgeting with the remote.

There was Kenny, hairsprayed to the nines, his face so full of Botox and fillers, he looked like a Macy's Thanksgiving Day balloon. He wore an expensive pinstripe suit, his tie looking high and tight enough to cut off ninety percent of the oxygen to his brain. Kenny couldn't spare the oxygen. The supposed pundit of the people, as long as the people were on one side of the looney aisle, looked into the camera, into our souls, and began his nightly newscast, or, as my friend Ramses said, half hour op-ed monologue bordering on an infomercial for the criminally ignorant.

My knuckles whitened as he droned on about the supposed grand malfeasance a governor had committed, calling for his impeachment.

"Look at you," Aja said from over my shoulder. I dropped the remote. Even tipsy, the woman walked around the house like a four-pound cat. "You look so uptight, you'll need to pop a box of Imodium just to fart. Don't you think you have enough stress without subjecting yourself to this blowhard every night?"

I sucked air through my teeth and tried to ignore her.

Kenny moved on to his support of updating the dictionary to include a half dozen new pronouns. I'd bet a majority of the people calling for such a thing couldn't pick out a pronoun in a sentence if they were given the noun and the verb.

"I'll never understand this for as long as I live," Aja said. She'd tied her short dreads back, holding them together with a bright yellow band. Her emerald eyes were glassy. I could smell stale wine and staler crackers on her breath.

"I never asked you to understand."

"What, do you have the hots for this guy or something?"

She was in her let's-press-Sam's-buttons mode. I wasn't in the mood. I hadn't been for quite some time.

"Hey, next time you're sexting him, ask him if he's into guys for me," I said, keeping my eyes glued to the TV.

"Screw you."

"Not on your life. That ship sailed, took a flaming arrow from the skies, burned up and sank to the bottom of the Mariana Trench."

"I bet you wish I was on that ship."

Now I turned around. I put on my best shit-eating grin and easily ignored the fact that Aja was wearing a low-cut t-shirt and short-shorts and was stunning enough to have been a model if she were just a few inches taller. "Well, look at that. A broken clock *is* right twice a day. You still have a few hours to be correct about a second thing."

Aja sneered at me. "You're a real asshole."

"If I am, I have you to blame."

"Keep throwing it in my face. See where that gets you."

Kenny slid into something about immigration. I was too distracted to indulge in my usual hate viewing. Not that I needed it, but in a strange way, it felt good to direct my ire at someone not living under my roof.

"I keep hoping it'll get me alone and happy, but the world is against me."

She threw some verbal jabs at the back of my head. I'd grown a callus there and nothing penetrated. A big drop of sweat ran down Kenny's face. I was going to tell Aja she was even pissing Kenny Silva off when the anchorman stopped midsentence, threw his head back and sneezed hard enough to send his earpiece flying.

"My apologies," Kenny said. He looked over to his right, probably at his producer, and winked. "Sometimes they just come on without not—"

Kenny's head burst into flames.

When his hands went to the sides of his face, they ignited as well.

The poor guy screamed bloody murder. The camera caught someone rushing to the desk toting a fire extinguisher just before the feed went to black for ten seconds, and then a commercial about incontinence.

I sat there with my mouth wide open.

Aja started to giggle. "Thank God. At least something good came out of this mess."

A slew of commercials played for the next twenty minutes. For some reason, I kept expecting Kenny to come back on the air with maybe some soot marks, a bit of hair singed, assuring us that he was all right. Everything was all right.

But it wasn't.

It hadn't been for some time now.

We'd all seen pictures and videos of other people going combustible, as the world had come to call it. I'd even walked by the blackened remains of some poor soul in the middle of the street one day when I was coming home from the liquor store. It smelled like barbecue and got garbage and his corpse was still smoking within the ring of stunned onlookers.

This was the first time I'd seen it happen to someone I knew. Not that I knew Kenny Silva. Not enough to tell anyone what he liked to do on weekends or his favorite cocktail. Years of hate watching the man had formed an artificial, one-way bond that had just been ignited like a devilish kid taking a lighter to a spider's web.

It was horrible.

Or amusing, if you were a cheating wife who only loved her phone and wine.

It sucks to say that watching a stranger you think you knew go combustible was the moment that really brought the whole dire picture home.

The whole spontaneous human combustion thing was something to worry about, but not so much me and mine. It was a problem others had to face. If it was actually real and not fake news. Kenny had warned us that it was all a hoax, some kind of false flag operation to keep people scared and happy to hand over what little rights they had left to the government.

"Shit."

I suddenly felt hot. And scared. I raced to take a cold shower. In the adjoining guest bedroom, Aja played some insipid game on her phone, electronic beeping and chirping stabbing me in the ears while I worried that if I didn't cool myself down fast enough, Kenny Silva was about to have company in either the burn ward or that great, white tunnel to the beyond.

TEXT

My friends enjoy mocking me and calling me a Luddite. Just because I don't have my phone or tablet permanently attached to my hands does not make me a technical ignoramus. I don't do social media (I mean, why would I want to talk to all the assholes I was happy to get away from when I left school in the dust, reconnect with old work colleagues or worse yet, interact with complete strangers?), take selfies, record funny videos or listen to podcasts. You'd never find me tripping down a YouTube rabbit hole.

That being said, I know what I'm doing when it comes to computers. I can order things online, take advantage of virtual banking, use Google navigation when I drive somewhere new, and hell, I'm on a computer all day at the office. And until recently, I practically lived in that office. My eyes aren't what they used to be thanks to all the hours spent staring at a monitor.

What I don't feel the need to do is share my life with every fucktard with a phone or peek into their fake, miserable existences. The entire world is anxious and depressed and the pharmaceutical companies love it. I'll bet you could graph

antidepressant prescriptions with the increase in internet pene-
tration and find they form a common curve.

Railing against technology gets you nowhere. My philos-
ophy is to use it when I need it, avoid the triggers to addiction
and keep my opinions to myself. Folks can do whatever floats
their goats. Baaaa.

I was very cognizant of the fact that Aja and her phone were
starting to become inseparable just before the end-of-year holi-
days. She'd check it repeatedly during movie night, when we
were out to dinner, every time we were in the car. If I woke up to
pee in the middle of the night, her side of the bed would be
bathed in the blue glow of that damned screen.

I'd ask her what she was looking at that was so engrossing.

"I'm talking to Sheila this girl I went to grammar school
with."

"It's just this stupid game on Facebook."

"Just one more video and I'll turn it off."

I thought my laissez-faire attitude made me enlightened.
Confident. Maybe even a little superior, if someone were to put
the screws to me until I confessed.

It actually made me stupid.

Aja made the mistake of leaving her phone on the bathroom
sink the night before Thanksgiving. We'd set the alarm early so
we could make the drive to our mutual friend Marcus's house in
Mystic.

I noticed the phone and picked it up to move it aside so I
could brush my teeth. It pinged and her home screen lit up. By
dumb luck, the screen lock hadn't been activated yet and my
thumb hit it just right when I grabbed it.

The text read:

U taking that shower yet?

I stared at the phone. What in the blue hell?

Follow up:

I want u to get all wet and soapy 4 me.

I can't exactly recall everything that was said from that

moment on. My ears rang and my body floated several inches off the floor. I was both numb and in agony as every pore felt as if sharp needles had been jammed into them.

Did I see red? Oh yeah. And black and a kind of fuzzy white that blotted out the edges of my vision for a spell while I screamed until my throat was raw and my temples pulsed to the savage beat of my wounded heart.

Aja angrily swiped the phone from my hand. The one thing I can't forget is when she said, "How dare you touch my phone!"

"How dare me?" I know my mouth flapped open and closed enough times to be comical. My brain misfired from being swatted by the most ludicrous thing I had ever heard. Eventually, I came out with, "How...the fuck...dare you...destroy our marriage!" Or something like that. Like I said, I was in a sort of blackout, but not the kind where you come to with blood on your hands, a body at your feet, and a neighbor pounding on your door.

Actually, our upstairs neighbor did give the floor a few raps with her cane. Mrs. Passick was so deaf she'd sleep through a fireworks display in her bedroom. It was a testament to how heated our argument became. And I didn't give a cat's cooch if she called the cops. I was the victim. Could I press charges against Aja for sexting? It seemed reasonable to me at that moment. Surely the cops would understand.

"Get the hell out of my house," I shouted when I felt my body and mind on the brink of a shutdown and just needed to collapse in a corner.

"It's my house, too. What are you gonna do, throw me out? Come on. I dare you."

My head spun. Who was this woman? This couldn't possibly be the Aja who grabbed my hand during scary movies or cried on my shoulder whenever she watched those commercials about rescue dogs or kids in Appalachia with cleft palates. This wasn't the Aja that had shared my entire adult life with me, the great and the rotten parts, and had often talked about how amazing it would be when we celebrated our fiftieth wedding anniversary many years from now, surrounded by the incredible family we were destined to make.

This Aja vacillated between a trapped animal and an apex predator.

There were no apologies. No asking for forgiveness.

She'd been busted and went on the offensive to keep me unbalanced.

"It's just texting," she said. "I never even met the guy."

"Oh, so that makes it okay? I should only be concerned if you got all wet and soapy while he was in the shower with you?"

"What?"

She hadn't read her cyber lover's last text. It made me feel good to see her brows knit like that. Aja was always so sure of herself. Moments like this, it was nice to see her foundation rock a bit.

"You're a real piece of trash. Throwing away ten years of marriage so you could sext someone who for all you know is a seventy-year-old lesbian from Romania!"

She rolled her eyes. "He's not."

"Oooh. And how do you know that if it's only texting?"

"He's sent me pictures."

I put my hands up. "Thank God! No one has ever been known to be deceptive on social media. I'm glad you made sure you got the perfect catch before chucking everything we built together."

"You're being dramatic."

"And you're being a whore."

It went on like that for too long. In an alternate universe, that spat continues in an infinite loop, neither side growing wiser or cooling down.

When we were both winded and empty and broken, Aja grabbed her pillows and our comforter and went into the guest bedroom, slamming our bedroom door hard enough to knock two pictures off the wall.

I had to drink a half a bottle of vodka to settle my nerves down. Bordering on drunk around one in the morning, I snuck into the guest bedroom and got ahold of her phone. It made a wonderful banging sound as it pinged off the steel walls of the garbage chute.

SEPARATE BEDS

The lockdown orders came pretty fast. This was well before Kenny Silva morphed into one of my favorite members of The Fantastic Four in front of millions of eyeballs.

RIP Kenny.

Ground zero for the SHC pandemic in the United States could be found in Bluffton, South Carolina. Sixty-year-old Buster Garabedian, a transplant from the Bronx, had just settled into his tattered reclining chair to watch the Atlanta Falcons game. He'd eaten a dinner consisting of frozen clams casino, pasta, and a side of escarole salad. He'd washed his meal down with a six-pack of Pabst Blue Ribbon. Since his stomach had been burned to ashes, forensics gleaned this information from the empty PBR cans on top of his trash, mingled with the frozen dinner box and plastic container containing bits of salad makings.

Half a glass of cheap bourbon was still in the glass on the side table, just six inches from the charred remains of Buster and his barca lounger. They said it was difficult to see where man ended and lounger began. Buster's feet and left hand were all that was left, the skin only slightly blistered.

Somewhere before halftime, Buster went combustible. No

one in his condo complex heard any screams. For some reason, the smoke alarm in the adjacent kitchen never went off. It wasn't until a neighbor walking her dog saw smoke billowing out from under Buster's door that anyone realized something was amiss.

Buster (with the exception of his hand and feet), the lounger and a bit of carpet were a coal-black pile of ash by the time firefighters arrived. The fire had extinguished itself. First responders noted a sickly odor outside the realm of their normal experience when stumbling upon a crispy corpse. The medical examiner drew attention to a greasy substance coating Burt's remaining extremities.

The fact that Burt Garabedian had a box of cigars on his mantle and one unlit stogie on the table beside his glass of bourbon led officials to list his cause of death as accidental. He must have had too much to drink, went to light his cigar and dropped the match on his shirt or the lounger. Once the chemicals in the lounger and his clothes, along with his own fat, had burned themselves out, the fire had nowhere else to go and just called it quits.

That would have been that if not for an army of Internet sleuths with little else to do. They started to ask questions.

Why was the cigar, which was right next to his burning body, still perfectly intact?

How come there was only a small burn mark in the ceiling and how did the rest of Burt's cheap furniture not go up as well?

Why were there no char marks on his extremities?

What exactly was the smell and what could they attribute it to?

And what about that greasy residue? Had someone doused him with a chemical and watched him burn? Digging through his online presence revealed a predilection toward gambling. The man loved ponies, cards and slots. Was there an angry bookie out there with blood on his hands?

Burt Garabedian's death had drawn more attention than anyone expected, but it didn't exactly go viral.

At least until Violet Martin, aged seventy-two, was found incinerated in her home a week later. Her whole left arm was resting atop the ash pile, her fingers drawn up as if pleading to the gods for salvation. Violet lived less than thirty miles from Burt in a cozy cottage in Savannah, Georgia.

Both deaths were mysterious (how did their houses not burn down?) and neither Burt nor Violet was the picture of health. Burt had diabetes and poor Violet suffered from heart and kidney issues. They both liked a drink with and after dinner. Burt puffed on cheap turd torpedoes and Violet, very much against her doctor's orders, snuck a Virginian Slim every now and then.

Now things went viral.

Spontaneous human combustion used to be fodder for poorly made TV shows in the seventies and eighties. Because most furniture made back then was seemingly of the highly flammable variety, the world assumed they were the victims of poor taste in places to park their carcasses.

Manufacturing had changed and the slight craze over SHC had died down.

Until Jenny Overton from Appleton, Wisconsin, an adorable ginger with a freckle face, ignited in a playground two blocks from her house. The second grader was playing with two of her friends when they said she just, "turned into fire." Jenny's mother had managed to put her out using her coat to tamp down the flames, but it was too late.

But it wasn't over. Jenny's body went combustible a second time while in the back of the coroner's van. This time, there was nothing left of the seven-year-old.

From that point on, there was a report of at least two people going combustible every week. It seemed to only happen in small towns with little to no witnesses to tell the tale of how it started. Kind of like UFO abductions.

SHC made the top of news feeds for a month after that, sending the foibles of reality stars and politicians to a hearty scroll down away. It was an almost perverted amusement for some, for others, an intriguing mystery. Sure, each was a tragedy, but it kind of made sense that it was happening to a bunch of yokels. Who knew what kind of shenanigans they were getting into in order to cut through the boredom of small-town life?

Naturally, the shit really hit the fan when SHC came to visit New York, Chicago and Los Angeles. Now the newscasts stopped playing X-Files music in the background of the stories.

Sensing a rising pandemic of sorts, the government went back to the well they had dug previously and shut everything down to stem the swelling tide of panic.

Just like before, it was a mistake.

With people sequestered in their homes, SHC still struck, only anyone sleeping next to a person who went combustible found themselves too hot to handle. The burning bed wasn't just some old movie. It was a reality, a fear that dogged everyone on the planet like a cloud of gnats.

In poorer towns or cities, with people crowded close together, entire families were lost. In some cases, buildings or whole blocks were embroiled in the mysterious, ravaging fires.

Those who had room to separate did so. Sleeping in the same room was socially and morally unacceptable. Polls showed that people were having less and less sex. A, sex meant you were in the same room. B, there was a growing fear that getting hot and sweaty led to going combustible. Better to wave at each other from across the room and conjure visions of the oldest person you knew giving themselves an enema to keep your hormones at bay.

Aja and I had been sleeping in separate rooms before it became the stuff of constant PSAs.

So, for once, we were ahead of the curve.

Score one for infidelity.

FRIENDS AND FAMILY

Aja and I may have had our fair share of differences.

She's Black, I'm White.

Her temper ran hotter than the sun's core, whereas mine takes a while to ramp up, and even then, you won't need sunscreen to stand beside my wrath.

She loves all the trappings of pop culture, from reality television to supermarket rags and saccharine music. My movie taste is stuck in the seventies ("You talkin' to me?") and I consume science fiction book series, the kind with teeny tiny print and lots of dragons, like they were Pringles.

She loves packed clubs. I prefer quiet bars.

We couldn't even find equal ground in sports. She's a huge Yankees fan. I'm Bosox, all day, every day.

When people meet Aja, they inevitably ask her if she's a professional model. Her flawless skin, green eyes, long legs and a lean body were certainly traits she could cash in on. I look like a guy who enjoys craft beer (which I do) and shops online for beard oil (again, guilty).

But there was one huge similarity that drew us to each other initially. Well, I know on my part, I was first captivated by her beauty when she was introduced to me at an after-work party by a mutual friend. How could I not be?

Aja and I are both orphans.

We had no family to speak of, unless you wanted to count innumerable foster families, which we didn't.

Being an orphan had felt like a hidden disability until I met Aja. For my part, the hurt of being abandoned lessened when I saw that even someone as perfect as Aja could be shunned by her parents.

Maybe being orphans is why we clung to each other so tightly. We felt we had to become our own family. Circle the wagons. Grow some roots.

Being orphans had its benefits.

When we got married (a ceremony of ten on a beach in Bermuda) there were no parents to ask us by the end of the wedding night when we were going to give them grandchildren.

Family drama was the stuff of fiction for us.

Now, with the way things were going with SHC, there were four less people in our lives to worry about. I couldn't imagine being separated from an older parent and fretting day and night over the state of their health. Had Mom gone combustible while making dad his morning oatmeal?

Our friends, carefully curated over the years, were our family. They were young and bright and funny and loyal. I worried less about them because like us, they were too with it to be anything less than invincible.

"How you holding up?" I asked when Dave Colon, my best friend, picked up his phone. We'd met working in a shoe store in the mall when we were eighteen. He now managed that very same store.

"I'm not gonna lie, this is freaking me out, man."

"Me, too. It's like something out of a horror movie. How's being trapped in your apartment treating you?"

"If I don't get out soon, I think I'm going to lose it. I would give my left nut—no, both nuts—just to be able to go to The

Rambler and tie one on with all of us having complete control of the jukebox. I wonder if that ass hat who hacked it is combustible by now. How are you and Aja holding up?"

I looked across the apartment at Aja. She was flipping through an old issue of *People* magazine. She must have felt me looking at her, because she threw a quick, I-know-what-you're-doing glance my way.

The day after our big blow up, she'd said, "I bet you can't wait to tell all your little friends what a piece of shit your wife is."

Those little friends were hers as well. Especially Dave, who had been the best man at our wedding.

Since that comment, I refused to give in and tell a soul. I wouldn't give her the satisfaction.

I sighed and said, "Hanging in there."

"At least you have someone to beat your meat for you. I sit on my left hand until it falls asleep just so it feels like someone else is touching me."

I couldn't stop myself from laughing. "You've already resorted to the stranger?"

"These are tough times. A man's gotta do what he's gotta do."

I could see Aja wasn't pleased that I was laughing, so I intentionally brought up old exploits with Dave that never failed to crack us up. When we hung up, Aja tossed her magazine down.

"He knows," she said.

I sighed. "If he does, it didn't come from me."

"Yeah, right."

"Believe me or don't believe me. Your perception of things is not my problem. Not anymore."

But I remembered when it was. And when Aja stormed into her room, I felt that emptiness, like an organ that had been surgically removed by an unskilled surgeon.

THE NOSE KNOWS

It turns out Kenny Silva did not die in vain. In fact, his fiery passing sparked the exact kind of paranoid mania that he used to rail against. He would have been rolling in his grave if there's been anything left to roll.

"Jesus, Sam, I think I'm gonna sneeze!"

Aja came running into my bedroom wide-eyed and terrified. She fanned her hands in the air and did a little two-step, all while trying to bunch up her nose.

I was working on a spreadsheet that if printed would wallpaper ten houses. My eyes were getting bleary and it was a well-timed break.

"Why don't you pinch your nose closed?" I said.

She drew in a massive gulp of air and tears started rolling down her cheeks. "I don't think I can stop it. I don't wanna die!"

I got off my perch on the edge of the bed and clamped down on her nose with my thumb and forefinger. For a moment she struggled against me and I thought she was going to slap the side of my head with one of her wildly gesticulating hands.

I don't think I'd ever seen her so scared.

"Shhh, shhh. Just calm down. Take a slow breath through your mouth. That's it. Now, let it out slowly."

We hadn't spoken to one another in three days. I couldn't remember what had set off the wall of silence. Not that it took much.

For a moment, at least, I forgot why I was angry with my wife and just wanted to take care of her. I put my other hand on the back of her neck and massaged it the way she liked.

"You're going to be fine. Every sneeze doesn't result in going combustible."

"Bud ebby combustible starts wid a sneeze."

"Nobody knows that for sure. They haven't gotten near enough data to be sure of anything. Most times, a sneeze is just a sneeze."

"Until it isn't."

Aja visibly started to settle down. Her hands hung at her sides and her nose wasn't attempting to flare as much under my fingers. I didn't think getting into a debate on the latest uninformed combustible conspiracy theory would help matters.

"Remember when I had that real bad sinus infection and you bought that neti pot because your friend at the office said it worked better than antibiotics?"

The makings of a smile turned the corners of her mouth. "Wendy said it worked for her fambly all the time."

"Wendy is a witch doctor. When I tipped the pot, that nasty salt water went right down my throat. I nearly choked to death. And you stood there laughing the entire time."

I let her nose go.

"Because I knew you'd be okay. Men are such babies when they're sick."

"Oh sure, laugh at the sick guy drowning in saline and snot water."

Aja's head reared back, and she snorted with laughter. Even I snickered a bit.

"Still feel like you have to sneeze?" I asked, wiping my fingers on the side of my pajama pants.

She shook her head. "No. Thank God. I was so scared."

"I could tell."

She wiped her tears away and walked out of the room. I shrugged and got back to my monstrous spreadsheet. Working from home was cool, but it also meant I worked longer hours than ever, which wasn't a bad thing. I needed the distraction.

A few minutes later, she popped her head back in. "Thank you."

When I turned around, my eyes were drawn to the tampons sticking out of her nostrils.

"What are you doing?"

"Not taking any chances." The tiny strings danced in the air as it was expelled from her mouth. "Here's a couple for you." She tossed two tampons in their packets on the bed.

"I'm not putting those in my nose."

"Suit yourself."

She disappeared back into her room. I looked at the tampons. Is this what the world was coming to?

Then I thought of the businesses big and small that were probably already pushing to get sneeze-restricting products into the freaked-out world. Whoever came to market first and whoever did it best stood to make a killing.

The spreadsheet called, and so did my boss from his home in Wyoming. It was his summer home somewhere by a river. When things started to go south, he picked up the family and went out west. I suspected he was doing more fishing than work. Good for him. I would if I were in his shoes, too. At least if I had a house in Wyoming, I could escape this apartment and forced confinement of two people who didn't want to be in the same continent, much less a twelve hundred square foot apartment.

When the video call ended, Aja was at my door again.

"I need you to come here."

I was going to point out that we were well past the days of her telling me what to do. But I was tired, and she looked ridiculous with those tampons in her nose. A little amusement would be a good way to end the day.

I followed her into the living room. She pointed out the bay window.

"Good to see Mr. Molina out and about," I said. The old man lived in the house across the street and had been a fixture in the neighborhood since Nixon had tamped the flop sweat off his face. The man lived for his garden, but I hadn't seen him in weeks. I'd assumed he was either in the hospital or worse. The usual lines of washwoman gossip had been cut since people were too afraid to get close to one another. I looked back at Aja. "Am I missing something?"

"He's been holding back a sneeze for the past five minutes. His eyes shut and his mouth opens, and he goes for that bandana in his back pocket. But each time, it dies before it comes out."

"So, you want me to stand here and wait for him to sneeze?" I wish I could have said I had better things to do.

"Exactly."

"Wouldn't it be more neighborly, or better yet, humane, to go down there and give him your tampons? Or at least warn him?"

She chewed on her full bottom lip. "I didn't think of that."

A lot of people had not been doing a lot of thinking lately.

"You think I should?"

"If you believe in the sneeze theory, then yes. It's the same as watching a blind man cross a busy street. You know something bad is going to happen. You're obligated to try and stop it."

She put her hands on her hips. "So why don't you go down there?"

"Because I don't think there's a correlation between sneezing and going combustible. However, the person stopping her nose's time of the month does."

Aja thought about it for a moment and I saw the resignation on her face. "Crap. You're right."

She was about to rush to her bathroom to grab some tampons when Mr. Molina let loose with a sneeze that should have knocked him off his feet. He wiped his nose with his red bandana.

"He looks fine to me," I said. I knocked on the window to get his attention. Mr. Molina looked around for a bit, met my eyes and waved.

"Huh," Aja said.

"Yeah. Huh."

Just for good measure, Mr. Molina sneezed again.

"Now will you calm d—"

The fire started at Mr. Molina's feet and raced up his body in less than a second. He was a spinning pyre of flame, the heat and smoke choking off his screams.

It didn't take long for his legs to give out. He fell to his knees, and then pitched forward. Black, oily smoke spiraled off his charring corpse. We both turned away. We'd already seen too much. There was no point calling the fire department. He was a lone combustible out in the open. It was too late to save him, and the fire would burn itself out.

To Aja's credit, there were no I-told-you-so's.

I found sleeping with tampons jammed in my nose difficult, but it beat the alternative.

RAMP UP

Naturally, if a sneeze could trigger SHC, it had to be a virus. The government threw billions of dollars at the medical community to find a cause and a cure.

So far, no good.

If people steered clear of one another for fear of catching a lick of flame or two, now they went full-on turtle and retreated deep into their shells.

"We need food," Aja said. She had the refrigerator door open, and I could hear mostly empty bottles and storage containers sliding around the shelves.

"Then place an order."

The spreadsheet had taken over my life, which was a good thing. I wasn't even sure what its ultimate purpose was anymore, other than to keep my mind off far darker things. Spreadsheets were mind-numbingly banal and there wasn't a person on earth who wouldn't give their right arm for a lifetime of spreadsheets about now.

"Don't you think I already tried that?" Aja was itching for a fight. I knew that tone. "The earliest delivery will be in two weeks. By that time, one of us will be eating the other after they drop dead from starvation."

I thought about how much food there would still be left if I had thrown Aja out when I found the texts.

She banged about the kitchen, griping and karping, opening and slamming cabinet doors.

"There's always the vegemite Dustin brought back from Australia," I said.

"You want it? You eat it."

"Trust me, I will."

That jar of pasty goo had been in the back of the pantry, unopened, for close to three years. Dustin said it tasted as bad as its reputation. Not being adventurous eaters, Aja and I happily relegated it to the pantry. If I remembered correctly, vegemite was packed with vitamins. It might be wise to just suck it up and try it.

Giving up on the kitchen, Aja slumped on the couch and turned on one of the twenty-four-hour news stations. Of course, just about every station was nothing but news about SHC.

She cranked the sound so loud, it charged like a bull through my closed door.

"All right! Enough!" I cried out.

Aja hit the mute button on the remote and gave me a what-did-I-do look. "What?"

I yanked open my t-shirt drawer and dug through it. "There has to be someplace that's open."

The Great Van Fleet shirt she'd bought me when we went to see them at the Palladium would do. I put scissors to shirt and created a makeshift mask I could tie around my head and cover my nose and mouth. I inserted tampons in my nose and was ready to go.

When Aja saw what I had done to the shirt, to the memory, her mouth opened for a second and then she turned away.

As I headed to the door, she called out from the couch, "Don't you want my list?"

I slammed the door.

A list. I was lucky if I could score a can of beans and maybe some clam chowder.

Outside was eerily quiet. We didn't live on a main road but even on a slow day, there was always a car or two driving down the block and people walking about.

The gray skies birthed a desperate breeze that had nothing better to do than scatter litter from one side of the street to the other. I walked past Mr. Molina's house with my hands deep in my pockets, expecting to see him pop up from behind his hedges.

I didn't want to be out here.

But I didn't want to be in there, either.

I wondered if Aja watched me from the bay window. Pride kept me from looking back. Odds are she was glued to the television, watching the horror totals tic up in real time.

A pair of dogs raced around a Honda Accord, its rear tire flat as a postage stamp. I spotted cats peering at me from hidey holes in shrubbery and narrow alleys. Had there always been so many cats in the neighborhood? Or had they lost their owners to SHC? At least now, if you went combustible alone with your car or dog, they couldn't tuck into you like a Thanksgiving feast.

Singa's Mini-Mart was just a couple of blocks away. I'd seen the news coverage in the big supermarkets. Pure chaos. Americans are greedy consumers. When we get scared, we need stores large enough to house the things we gorge upon.

Singa's just might have been overlooked by the panicked masses.

A glimmer of flame caught my periphery. A burning column of fire roared in an apartment across the street. I stopped, the aroma emanating from the building making my stomach roil. It's not that it smelled especially bad. In fact, it's the opposite. I'd been to a few pig roasts and the similarity flushed me with shame and nausea. I wished the tampons did a better job of filtering smell.

There were shouts within and then banging, followed by the distinctive sound of splintering wood. I watched a man rush into the room and douse the flames with a handheld fire extinguisher. I got to walking before the smoke settled. I had a pretty good idea of what I'd see and my day was already shit enough.

I hurried around the corner and almost whooped out a hallelujah when I saw the gate to Singa's was up.

My enthusiasm was tempered when I looked through the window. The place had been ransacked.

Singa, at least that's what I assumed his name was since he was always there, sat behind the counter reading an old newspaper.

"What happened in here?" I said.

The shelves had all been knocked down, glass to the cold cases reduced to pebbles, boxes, bottles and cans strewn about as if the entire store had been invaded by a mosh pit.

Singa, who had been old to begin with, looked like he'd aged twenty years. The bags under his eyes were dark and had an almost crispy texture. Those umber eyes held back tears that threatened to fall any second. He looked around the remains of his store in a daze.

"Humanity happened," he said, his voice, like his gaze, far, far away.

I put a fifty-dollar bill on the counter. "You mind if I see if there's anything worth saving?

"Keep your money." He either avoided my gaze or thought he was talking to a ghost. "Money burns. We all burn."

I snatched a reusable bag from the floor and got on my hands and knees, looking for anything that had been left whole. I came up with a box of elbow macaroni, a can each of beets, sliced potatoes and artichoke hearts, three bottles of off-brand water, and a box of stuffing mix. It wasn't much, but it was better than nothing.

I slung the bag over my shoulder. "Is...is there anything I can do for you?"

His eyes slowly found mine. "Yes." He opened his palm. In the center, I saw a tiny pile of black specks. "Run."

Singa dipped his head and inhaled the powder like a coke-head fresh from rehab.

The sneeze came instantly.

The flames seemed to burst from every pore of his body.

I jumped back and slipped on a pile of debris, sure that the heat had singed my eyebrows.

Poor Singa slumped into his chair and burned without a sound.

It took a few attempts to get to my feet and run out of the store. In my mad dash back home, my heavy breathing popped the tampons loose. I didn't stop to look for them.

I noticed fires in other windows.

The one that had been put out earlier was back, blazing again. SHC was like that sometimes. Someone on the radio had called it 'almost sentient.' It didn't like it when people put it out. So, it came back with a vengeance. This time, no one tried to extinguish it.

In fact, there were tendrils of smoke everywhere as far as I could see. And nowhere could you hear the sound of a single fire engine. What was the point?

Oddly, what disturbed me most was when one of the feral cats hiding under a car gave a loud sneeze. It burst into flame immediately. The fleeing blur of burning hair and flesh went headfirst into a wall, made a sharp turn and disappeared down an alley, leaving grayish smoke in its wake.

It smelled like Aja's hair when it got caught in the blow dryer. And spoiled meat on the barbecue.

Hunger wasn't an issue when you didn't want to eat.

ROAR

THE BRONX ZOO, THREE MONTHS AGO

Paulie tugged on his mother's arm.

"Come on, Mom! They're going to feed the giraffe!"

"Calm down, honey, we'll get there in plenty of time."

"But Mom!"

"But yourself. Here, drink something before you dehydrate."

Paulie took the juice box and sucked down some apple juice. He was sure they giraffe was eating right now and would be done by the time they got there. His mother was sooo slow.

A girl his age walked past him wearing a parrot hat. He wanted one, too. Maybe after the giraffe, they could go to the gift shop and get one. And then maybe find a concession stand that sold chicken nuggets. He was as hungry as a giraffe.

The crowd got thicker as they approached the giraffe enclosure. Paulie's mother had a death grip on his hand. He normally would have complained, but he didn't want to upset her and risk not being able to stay for the feeding.

What he saw as a problem was getting close enough to watch it. There were so many adults and kids packed around the rail, he'd need to get on his mother's shoulders to see anything. If his dad was around, that would be easy. Not so with mom. She wasn't as tall and strong and was always complaining about her bad back.

"Look, a giraffe!" he said, excitedly pointing.

Sure enough, a large adult giraffe gracefully approached the rail, staring at all the people with its huge, dark eyes. Paulie wondered what it thought of them. He hoped it loved him as much as he loved it.

His mother jostled through some people to get closer, but there came a point where they hit a wall of humanity.

Hands were held high with their phones recording the giraffe.

Forget the parrot hat, Paulie thought. *I want a giraffe hat. I hope the gift shop has one.*

The giraffe lowered its head until Paulie couldn't see it anymore. That frustrated him to no end.

Suddenly, the giraffe's head snapped up.

Its long tongue popped out of the side of its mouth.

It squinched its eyes.

And then it sneezed, splattering anyone close enough with giraffe boogers. Some people oohed, others screamed, and still others laughed. Paulie was one of the laughers.

That'll show them for taking up the best spot!

Poof, a cone of flame broke out on top of the giraffe's head. The fire quickly engulfed its head and ran down its long neck.

Now the screaming turned to screeching.

It sneezed again, only this time, the fire had turned the majestic giraffe into a dragon. Twin jets of flame shot out of its nostrils. Anyone within ten feet of the rail was set on fire. They ran, blind to where they were going, setting other people on fire.

Paulie watched it unfold in mute horror. His mother yanked his arm and pulled him off his feet. She ran as fast as she could from the wailing, stumbling human torches.

They just managed to get away, but not before hearing more screams throughout the zoo. Paulie heard a man say a lion had just gone up in flames. A woman said all of the gorillas were burned to a crisp.

His vision blurred by tears, Paulie couldn't make sense of what he was seeing. He guessed this meant he wouldn't get to go to the gift shop or eat chicken nuggets, and that made him sad.

Two weeks later, he was watching his favorite cartoon when one of those dumb special announcements broke in. Normally, he'd walk away. But this time, he sat in rapt attention as the old newscaster went through the list of animals that were affected by SHC.

Domestic pets like dogs and cats and hamsters were now considered dangerous to have around. Mice and rats, so far, appeared to be fine.

All large mammals, from tigers to rhinos and bears, could go up in flame any time. Forest fires raged out of control on every continent.

Squirrels and raccoons were safe from SHC, as were many species of birds. But some birds, like sparrows, blue jays an pigeons, were like flying hand grenades.

Lizards were flame proof.

Paulie hated snakes. It figured.

FALLING STARS

The first plane fell out of the sky on a sunny day in Portland, Oregon. The pilot, a thirty-two-year veteran of American Airlines, had apparently sneezed just as they were making the climb to cruising altitude. He ignited immediately, as did his nearby co-pilot.

When the plane crashed, it took out most of an entire neighborhood, claiming hundreds of lives on the ground, but very few in the plane because most people weren't leaving their houses to fly.

I watched the news report and felt my stomach drop as quickly as the plane. The whole disaster had been captured by someone using their cell phone. Thankfully, the video cut away before it hit the ground, though the on the scene news crew showed plenty of the burning wreckage.

That night, I sat by my bedroom window and watched several planes burst into flame and make death spirals into the area too far away for me to see.

All I could think of was falling stars.

I wanted to call Aja to watch it with me, to witness the end of man's conquering of the skies.

Instead, I watched it alone, and I cried.

HANGRY

Tensions ran high.

It was to be expected when you were starving and scared and living with the aftermath of a marriage betrayed. In a compassionate world, we would be living on other sides of the country, if not separate continents.

Close confinement did us no favors.

Aja would cry out, "We're out of paper towels!" with the kind of desperation reserved for someone on a sinking ship realizing the last lifeboat had hit the water.

Then she'd glare at me from across the room, into my room where I had stupidly forgotten to close the door.

After feeling her stare dig under my skin like nesting fire ants, I spun in my ergonomic chair and said as coolly as possible, but with enough simmering contempt to get my point across, "What do you expect me to do about it?"

"We should have conserved them." She waved the cardboard tube like a baton.

"We did. That's why I put all the dishtowels on the counter so we'd use them first."

Dirty dishtowels. That reminded me that we were running out of laundry detergent.

"I distinctly remember there being half a roll just yesterday. Where did all the paper towels go, Sam? Can you tell me that?"

Normally I'd give my entire epidermis to avoid this kind of fruitless, mind-numbing confrontation. But lately, I'd been leaning into the anger and found myself enjoying it.

"You might want to get a mirror and a flashlight and take a look up your ass."

Aja chucked the cardboard tube at me. It landed a good twelve feet short.

"You're such an asshole!"

"Take your drama to someone who gives a crap."

I turned in my chair so my back was to her. I flinched when her door slammed.

And then I smiled.

The acrid, porky smell of combustible smoke wafted into the apartment several nights later. I jumped out of bed, sniffing the air, searching for the source. When I went to turn my bedside lamp on, nothing happened. I yanked the blinds open to allow some moonlight into the bedroom. Opening the window, I took a deep breath. The slow, combustible burn of society was a constant now, like the faint aroma of a roaring fireplace an hour after it's burned itself out.

This scent was closer.

The streetlights were out, which meant all the power was down. I prayed there was someone left to try to get it back on but wasn't going to hold out hope. A few planes had knocked out power grids. Neglect and a lack of people to work them was taking care of the rest. We were lucky we'd had it this long.

Using the phone's flashlight app, I made my way out our door and into the pitch-black hallway. There were only four apartments on each floor and four floors to the entire building. The Sawyers next to us had been on vacation in Vermont when things got bad and never came back. Ed, the divorced guy— we'd never learned his last name—from across the hall was a firefighter. We hadn't seen him in weeks. I suspected the worst. As for Gilda and Jean down the hall, a pair of octoge-

narian lesbians who always invited me in to share their afternoon Budweiser, we'd heard from Ed before he disappeared
into the smoke that Gilda had gone combustible in her
doctor's office waiting for her quarterly check-up. Jean had
been sitting next to her when it happened. Her coat caught
fire, and she'd been rushed to the hospital to treat her for
third-degree burns. It was a race between time and a lurking
sneeze to get her.

In fact, from my last inspection of the building, there were
only a handful of people left. I'd go up and down the halls,
knocking on doors, asking if anybody was home and if they
were, I'd ask if they were okay. I only received muffled replies
from Mrs. Passick and Donte and Patti Rojas, who lived on the
same floor as Mrs. Passick. The rest had either fled or died.

Three hard raps on Donte and Patti's door elicited nothing
but silence.

"Donte. You still there?"

That left Mrs. Passick.

I shone my light onto the floor and saw fingers of oily, gray
smoke.

"Dammit."

Her doorknob was warm, but not blazing to the touch.

Maybe she'd left her oven on and went to bed.

"Mrs. Passick."

I knocked loudly. Even on a good day, you'd need to smash
her door with a battering ram to get her attention.

I took a chance and turned the knob.

The door was unlocked.

Smoke filled the small foyer to the right of her galley
kitchen.

A column of fire dominated the living room. It stayed
contained within itself, wrapped around Mrs. Passick like a too-
warm blanket.

She must have been burning for some time, because her left
foot had separated itself from her leg and lay on its side,
unharmed, clear from the conflagration.

I looked around for a fire extinguisher. The old woman didn't appear to have one.

The last thing I wanted was for the fire to expand and torch the building.

I dashed to her bedroom and ripped the comforter off her bed. My plan was to throw it on her and smother the flame. The heat, however, was so intense, I feared the fabric would only add more fuel.

I pulled a chair from her kitchen and propped it in the doorway. A quick rummage through her refrigerator landed me a bottle of white wine. I uncorked it with a steak knife and drank from the bottle, keeping a fire watch until there was nothing left of Mrs. Passick or the half of the couch she had been sitting on.

Drunk and satisfied that our home was safe for the moment, I stumbled downstairs and passed out face down on my bed.

Aja woke me up with a hard poke to my side.

"The electricity's out."

My temples throbbed. For a moment, I couldn't place where I was or who was the angry woman standing over me.

"Still?" I said, my mouth dry and tongue sticking to the roof of my mouth.

"We have to call someone."

"Be my guest."

"I forgot to plug my phone in. It's dead. Give me yours."

I looked at her incredulously. "You honestly think the power company has someone waiting to take your irate call?"

She spotted the phone on my bed and snatched it up. "It's better to try than just lie around like some loser."

I turned away from her, caught the sun spilling through my window. It was like being stabbed in the eyes with cocktail forks.

After a few minutes, I'd drifted off to sleep. Aja woke me again, this time shouting, "Ugh! It's just a recording that takes you nowhere! If we lose power, we're done. Do you fully grasp that?"

That statement told me I had grasped our situation well before her.

No power meant I was free from that spreadsheet. What was once a distraction had become an obsession, even though I hadn't heard from my boss for days.

I couldn't help but smile.

"What are you smiling at? I think you've lost it. Like, seriously."

"Ah, but I still have you."

FORAGE OR FAMINE

It had never occurred to us as we starved in our apartment prison to pay visits to the empty units in the building to see if anything had been left behind. We were not the Greatest Generation. Not by a long shot. I was amazed we had actually lasted as long as we had. All of our skills revolved around turning on electronic devices that did all the heavy lifting for us.

"How many bags do you have?"

Aja rattled the reusable shopping bag filled with other bags. "One-two-three-plenty. Let's just get this over with."

I'd insisted she come with me to help carry our pilfered goods. Was it stealing if everyone was either dead or gone, most likely for good? It sure felt like it.

We'd run out of tampons and had taken to jamming bits of fabric we'd cut from facecloths up our nostrils. Funny how you can get used to just about anything.

We went to the one apartment I thought would be our best shot. The Sawyers were a rambunctious family of five who had headed for the hills months ago. They may have assumed they'd be back in a few weeks and left some food behind.

Naturally, the door was locked, but I tried the handle anyway.

"How are we supposed to get inside?" Aja huffed.

"Like this." I kicked the area just under the handle as hard as I could. I didn't expect the door to give way on my first kick. I also didn't expect the shockwave of pain that reverberated up my leg on a one-way path to the top of my skull.

Aja covered her mouth when she tittered.

Now properly pissed, I kicked at it again. And again. And a few more times until my hip promised me that if I tried one more time, it was going to split in two.

Because I wasn't in enough pain, I stepped to the opposite wall, got a tiny shred of momentum and whaled my shoulder into the door. My teeth clacked and my shoulder made a strange sound that was akin to uncooked spaghetti being snapped in half.

Now Aja was outright laughing.

"You're all about equality. Why don't you give it a try?"

"Because I'm not an idiot."

She dropped the bags, went into our apartment and came back wielding the aluminum bat I'd bought way back when my company had a softball team. She held it out to me, handle first. "Have at it, slugger."

I grabbed the bat and thought of Ralph from The Honeymooners. I wiggled the bat at Aja and murmured, "Pow. Right in the kisser."

"What?"

"I said thanks."

I brought the bat down on the handle the way you swing a mallet at those strong man attractions at fairs. The bat vibrated violently in my hands and came back up at my face too fast for me to avoid. It made a hollow dinging sound as it connected with my forehead and I saw stars.

Reeling until my back hit the wall, I tried to focus my eyes.

"Open sesame," Aja said as she strolled inside with the bag of bags swaying on her arm.

The bat had been very efficient at getting us inside the apartment and eradicating several thousand of my brain cells. I staggered after her, disturbed by a distant ringing in my ears. I felt the lump start to erupt on my head.

It was bright outside and Aja had to open the curtains and blinds so we could see our way around. The place was in disarray. Not the *we've-been-burgled* kind. More like the field of detritus left in the wake of a young family.

First thing I noticed was the stocked bar. There were bottles of vodka, vermouth, scotch, and Jägermeister. If we didn't find food today, I figured I could at least go numb into that dark night.

Aja went straight to the refrigerator.

"You might not want to open that," I warned her.

"Why the hell not?"

She had to tug hard to get it to open. I knew the smell had smacked her good by the face she made. She quickly slammed it shut.

"I'm sure there's food that's gone pretty bad in there," I said, grinning.

"Wisdom from a unicorn."

I tapped my forehead bump and winced.

While I loaded up bottles of booze, Aja found boxes of pasta, mac and cheese, cans of vegetables, peanut butter, and an unopened box of crackers. It was actually a pretty good food haul.

My bag of booze felt like it weighed a hundred pounds. I carried it as if it were unstable explosives. The last thing I wanted was for a single bottle to break.

"Sweet!" Aja found a case of water in a lower cabinet, two big bottles of some sports drink, the kind that comes in colors not found in nature, and a brick of juice boxes.

"We'll come back for the drinks," I said. My head throbbed and I was sure I'd fail a sobriety test by the way I was walking.

"Oh, wait."

Aja ran toward the bedrooms.

She came back, shaking her head. "Pads. What grown woman wears pads?"

"I wouldn't know."

It took two trips to hustle everything back to our place. I collapsed on the sofa. The other apartments could wait. My head needed ice in the worst way, and of course, there was none to be had.

Despite my pain, my brain conjured up a ray of clarity that almost made me forget the pain.

"I just thought of something," I said to Aja as she stowed the groceries away.

"It must be dying of loneliness."

I didn't rise to the bait.

"The whole building is one big vacancy sign."

"So?"

"So, I think it's time you moved out."

HONEYMOON

The apartment was the first place Aja and I had ever lived together. We'd picked it out three weeks before our wedding, slowly moving secondhand furniture and engagement party gifts in between wedding rehearsals, picking up tuxes and dresses and all the last-minute madness that goes with modern-day nuptials.

I even carried Aja over the threshold the day we got the keys. We were giddy and excited and in love and were pretty damn sure it would be that way until the day we died. We split a six-pack of some craft beer I'd bought at a gas station and made love on the bathroom sink. And the kitchen sink. And the living room floor after I'd laid down some comforters.

Two bedrooms seemed to us at the time an extravagance. It was, considering we were fresh out of college and owners of next to nothing. We designated the second bedroom a party room. I'd bought an old ping-pong table from a garage sale and we used it to play beer pong when our friends came over, which was often at the time. Aja bought a karaoke machine that we set on a table in the corner, and I found a mini fridge at a yard sale that we filled with cans of IPA.

Thinking back on it now, we were the worst of neighbors—

young, loud, and irresponsible. The wedding party rolled into the honeymoon bash that slid into the after-work chill out and weekend party hearty scene.

There were complaints, and to our credit, we settled down when it was brought to our attention that it was late and we were getting obnoxious.

I loved waking up to us both naked and a little hungover, counting the hours at our middling jobs until we could be with each other and either party for two or have the gang over (where partying for two ensued later).

"Do you know how much I love you?" Aja would say, her bronze skin shining by the sunlight streaming through our window. She was the most beautiful woman I had ever seen, and I still woke up sometimes wondering if it had all just been a dream.

"No. How much?"

She'd hold her thumb and index finger as close together as she could without them touching.

"That's not a whole lot. Should I be worried?"

Giggling, Aja would say, "No. It goes from the back of my thumb all the way through infinity and to my pointer finger."

She smelled and tasted like coconut and her moans alone got me to recounting the football highlights, and when that wouldn't work, the scowling faces of the nuns in my grammar school.

"We should really start saving for a house," I said one day while we ate oatmeal at the kitchen table, each of us reading the Sunday paper on our tablets.

"Why? We have everything we need right here."

"Yeah, but renting is a sucker's game. The smart thing is to buy and build equity."

"You don't even know what that means."

"Yes, I do. At some point, we need to think about our future."

She put her tablet down, pushed the chair out from under the table, stood and let her silk robe drop to the floor. "This is our future. You and me. Nothing else matters. We'll always find a way. Now get those clothes off before I finish what I started all by myself."

It took two years before the party room became the office. I'd gotten a promotion at work and could work remotely from time to time. Aja went from drawing random doodles to taking her art, a natural gift with no training, seriously. We split the room down the middle and could do our thing simultaneously in the room without disturbing one another because, well, because we wanted to be close, all the time.

Afternoon delight was more than just a song.

Until we wanted a baby.

Then it became a chore, especially when nothing happened right away. The joy of sex without a condom was short-lived. Then it was ovulation charts and taking temperatures and timing. I'd almost crashed my car racing home one afternoon because Aja had called and said we had to do it right away.

In the end, and after some nervous consultations with doctors, it was down to me. Not enough swimmers on the team. Insurance didn't cover procedures that could have helped, nor did it lend a dime of help toward adoption.

Why do they make adopting children—children that desperately need a loving home—so expensive? The system should pay people to adopt them, not the other way around.

I digress.

That was the official end of the honeymoon.

Things were different after that, but my love for Aja never changed. No matter how many times she told me she didn't resent me, I could never fully believe her. Was I projecting? Probably. Most likely. It didn't matter. I couldn't change the way I felt.

Marriage was easy until we had to work at it.

There was love. There would always be love. There just wasn't always fireworks and orgasms. Work life grinds you down. Becoming responsible adults grinds you down. Realizing you would never have children of your own did more than grind you down, it hollowed you out. It murdered a hope. A dream.

Like all married couples, we fell into a routine—and not the fun kind that involved beer pong and going to work drained and still buzzed.

We adapted. Our love changed, but in a good way.

I couldn't imagine my life without Aja.

Until she could imagine hers without me.

I couldn't foresee something like that ever happening to us, just as no one could predict that the world would come to a crashing end because of a pandemic of spontaneous human combustion.

Luckily for us, both happened at the same time.

And now here we were, moving Aja into the Sawyers's apartment, neither saying a word as we shuffled boxes and bedding back and forth.

When we were done, a pink and purple dusk had settled over the town. Exhausted and unsure how I felt about the whole thing, I randomly played with the light switch to the kitchen while contemplating what can to open for dinner. Creamed corn seemed to be the clear-cut winner.

The light turned on.

I banged on the wall.

"Electricity's back."

I got a quick thump in return.

Eating my creamed corn, I couldn't decide if I missed Aja or if I was just afraid of facing the end of the world alone.

HUMAN NATURE

With Aja gone and no more work (I hadn't heard from my boss or coworkers in over a week), I woke up still sore from trying to break the door down and settled onto the couch to watch the news. The constant assault of negativity drove me nuts when Aja was here. Now with her gone, I thought I could handle at least a few minutes.

Things were going from bad to worse.

Every corner of the globe was afflicted by SHC.

The climate change people were blaming our wasteful ways. It wasn't just the planet that was heating up.

Christians blamed Muslim terrorists for concocting some as yet unknown poison that superheated human cells.

These were the days of Revelation, and that made some folks pretty damn happy.

Take the Skipps, for instance. The smiling family of four recorded a video in their yard, waving at the camera.

Walt Skip, patriarch and chief looney in charge, said to the camera, "These are glorious days. Days that the chosen have been waiting for since Christ ascended into Heaven. We are not afraid because we have lived just lives in the Lord." He paused to look at his wife, son, and daughter. They were downright beaming. "For the wicked, these are times of worry and fear and strife. Today, we are ready to enter the warm embrace of God our savior and leave this world of sin and inequity behind. Do not shed a tear for us. Instead, give your hearts to God and join us in the wonder of eternal life."

Walt shook handfuls of pepper into his family's palms.

Something looked off about his son, who appeared to be in his late teens. I knew what made eyes that glassy and red. Walt, his wife, and daughter quickly inhaled the pepper. In seconds, they sneezed. Not long after that, they burned from the head on down. Their screams didn't sound like they were happy to be on the entrance to the gates of Heaven.

Stoner son and brother watched it all for a moment and I thought for sure he was going to run off camera, the weed having given him enough insight to realize this was crazy.

Nope.

He looked into the camera, snorted the pepper and said, "Adios, motherfuckers!"

Just like that, he went combustible.

The anchor, a nervous young guy I'd never seen before, wax plugs in his nostrils making him sound like he had a cold, came back on the screen. "The suicide rate across the country is incalculable, according to authorities. They are asking anyone who considers suicide by SHC to call the suicide prevention hotline, any time, day or night."

A toll-free number popped up under the anchorman.

I decided to give it a try.

"All of our representative are currently assisting other callers. Please wait on the line and someone will be with you momentarily. If this is an emergency, please call nine-one-one."

I put my phone on speaker and listened to the recording repeat itself for ten minutes before hanging up. Not that I was thinking of making myself combust. I just had a sneaking suspicion—now proven—that there wasn't anyone out there to really help.

Bombings in the Middle East escalated as the ever-present holy wars were heated up by SHC.

I scratched my head. If everyone, regardless of race, religion or location, was going up in flames, how could any one party be given the blame? It wasn't a matter of who was right and who was wrong. It was just a good excuse to go out and kill some people.

If things kept up at this pace, cold and flu season would finish us all.

A news report out of Moscow said scientists in a lab there had definitively located the source of SHC. A volcanic explosion that had occurred in Iceland seven months ago had spewed a great cloud of volcanic ash that spread up and out and seeded the lower atmosphere with a spore that seemed to be at the heart of SHC. They were racing to find a way to inactive the chemical reaction that the spore created when ingested and incubated in the lungs.

They'd even named the spore. Sure, it had some technical, boring label that was a series of numbers and some Latin, I think. But I preferred THE RED MOLD. It sounded as ominous as the pandemic itself.

The rest of the newscast was spent downplaying the Russian's claims about THE RED MOLD because they were, after all, Russians and not to be trusted. More likely, it was something they'd concocted in some lab that had gotten out on purpose or by accident and backfired, killing its creators with as much zeal as their enemies.

"Icelandic spores from a freaking volcano," I said to my empty living room. Out of everything I'd been hearing, that one sounded right to me.

I turned off the news. That sure didn't make me feel any better.

Neither did a cold can of Spaghettios.

If the SHC didn't kill us, our own anger and stupidity would finish the job. It seemed inevitable even before SHC, but now that the doomsday clock had gone warp speed, I was both afraid and disgusted.

Scientists needed to find the cause and a way to stop it quicker than a virgin's money shot. But distrust was now a way of life and whoever was left smart enough to end it would do so in an echo chamber of least resistance. Not a recipe for success.

In fact, I remembered reading online that the premier scientific team in Switzerland tasked with finding the root cause of SHC had all gone combustible just last week. I wondered how long those scientists in Moscow would hold out.

If a stray burning cat didn't torch the building, some misguided, pissed off flat-Earther-doomsday prepper-social justice warrior-cancel culture cretin would end up smoking us out for shits and giggles.

I had to get out of here.

As much as it pained me, *we* had to get out of here.

I knocked on Aja's door. She wrenched it open, clearly unhappy to see me.

"What?"

The television was on and her fingertips were stained orange from snacking.

"You know that sooner or later, we're going to have to leave, right?"

"You don't even want me in the same apartment as you. What makes you think I'd go anywhere with you?"

She had a good point. I could remind her that we loved each other very deeply once. Problem was, I couldn't get my mouth to say the words.

"It's not safe here."

She looked across the apartment to the open window. The sky was gray with ash. "Oh, but it's so much better out there."

My blood boiled. Here I was, offering an olive branch of a sort, and she stomped on it.

"Fine. Stay here. It's your funeral."

She slammed the door in my face.

That didn't go well.

Though it did go as expected.

THE PLACE

The lights had been flickering on and off for days. Aja and I hadn't spoken for just as long, though I did hear her television through the walls twenty-four-seven.

I'd spent the entire time scouring the Internet. Social media posts were on the decline because there were fewer and fewer people around to post selfies, announce their gym gains or be pissant trolls.

The news sites were buzzing, but what it all boiled down to was people are burning and all of our infrastructure was on the verge of collapse. I skipped anything that even had a whiff of an opinion piece. Opinions were like assholes. Everyone had one and they were usually pretty crappy.

What I looked for was anyone talking about a place that wasn't affected by SHC. I concentrated on locations that were known to have wet, damp climates, such as Ireland and Seattle. In my mind, it was hard to fan the flames when you were wet. I was wrong. People went combustible in driving gales, the flames being doused by the rain for a moment, and flaring back the second the victim started to dry off.

I feared that my search was in vain, or if it wasn't, we'd lose power for good before I found it.

For the first time in a dog's age, lady luck gave me a little side-eye.

A post on an obscure message board I'd found said:

No combustibles at Consumption. Taking my family there tomorrow. Spread the word.

Someone replied with:

Don't believe everything you hear. Hardly anyone lives there to being with. If you haven't heard of any combustibles up there, I'll bet it's because they don't even have Internet.

The man with the family responded three days later.

You're wrong. We're two days out from Consumption. Not the only ones on the road there. Spoke to several along the way that confirmed it. Zero cases of SHC. Not sure why but I don't care. All that matters is that my family is safe.

Then came a string of posts:

Good luck and God bless you. I'm in a wheelchair and wish I had someone to take me there. I know they say we all die alone, but I'm tired of living alone.

You're crazy. Like some dumb ass town in Bumbfuck, Canada is immune to SHC. Common sense has gone out the window since this thing started. Anyone else thinking of going to Consumption, you should know that if you don't burn up, you certainly will freeze to death.

I heard the same thing from a cop in Regina. He said he was going there with his wife. Think I'll follow him.

If you want to fuck my beautiful, big tits, come visit my cam show at...

Consumption, Canada.

A place named after a disease that was immune to another. The irony wasn't lost on me. I pulled up a map of Canada. It was way up in the Northwest Territories. That person who wrote about freezing to death was right. It was going to get downright frigid up there soon.

POWER

I collected all the information I could about Consumption. By the last census taken a decade ago, it had a population of less than five hundred. Come winter, the temperature could easily dip below minus twenty degrees. Where we lived now, everyone threw a hissy fit when we woke up to a thirty-degree morning.

Consumption was a quiet lake town and had no tourism to speak of. There were a few pictures of houses on the water's edge that looked like they'd barely survived the harsh winter.

It got me wondering. Word had gotten out that Consumption might be the only place, at least in North America, that SHC hadn't touched...so far. If enough people braved the trek, it sure didn't sound like a town that could handle the influx of refugees. Dark Lake didn't look as if it contained an unlimited supply of fish to feed everyone. Odds were pretty high that Jesus hadn't set up camp and was whipping out loaves of bread from his pockets. And there sure as hell weren't enough places to stay. Consumption could be easily overrun and collapse under its own weight. Winter was going to come no matter what. When the spring thaw arrived, how many human popsicles would melt under the sun's long awaited glare?

Dark Lake. I couldn't get over how ominous it sounded. There was very little information online about the lake itself. In the few pictures I saw, the waters did indeed look quite dark. Was that how it got its name? Or was there some sinister legend behind it?

Maybe it was like nicknaming a huge dude Tiny.

Neither Dark Lake nor Consumption sounded inviting. I got the feeling the inhabitants planned it that way.

The power went out for good on a Wednesday afternoon. My computer lost connection with the Internet and went to battery mode. I heard Aja shout something in the next apartment. When night came, there was a knock at the door.

"I need my candles."

"All yours."

Aja had a massive collection of scented candles. We could burn those things twenty-four hours a day and have light for a year. She went to her bathroom, and I heard glass containers clinking against one another and she gathered them in a canvas bag.

"Did you leave me any?" I asked.

"Yes. A few."

"Please don't tell me it's the pumpkin spice ones." She knew I despised all things pumpkin spice.

"No. There's a couple of pipe tobacco ones and a cinnamon," she replied curtly, turning to go.

I almost reached out to grab her arm but thought better of it. "Wait. We should talk about some things."

"I'm not leaving here."

"We can't stay here forever."

She put a hand on her hip. "You know all those movies we've watched where people wander all over the place searching for a safe haven? This is exactly what they look for. We're safe. We have supplies in the other apartments. We even have fireplaces when it starts getting cold."

"Yes, but it won't last as long as you think."

Her fingers tapped against her hip bone. It was a nervous tic of hers. She must have been jonesing for her phone. Too bad the power hadn't gone out months ago. Maybe we'd still be living in the same apartment, scared but happy and together.

Fuck Thomas Edison.

"Can I go now?"

My shoulders slumped. "Fine."

"Thank you."

She didn't slam the door, which was an improvement.

I fell asleep beside the legal pad of notes I'd made about Consumption. I dreamed of drinking an ice-cold beer from a frosty mug. Aja and I were at a tiki bar in a Florida resort. She wore her red bikini, water droplets shining like diamonds on her skin.

"One more beer, then a quick dip and I'll towel you off good in our room," my dream self said.

"Why wait?"

We made love on the tiki bar while vacationers watched and applauded.

I woke up with a knot of wood in my shorts and a terrible thirst. A warm can of beer was a poor substitute. So was my hand.

Once my head cleared, my mind was consumed by Consumption. I called Dave while my phone still had some battery life.

"You have power," he said without a hello. My heart fluttered, ecstatic that he was still alive.

"Nope. Went out yesterday."

"Same." Dave lived the next town over.

"I'm thinking of getting out of here."

"That's good. Go for a walk. Just be careful."

"No, I mean getting out of town."

Dave chuckled. "Not really the best time to take a vacation. I'm pretty sure all the hotels are closed."

"You ever hear of Consumption in Canada?"

"All I know about Canada are the cities that have hockey teams. Consumption ain't one of them."

I told him what I'd learned.

"Sounds like fake news to me," he said. "And a one-way ticket to a bad end."

"I don't see a good end just hanging around here waiting for the food to run out or to catch a serious cold and sneeze my way to being the Human Torch."

Dave was quiet for a moment. "I hear you. But still. It's a big risk."

"What isn't at this point?"

"What does Aja say about it?"

I looked at the wall connecting the apartments, wondered what she was doing. "She needs convincing."

"I don't doubt it. You got a whole building to yourselves."

I'd texted him about our breaking into the apartment next door. He dropped a lot of LOLs when I told him how I'd hurt myself. I aim to entertain.

"I can't shake the feeling that something bad is going to happen. If someone came here to take our stuff, who am I to stop them? I'm not going to suddenly become a warrior or find a gun and discover I'm the reincarnation of Billy the Kid or something."

"No, you're more like the fat sidekick in a comedy."

"I'm not fat."

"Technically, no. You wear most of your fat in that furry face."

The beard had only gotten bushier, but I'd definitely lost weight. How could I not have?

"You're one to talk. Your baby fat is so old, it collects social security," I said.

"Very funny."

"I just want you to think about it."

"I will. Not much else to do."

"Turn your phone off to conserve power. I'll call you in three days at noon."

Groaning, Dave said, "Shit. I don't have a single analog clock. How am I supposed to know when it's noon?"

"Go find one. The world is one giant department store and they don't want your money. Talk to you in three days."

"Say hi to Aja for me."

I didn't.

B&E

I nearly had a heart attack when I woke in the middle of the night and saw a dark figure standing over me.

Too terrified to speak, I did a kind of spin, crab crawl, drop kick off the bed. My legs got tangled in the sheet I'd dragged down with me.

"Shh! What's the matter with you?"

When I opened my mouth to speak, I worried that my heart would flop right out. "What the hell are you doing in here?"

"Keep your voice down," Aja whisper-hissed.

Still half in a rapidly fading dream, in pain from hitting the floor and the cold confusion of reality, I replied in as many syllables as I could muster, "Why?"

A small fire blazed, and for a moment, I thought Aja had started to go combustible. I jumped to my feet, or tried to, but my ankles were bound in the sheets. This time, I was lucky enough to fall on the bed. When I looked up, I saw Aja's face lit by the glow of a lighter's flame. She pressed her finger to her lips and pointed down.

I crawled to the edge of the bed and looked at the floor. I saw my slides and a book I'd been reading before I nodded off to sleep.

As I was about to ask another long-winded question, Aja pinched my lips closed.

"Somebody's down there," she mouthed.

The loud thump came in confirmation as quickly and surely as the hidden assistant for an old-time spiritualist at a séance. I heard footsteps. Whoever was down there wasn't concerned about being heard. They probably assumed the building was empty.

At least I hoped.

The other option—that they weren't afraid because they would take care of anyone who got in their way—had my stomach in an instant knot.

I slowly disentangled myself and got off the bed. "Did you lock the door?" I whispered in her ear. I got too close to the lighter's flame and felt the burn on my cheek.

"Sorry," Aja said. And then, "Of course I did. You think I'm stupid?"

I looked her in the eye for a long moment. "Now's not the time to debate that. Stay here."

Walking as gingerly as I could in my socks, I crept to the closet and oh-so-carefully rooted around for anything closely resembling a weapon. What I found was a bowling ball (from when I was on the bowling team in high school) and a yard-stick. I was neither Walter from *The Big Lebowski* or a nun. I needed something more threatening, yet not as intimate as a knife, where I would need to get too close to the intruder should he or she or they try to break into the apartment.

I jumped and nearly yelped when Aja touched my back.

"I'm scared."

I would have said me, too, but I couldn't catch my breath.

"Maybe if we just stay here real quiet, they'll keep to the downstairs and move on."

"But what if they don't?"

I set Aja on the bed. "Just...just stay here."

A weapon. What could I use as a weapon? A real man would have power tools and rebar and hell, guns. My anti-gun stance suddenly seemed like one of my life's poorest decisions.

I saw Aja's silhouette in the bedroom. Well, it wasn't the poorest.

Then I remembered the Sundays Aja would drag me out to seek out every yard and tag sale within a ten-mile radius. Our coat closet was a collection of used goods that we kept talking about having our own tag sale to unload them.

The hinge squeaked just enough to make me stop and hold my breath.

More stomping downstairs and what sounded like drawers being opened and closed.

I quickly pulled the door open the rest of the way. It was too dark to see inside the closet and I didn't want to make a ton of noise rummaging around.

"I need your lighter," I whispered.

Aja tiptoed over. "What are you looking for?"

"The box of lawn darts."

"This isn't game time," she said. I shot her a nasty look and swiped the lighter from her hand.

Naturally, the battered box was buried under a heap of junk.

"Hold this and keep it on." The light wavered thanks to Aja's shaky hand.

"I still don't understand why you want the lawn darts."

"Because they're the ones that were outlawed years ago. They're basically spears."

"Oh."

"Yeah. Oh."

After what seemed like an eternity of gingerly removing boxes and bags and old boots, I laid the lawn darts box on the kitchen table. As I took off the lid, we heard someone coming up the stairs to our floor.

I recalled reading on the box that the deadly yard game had come out in 1974. The steel darts looked like something a samurai would use to impale his enemies in a kung fu movie. Who the hell thought this was safe family entertainment?

At the moment, I was thankful for the creator's short-sightedness.

Aja grabbed my arm as the footsteps approached our door. I plucked a lawn dart in each hand.

In the game, you had to lob them across the yard so they stuck in the grass. Kind of like shuffleboard, but with the fear of impalement thrown in for good measure.

I hefted the one in my right hand and held it at shoulder height. I'd played a lot of darts in a lot of bars, though never with one this large and unwieldy.

The doorknob turned.

Aja clapped her hand over her mouth to stifle her crying.

"Go into the bedroom and lock the door," I murmured just an inch from her ear.

She shook her head so hard, I was whipped in the cheek by her dreads.

"Fine. Just back up a little."

She was plastered to me. I couldn't cock my arm back far enough to get good momentum on the lawn dart.

We nearly hit the ceiling when something hit the door with a loud thunk. The wood of the doorframe sounded like it was starting to splinter.

Whoever was on the other side must have been trying to wedge their way in with a pry bar or something. Aja whimpered behind me. My heart raced so fast I was lightheaded.

The drunker I got, the better I played at darts. The wooziness might work to my advantage.

With the final crack, the door flew open.

I let loose with the lawn dart as hard as I could throw it.

The banished game piece stuck into the wall. The dark shape in the doorway leaned in to look at the embedded lawn dart.

With a quick transfer of the lawn dart from my left to my right hand, I chucked it at the shadow.

The sound it made when it hit home will haunt me forever.

MURDERER

"Holy shit!"

It was all I could think to say. My hands shook.

The shadowy shape lay on its side on the floor. In the darkness, I couldn't tell if it was breathing or not.

"Is he dead? Is he dead?" Aja cried.

"I don't know." I tried to shush her. While she was fixated by the impaled intruder, I listened out to hear if he or she had an accomplice. I prayed it wasn't a she. I was brought up never to lay a finger on a woman in anger. Not even in self-defense.

I wasn't sure if a court of law would rule this self-defense or straight up murder.

When I was sure there wasn't someone else creeping about the apartment, I asked Aja for her lighter. We took a knee on either side of the body. Sucking in a deep breath, I flicked the lighter.

Part of me wanted to say, "Thank God," and sigh with relief when I saw it was a man, white with a ten o'clock shadow, possibly in his thirties.

Seeing the lawn dart protruding from his ruined eye socket, blood and goo I assumed was his actual eyeball running down his cheek, sent me fleeing to the sink where I lost the can of string beans I'd had for dinner.

Aja picked up the lighter where I'd dropped it and stared at him long and hard. "I don't see him breathing. Wow. That was some shot. You really nailed him."

She wasn't quite as horrified as I expected her to be. Wiping my mouth with a dishtowel, I said, "Now's not the time for puns."

"Huh?"

"Never mind. Here, let me check for sure."

Steeling myself, I pressed my fingers against the side of his neck. Yep, he was dead.

"What do we do now?" I said.

"What do you mean?"

"I mean, I just killed a man. Shouldn't we call the police? He did break into the apartment. That's justifiable homicide, right?" I had no idea what the hell I was talking about.

"Do you honestly think there are any police still on duty?"

My nerves were frayed, and Aja was right.

"What do we do with him? We can't just leave him here. Sooner or later, he's going to start to...to...to rot." My stomach flip-flopped again.

"I don't know. Let's just wait until the morning."

"I'm not going to be able to sleep knowing there's a man I killed in the next room."

Aja took my hand. "Then come stay with me. Come with me and sit down for a minute."

She guided me to the couch, closed the door, and poured a glass of bourbon. I drank half of it in one gulp.

"I'm a murderer."

She rubbed my back. "No, you're not."

"Then what do you call a person who just killed someone?"

"A guy defending his home." I took another sip. "And his wife."

"Was I really? Yes, he broke into the apartment, just like we did a week ago. Did we deserve to be killed the moment we walked in the door?"

"That was different."

"How?"

"Because we needed food and water and they were our neighbors. We know they wouldn't have denied helping us if they were home."

"Actually, we don't know that. The world ain't what it used to be. They might have told us to get lost. They had their kids to think of."

"I seriously doubt that."

I finished my drink and Aja was quick to refill my glass.

"He was probably just like us. Hungry and scared and desperate. Why didn't I at least try to talk to him?"

Aja hovered over the body. "Because he broke our door down like a maniac."

I peered over the couch and saw her rifling through the man's coat and jeans pockets. "What the hell are you doing?"

She held a handgun with her thumb and index finger. "Aha. Still think he was a good guy?"

"With the way things are, if he was walking the streets, it's a smart thing to have." Smarter than a lawn dart. And a much better deterrent.

She put the gun on the counter and found another tucked in his waistband. "How about now?"

"Having a backup shows he wasn't dumb."

She also found a switchblade and a hefty Bowie knife in a holster strapped to his leg. It got harder to defend my stance. I wasn't sure why I wanted him to be innocent. Maybe I felt I deserved the crushing guilt.

What I got was my third glass of bourbon in less than ten minutes. My stomach burned but at least I wasn't nauseous anymore. Normally, I would be on the cusp of slurring. The booze had a tough time fighting through the swell of adrenaline in my system. In the back of my head, I knew I was headed for a crash and wished it would hurry the hell up.

"Ew, gross."

Aja pulled women's panties out of the man's coat pocket like a magician tugging multicolored scarves out of his mouth.

"At the very least, he was a major creepo."

I couldn't tell if that was what made me feel better or the fuzzy effects of the bourbon.

"You should check them to see if they're clean," I said.

"Feel free. I'm not adding panty sniffer to my resume."

If they were used, it would put a deeper blight on the man's character. It was twisted logic, but I needed the assurance.

"I will."

"You won't. That's disgusting."

"There's a dead body with a dart in his eye. Some slightly worn panties pale in comparison."

"I'm cutting you off." Aja swiped the bottle of bourbon off the kitchen counter and tucked it under her arm.

"Fine."

I got up to check the panties. Aja had scattered them around the corpse.

The moment I stood up, the entire room spun and flipped me like a pancake.

I vaguely recall Aja trying to help me to my feet. I had fallen on the dead man. When I put my hand on his head to balance myself, I felt the squish of the dart burying itself deeper into his cooling head.

BODY

Waking up in a strange apartment on a strange couch did not help my hangover. Once I realized I was in "Aja's apartment," the vivid memory of what had happened the night before, hit me like a dump truck.

The hope that it had all possibly been a nightmare quickly died when Aja, who had been in the kitchen eating dry cereal, said, "I think I know where we should take the body."

"Can I take a piss first?" My body ached and my head was ready to split in two.

Aja followed me to the bathroom. "At first I thought we could just chuck it out one of the back windows into the yard, but that stink will get bad real fast," she said through the door. My bladder ached but I couldn't go. Not with her talking about how to dispose of a dead body just two feet away.

Ignorant of my plight, she continued, "We can either bury it, which is a lot of work if you ask me, or leave it in Mr. Molina's shed. It'll be far enough away and out of sight. What do you think?"

I leaned my forehead against the cool tile wall. "I think I'm going to die."

"Wow. Even with the world ending and a dead man next door, you still have a shy bladder?"

I thought I heard her give a tsk sound as she walked away. My bladder registered that she was out of earshot and exploded.

When I came out, Aja had a bottle of water waiting for me. "Thanks."

"When you feel up to it, we should get it over with."

I didn't have the strength to argue. I also wasn't sure if I'd ever feel up to it.

"Let's just do it now."

I opened the door and checked the hallway first to see if anyone else had snuck inside the building overnight. When the coast was clear, we went into our apartment.

The first thing I noticed, much to my stomach's dismay, was the buzzing of the flies. I'd left one of the bedroom windows open and they had found an irresistible feast.

Second was the smell. The body had already had that sweet, spoiled meat funk about it. We both pulled the collars of our shirts over our noses.

Third was the deep, dark discoloration on the man's face where it met the floor.

"Blood pooling," I said.

"What?"

I hadn't realized I'd said it out loud. "His face. It's that color because all the blood is settling there."

"I wish I hadn't eaten. I thought it would look more like the way they show bodies on TV."

"Networks realize people like to eat while they watch their shows."

"Do we wrap him in something?"

"It would be a good idea, unless you want to touch him. Plus, despite the way things are, I don't think we should be seen carrying a corpse around."

Aja looked in the kitchen cabinets. "How about a garbage bag?"

The man had been at least six foot and broad. "Does he look like he'll fit inside a thirteen-gallon bag?"

"Well, no."

I looked at the area rug in our living room. Aja saw where I was looking and said, "No. That was a wedding gift from Sheila."

It wasn't lost on me that this was a perfect use for anything associated with our wedding. "You have any other ideas?"

I gave her a minute of silence, which actually feels quite long when there are no other sounds or distractions. "Okay, help me move the coffee table."

Aja looked on the verge of tears as we cleared our stuff off the rug and dragged it over. We positioned the rug so it was up against the body.

"I'm not rolling him up," Aja said. She gave an exaggerated shiver. "Besides, you worked in that Mexican restaurant when we were a kid."

"What does that have to do with anything?"

She flicked her fingers. "It'll be like rolling a giant burrito."

I didn't bother telling her that was the dumbest thing I'd ever heard. But I did feel the need to correct her. "Not going to need to tuck in the ends and roll. More like an enchilada."

"Whatever."

Waving the flies away, I crouched on the other side of the body and put my hands on his upper arm and side. What I wanted to do was jerk my hands away, head for the bathroom, and lock myself inside for a week.

Instead, I pushed.

At first, the body didn't move.

Aja looked at me.

I looked at Aja.

I pushed again, this time harder.

His body started to move but his face was reluctant to follow. The wet, tearing sound told me the blood was making his flesh stick to the floor. Choking back bile, I gave one great shove and heard a hard thunk.

"Oh crap," Aja said. She'd tied a dishtowel over the bottom half of her face.

Oh crap was right. The lawn dart propped the body up, preventing it from fully turning over.

At that point, I was fine with leaving him there for eternity. The whole neighborhood would be nothing but one big waste-land soon enough. No sense in my trying to keep this little slice of heaven in order.

"Nope. I'm not gonna do it," I said.

"But you have to."

"Says you."

"Fine. I guess you'll have to stay with me. Or move all your stuff to one of the other apartments."

Neither option sounded appealing.

"Step back," I said to her. She stood by the head, eyeballing the source of my displeasure. "A little further."

I waved at her until she'd backed into the kitchen. "Why do I have to be way over here?"

When I touched the end of the lawn dart, my teeth clamped shut as a protective measure. "Just in case I projectile vomit."

My skin crawled and my soul left my body to take a walk around the block as I slowly extracted the lawn dart. It made a squelching noise that ended with a burp and a pop. Blood dripped off the deadly tip. "Where should I put it?"

I fought nausea and vertigo.

"Just drop it on the rug."

I was happy to oblige.

After that plummet into horridness, wrapping the man up into the rug was easy. I sealed it up with duct tape, using half a new roll just to be sure the body couldn't slip free.

I did most of the work dragging him out of the apartment, down the hall and the stairs. Aja tried, but she kept having to pause to gag, especially when a fly wriggled its way from out of the carpet folds and into her mouth.

If I'm being honest, I found it kind of funny.

The revulsion on Aja's face was unparalleled. She ran back

into her apartment, where I could hear her retching over the toilet.

The head thunked on each step as I let gravity do most of the work.

Carrying him across the street and up into Mr. Molina's yard took over an hour with a lot of starts and stops. Thankfully, no one was around to ogle our plight.

The shed smelled like earth and gas and grass clippings. We had to take Mr. Molina's mower out to make room for the body. I opened two twenty-pound bags of topsoil and covered him with it. It was at least an added layer to keep the stench at bay.

"Look at this place," Aja said, wiping sweat off her brow and looking at the expansive yard. The grass and weeds were almost knee high. "Mr. Molina would be so pissed."

I looked over at what remained of the ash pile that had been Mr. Molina.

"I don't think he cares all that much."

I remembered sharing a beer with Mr. Molina now and then on summer nights when the lightning bugs lit up his perfect yard and he talked about baseball and the way it used to be played. The man was a walking, talking baseball almanac.

"I need a shower," Aja said.

"I need an acid bath."

When we got into our respective apartments—mine now adorned with a pool of coagulated blood and lingering flies—we both discovered that running water was another thing to add to the list of things that we took for granted and now were no more.

ESCALATION

The next intruder, or better yet, forager, came two nights later. This time, I kept the lawn darts in the closet and stayed with Aja behind her locked door.

"Guess there won't be anything left for us on the first floor," I said to her after I saw the dark shape amble out of the apartment and down the street, dipping through the broken window of a house.

"We should board up the front doors so no one can get in."

"That's like painting a giant sign that screams, HEY, WE HAVE SOME GOOD STUFF IN HERE. BET YOU CAN'T BREAK THIS DOOR DOWN!"

Aja rolled her eyes. "If we barricaded it right, no one could."

"Neither of us can be considered a master builder. Remember when we took that pottery class on that cruise to the Bahamas? We couldn't even make a simple cup."

"This isn't pottery."

"No, it's more complex than spinning clay. Face it, when it comes to using our hands, we're useless."

"Maybe you are."

I wasn't in the mood to get into it. Aja had a hard time getting her phone in a new phone case. Between the two of us, the effort of installing some kind of barricade would be laughable and far from impregnable.

"I have to get back to my crime scene," I said, leaving her in the dark.

No matter what I did, I couldn't get the smell out of the floor. I was sure it was all in my mind. But the mind is a powerful thing, and it can really fuck with itself when it wanted to. I'd put beach towels over the spot where the body had lain as a way to make sure I avoided stepping on it.

Whenever I tried to sleep, I kept smelling the rotting body and hearing the door crash open. The bourbon I'd swiped from the Sawyers' apartment was running low.

The next night, I sat vigil by the windowsill and watched a man and woman slip into our building. It didn't take them long to realize the pickings were slim downstairs. Aja came padding into our apartment.

"There's more," she said breathlessly.

"I saw them."

We could hear them coming up the stairs. "Did you lock your door?" I asked her.

She shook her head hard enough to make her dreads fan out.

I sipped my bourbon and Aja paced as we listened to them ransack the cabinets next door. It wasn't lost on me that my door was unable to lock. I hoped they would find more than they needed and walk away.

They didn't.

When I heard them step into the hallway, I brushed past Aja and opened one of the kitchen drawers.

"You kept them?" Aja asked when she saw the handgun. Her tone was a mix of angry and disappointed.

I palmed the gun. "Yep."

I was feeling pretty brave, thanks to the bourbon.

"We don't do guns," she whispered.

"When the most dangerous thing we did in a year was eat those wings with the ghost pepper sauce, yeah, we didn't do guns. Are you pretending to be this dense? If you haven't noticed, the pacifists lost."

I could tell she wanted to raise her voice.

The doorknob started to turn.

"Occupied," I said, putting as much bass in my voice as I could muster.

The turning stopped. The door didn't open. If they only knew a sneeze could fling it wide.

The couple on the other side didn't move. Which meant they were contemplating their odds.

Recalling all of the action movies I had ever watched, I cocked the gun. In the absence of background noise, it was actually quite loud.

Apparently, it was effective, too, because the clomping of hurried footsteps quickly followed. I went to the window and watched them depart, wondering if I should hurl a sassy one-liner their way.

When I turned from the window, Aja was glaring at me with her hands on her hips. "I don't even know you anymore."

"I could say the same. And my wife changed when things were good."

She stormed out of the apartment. I went back to the bourbon.

THE DECISION

I tried calling Dave several times. His phone went directly to voicemail. Either his phone was dead or he was swiping me to voicemail. I put my money on the former. I tried not to think of the third possibility.

It was time to get out.

This place was turning into a quickie mart. Sooner rather than later, we were going to get hurt by someone or *someones* desperate for food. I wasn't exactly up to putting notches on my belt for each kill. Hell, I could barely sleep for more than two hours in a row without waking in a cold sweat from the nightmare of killing the man who was now decomposing in Mr. Molina's shed.

The stench of smoke was just a part of the air now as Manhattan, just across the Hudson River, burned non-stop. Even the wads of fabric we kept stuffed in our nostrils couldn't keep the acrid smell at bay. When I mentioned to Aja that a lot of what we were smelling was people, she said I was a sick fuck and left the apartment. At the time, I felt, mission accomplished. But my words haunted me.

Canada's Northwest Territories at least promised fresh air. It was a good place to spend before going combustible like everyone else. Consumption may have been a pipe dream, but it was enough to keep me going.

And I was ready to go grab an RV and Dave and hit the road.

We didn't own a car because why bother when you could get an Uber ride in minutes? I regretted that life decision now. I remembered there was a place that sold used cars and RVs over on Summer Street. It was part of a long strip of car dealerships that was about five miles away.

Again, if I had any street skills, I could hot wire a car and drive there. Five miles wasn't a long walk, unless it was the apocalypse and you worried about what was lurking behind every corner.

I had to hope there were some RVs left and I could find the right keys. Then I'd swing back home, load it up with the little I had that was of value on the road, and hope Dave was still alive.

I told Aja my plan when she came over to get more candles.

"So you'd rather die in Canada?"

"I'd rather take a chance and try to *live* in Canada than wait to die holed up in this place."

"This place is our home."

"Was our home, Aja. Now it's a prison. A prison, mind you, that inmates like to break *into* every night."

She crossed her arms and shook her head. "Well, then I guess this is the end, then."

There was a time, not long ago, I would have begged her to come with me. If she'd said no, I would have stayed.

Now, I shrugged my shoulders. "Guess it is. The lawn darts are all yours, since you're still anti-gun and all."

I stormed out of the apartment. I had one of the pistols in my pocket, hoping I wouldn't shoot my dick off as I walked.

The skies were hazy with clouds and smoke, narrow rays of sun breaking through here and there. There was a cold wind that I assumed had come from Canada to give me encouragement. Pulling my wool cap down until it met my eyebrows, my nose plugged with bits of a torn-up shirt and a bandana over my lower face, I set out for Summer Street.

I hoped I looked badass enough for anyone who happened to be around to give me a wide berth. It was doubtful. More like I looked like a lost hipster who was playing cops and robbers.

Taking a right on Palisades Street, I spied a mound of what looked like dumped coals from a barbecue against a fenced empty lot. There was an unharmed thumb and three fingers on one side of the ashes, and a leg from mid-calf down on the other. The links in the fence looked to be coated with grease or wax.

I hurried on, denying my inner rubbernecker. Some poor soul had sat by the fence and gone combustible. Recently, judging by the state of the remains. I wondered how long it would take before a hungry dog or some big birds came for the fingers and leg.

Dogs. I hadn't thought about packs of wild, starving dogs roaming about. There weren't many owners left to feed and care for them. Even though dogs could go combustible, too, I'd seen quite a few out and about or waking me up with their howls and barks at night. They say if you die in a locked home with your dog, it will start eating you within three days.

SHC had been laying waste to the world for far longer than that.

Suddenly feeling too exposed, I searched around until I found a two-foot-long section of pipe at the back end of the vacant lot.

Three blocks away, I saw a minivan cruise down an intersection. I smiled as I watched it disappear, knowing there was life in that van. Good, bad or indifferent, humanity needed whatever it could retain to keep on trucking.

Ambling onto Washington Boulevard, I thought I spotted an old woman watching me from a window. The curtain billowed slightly when she ducked out of sight. I was tempted to knock on her door and ask her if she was all right and if she needed anything.

The words, *granny with a shotgun*, floated into my head.

I kept walking.

I jumped at the rumble and thunder of a motorcycle with a sidecar as it sped past me. Both riders wore black helmets and I couldn't get a bead on whether they were men or women. They didn't stop to acknowledge or accost me, so I counted my blessings.

The ashen remains of another person were on the stoop of a three-family house. Only the head was left, and the expression on the man's face chilled my soul. There was no peace in his last moments.

It was eerily quiet for the most of my walk. Weehawken had dropped the mic and it was the silence that got to me most.

About a mile from the RV dealership, I heard the whoop-whoop of a police car approaching. Turning on my heels to search for it, a bubble of hope that all was not totally lost rose within me.

The black-and-white cruiser had its lights flashing, siren wailing.

Smoke poured out of the windows.

As it came closer, I saw the flames within.

The passenger door opened and a man dressed in plain clothes spilled out on the street. As the burning car passed, I spotted some semblance of a man within the flames, his arms locked, hands still on the wheel. The police cruiser sped down the street and out of sight. Seconds later, I heard the crash—metal crunching, glass breaking.

Realizing I should be more concerned about the person who jumped out of the car, I ran over to him. His jacket was smoking on the side that had been close to the immolated driver. He was young, late teens at most, with a tattoo of a deck of cards on his neck.

"Are you all right?" I said, offering my hand to help him up.

He pushed himself to his knees and looked down the street. "Fucking Jimmy, man. We was driving and shit and just having some fun and then BOOM! He went all combustible and I couldn't get that freakin' door to open."

He brushed off his sleeves and pants and got on his feet.

"What the fuck you lookin' at?"

I took a tentative step back. "Nothing. I just thought you might be hurt."

"So?"

I had to think for a moment. "Well, if you were, I could help you."

"You think of hitting me with that pipe and you'll wish you were Jimmy." He brandished a hand cannon that had been hidden under his coat and pointed it at me.

I looked at the pipe, having forgotten I was even holding it. "I wasn't going to do anything but help you if you needed it. Which you clearly don't. So, I'll just be on my way."

He stared at me for a bit, and I could see very little mercy in his hard eyes. After I started to back away, he tucked the gun back into his coat.

"Word of advice," he said. "Keep to yourself. Ain't no point helping nobody, cause ain't nobody gonna be saved for long. Just do you. Might help you live a little longer."

With that, he sprinted away.

His road wisdom wasn't entirely unsound.

Which is why I was very sad for the rest of my trek to the RV dealership.

RV

Big Donnie Nelson's Truck and RV Emporium loomed large up ahead. I nearly dropped to my knees and wept when I saw there were still some vehicles left in the lot. Not many. They'd either been pilfered like I was about to do, or Donnie had one hell of a blowout sale before everything shut down.

Big Donnie was a fixture on late-night local television. His commercials looked like they cost about thirty-seven cents to make, but that was part of their charm. Donnie Nelson had pitched in the big leagues for four years and always said he'd never throw a curveball at his customers. He was big in many ways. The gut he sported I figured would make it difficult for him to even play in a beer softball league now.

First, I checked the showroom to make sure it was empty. The double doors were locked, but the glass had been blown out. Pebbles of it fanned out in the entryway.

I poked my head inside. "Hello. Big Donnie?"

If Big Donnie had gone combustible, I imagined it must have been one hell of a fire.

I scooched my way inside, my footsteps echoing in the vast showroom. Four model RVs were parked behind the gathering of sales desks. I ran my finger over one of the desks. It was covered in a fine layer of ash.

How much of this stuff are we breathing in every minute of the day? I thought. Better yet, how many dead people were now a fine sediment in my lungs?

Shaking off my morbid thoughts, I searched for where they kept the keys. They had to be in a back office. I found the break room. A moldy Danish was on a paper plate in the center of the table. The fridge had three bottles of water, two cans of Diet Coke and two cans of Red Bull. I found a plastic bag and loaded them up. No sense passing up free provisions.

The refrigerator was also jammed with Tupperware and takeout boxes filled with rotting food. I extracted the drinks quickly, desperate to avoid the odor of all that rot.

A couple of offices yielded little, but then I knew I hit the jackpot.

Big Donnie's office was adorned wall to wall with pictures of him in his playing days with the Brewers. There were other photos of him with various celebrities, politicians and even a couple of once-famous musicians.

A baseball in a glass case was on his big oak desk. I read the tiny placard on the base.

No Hitter, July 14th, 1998, Donnie Nelson

"Look at you, Big Donnie. Nice one."

On the right wall was a black metal box with a yellow sticker that read KEY TRAK. There was a keypad next to it.

Lacking a code or electricity to power it, I was about to whale at the box with the pipe when I touched it and the door, now that I could see, was a tad dented, slowly opened. There were keys inside but more empty pegs.

I dumped a pile of slick brochures out of a nearby box and filled it with the keys. Tucking it under my arm, I carried the box, bag of drinks and pipe to the lot.

A dog barked in the distance. I hoped it wasn't some kind of junkyard mongrel that hung around car lots waiting for its next meal.

Huge RVs the size of city buses dominated the first row in the lot. Most were new and still held some shine. I had to crane my neck just to take them all in from top to bottom. I was sure their interiors were spacious and decked out better than a five-star hotel.

It was tempting to take the first one I saw, but there were a couple of problems.

First, I hadn't driven so much as a car in two years. I wasn't sure how well I'd be able to handle something that big.

Second, they must get like five miles to the gallon. With the electricity out, getting gas was going to be a major issue. I needed something that consumed less dinosaurs.

I trolled the lot, waiting to hear the approach of footsteps from a waiting salesman who would clap me on the back and say, "So, you ready to take your home on the road? I've got a beauty that you'll love so much, you'll want to have it buried with you when you pass on."

Instead, I had the constant, eerie sensation of loneliness that, for my money, was worse than strolling down a bad neighborhood at night.

There were RVs no bigger than vans. One of the doors was unlocked, and I looked inside. Not much room for me, Dave, and Aja.

Aja. Was she even going to come? Would I throw her over my shoulder caveman-style and carry her out of the building?

It was a sad realization that I didn't know. The woman I had shared every part of my life with for over a decade had become a stranger to me. It was nauseating, the hollowness I felt inside when I thought of her. Yes, I still loved her, loved what we had once been, but was it enough to get on my knees and beg her to come with me?

"Fuck me."

My legs were tired from lack of use and the sun was going to set sooner rather than later.

And then I found it.

She was a mid-sized RV, the kind that looks like the front of a pickup truck with a camper soldered around it. I pulled on the door. Locked.

I set the bag and pipe down and rifled through the box, trying different keys and not having any luck.

At least until I looked at the name painted on the side of the RV.

It read in blue lettering—Freedom Elite.

The front grill had a Ford logo.

I looked at the keys in the box. The keychains bore the name of the company. On the back, someone had used a label maker to delineate which RV they belonged to.

There were three sets of Freedom Elite keys and only two of the RVs in the lot.

"Let's see what's behind curtain number one," I mumbled. The barking dog sounded as if it were getting closer. My fingers fumbled getting the key in the lock.

The handle turned on its own and I was slammed in the chest by the door.

Sprawled on my ass, I looked into the RV.

A heavyset man wearing a green jogging suit stood on the lone step. One hand was curled into a fist. The other gripped a steak knife. Not the most intimidating weapon he could have brandished, but it was enough to get my heart racing.

"Get the hell outta my house!" he snarled. His hair was curly and wild, and his upper lip was adorned with a drooping salt and pepper mustache.

"Whoa, whoa, whoa. I'm sorry. I didn't know you were in there!" I held my hands out in a feeble attempt to keep the man at bay.

He stepped onto the blacktop.

"Goddamn thief. What gives you the right to break into my home?"

Now, I realized that was not the time to point out that I was pretty sure he was not the owner of the RV.

"Hey, look, I was trying to find an RV...an empty RV...to roll on out of here. My apologies. If you don't mind, I'll just move along now."

When I tried to get up, he shook his closed fist at me.

"Don't you get any funny ideas."

I couldn't come up with a single funny idea.

"You know what I have in this hand?"

I shook my head. I didn't and wasn't the least bit curious. An image of a monkey flinging his poop through the bars of his cage came to mind.

"Sneezing powder."

A shock ran through me. He might as well have been pointing an elephant gun at my head.

"I don't want any trouble."

"Well, you got some."

My nose was plugged up and I had the bandana over my face, but would that be enough? And where the hell did he find sneezing powder? Was that really a thing?

I held out the bag of drinks. "Here, you can have them. Just please, let me see if that RV over there is vacant and works." I nodded at the other Freedom Elite. He took a quick glance over his shoulder.

"Nobody's in there," he grumbled.

Slowly getting to my feet, I kept my eyes on that hand of his, wondering if the pipe would reach should he look like he was about to release the modern-day equivalent of germ warfare. I set the bag between us.

"Are we good?"

He wiped his mouth with the back of his steak knife hand. "Where do you think you're taking that RV?"

There was no way I was going to tell him about my road trip plan to Canada. What if he insisted he come with me? I didn't relish the thought of making the long trek with the threat of getting a handful of sneezing powder thrown in my face looming over me.

"I'm not sure. Anywhere that's not here."

"You got the cash to pay for it?"

Cash? Holy crap, I was going to be robbed by a fellow RV thief.

"What? I, well, I..."

The man busted out laughing. "Look at you. I'm surprised you lasted this long. That road is going to eat you up and shit you out. Go on, take it. But you see anyone else sniffing around here, you tell them to leave me be." He looped his index finger through the bag's handle.

"Um, yeah, sure, I'll tell them."

His smile fell off his face. "No you won't. You might want to work on your bullshit game, son. You're gonna need it."

He turned to go back inside and for some ungodly reason, I felt the need to ask him, "Hey, is that really sneezing powder in your hand?"

One of his eyebrows raised. "What do you think?"

He slammed the door closed and I exhaled so thoroughly, I felt as if I'd emptied my soul.

The next RV was mercifully free, but the battery was dead. I had to run back to the garage area of the lot to find one of those portable battery chargers. Once I fired up the RV, I pumped my fist and gave an idiotic whoop when I saw the gas needle go all the way to full.

By the time I pulled out of the lot, night had fallen, making it easier to spot the flames around me and in the distance as I hurried home.

END OF THE WORLD STUBBORNNESS IS THE WORST KIND

I pretty much demolished the bumpers of the cars in front and behind me as I tried to parallel park the RV across the street from my building.

When I hopped out, a breeze came from the east through Mr. Molina's yard. This time, I could definitely smell the fruiting body of the guy I'd killed. I ran into our building and up the stairs to the apartment.

I heard music coming out of Aja's place when I passed her door.

Curious, I knocked.

No answer.

I knocked again, harder.

Still no answer.

I sniffed the air, searching for fresh smoke and cooked meat. Nothing than the usual background odor.

"Aja?"

I grabbed the doorknob and turned.

Why didn't she lock the damn door?

My pulse thrummed in my ears. What was I about to find?

I spotted the source of the music. A DVD player was on the dining room table, a pair of palm-sized speakers plugged in. An old Lenny Kravitz CD was spinning away. He was jamming to "Let Love Rule."

"Aja?"

Where was she?

The skin on the back of my neck prickled. It felt as if someone was going to jump out of the shadows any second.

The bedrooms were empty. I wished I had a flashlight on me.

Light.

I went back to the dining room, spotted one of Aja's candle jars and lit it.

What if Aja wasn't here? Where could she be? Why would she waste whatever battery life was left in the CD player in an empty room?

Creeping through the hall with the flickering light of the candle, I feared the worst. Or worst adjacent to going combustible.

My body tensed when I saw light coming out from under one of the bathroom doors.

I almost knocked. What if someone other than Aja was behind that door? It was better to take them by surprise. Just what I would do if it was anyone other than Aja was a mystery even to me.

I twisted the knob and threw the door open.

Aja was in a tub filled with bubbles, surrounded by candles. The confusing perfume of too many conflicting aromas cut through everything guarding my nose.

Aja's eyes flew open and she screamed bloody murder, kicking bathwater and bubbles over the lip of the tub.

"It's just me! It's just me!"

She covered her breasts with one arm and shouted, "What the hell are you doing in here?"

"I thought something had happened to you."

"What the hell! How can taking a bath make you think something was wrong?"

I nearly choked on a dry swallow. "I knocked. I called out your name. How could you not have heard me?"

Then I spotted the empty bottle of wine and wineglass on the floor.

"I think you're tired of beating your meat and wanted to see if you could get some."

Now, there was a time she would have said that with a sly smile and world-class bedroom eyes.

"Yes, I came to take advantage of you," I replied, suddenly exhausted.

"Hand me that towel and turn around."

"Are you serious? I've seen you naked more times than I can ever count."

"Turn around."

I handed her the towel, sighed, and gave my back to her. "Are you decent now?"

"Yes."

She bumped into the sink when she tried to get another towel for her hair.

"How was the wine?"

Aja curled her upper lip at me. "Don't drunk shame me. That's funny, coming from you."

"I think we can finally get past all the shaming nonsense now. I came to tell you that I went out today and scored an RV. From the looks of it, it will sleep six or more. Not that I plan to fill it up."

She tucked her hair under a towel and turned to look at herself in the mirror. "So what does this have to do with me?"

"I figured we'd use tonight to pack and then head on over to Dave's first thing in the morning."

She spun on the balls of her feet to face me. "I'm not going anywhere with you."

"Are you crazy?"

"No. Are *you* crazy? You're the one that cut me out of your life. Why would you even want me with you?"

"Really?"

"Yes. Really."

"You can't stay here alone. I mean, Christ, you left your door unlocked, and you were passed out in the bathtub. Anyone could have come in here."

"Anyone did." She went back to mirror gazing.

"I'm being serious."

"So am I. You made it pretty clear that we're done. Now you and your little friend Dave can go off to Canada and have fun."

I wanted to pull my hair out. "Oh yeah, it's going to be a laugh a minute. Can't wait. You're out of your goddamn mind."

She glared at me through the mirror. "That's one thing I'm not. Look, I know what I did was wrong. You can't forgive me, I understand that. That's you're right and if I'm being honest, most people in your shoes would feel the same way. I'm cool with that. I can live with it. There's no way I'm going to live in a freaking RV with you when I know deep down you hate me."

I opened my mouth to reply, but pulled back. The easy thing to say would be that I didn't hate her. Sure, there were times over the past few months when I felt I truly did, but it was impossible to forget that we loved each other deeply before this mess.

So why couldn't I just say it and maybe move us beyond what I believed on her part to be a suicidal impasse?

"See," she said. "You know I'm right. Now if you'll please get out of my bathroom."

I slammed the door on my way out and shouted, "At least lock the damn door!"

My night was spent deciding what was worthy of packing and what could stay behind forever. Through it all, I kept wondering what Aja was doing, trying to convince myself that I didn't care.

JERK

I tried calling Dave again just as the sun was coming up.

No dice.

Worry started to creep in.

Just chill, I told myself. *You'll find out soon enough.*

I heard movement coming from next door. Whenever Aja drank, she made it a point to wake up early the next day and do yoga. She said it got all the toxins out. She used to try to get me to do yoga, but quickly learned that my inflexibility was probably the one thing keeping me together.

The to-do checklist I'd made the night before was taped to the screen of my defunct TV. I freshened up, changed, had a breakfast of a granola bar and bottle of water and double checked the three bags I'd packed. I'd stuffed a lot of my winter gear for the trip, figuring it would be pretty cold by the time we made the Northwest Territories.

I also had the guns, just in case. It was smart to constantly remind myself that pacifism died the moment SHC crept into the world.

I was about to grab a couple more paperbacks when I heard someone outside say, "Oh yeah, baby, show me those tits."

Standing across the street was a man in his early thirties

who looked deranged at worst, homeless at best. His pants were off, and he was stroking a considerable erection. I followed his glassy-eyed gaze to Aja's window.

Crap.

She must have been doing her stretching by the window. And now she'd garnered the attention of the only person walking about for God knew how long.

I knocked on the wall. "Aja. You have an admirer."

There was a pause, and then a return slap. Did that mean she knew what I was saying, or dismissing me?

"Look out your window."

I did. The man was still going at it.

I went over and knocked on Aja's door.

"I'm busy."

"Can you please look out your..."

I stumbled back when the door whooshed open. Aja was in a bra and panties, her dreads tied up in a thick band. "What now?"

I took her by the hand and started walking. She pulled back, standing her ground. I let her hand go. "Can you please just come to the window?"

"I thought you would be on the road by now."

"For once, just listen to me."

To my surprise, she followed me. I stepped over her yoga mat and looked out the window.

"I don't see anything."

"Some crazy guy was right there beating his meat to your yoga workout."

"Ha ha."

"I'm not kidding."

She pointed to the doorway. "Go. Pick up Dave so you guys can freeze to death in Canada."

And that took us to another point. I'd promised myself I was going to make one more attempt to get Aja to go with us.

Unable to meet her irritated gaze, I instead looked at a stain in the rug shaped like the state of Maryland. "I really think you should come with us. It's not safe here."

"But it'll be safer in a car on steroids? I don't think so."

"You shouldn't be here alone."

"I can take care of myself."

I was about to remind her about the night before when the street masturbator came running into the apartment. His pants were completely off, and his boner slapped against his stomach as he sprinted toward Aja. Seeing him up close, catching the utterly demented look in his eyes, I knew we were in trouble. I pushed Aja out of the doorway and onto the bed.

"I want those titties!" the crazed man shrieked. He made a quick pivot, locking onto Aja on the bed and throwing a hip check my way that nearly sent me sidestepping out of the window.

He leaped onto the bed. Aja scrambled to the other side and jumped off.

Regaining my footing, I lunged at the man. My hands missed getting a hold on his bare ankles. His skin was streaked with filth. The stains on his ass cheeks nearly had me hurling.

As he reached out for Aja's breasts, she brought a knee up to his lower jaw. The clack of his teeth crashing together set my own teeth on edge.

The man's eyes rolled up into his head and he wobbled on the edge of the bed. Aja grabbed a lamp and smashed it on the back of his head. He collapsed face down on the bed, his muscles letting go as he evacuated his bowels on the twisted sheets.

Aja waved at the air in front of her face. "Oh my god, that's so nasty I think I'm gonna get sick."

She scurried out from the side of the bed and fled the room.

I checked to make sure the man was still breathing, unsure if I wanted him to be alive or not. His back rose and fell gently, and he even started snoring. I joined Aja in the living room.

This time, I looked her square in the eye. "You're coming with me, and that's that."

Her eyes flicked over my shoulder to the scene of the near crime.

"You can argue with me all you want...when we're in the RV," I said as I made sure to lock her door just in case he wasn't a lone jerker.

"You just don't want to feel guilty," she said.

I gritted my teeth.

"Look, when I married you, I took our vows seriously. And even though you didn't, I'm still responsible for you."

"You're not my father." Never mind that she hadn't known her father.

"No. I'm your husband, despite everything, which is more than anything you've ever had. So, pack your stuff before this nut job wakes up and let's go."

We had a bit of a standoff, complete with an unspoken staring contest.

Aja blinked first.

She huffed all the way to our apartment to get her bags. I kept an eye on the crazy man when she returned and packed. Or more like overpacked.

Neither of us said a word to one another as we transported the remnants of our old life into the RV. Aja broke the silence when she stepped into the house on wheels. "I thought it would be bigger."

"You didn't say that the night after Gina's party."

She settled into the passenger seat and looked away. I wasn't sure if it was out of disgust with my bringing up our first night together or to hide her expression.

I started the Freedom Elite up and knocked the fender off the car in front of me as I pulled out.

We were just past our building when I hit the brakes.

"What now?" Aja said.

I pointed to the side-view mirror. A gang of men and women wearing leather and Halloween masks, had turned the corner. All had various blunt weapons in their hands. Two men at the lead towed what looked to be a wide cart on wheels. They spotted our building and swarmed inside.

My heart raced and the acids in my stomach curdled as I heard things breaking inside. These looters were prepared, fearless and looked like they would kill you without a second thought.

I gunned the engine, catching the attention of those who had yet to enter the building.

"Holy shit," Aja said, her hand over her heart. "I mean...holy shit."

"One thing about a car on steroids," I said as I turned the corner. "It's got wheels, which means you can just drive away from trouble."

DAVE

The closer we got to Dave's house, the more devastation we came across. Entire blocks of row houses were razed to the ground, some of the piles still emitting columns of smoke. So much ash collected on the windshield, I had to keep the wipers on (after pulling over and spending too much time figuring out how to turn them on).

"He probably left already," Aja said.

"We don't know that for sure." I concentrated on the road. The streets here were littered with bicycles, trash, broken glass, discarded bits of construction material from the collapsed houses, and in some spots, the remains of people. I especially didn't want to roll over their ashes and leftover body parts.

"I know I would have."

"Says the woman who was going to stay in our building."

She crossed her arms over her chest and ogled the post-apocalyptic scenery.

I breathed a sigh of relief when I spotted Dave's two-family house. The blue shingles were a little toasted on the side next to the half-burned house. "At least it's still standing," I said, pulling into the driveway.

"It doesn't look like anyone's home."

"None of the houses do. But we're testament that there are people left. And I don't think homelessness is a problem anymore. Too many empty places to choose from." I opened the door and reached behind me for the pipe I'd carried with me to the RV lot and back. I felt it had a bit of luck on account of I'd made it back alive, with my goal, and without having to use the pipe on anyone.

"I'm not waiting here alone," Aja said.

We closed our doors quietly.

"How do you go from wanting to come with me to not being able to wait in the RV?"

"This neighborhood gives me the creeps. Why were there so many fires here?"

We cautiously walked up the steps. "Too many houses in too little space. You get so many people jammed against one another, that's a lot of combustible potential." I reached out and almost rang the bell. Aja eyed my extended finger and shot me an *are you kidding me* look. "Force of habit."

The door was locked, so I knocked. When there was no reply, I knocked again and put my ear to the door.

"You hear anything?" Aja asked. Her head was on a swivel, looking up and down the block for potential trouble.

"No."

"Maybe he headed up to Canada without you."

"He wouldn't do that. Especially since I'm the one who told him about it. One thing Dave isn't is a lone wolf."

A chill wind skittered down the street Aja hugged herself. "I just hope he's okay."

I used the bar to break one of the little square panes of glass in the door. "Yeah, me, too."

Like us, Dave was an orphan. He'd grown up with parents, but they had been killed when driving home from a work event by a drunk driver. He had no siblings and his extended family were distant at best. We had been each other's family now for quite a while.

No sooner had I opened the door than I heard the rush of

heavy footsteps above. What could best be described as a throat-ripping war cry followed.

I instinctively pushed Aja behind me and raised the pipe with one hand while fumbling in my pocket for the gun with the other. I spotted a pair of legs scrambling down the stairs. I may have let out my own warning growl.

Dave had an aluminum baseball bat raised high over his head. He wore a trucker hat and a pair of boxers with bananas resting in the crease of peaches. His beer gut jiggled as he ran.

He came charging at us with abandon, without the slightest hint of recognition of who we were.

Just before he brought the bat down on my head, I pulled my mask down and took off the beanie I'd stuck on my head before I left the apartment.

Dave let the bat slip from his hands and it bounced on the steps. "Holy shit, it's you!"

He pulled me in for a bear hug before I could say a word. He smelled liked he'd passed his sell-by date and his back was sweaty.

When he looked up after pounding me on the back, he saw Aja and shouted, "Aja! Come here."

"I don't think so," she said, clearly appalled by his physical state.

Not that he cared. He let me go, and I turned my head to the side and took a hearty gulp of semi-fresh air. Aja was crushed against him. I noticed that Dave was crying.

"I was so worried about you guys," he said, his breath hitching. Aja kept her hands at her sides. He mercifully released her. "When I didn't hear back from you, I assumed the worst. And then my phone lost all its charge and I've been losing my mind ever since."

I couldn't help but smile. Dave's hair had gotten long in the back, morphing into a mullet. He hadn't shaved in a while and his beard game was terrible. There were patches on his face where nary a whisker grew. He stood there in his underwear with his hands on his hips.

"Didn't you hear me knocking?" I asked.

"Nah. I was asleep. Not much else to do, right? Come upstairs." We followed him up and into his apartment. Aja pinched her nose and rolled her eyes. I motioned for her to keep it to herself.

"Sorry about the mess," Dave said.

Mess was an understatement. If I hadn't known better, I would swear he'd been robbed. Empty cans of beer and pre-made pasta were everywhere, along with dirty clothes, napkins, balled-up tissues and a considerable stack of nudie magazines next to the couch. He saw me looking at them and positioned his body so Aja couldn't see the pile of smut.

"Where did you get those?" I whispered to him while Aja hung back, surveying the nightmare.

"Stationery store two blocks over. Once the power was out, free porn videos were gone, I had to do something. It's where I got all the beer, too."

"I'm surprised they weren't already gone."

"The owner was still there holding down the fort. He was a former Marine in Vietnam and a retired cop. Tough old bastard. I paid for all of it, like a good citizen."

"You are not allowed to let the RV get like this," Aja said.

"RV?"

I smiled. "I got us some wheels so we can head to Canada. Check it out." I opened the blinds to the window overlooking the driveway.

"Is it true what they said about Consumption?"

"Honestly, I don't know. But I'm willing to give it a try. No sense staying here."

Aja tapped Dave on the shoulder. She'd hooked a pair of sweatpants on her finger. "If you don't mind."

"Yeah," I added. "There's a lady present. Show some class."

For the first time in I couldn't remember how long, Aja and I both laughed.

"Oh, shit, right." Dave dipped into his bedroom and came

out seconds later wearing the sweatpants and a Daffy Duck t-shirt. "I take it we're hitting the road now."

"Yep," I said.

"Okay, I gotta pack. Crap, I don't think I have any clean clothes."

"We'll find a way to air them out," Aja said. "You have a laundry bag?"

"Of course."

"Fill it with your clothes. How about some rope?"

"What are you talking about?" I asked her.

"We'll poke holes in the bag and tie it to the roof. Let Mother Nature de-funkify his stuff."

Dave frowned. "Hey, I'm right here, taking offense."

"And find something to stick in your nose," Aja said, stepping over his porn stash. "You are not sneezing and turning that RV into an Easy Bake oven."

THE ROAD

After Dave bathed using a jug of room temperature water, we loaded up his stuff and all the food and drink he had into the RV. It was going on noon by the time we hit the road. His bag of dirty clothes was lashed to the roof and I hoped it stayed that way.

Although, if it did become a road casualty, we could always stop at a store and grab some new clothes. I'd watched him pack up a Britney Spears concert t-shirt from 2001 and several pairs of sweatpants, all of them with considerable stains and one with a rip in the crotch. The man could stand a wardrobe revamp.

Dave settled into the padded seat of the dinette area while Aja rode shotgun. I wanted to roll the windows down, but the air streaming in was anything but fresh.

"This is a pretty sweet ride," Dave said as he spooned cold Spaghettios from a can. "When did you buy an RV?"

"I didn't exactly buy it," I said, catching a portion of him from the elongated rearview mirror.

"Oh, yeah, right. How come you didn't grab one of those huge mamas with pop out sides and more bells and whistles than a house?"

This coming from a man who'd never gotten his license.

"How about I drop you off on that corner and you can whistle 'You Don't Know What You Got, Til It's Gone' all the way home?"

I didn't have to force a laugh or a smile of shout, "LOL!" for Dave to know I was messing with him. His spoon scraped against the can as he said, "Did I tell you how sweet this ride is?"

I spotted a gas station and pulled in.

"We out of gas already?" Aja said.

"No, but we should grab as much as we can whenever we can. Plus, I need a map."

She cocked her head at me. "You don't know how to get there, do you?"

I steeled myself. "I know we're going to head west on 80, and then at some point we'll have to go north and cross the border. I drew a map, but I don't know how accurate it is."

Aja threw up her hands. "So you make this big plan to take us all the way to nowhere and you don't even have a clue how to get there?"

"I'm not sure if you noticed, but Google Maps is down due to technical difficulties. All the systems died before I could map the whole trip out. It'll be fine. People got to where they were going before they were dependent on their frigging phones."

I thought I heard her mutter, "Idiot," as I got out of the RV. I heard Dave say, "I'll go with him." He came out the side door, his nostrils now filled with bits of cork from a wine bottle.

"Trouble in Paradise?"

I regretted not telling Dave our issues back when they had started. I'd asked myself why many times and had come to the conclusion that I was embarrassed. And maybe ashamed. Not just for me but for Aja and us.

"What's Paradise?" I said as I walked into the station's mini-mart. I saw a lone, red plastic gas can underneath a shelf of wiper fluid and grabbed it.

"That whole quarantine was a bitch," Dave said. "It sucked

being alone, but in a way, at least I didn't have any friction, which is only natural when two people are cooped up for too long."

All of the shelves that would normally hold snacks were empty or pulled down. I searched in vain for a rack of maps. In the cold cases, all that was left were some cartons of very spoiled milk.

"Not even a bag of Cheetos. Man, people suck." Dave kicked a can of motor oil across the floor.

"Well, at least we can try to fill this up," I said, shaking the empty gas can.

"I got it." Dave swiped the can out of my hand and jogged to the nearest pump. He looked perplexed when nothing worked. I shook my head and dipped into the one-car workshop.

"You need electricity for the pumps to work," I said when I came out.

"So how do we get gas?"

"With this." I held up a rubber hose.

Dave looked perplexed. "And how is that going to help?"

"You never heard of siphoning gas?"

"Nope."

"But I bet you can tell me the top ten porn stars before SHC started."

Now he smiled. "Well, there's Bella White, Ashley Spanx, Lita B…"

"I get the point. Here, I'll show you because we're going to be siphoning a lot of gas on this trip. Keep your eye out for gas cans anytime we stop at a gas station. We'll need them as much as we need food."

I spotted a Camry parked on the side of the garage. "I'm sure there's some gas in that tank."

"This I have to see," Dave said.

I had to run back into the garage to get a screwdriver because we couldn't pop the cover to the gas cap. "We should fill up a toolbox before we go. We're going to need them."

After prying it open, I unscrewed the cap and fed the hose down into the tank. We squatted around the gas can.

Dave looked at me. "Now what?"

"You really never heard of this?"

"I'm serious."

"Anyway, all I have to do is suck on this for a little bit and the gas will come pouring out into the can."

"That's it?"

Now I had my doubts. I'd only ever seen it done in movies and I think in a Woody Woodpecker cartoon. "It should be."

I put the tube to my mouth and inhaled. Noxious gas fumes immediately went to my brain, making me lightheaded.

"How do you know when it's working?" Dave asked.

I turned to look at him and shrugged. A half-second later, my mouth was filled with a flood of gasoline. The introduction of a fluid so deadly and horrendous set off alarm bells. I felt a panic attack coming on.

Immediately spitting the poison out, I had the presence of mind to stick the hose into the gas can.

Dave laughed.

I threw up in his face. By accident. Though maybe there is a little intent coming from my subconscious.

Dave shot to his feet and threw up on the Camry's trunk.

I ran to the RV, spitting with every step, and opened the door so hard it almost came off its hinges.

"What happened?"

Aja was sitting on the sofa reading a magazine. She jumped up when I came rushing in.

I couldn't speak. I opened the refrigerator and grabbed a can of Coke, guzzling half the can until the carbonation and gas sent it all rocketing back up my throat. I vomited into the mini sink this time.

"Sam?"

I waved Aja off, slowly drinking more Coke and carefully spitting into the sink. In between sips, I tried to catch my breath.

"It stinks like gas," Aja said, waving at the air.

I opened my mouth and pointed. The fumes were so rich I thought I was going to pass out.

"Did you siphon gas?"

I nodded.

"I bet you sucked on the hose and got a mouthful."

I nodded again.

"There's an easier way." I thought I detected some sympathy, but it was hard to see behind the wall of superiority. "I can show you next time."

I pushed past her to get some air outside. Dave was staggering to the van, covered in my and his vomit. "I fucking hate you."

I gave him a thumbs-up.

The RV door slammed, and I heard it lock. Aja moved to the passenger seat and rolled down the window. "Don't think either of you are coming in here until you clean up."

We went back to the shop and found a roll of rough, brown paper towels. I loaded up a toolbox and Dave grabbed two fire extinguishers.

"I guess this makes us even," Dave said as we walked back to the RV.

"Even? For what?"

"Remember when I threw up on your pants and shoes when we had that liquid lunch at The Bayou?"

I stopped. "That was you? I'd always assumed I did it to myself."

Aja had left a bowl of water and a bar of soap on the ground for us. We did a quick lather up and hit the road in search of a map.

OUT FOR WALKIES

It took three more gas station stops before we found some maps. A couple would guide us to the Canadian border. I'd hoped Canadians were less reliant on technology and stocked more maps in their gas stations and rest areas.

In one of the stations, Aja came out with us and found some more tubing, which she'd cut into a foot-long tube.

"This is how it's done," she said, inserting the long tube into the tank of an abandoned car, and then the small tube. She covered them with a cloth, blew into the small tube and gasoline instantly poured out of the larger one into another gas can we'd found.

"How did you know how to do that?" Dave said.

"I saw it on YouTube one night when I couldn't sleep. Don't ask me how I stumbled into gas siphoning vids. I thought it was a cool life hack, so it stuck."

I mumbled a thank you.

Aja's nose wrinkled. "Your breath can still melt glass."

I pulled Dave to come along with me to get the other gas cans we'd found and stored in the RV. "And you can kiss my ass," I said, though I'm not sure Aja even heard me.

"Thank God for her," Dave said. "I don't think I could have

handled getting a mouthful of gas and I'm sure as shit not going to get puked on again."

"Yeah, she's such a blessing."

Dave paused and gave me a look. I made it clear I wasn't in the mood to elaborate.

On the road with proper provisions and almost thirty gallons of gas, I headed toward the entrance ramp to I-80. The streets were relatively clear. I had to swerve around a burned-out shell every now and then. I slowed down long enough to look down into one. The driver's seat was blackened with a pile of ash in the center. The bottom half of the steering wheel had literally melted away. A whole right arm lay on the unharmed passenger seat.

According to the map, we were about a quarter of a mile from the highway when Aja leaned forward in her seat and point out the window. "Look."

What looked like a considerable campfire burned on the sidewalk up ahead. As we got closer, we saw a writhing shape within the flames.

"Stop. Stop!"

Aja jumped to my side and tugged the wheel hard enough to send the RV hurtling toward the curb. I mashed the brakes to keep from going through the plate-glass window of a pharmacy. Its door had already been smashed open, but why add to the mess?

Aja was out the door before the RV came to a full stop.

I looked out the windshield and saw why.

A Siberian husky puppy tugged at the end of its leash, frantic to get away from the fire. The only problem was, its owner in the center of the fire still had the strength to keep a firm grip on the leash. He or she was on their knees, head bowed, turning crisper than burned bacon (and smelling disturbingly like it), but half the arm that held onto the leash was untouched by the flame.

Aja wrapped her arms around the dog and fumbled with its

collar, trying to set the dog free. The husky hopped on its hind legs, yipped and howled piteously.

Dave and I scrambled out of the RV. Aja turned to me with a desperate look on her face. "Help me!"

The dog snapped at her in its terror. Or maybe it hated people.

I wasn't a big fan of dogs. I'd been bitten by a poodle when I was seven and then a bulldog when I was sixteen and had jumped a neighbor's fence to go pool hopping. Apparently, dogs weren't a fan of me, either.

Thankfully, Dave loves all animals and grabbed hold of the leash and tugged. The arm pulled away from the burning body and the dog started to run. Aja practically tackled the thing while Dave stomped on the burning section of the limb.

It may have been wrong to find the whole scene funny, but so what?

Aja wrapped the mid-section of the leash around her wrist and dug her heels in to keep the dog from darting down the street. "Get over here, idiot!"

I'm still sure why I rushed to help her. But I did. Together, our combined weight was too much for the dog. He stopped scrambling and turned to us as if to say, *fine, you win.*

I looked over at Dave. He'd tamped down the flames and pried the end of the leash out of the fingers, each one cracking loudly in the process.

"I think I'm gonna get sick," Dave said, handing the loop over to Aja.

"No, you're not," she said to him.

He looked down at his sweatpants. The bottoms were poked full of burn holes. "Oh man, it ruined my best pair."

All I wanted to do was get away from the burning body and back on the road. We'd barely gone ten miles the whole day, what with all the stops. At this rate, we'd get to Consumption right around my retirement age.

"Come here, baby. It's all right. Come on. Yes. You're okay."

The husky hesitantly approached Aja, and she petted its black-and-white fur, talking to it as if it were a baby.

"Okay, we saved a dog. A deposit for the karma bank," I said, watching the sun in the western sky. "Time to hit the dusty."

Aja gathered the leash, looked at the husky, and said, "Come on, puppy. Come on," as she led it into the RV.

"I didn't say to take the dog with us."

Aja whirled around. "Oh, you want to let the puppy just fend for itself?"

"That's exactly what I was thinking. We can't pick up every stray along the way. This is an RV, not an ark."

"He's coming with us."

"He'll be fine. The stray dogs I've come across don't look like they've missed a meal."

"He's a puppy. He needs us."

The husky went from wagging its tail at Aja to snarling at me.

"I don't think so. Last thing I need is some dog biting me while I'm trying to drive this thing."

Aja rolled her eyes. "He won't bite you. Dogs are sensitive. He senses you don't want him here."

"Seems smart enough then to make it in the big world."

"I told you, he's coming with us."

I took a deep but less than calming breath. "For someone who didn't even want to make this trip, you sure are bossy. For my money, you should have left your HBIC hat back at the apartment."

She looked away from me and buried her face in the dog's neck. "You're an asshole."

"And you're a cheating bitch with a 'my way or the high-way' complex."

Aja snarled just as the dog had. "Oh, fuck you."

My blood boiled.

"No, fuck you!"

Dave stepped into the RV with an armload of cans of dog

food, looking like a lost puppy himself. "Am I interrupting something?"

ROAD FLARES

Dave and Aja played with the dog while I drove. The dog made occasional weird howls that sounded like a person impersonating a sick werewolf. Disturbing.

While I drove, I kept hitting the seek button on the radio to find any stations still broadcasting. So far, all I got was static.

"Gimme your paw," Dave said.

I looked in the rearview and saw Dave on his knees with his outstretched hand. The husky cocked his head, looking at my friend's palm. "You can do it."

"Can you sit for mommy?" Aja said in a singsong voice.

The husky sat, his tongue hanging out of the side of his mouth.

"Good boy." Aja reached into a bag of dog treats and gave one to the husky. Dave had grabbed every bit of dog food left in the pharmacy's shelves. Aja and Dave were enjoying this Hallmark moment, forgetting we were living in a grindhouse flick.

I turned back to the road just in time to spot the abandoned motorcycle in the center lane. I cut the wheel hard to the right and swerved around it. I heard Dave, Aja, and the husky side along the floor, all protesting loudly.

"What the hell is wrong with you?" Aja said.

"Would you rather I drive through every car and motorcycle I see?"

My hands were shaking, and sweat beaded on my hairline. That had been too close. I spotted waves of ash spiraling from the motorcycle in my side-view mirror.

"At least give us a heads up," Aja said.

"I'll remember that for next time when I have a split second to react and not get us in an accident. My apologies."

"Hey, no harm, no foul," Dave said, trying to keep the peace. "Thank you for doing the driving and not getting us killed."

"Maybe I should take the wheel for a while," Aja said. She'd eased her way into the passenger seat. I watched her rub her elbow from the corner of my eye.

"It's getting dark soon," I said. "I'll probably just pull over for the night."

"Fine. I'll take first shift in the morning."

We'd see about that. Aja hadn't been behind the wheel in a long time. Even when she drove, she'd never been a master of the road.

Then again, neither had I.

So far, I'd only seen one other car on the road, and it was going in the opposite direction. There were cars and trucks pulled to the shoulder here and there. I suspected I'd find a lot of ash and hands and feet roasting away in the sealed vehicles. Nothing I could stuff in my nose would ward off that smell.

"Uh oh," Dave said.

"What?" I asked.

"Little guy just had an accident. I wonder if he'd been able to do his business before his owner went combustible."

I slapped the wheel with my hand. "Fantastic. We have a shortage of paper products, and what we do have is going to go toward mopping up piss."

Aja shot me a look and went back to the dog. "That's okay, puppy. Everyone has accidents. We'll take you for a real walk soon."

We'd just passed the last exit for the Poconos. I saw a sign that Scranton wasn't too far. It would be kind of cool to spend a night in Scranton. Aja and I had watched every episode of *The Office* about five times over. It was a definite comfort watch for us.

Come to think of it, Scranton wasn't going to be such a cool stop. I planned to take the next exit when I saw flames in the dying light.

I slowed down, coming to a stop next to a similar RV pulled to the side of the interstate.

Behind the RV burned four fires—two large and two small.

A family.

Had they all gone combustible at once?

Or had one gone and the others willfully followed?

Or, and this made my stomach cramp, had they had enough and taken their lives as a family unit? It didn't take much to induce a sneeze.

Acid burned the back of my throat when I spied a tiny hand outside one of the human bonfires.

"What is it?" Aja and Dave asked. They walked to the front of the RV to get a look. I held out my hand.

"Don't."

I hit the gas too hard, sending Aja and Dave on their asses. Aja was none too pleased. Dave laughed.

I wanted to cry.

TOO SPICY

I drove another ten miles and pulled into an empty rest area for the night. It was unsettling to be right near a dark and quiet highway. Normally, I'd bet this rest area would be buzzing with cars unloading passengers so they could hit the bathroom, grab some snacks from the vending machine, stretch their legs, or walk the dog.

"I'm going to take the dog out for a walk," Aja said.

It was dark outside. Too dark, because the overhead lights weren't on.

"I'm not sure that's such a good idea."

Dave was rustling through the dinette cabinets.

"You want him to have another accident and use up your precious paper towels?"

The husky glared at me with canine contempt.

"I don't know if you're being willfully ignorant, but yes, paper towels are precious."

She opened the door. "Which is why we're going for a walk."

A part of me wanted her to step out that door and keep walking. I'd start the RV up and shove off.

"Take this." I opened the glove compartment and gave her one of the guns.

"No way."

"Just in case. You don't know who could be hiding out there."

"At a rest stop in the middle of nowhere? Not too paranoid."

I put the gun on the retractable dining table. "Fine. Don't take it. Have fun roaming around the dark."

"Why don't I go with her?" Dave said. "I'll even take the gun."

"That would be cool," I said.

The door slammed shut.

"Or not," Dave said. He had a pot in each hand. "I'm sure you don't need me to tell you, but your vibes are way off."

I slumped onto the sofa. I had read in the manual left in one of the consoles that it pulled out into a bed. "You have no idea."

"How long has it been like this?" He put the pots away, found a frying pan and put it on the three-burner stove. He then pulled off the tops of a couple of cans of Spam.

"Too long and I'm too tired to get into it." I lay my head back and closed my eyes. "What in God's name are you planning to make?"

"My world famous, if the world would only stand up and take note, spicy Spam and rice."

"I hate Spam."

"Have you ever tried it?" I heard him digging the meat paste out of the can.

"Once and that was enough."

"The key is, you have to fry it and season it just right. Now that we live with our noses plugged up, I'm going to amp up the spice to cut through. Then I'll cube the Spam, toss it into some rice and *violet*! Spicy Spam and rice, complete with enough carbs and protein to keep us going."

"Violet?"

"It's my catchphrase. You know, for when I get my own cooking show."

"What's the show gonna be called? Single Dude Dines In?" Dave chuckled. "I have to write that down!"

I settled deeper into the sofa, fighting the urge to look out the window for Aja and the dog. Soon, the RV was filled with the sound and smell of sizzling Spam. The microwave chirped and hummed. It all sounded so normal, even though nothing was within ten galaxies of normal about this trip.

The cooking Spam and rice made it through my nose plugs, and I had to admit it smelled good. Like the split, grilled hot dogs I used to get at this corner luncheonette by one of my foster houses when I was a kid.

When the door opened, I jumped to my feet.

The husky ambled in first, looked at me sideways, and then nuzzled Dave's legs.

"Calm down, killer," Aja said to me. I realized I had my fists up in a very poor imitation of a fighter's stance.

The husky started barking, front paws seeking purchase on the lip of the stove. His tail wagged furiously.

"Somebody likes my Spam," Dave said, offering the dog a piece that was greedily devoured.

"No jumpies," Aja said, tugging on the leash. "You're going to get burned."

I thought of the dog's owner, engulfed in flames just a few hours ago. Suddenly, the Spam didn't smell so good.

The dog went wild and Aja had a hard time controlling the puppy. "I'll put him in my room for now."

She and the dog disappeared into the master bedroom at the rear of the RV. Dave looked at me and mouthed, *"My room?"*

I shrugged and went back to the sofa. My bones felt like they were made of rubber. "You can take the bed the above front. I'll be fine right here."

"It's gotten to separate beds for you and Aja now?" He sprinkled some orange and red spice onto the microwaved bag of rice.

"Separate everything."

"What the hell happened? You were the couple everyone

aspired to be, man. It's why I never settled down. I couldn't compete."

I grinned. "You didn't settle down because you couldn't find someone dense enough to say I do."

Dave waved the spatula at me. "I'd have a snappy comeback if it wasn't true. Dinner's almost ready."

"That was quick. I was hoping to get a power nap in before I ate."

He transferred the Spam and rice into a pot and stirred.

"You can nap later. And stop changing the subject. What went on between you two that has you like this?"

Maybe it was because I was tired, or maybe I felt he should know since he was going to be living with us in cramped quarters, but I finally resigned myself to spilling the whole story. "Just before SHC went into overdrive, I woke up one night to pee. When I got up..."

The master bedroom door opened and Aja and the husky emerged. "I'm starving." She'd changed into stretch pants and an oversized shirt. "What's on the menu?"

Dave grabbed a bowl and spooned some out for Aja. "I present Dave's world-famous spicy Spam and rice."

Aja looked into the bowl the way a student would gaze at the frog they were about to dissect against their will. "Spam?"

"Try it. Trust me, you'll like it."

"Beggars can't be choosers," I said. "If you want fresh meat, you're gonna have to kill it, skin it and butcher it." Aja dismissed me with a cutting look.

She tucked her fork in the bowl and filled it up. "Maybe now's a good time to go vegan."

Dave clucked his tongue. "You need protein. Just give it a shot."

The husky whined.

"See, he knows it's good."

"He's a dog who would probably eat another dog's shit," I said.

Aja shook her head at me and took a bite. She went from squeamish to smiling in a nanosecond. "Hey, not bad."

Dave beamed. "See. I told you!" He made another bowl and brought it to me. "Dig in, brother."

Dave jammed a spoon in the pot and ate from it. I took a bite and was mildly surprised. "Not bad."

Not good, either, but I was hungry, and it went down fast. My brain had a hard time reconciling that I was eating canned meat. My stomach, on the other hand, was happy with Dave.

We were all finished in less than two minutes. Stress has a way of either wiping out or awakening an appetite.

"I'll wash the dishes," Aja said, putting her bowl in the small sink.

"Nope, I've got it," Dave said, taking my bowl. "It's the least I can do for you two saving me from my apartment."

I was ready to go to sleep even though it was barely seven o'clock. The day had felt like a year and may have taken that much from my life.

While Dave worked at cleaning everything up, the husky couldn't help itself from jumping on him, begging for attention. Aja attempted to corral the pooch with very little success.

"I know, dude, I'm awesome. Just let me finish up here," Dave said to the dog.

The husky leaped and knocked into the counter. I saw the bottle of spice fall in slow motion. The top wasn't on. Colorful granules spilled from the holes in the top, raining down on the dog's head.

It backed away and looked up, sucking in the spice.

First, it barked.

Then it yipped.

Next, it howled, I'm sure in pain as the spicy concoction assaulted the membranes of its nose.

Aja went to console the dog.

Dave dropped the pot and reached down to grab the spice, sending more into the air.

I saw the husky's eyes close. Its face bunched up.

"No!" I shouted as I bolted from the sofa. There was a mini fire extinguisher clamped to the wall by the stove. I vaulted over the dog and ripped the extinguisher free, body-checking Dave in the process. Dave spun out of the kitchen area and down the narrow hallway to the bathroom and master bedroom. "Aja, back away!"

She looked to me as if I'd gone mad.

And then the dog sneezed.

My fingers gripped the lever on the fire extinguisher. If SHC had any mercy, it would give us a few seconds before the dog turned into a ball of flame and destroyed our ride.

Even Aja scrambled away from the dog.

The husky sneezed again. And again and again.

But it didn't go combustible.

I didn't realize Dave was at my back until he spoke and nearly gave me a heart attack. "Why isn't he flaming out?"

"I don't freaking know."

In between sneezes, the dog wailed in agony.

"We should take it outside, just in case there's some kind of delay," I said.

This time, I didn't see Aja volunteering to take the dog. "You just had to take the fucking dog with us," I growled.

"Because I'm not an uncaring piece of crap," she shot back.

"I care. I care about us surviving!"

I grabbed the leash and practically had to pull the dog out of the RV. I jogged us away from the mobile home, stopping at a worn picnic table beside a glass-encased map of I-80. I tied my end of the leash around one of the table's legs.

And then I watched.

The husky had the sneezing fit of all sneezing fits. Its eyes leaked like waterfalls. I found myself feeling sorry for the dog. It was in real agony.

The fire should have ended its pain. Why was the dog not burning?

Dave and Aja watched from the open door of the RV.

After a few minutes, the sneezing stopped. The husky licked its nose constantly. It wagged its tail.

Dave broke the silence. "Not that I wanted to see the little guy go combustible, but what the hell, man?"

I shrugged. "Beats me. Seems to be okay now."

In the light escaping from the RV, I could make out tears running down Aja's face. "The poor baby." She ran to the dog, dropped to her knees, and wrapped her arms around its neck. "I knew there was something special about this guy." The dog slurped at her face.

It was a mystery. I kept waiting for the dog to ignite. After waiting an hour or so, I said I was going to bed.

We were a mix of mystified and glad the dog didn't suffer the same fate as its owner.

But even Aja didn't balk when I said it should sleep in the rest area's bathroom.

ROAD BLOCK

Aja woke up before Dave and I so she could walk and feed the dog. I was awakened by the dulcet tones of the husky barking its head off when she led it into the RV.

I heard a thump, and then Dave shouting, "Dammit! My head."

"Hell of an alarm clock you got there," I said, sitting up. I hadn't bothered pulling out the sofa. It was comfortable enough as is, though a little on the short side. My feet hung over the end all night, not that I cared.

Dave hopped down from his sleeping area, rubbing his head. "I see the little dude made it through the night."

"I decided to call him Miracle," Aja said, ruffling the dog's fur.

"How about flame retardant?" I said as I stretched my arms over my head.

"Or asbestos?" Dave added, laughing.

"You're both idiots. But despite that, I did score this for your breakfast."

Aja tossed a pack of Pop-Tarts to each of us. Mine was blueberry frosted. My favorite. Dave seemed happy with his brown sugar cinnamon.

"Where did you get these?" I asked with my mouth full of the sugary pastry.

"Vending machine."

"It still works?"

"When you throw a rock into it, yeah."

Dave and I devoured our Pop-Tarts while Aja nibbled on some crackers. When Dave was done, he started rubbing his belly. Before he could amble to the bathroom, I put my leg out to stop him.

"While we're stationary, ones and twos should be done outside."

"What? Why?"

"Because I don't know how much the waste tank can hold and I'm hoping to never have to find out. And knowing you, you'll clog the toilet up."

Aja made a disgusted face, then turned her attention to Miracle, the dog that defied SHC.

With a dramatic sigh, Dave said, "Fine." He took a roll of toilet paper from one of the cabinet and went outside.

"Thank you," Aja said.

I got up to get a bottle of water. "For what?"

"For saving us from Dave's morning crap. I can only imagine what that Spam is like twelve hours later."

I went to the bathroom to splash some water on my face, brush my teeth and change into a clean shirt. Then I went outside to pee. At first, I looked for some bushes or a wide tree. But, since no one was around, I decided to walk up to the edge of the highway and let it fly. Who knew public urination could be so freeing?

Back in the RV, Dave and Aja were petting the dog.

"I think I know why Miracle didn't go combustible," Dave said.

"This I have to hear," Aja said.

"Because it's spontaneous *human* combustion. Miracle is definitely not a human."

I shook my head. "I've seen animals go combustible. Plenty

of them. Did you see that video taken in Africa of those stampeding gazelles that were all on fire?"

"Huh. You're right."

Miracle licked the side of Dave's face.

"Yep. Huh," I replied. I took the keys out of my pocket and headed for the driver's seat.

"I want to drive," Aja said.

"That's okay. I think I got it."

"You don't trust me?"

That was a loaded question. I decided to stick with the whole driving aspect. "In a word—no. We'll be stuck in a ditch or wrapped around a tree before we know it."

"That's some sexist bullcrap."

I noticed Crag back away, pretending to study the bathroom door.

"That's going for the low hanging fruit," I replied, starting the RV up. "I don't want you to drive because on a good day, you're a terrible driver. Even if you had a penis and a mustache, you'd suck."

"You suck," she snapped back.

"Oh, good one. I'm wounded to my soul."

A dog biscuit whizzed past my ear and bounced off the windshield. I didn't bother turning around. Just kept my mouth shut and eased the RV onto the road.

Dave took shotgun this time. Aja was back in the master bedroom with Miracle.

We passed by some cars that had pulled over to the side of the road, but there were no signs of their occupants.

"This is really kinda creepy," Dave said, staring out the window as I slowed down to look at a white Chevy Malibu with all of its doors open. "I mean, there have to be other people around. Where the hell are they?"

I waited for a bit, honked the horn, and when no one came out from the tree line, hit the gas.

"Maybe hunkered down, waiting for the end. Or a rescue," I said.

"Or maybe there really is no one left in these parts."

That made me laugh. "In these parts? You all of a sudden from the south?"

We came around a bend and that's where I saw the pile up. The entire westbound side of I-80 was clogged with cars and trucks. At the front of the jam, there was a logging truck lying on its side, the cab burned to a cinder. Several other cars were singed as well, though not from the truck fire. You could tell the fires had started inside them, the flames licking the doors and rooftops.

"Holy cannoli," Dave said. "There must be a dozen cars."

At least. I saw tire tracks in the grass, signs that smaller cars and a motorcycle or two had come upon the wreck and driven on the sloping, grassy median to get around it.

My concern was that if I tried it with the RV, it would tip over on its side.

I stopped the RV and got out to survey the damage. It was bad. I was sure if I got close enough, I would find ash piles and rotting extremities in some of those cars.

Dave hopped out and stood with his hands on his hips, shaking his head. "This is fucked. Maybe we can turn around, get off the last exit and take side streets until we get to the entrance after this."

"I don't think our maps have that much detail, but we'll have to do it."

As a cloud passed, the sun glinted off the windshields and blinded us. "Should we gas up while we're here?"

"I guess so." I really didn't want to look inside those cars.

Dave emptied three of the gas cans in the RV tank and I gathered the tubing I kept in one of the exterior compartments.

"Why don't we just drive around it?" Aja said as she walked out of the RV with Miracle.

"Because that's a steep angle and we're driving a top-heavy vehicle," I replied.

Dave hurried past us and got to work siphoning gas out of a Dodge.

"You can at least try."

I grit my teeth. "Failure means we lose the RV and have to walk to the nearest town in Bumfuck, Pennsylvania. Not gonna happen."

"Whatever."

"Yeah. Whatever."

"Come on, Miracle." Aja shook her head at me and led the dog away. The husky gave me a lingering look before following her.

I helped Dave load up on gas. It only took a few minutes, and I was careful to keep my eyes averted. At least the stop wasn't a total loss.

As we loaded the gas cans in the RV, I thought I heard Aja talking to someone. Dave must have, too, because he cocked his head and then turned to me.

We walked to the back of the RV.

Aja was in a conversation with a tall, thin brunette dressed from head to toe in camouflage. Her nose was pinched by the kind of clip swimmers wore. I couldn't hear what they were saying, but the message became pretty clear when the woman brandished a gun with a long barrel that looked like it could turn Aja's head to a pink mist faster than I could blink.

WE HAVE A GUEST

I'd seen enough zombie apocalypse movies to know that the real monster is man. And here was an example of the species—albeit it a pretty attractive monster holding a very unattractive gun—looking like she was going to end our trip to Consumption in a hurry.

The husky, instead of protecting Aja, went over and licked the woman's leg.

"We should get your gun," Dave whispered in my ear.

Aja, to her credit, stood her ground, apparently unconcerned that there was a gun in her face.

I pulled Dave to the other side of the RV so they couldn't see or hear us. "And do what?"

"Take G.I. Jane out."

"I'm just as likely to shoot Aja. Or myself."

"We can't just stand here."

"I know that."

Dave chewed on his bottom lip. "So?"

Just then, we heard Aja say loudly, "You'll have to ask them."

"There goes the element of surprise," I said, slipping into

view. The woman swung her arm and pointed the hand cannon at me. I instantly raised my arms. "Don't shoot."

"I need a ride," the woman said.

"Where to?" I asked, hating the tremor in my voice.

"Where are you headed?"

Aja said, "He thinks that—"

"Wyoming," I said, cutting her off. "My parents have a place out in the boonies in Wyoming. Very remote. We're hoping things are better there."

The woman looked to Aja. Aja shrugged, telling her without words that I was full of crap. I knew we were in bad place, but was it at the point where Aja sided with an armed stranger over me?

"Works for me," the woman said. She had eyes so brown they bordered on black. They were very hard to read.

"Any chance you can lower your gun?" It was worth a try.

"Not until I think I can trust you."

"Says the woman holding us at gunpoint," I said.

"I'm sorry, but I can't be too careful."

"I can see that."

"She's all alone," Aja said to me. "Show some sympathy."

"How do we know she's alone? Oh, is it because she told you that?"

"Yes." Aja narrowed her eyes at me. "I believe her."

Now I threw my hands up in the air. "You believe the woman who stuck a gun in your face. I think we can safely say you're not a good judge of character."

She looked me up and down with a look of disgust. "You can say that again."

My blood boiled. "Don't even think of putting your shit on me. I'm not the one who wrecked everything."

"Hey."

We both turned to the woman. I'd forgotten she was even there for a moment. Her gun was now at her side.

"Fine," she said. "Only thing to worry about here is you two killing one another."

Miracle barked at me, and then looked up at the woman and wagged his tail. I was outnumbered.

That's when Dave seemingly fell out of the sky, arms stretched out, screaming his fool head off. The woman glanced up and stepped a foot to her left. Dave hit the ground hard enough to knock the wind out of himself. He rolled onto his back, gasping for air. Now the gun was leveled at his chest.

"He's with us!" Aja said.

"What the hell were you trying to do?" I asked him.

His mouth opened and closed, and his eyes watered. He made a strange barking sound as he tried to hold on to the tiniest wisp of air.

"Just settle down, Dave. Try to relax. You'll breathe again," I said, hand on his shoulder, cognizant that I was in the line of fire.

"You look hungry. You want something to eat?" Aja asked the armed woman.

"Actually, I'm starving."

"Come on, let's see what we can cook up."

The women left us in the dirt. I helped Dave sit up and he started to take small, steady breaths.

"Haven't had that happen since senior year gym class," he finally managed to croak.

"You okay?"

He nodded.

"I can't believe you jumped off the roof of the RV. You think this is a wrestling match? She could have shot you like a fat clay pigeon."

"I thought I had the element of surprise."

"Big guys leaping off rooftops while screaming their head off are the polar opposite of stealth."

"I know that now." Dave winced and clutched his ribs as he got to his feet. "Looks like we have one more for the road."

I scratched my head, but not because it was particularly itchy. "At this rate, I'm going to have to hot wire a tour bus. I'm sure Bon Jovi's bus is left on some dusty rode somewhere."

Dave dusted himself off. "One way to look at it. There's safety in numbers."

I eyeballed the wreck up ahead. "Yeah, until you cram them all into a tin can with weapons on board."

HELLO, MY NAME IS MINDY

We learned our new passenger's name was Mindy Daddario, and she had grown up in the area but had moved fifty miles away when she turned eighteen. She happened to be in town visiting her mother when the SHC shit hit the fan. She guided us around the side streets and back onto I-80 ahead of the pileup, all while chatting with Aja over the dinette table and eating soup.

When she was done with the soup, she asked Aja if there was anything else. Aja made her a can of store brand ravioli.

I drove in silence once we were back on the highway. Dave kept stealing glances at Mindy through the rearview mirror. I could see why. She was his type—meaning a living, breathing woman.

Actually, she was rather pretty, once you got past the Army surplus store get up.

"Is your mother..." Aja waited for Mindy to step in.

"Dead? Yeah. She caught a cold and it wasn't long after. I was out at a meeting and when I came home a couple of hours later, all that was left of her in the kitchen was a part of her right leg."

"I'm so sorry."

"It's fine. We'd never gotten along. I was trying to see if we could patch things together. To be honest, it wasn't really working. Which is why I left to go to a meeting."

Dave piped up with, "What kind of meeting?"

I backslapped his arm.

"What?"

Mindy looked directly into the rearview mirror so we could see eye-to-eye, so to speak. "I'm in AA. Got four years sobriety. I figured it was time to see if I could salvage anything with my mother. She was a dry drunk and just as angry as I remembered her."

I recalled the bottles of booze we'd loaded into the RV. They were stuffed in cabinets and under the bed in the master bedroom. I wondered if that was going to be a problem.

If Mindy was going to be a problem.

I mean, she had started this whole thing by pulling a gun on Aja.

And why was Aja suddenly so friendly toward her?

It could have been that she simply liked having another woman on board. It was nice when all we needed was each other. Well, until...

"I was fine with my mom going combustible. At least until her boyfriend came over and saw the state of her. He got all crazy. Started saying I'd done something to bring the SHC on. I told him to get the hell out of the house. He stormed off. Only he came back an hour later. He had two containers of baby powder in his hands. I jumped out of my chair when he kicked the kitchen door in. Next thing I know, he was squirting powder in my face, trying to get me to sneeze." She tapped the nose plug. "Guess he thought he'd catch me without it on. His whole plan backfired. He let out a whopper of a sneeze. The SHC came on so quick, for a second there, I think he breathed fire like a goddamn Godzilla."

Dave had turned fully around in his seat, riveted. "I can't believe he tried to kill you."

"It was no loss to society. Though he did burn the house

down. Since then, I've been looking for abandoned houses and killing time. Problem is, most houses have, you know, ashes and...parts in them. Not comforting."

Aja put her hand over Mindy's. "I'm so sorry."

Mindy shrugged. "No one has it easy now. Had some issues with the others and then I decided to hit the road, maybe find a working car on the highway and head west. If I'm going to be stuck by myself, might as well go to where the winter will be warmer."

"What others?" Dave asked.

"Nothing much to speak of. There was the guy who tried to rape me. There's always a guy like that when things get bad. Had a family of Quakers who took me in, but the wife didn't take so well to me, and well, that ended." She leaned back in the booth. The leather burped as she settled in. "Oh, and that guy wearing the prison jumpsuit." She snorted. "That didn't last long."

Why did I have the feeling Mindy left a lot of bodies in her wake? She didn't seem like the type to just up and leave. Maybe it was because she was packing and seemed completely disassociated from her recent history.

Had we just allowed a psychopath on board?

I wondered if there was a bumper sticker for that. Probably was online, if the Internet still existed.

"I'm sorry about the gun," Mindy said. "Things just haven't been easy and I had trust issues before SHC. Thought that and my outfit would make people clear away. Until I saw Aja and this little pup and got a little hope. My first impressions always suck."

"Don't you even think about it," Aja said, waving her hand. "You look exhausted. Why don't you take a nap?"

"It's been a while since I was able to sleep without one eye open."

"Take my bed. Come on, I'll get you all set up."

Aja, Mindy, and Miracle went to the back of the RV and shut the door.

"She's kind of a babe," Dave said.

"Who may have killed some people. Including a Quaker. Who would want to kill a Quaker?"

My hands gripped the wheel until my knuckles hurt.

"She didn't say she killed anyone."

"It's called reading between the lines, dude."

Dave stared longingly at the closed door. "I think you're being paranoid."

"For once, I don't want to be proven right. I think you and I should sleep in shifts tonight. Just to be safe."

"Sounds a little extreme, but fine by me. I'll take whatever shift Mindy is awake for."

I shook my head as I weaved the RV around an overturned, burned-out SUV in the right lane. "Just try to keep it in your pants."

"My odds are pretty good. You never know, pretty soon I could be the last available man on earth."

Aja came out of the bedroom alone and shut the door.

"As soon as she laid down, Miracle cuddled right up next to her. Poor girl was out before I got to the door."

It shouldn't have bugged me that a stranger was allowed in Aja's bed, and I wasn't. But it did. Nothing about a demolished relationship had to make sense.

"Maybe when she wakes up, you can paint each other's nails and do your hair," I said.

"You're an idiot, you know that?"

I looked at the map to confirm we still had a long way to go before we left I-80. Pennsylvania seemed to go on forever, and there wasn't much to see. "I'm afraid to stop driving and see who or what else you'll invite along with us."

"I'm not sorry that I care for a puppy that could have been burned alive and a woman in need."

Dave suddenly found himself very interested with the cup holders.

"Everyone's in need. And this RV is getting more crowded

by the day." I was tempted to stomp on the brakes just to pitch Aja across the RV and disturb Mindy's sleep.

"Well, maybe we'll need to get a bigger RV."

"That wasn't the plan."

"Plans get changed all the time."

I locked eyes with Aja through the rearview. "You can say that again."

WELCOME TO OHIO

We stopped somewhere in Ohio to gas up and pull behind a barn for the night. There was a used car lot ten miles before we spotted the farm, and Dave and I filled the RV and the gas cans up.

I'm no fan of remote places and this stretch of Ohio was nothing but flat land, farms and grain silos. I felt safer keeping the RV out of sight of anyone passing by the road.

Speaking of which, we did see a car going eastbound on I-80 that afternoon. We both slowed to get a look at one another. They drove some kind of muscle car—I'm not a gearhead—with what looked to be four girls in their late teens. They all sported dyed green hair and went heavy on the goth makeup.

I wanted to tell them there was a whole lot of nothing in the direction they were headed. What stopped me was a fear of them telling me the same thing about the west.

The longer we traveled, the more apprehensive I became. Where were the people? Had SHC wiped out most of the population? It was entirely possible, considering how difficult it was not to sneeze. Even with my nose plugged, I'd had several terrifying moments when one almost came out of nowhere and took me to a burning hell. And what if I sneezed in my sleep?

Another thing that bothered me was Mindy, the possible murderer of convicts, asshole boyfriends, rapists and Quakers.

Dave and I sat outside on lawn chairs we'd found in the empty farmhouse. We'd checked it before settling in just to make sure no one was home.

There were bits of people and a lot of ashes and greasy walls, but no one among the living. They did leave behind some good food, including too many jars of fresh tomatoes, mini potatoes, pickles, and fruits to fit in the RV.

Aja and Mindy's laughter drifted out of the RV's windows. Every now and then, Miracle barked excitedly.

"Man, these pickles are delicious," Dave said. His chin glistened in the moonlight with brine. "You really don't want one?"

"Pickles are the devil's food," I said. I munched on a bag of corn chips. "I hate it when a pickle hides within all the good stuff on a burger."

Aja said loud enough so we could hear, "Sam can bunk with Dave. This pull-out sofa is more comfortable than I thought."

Dave wiggled his eyebrows. "You want to be the big or the little spoon?"

I dropped the bag of corn chips in disgust. "Pretty soon, she'll have me sleeping on the roof."

Dave screwed the lid on the mason jar of pickles. "What really happened between the two of you? It's making me super uncomfortable, and you know me. Oblivious is my middle name."

He was right. It was a good reason why Dave was still single and hoarding nudie mags.

I wished we had a fire, but I was afraid the smoke would give us away. Maybe if I told our story to the flames, they would burn it all away and we could start fresh.

Then again, look at all the good fire had done the world.

I took a long pull from the whiskey bottle that was at my feet and looked up at the stars. It never ceased to amaze me, the brilliance of the night sky when you were out in the country.

"Aja cheated on me."

"What? No frigging way. Not Aja." Dave leaned so far back in his chair it almost tipped over.

"Yep."

"Dude, when? How? With who?"

"I think it's *with whom*." I took a deep breath that did little to calm me. I could feel my pulse quicken. "It was just before SHC went ape shit. And I mean just before. If I'd found out earlier, I would have kicked her out."

Dave grabbed the whiskey bottle and chugged a fair amount. "I can't believe this. Did you find her, you know, with another guy?"

"In a way. She'd been on her phone a lot."

"Aja was always on her phone."

"I mean, like a lot more than usual." I looked over at the RV, heard the women talking, and lowered my voice. "I found her phone in the bathroom one night. It was chiming like crazy, so I picked it up."

Dave's eyes bulged. "You looked at her phone? That's invasion of privacy."

"Yeah, well, there was an invasion of my marriage going on on that fucking thing. I see this text string so long, if I printed it out, we could probably drive on it all the way to Consumption. I didn't read much, but there was a lot of sex talk."

"No way. Just no way." Dave leaned his head back, staring open-mouthed at the sky.

The frank and beans I'd had for dinner curdled in my stomach. My chest hurt.

"And that wasn't the worst part."

"How much worse can it get?"

I swallowed dryly. "There were pictures. All of him. Mostly of his pathetic dick. I didn't see more because Aja came in and found me looking through her phone."

"What did she do?"

"That's the funny part. She attacked me. Like I was in the wrong. All that 'how dare you do that' and stupid shit. But I could see it in her eyes that she knew this was all on her, but she was like a cornered animal. We yelled at each other for the rest of the night. Our upstairs neighbor kept banging on the floor, but we didn't care. Not that night."

I wiggled my fingers to get the bottle back and took a drink. The burn only made my stomach hurt more. The idea now was to keep on drinking until I felt nothing.

"Sam, I'm so sorry. I wish you'd have told me sooner."

I looked over at my friend and could see the hurt in his eyes. The three of us had been friends for close to a decade now, because I didn't separate my wife from my friends. We were more than that. We were a family. Aja's betrayal had hurt more than just me, and I wanted to save Dave from that, especially when I didn't think we'd live this long after the outbreak.

After a long silence, Dave asked, "Who was it? The asshole she was sexting."

"Nobody. Just some random online that slid into her DMs and she fell for it."

"Was he local?"

I know what Dave was thinking. If he had been, and I had told Dave, we could have found the guy and beaten the crap out of him.

"Even Aja doesn't know. From the way he wrote, I'd say English wasn't his first language."

Dave's hands were on the sides of his head as if trying to keep it from exploding. I kept drinking, everything growing pleasantly fuzzier.

"Was she going to leave you for him?" he asked.

"She says no. According to her, she got sucked into the whole thing and it got out of hand."

"Did she at least apologize?"

I nodded. "Yep. A few times. But I didn't want to hear it. She blew it. She took the best thing about both of us and smashed it to pieces."

Something chittered overhead. I assumed it was a bat. I was no fan of bats, but I was feeling no pain and not in the mood to get up.

"And all of this was just texting, right?"

"Mmm-hmm."

"She was never physically with anyone?"

I shot Dave an angry look. "Please don't give me that load of horseshit. It was cheating, plain and simple. If I'd done it to her, you can bet she would call it cheating and never budge from that position. Just because she didn't swap spit with some adulterous ass hat doesn't make it any better."

Dave held up his hands. "Whoa, I was just asking. Sometimes a thing like that is just a gateway to, you know, more stuff."

I almost chuckled. "So sexting is the weed of the cheating world?"

"I don't know what I'm talking about. This is all just so crazy." He rubbed his eyes and stood up to pace around the chair. "I mean, you two were perfect. And I don't use that lightly. What hope is there for anyone if you couldn't make it?"

I swept my arms across the vast emptiness around us. "What hope is there anyway?"

Aja and Mindy burst into laughter. I took another long drag from the bottle.

Dave stopped pacing and asked, "Why did she do it? Why?"

My head felt like it was filled with helium. If I moved it too much, it would float up into the swath of glittering stars.

"I don't know."

"What does she say?"

I closed my eyes, willing my head to stay attached to my concrete body. "I never asked."

Our conversation ended there because I passed out before he could hurl another question to pick at the festering sore that was my life.

DESIGNATED DRIVER

I woke up being jostled around like loose lemons at the bottom of a shopping bag—reusable, of course. If we'd only know SHC would put an end to it all so soon, we could have saved ourselves from the war on plastic bags.

"Hey."

I sat up too fast and banged my head. After rubbing the ache away, I realized I was in the upper sleeping cabin.

And that the RV was on the road.

"Hey, good morning, Sam," Dave said. He sat in the dinette area, sipping from a mug of coffee. "How you feeling?"

My head throbbed, and I was sure it wasn't from smacking it on the roof.

"Like me and whiskey are no longer friends."

"Take this." He tossed a bottle of water up to me. I unscrewed the cap and drank half the bottle. "Who's driving?" I felt vulnerable and unsafe up there thinking that Aja was behind the wheel.

"Thought I'd give you a break," Mindy said from below. "And before you worry, I have a CDL license. This is like driving a toy for me."

Oh great, now the potential murderer controlled the RV.

Was I the only one concerned about our passenger? Were Aja and Dave so desperate to have any human contact, they were blind to the possibility that Mindy could be as bad for our health as SHC?

I slipped my legs over the side. Miracle, who had been lying on her side, got up to bark at me.

"Come here, Miracle," Aja said. The dog scampered to the passenger seat.

"Love you, too," I said to the dog as it slipped out of sight. I squatted between the driver and passenger seats. The day was bright and sunny. That was one nice thing about being away from a big city. There were a lot less fires, which meant goodbye to the ubiquitous layer of smoke that kept the skies gray and miserable. "I'm okay to drive."

That might have been a lie, but I wasn't keen on letting Mindy be the captain. What if she decided to jerk the wheel and drive the RV into a wall or down a ravine?

"You look like three shades of hell," Aja said. I thought I detected a note of genuine concern, but it was hard to tell through the throbbing in my skull and every cell in my body wailing for water. "Mindy's a really good driver. Sit back with Dave and let the ladies be in charge."

Dave piped in with, "Did I tell you I'm a feminist?"

Miracle licked Aja's face. "I could tell by your magazine collection."

His face reddened.

Mindy asked, "What magazine collection?"

"I'll tell you later," Aja replied.

Dave's cheeks looked like could fry some of his Spam on them.

Not in the mood or shape to argue, I slunk over to the dinette and sat across from Dave. I finished my water and put my head in my hands.

"You put a pounding on that bottle last night."

"My head is reminding me every second, thank you."

He leaned over the narrow table and whispered, "I don't

blame you. That's a lot you're dealing with. It's weird, too, because ever since you guys got me, I thought for sure you were the one who might have done something wrong."

I got another bottle of water and greedily sucked on it. "It's Aja's way of dealing with things when she's in the wrong. Keep on the offensive until you're tired of bringing it up. I didn't care when it was over little things, but I can't let this one go. It's all I think about, and I think it's driven me crazy."

"As if this whole combustible shit isn't enough."

"I'm beginning to wonder if the people who sneezed themselves out of existence aren't the lucky ones."

Dave's face darkened. "Don't say that, man. We're alive for a reason. We shouldn't take it for granted."

I closed my eyes and willed my headache away. Dave's optimism wasn't matching my mood...or outlook in general at the moment.

Aja and Mindy talked like long-lost friends. It was so un-Aja. Of the two of us, she had always been the quiet one, careful to let anyone get too close to her too soon.

She's trying too hard. And it's sad. And frustrating.

Was she bonding with Mindy to spite me? Or was it a case of apocalypse personality change? What was the sense of being a guarded wallflower when the world was crumbling around you?

I couldn't shake the feeling that Mindy was being used as a pawn to get under my skin. Thanks to Aja, I'd been kicked out of my sofa bed and now the driver's seat.

A cold trickle of panic dribbled down my spine.

What if Mindy thought the same thing? Would she off us like she had, in her words, *the others*?

"I gotta piss."

As soon as I got up, the RV swerved hard, and I crashed into the dinette table. The side of my thigh hurt like hell.

"Sorry," Mindy said, catching my scrunched-up face in the rearview. "Dead deer in the road."

I massaged my thigh and sucked wind through my teeth.

Did she do that on purpose?

"Is it weird to see an actual dead body instead of a clump of ashes?" Aja said.

"I think it's weird that your mind went there," Dave said.

Aja's mouth opened, and then closed, and then she turned away.

Dave had never spoken to Aja like that before. At least not when he was sober.

She knows I told him now, I thought.

Why not make our trip as uncomfortable as possible?

On the other hand, I was thankful for Dave. He beamed at me with his chubby cheeks. I gave him a thumbs-up. Solidarity in brotherhood.

After splashing cold water on my face, I filled a bowl with cornflakes and a dribble of condensed milk and started to feel a little more human after I'd eaten and finished the second water bottle.

"How long you think it will take to get to Wyoming?" Mindy asked.

I looked over at Aja who kept her eyes on the road, Miracle on her lap. We both waited to see what the other would say.

"I'm not sure. At least twenty or more hours," I said. I waited for Aja to correct me, to tell Mindy we were actually heading to some mythical town in Canada that was reportedly untouched by SHC, at least before everything went down.

When she didn't, I realized my wife had *some* reservations about Mindy. Oddly enough, it brought a small level of comfort to me.

"Of course, that's if we could go the speed limit all the way," I added. We'd had to slow down a lot to avoid cars and trucks left on the road. I suspected things would get worse if and when we had to pass through a major city.

"Cool," Mindy said. "I love driving."

In actuality, I thought it would take somewhere between fifty and sixty hours to get to Consumption. At what point in the trip would we drop Mindy off? Our route definitely did not include a pit stop in Wyoming.

"You need a refill on your coffee?" Dave asked her. She may have been a killer, but he was still on the make.

"Thanks, Dave," she said with a wide smile.

I wanted desperately to go back to sleep, but now that I was sober, I was less than enthused about sharing Dave's bed, even when he wasn't in it. I found one of my sci-fi paperbacks and settled onto the sofa while Dave flipped through an old issue of Sports Illustrated. I was impressed that it wasn't the swimsuit edition.

I was about a hundred pages into a Larry Niven book when the RV came to a sudden stop. I looked across and saw Dave was asleep.

"Something wrong?" I said, hoping there wasn't. I hadn't read this book since I was a kid, and it had its hooks in me. Maybe having another driver wasn't such a bad thing.

"Oh wow," Aja said with an air of dreamlike wonder.

I turned the book face down on the sofa and went to the front of the RV.

A sign denoting the road to Columbus was to our right. In the distance, the city itself was smoldering. A couple of its taller buildings still looked to be in one piece, but most were shells of their former selves. There were a few cars streaming out of the city, headed to God knows where.

"I used to go to hockey games there twice a year," Mindy said. "I dated an older guy who was big into the Blue Jackets. We were together for a couple of years, off and on. I got hooked on the Blue Jackets and kept going to games even after I kicked him to the curb. Now it's all gone." She pointed to where the coliseum once stood proudly. Now it was a charred wreck. "Fuck."

"I'm so sorry," Aja said, reaching over to touch Mindy's arm. I flashed her a look. Here she was, apologizing for something she didn't do or have any control over. Where was that same quickness to apologize when she threw our marriage down the toilet?

Maybe I was being irrational, but so what? This was the end of the world. Living with stuff crammed up my nose was normal now. Seeing more ashes than people was expected. Here I was waiting for my part in all of this to end, feeling very alone because my wife was both two feet from me and a thousand miles away.

I decided to take a cue from her playbook.

"You want me to take over?" I asked Mindy, putting my hand on her shoulder (and worrying she would slice it off with a hidden knife).

It looked like she was blinking back tears. "No, I'm good. Driving will help take my mind off it."

"Okay. Okay. You just let me know when you've had enough. I know this is a lot to take in."

"Thanks, Sam."

She sniffled a bit and put the RV back in drive.

Aja turned to me but I slipped away before she could convey anything with those eyes. We'd been together long enough to be able to communicate almost telepathically. I knew what she was thinking, and it made me feel warm inside.

I added, "If you need anything, a drink, food, you just ask. We're all here for you."

She drove around in a minivan facing the opposite direction. "That's very sweet of you. I'm so lucky I found you all."

I wasn't so sure she was all that lucky.

A WISH FOR BISCUITS

Mindy remained the driver for the day, as Dave and I had to get out three times to push cars out of the way. We were siphoning gas out of a Hyundai when the wind kicked up.

"Looks like a storm is coming," Dave said.

Black clouds were intruding on what I had assumed were gray ash clouds in the not-too-far distance. I was working the tubes and filling a gas can when the first gust of wind rocked the Hyundai.

"Holy crap."

"Nothing out here to block the wind," Dave said. Another gust whipped around us and suddenly Dave was on the ground clutching his face.

I let go of the hoses and ran to him. "What happened?"

"My eyes. Jesus-fuck-me-standing, it hurts."

"What happened to your eyes?" I asked, hoping he'd be a little more specific.

"I don't know. Something got in them. Feels like needles. I can't see."

"Stay right there."

I ran inside the RV and ripped open the refrigerator door.

"What's going on?" Aja said. She was feeding Miracle dog treats at the dinette.

"Something got into Dave's eyes. He can't see."

I grabbed a water bottle and hustled back out to him. Aja, Mindy and Miracle were hot on my tail. Dave sat on the ground beside the Hyundai with tears rolling down his face.

"Open your eyes," I said.

"I don't think I can." He was panting, clearly in a freakout.

"Unless you got Gorilla Glue in your eyes, I'm pretty sure you can. Come on."

His red, inflamed eyelids fluttered open. I poured the water on them, and Dave shrieked.

"Hold still."

Aja kneeled next to him. Miracle yipped and rubbed his nose on Dave's arm. "It's gonna be okay, Dave. Whatever got in your eye, we need to flush it out."

"F...fine."

He opened his eyes again and I tipped more water into them. He blinked hard, but didn't shut them entirely.

We heard the wind coming before it hit. Aja's dreads suddenly had a life of their own, undulating in the stiff breeze.

"Oh, not cool," Mindy said. I looked over at her. She was standing by the rear of the car. A stream of gray particles whooshed out of the Hyundai as the wind blew through the open windows.

For a moment, I thought I was going to be sick.

Dave had a person in his eyes.

I shook my head at Mindy and hoped she got the message. It took two bottles to flush his eyes and get him to the point where he could see well enough to get back in the RV. We settled him into a chair and Aja dried him off with a towel.

"I'm sorry I acted like such a baby," he said. Tears were still streaming down his face. "I can't take eye stuff. When I broke my wrist, I barely said ouch." He looked to Mindy. "I have a pretty high tolerance for pain. Just not when it comes to my eyes."

It was getting late, and Mindy and I moved to the front of the RV.

"He never needs to know," I whispered.

"Gotcha."

We went another ten miles and stopped at a roadside Cracker Barrel. There were no cars in the lot or rocking chairs on the front porch. It was the kind of sight I thought I would never see, even during Armageddon. I figured no matter what happened, people would be lining up at Cracker Barrel.

Mindy parked in the back.

Dave's eyes had recovered, though they were so red, it looked as if he'd spent the entire day hitting a bong.

"Who's down for some checkers?" I said.

"I'm going to stretch my legs," Mindy said as she got out of the RV.

Dave looked out the window. "It's eerie, man."

Why that would be stranger than seeing whole cities and neighborhoods deserted is something only a frequent purveyor of Cracker Barrel would know.

"I'm going to see if there's anything left inside," I said.

"Miracle needs to walk. I'll come with you," Aja said.

Dave's eyebrows shot up to the top of his head. That made two of us.

"Fine," I said.

"See if they have any of that biscuit mix. I would kill for steaming hot Cracker Barrel biscuits," Dave said.

Just the thought made my stomach growl.

"You want me to find a cow, milk it, and churn some butter for those biscuits?" I asked.

"Only if it's not too much trouble."

I smacked him on the top of his head with the rolled-up Sports Illustrated.

Aja, Miracle and I walked to the front of Cracker Barrel with its long covered porch. Miracle sniffed around and lifted his leg to mark the stairs. The double doors had been smashed in. I flipped on the flashlight I'd brought with me. The floor was littered with bits of glass, stomped candy, and crushed country CDs.

"We should be careful," I said softly to Aja. "No telling if there's someone hiding out in here."

She tied Miracle's leash to a post outside. "Don't want him stepping on glass. I hear all the vets are closed."

Miracle whined and wagged his tail, looking at us as if to say, *What do you mean you're leaving me outside? This is a joke, right?*

Her attempt at humor almost made me smile.

"Oh, look, candy," Aja said. Cracker Barrel's prodigious candy section still had a little left on the shelves. Aja grabbed a sweatshirt off a round rack and used it to load up on candy. It was filled with Sugar Daddy bars, Razzles, packs of Hubba Bubba gum and Raisinets.

"I still can't believe you like Raisinets," I said.

"They're delicious. God forbid actual fruit gets in the way of your sugar fix."

"I'm not the one literally robbing the candy store."

She stayed close to me because I had the flashlight.

Most of the tables and chairs in the expansive dining room were turned over. I spotted one of the peg games, the triangular block of wood still retaining its multicolored pegs and put it in the sweatshirt along with the candy.

When Aja looked at me, I said, "That game is addictive, and you don't need anyone else to play. Think of it as a video game for the end times. Or a healthy distraction."

"Whatever."

My foot touched down on something slippery and I went down, landing on my ass. The pain shot up my spine and I yowled. Aja picked up the flashlight that I'd dropped and scanned the floor.

When she started giggling, I asked, "What?"

"You're going to have some sweet jeans. There's pancake syrup all over the floor."

My hand came away from my jeans slick and sticky.

Wonderful.

Aja's titters turned to full out laughter. "Remember... remember when you had to go to the bathroom during the first act of Hamilton? And how you tripped over that guy's legs and fell on top of three people and all their wine spilled on you?"

It was not one of my finer moments, but they'd had a good laugh about it later that night. I didn't pay much attention to the musical after that. I was too busy stewing over my mishap and not enjoying the heady aroma of overpriced wine coming off my clothes. The worst part was I had to spend close to a week's salary for those tickets.

One thing I would not miss was Broadway.

I used the edge of an overturned table to extract myself from the gooey mess. "Yes, I remember. Some people never let me forget. Come on, let's see if there's anything left in the kitchen."

We pushed through the swinging door. My ass felt wet.

The place was a disaster.

"Looks like they had the running of the bulls in here," I said, shining my flashlight all around the carnage.

"I don't think we're bringing back biscuits for Dave."

"On that, we can agree."

Miracle started barking outside. We whipped our heads back to where we'd come. The door was still settling.

"Is that a scared bark? Or a warning bark?" I said.

"I *like* dogs. I don't *speak* dog. We should check on him."

We made it to the gift shop when it was Aja's turn to fall. Up went the sweatshirt and all the candy and peg game. Down went my wife. She'd walked right into a scattering of gumballs.

"See what I'm not doing?" I said, offering my hand. She took it and winced. "Laughing. Because I have empathy."

"Ugh. Can you break your ass?" She put her hand on her lower back and tried to straighten up.

"You can," a voice from the darkness said. My blood froze. "Especially when it's so damn bony."

ENTER SANDMAN

A man wearing a long leather duster and matching cowboy hat stepped out from behind the register counter. I shined my light on him, and he shielded his eyes with a gloved hand.

I almost laughed.

The guy looked straight out of some anime movie.

"Why are you in my place?" he asked, his voice low and gravelly as if he were trying to hide his identity.

"We're sorry, we just thought it was abandoned," Aja said, the pain still stark on her face.

"Yeah, like everything else," I said. Now that I got a better look at him, I figured him for maybe sixteen or seventeen. He was pale as a vampire with greasy hair and some acne on his cheeks. "Are you Mr. Cracker, or Mr. Barrel?"

"Sam," Aja hissed.

The kid hopped the counter. I saw him reach into his duster's pockets and when his hands came out, they were closed fists. Miracle's barking escalated to a whole new level.

"They call me Sandman."

"Who?" I asked.

He'd been walking toward us, but my question stopped him cold.

"What?"

"Who calls you Sandman? Are you with a group of survivors?" It would be good intel to find out if this apocalyptic cosplayer was alone or not.

"I've always been Sandman," he said in as intimidating a grumble as I assumed he could muster. Very close to Christian Bale's Batman. Again, I had to stifle a laugh.

He came closer.

"Why?"

He stopped.

"Why what?"

"Why do they call you Sandman? Do you put people to sleep or something?"

Aja grabbed my arm and squeezed, digging her nails into my flesh, her way of screaming at me to stop poking this walking hornet's nest. His getup would have been intimidating, if not for the pimples on his face and play acting at being the dark and mysterious Sandman.

"You're not very smart, are you?" Sandman said.

"I did pretty good on my SATs. Nailed a three-point-seven in college."

"Sam!"

Aja couldn't straighten up. It felt as if she were holding my arm just to keep herself semi-upright.

"Look, my wife is hurt, and I need to get her to lie down."

My wife. Sounded strange, but yes, she was still my wife. It just hadn't felt that way for too long.

"The Sandman doesn't care." He was now just a couple of feet from us.

"Oh, now you're doing the third person thing? I don't have time to play whatever cartoon or video game you think you're in. Are you supposed to be an X-Man or something? Just step aside so we can get out of *your* place."

Sandman sneered, and his leather gloves creaked as he tightened his fists.

"You White people think you own the world. Well, not anymore."

Now I was getting mad. "You White people? There's a mirror right over there. You might want to take a look in it."

That's when I spotted the grains of sand slipping from his fists. Or something that looked like sand. Whatever it was, I knew it was something that would induce sneezing. Our noses were plugged up pretty well, but at the moment, that wasn't all too reassuring.

Whoever thought the most terrifying thing in the world would be a simple sneeze?

"I'm not sure if you can see all that well, but my wife here is most certainly not White."

"If she's with you, she's just as guilty."

Aja hissed when we took a step back. She was really hurt, and I wondered how big the kid was under that duster. Should I just charge him and hope the plugs in my nose didn't fall out when we collided and all that sand or whatever didn't find its way up my nose?

"Just let us go, and it'll be like we were never here. No harm, no foul. Sound good?"

Sandman's face broke out in a world-class shit-eating grin.

"I'm here to finish what SHC started."

All right, this kid was a loon. The outfit kind of told me, but the look in his eyes confirmed it.

"You don't have to do this. Hasn't there been enough death?"

He shook his head slowly. "I'll trap every last one of you right here, in your white bread mecca. And once you're all gone, I'll remake the planet in Sandman's image."

"Please," Aja whimpered. "What did we do to you?"

He paused for a beat, tilted his head, and said, "You exist."

Sandman rushed at us.

I put myself in front of Aja and vacillated between punching him in the nose with everything I had (advice from an old friend who was a barroom scrapper) or kicking him in the balls.

I saw movement over his shoulder but was too busy deciding how to ward off his attack to make much note of it.

Sandman reared his right arm back, I assumed so he could throw the sand in our faces.

His black leather hat was knocked off his head, landing between us.

A slender hand snaked across his face and yanked out the cloth in his nostrils.

Another hand came forward, trailing a copious amount of white powder.

Sandman stopped in his tracks, hands releasing his payload of sand so he could bat the powder away from his face.

He spun around and dropped to a knee, his back heaving.

There was Mindy, looking down at him, one of her hands painted white with some kind of substance.

"No! No!" Sandman wailed as he worked furtively at his nose like a squirrel eating a nut.

When he suddenly took in a great breath, we all stepped back. Aja was practically dead weight and I thought we were going to collapse onto a rack of cookbooks.

Sandman sneezed. A humdinger of a sneeze that sent twin rays of powder into the air.

And nothing happened.

He looked back at Aja and me.

"I can't be killed. Do you need any more proof that I'm destined to be the last?"

I grabbed hold of a thick, hardcover cookbook. Maybe if I caught him just right with it.

Mindy shouted, "Goddammit!"

Sandman got back on his feet. The powder on his face made him look like a deranged mime. He reached back into his pockets. "Now, where were we?"

I heard a muffled *poof*. His left hand emerged from the pocket engulfed in flame.

"What? What?" Sandman's eyes grew as big as hardboiled

eggs as he watched the fire race up his arm, and then his neck, and finally his head.

His chest burst into flame at the same time as his legs.

"Come on," I said to Aja, tossing her over my shoulder to get away from the ignited Sandman. He spun and screamed and set fire to everything he touched.

Mindy grabbed ahold of my arm and the three of us ran out of the Cracker Barrel. She undid Miracle's leash, and we headed for the RV. Dave fell off his chair when we burst through the door.

"What the hell happened?"

I lay Aja down on the sofa, and she wailed in pain. Mindy and I were panting as much as the dog.

Dave looked out the open door and saw the flames inside the Cracker Barrel gift shop.

"I found your biscuit mix," Mindy said, holding up her powdery hand. "Unfortunately, I had to use it for something more important."

I started the RV up and got us the hell out of there, finding a Chevy dealership to hide behind a few miles up the road.

Mindy got Aja some painkillers and water, and Miracle jumped excitedly around the RV.

"Seriously, what went on back there?" Dave asked.

"The Sandman tried to kill us," I said.

"What?"

"I'll tell you when it doesn't feel as if my heart is going to explode."

PEOPLE

I drove the next day.

Aja stayed in bed, the bruise on her back getting darker and bigger. I worried that she may have broken her tailbone. Mindy gave her Motrin and stayed with her awhile, with Miracle on the bed for a short time until his puppy genetics made him antsy, and his prancing around made the pain worse, so he was relegated to the main cabin of the RV. He yipped happily at Dave and sent me a quick, unhappy bark.

Mindy eventually came out of the bedroom and squatted between the front seats.

"How's she doing?" Dave asked.

"She's in a lot of pain. I gave her a Benadryl, and that put her out."

"Benadryl?" I said. "It's not like she has a runny nose."

"No, but it makes most people sleepy. When you hurt, sleep is your best escape. I bet we could look through every drugstore between here and California and not find one true pain med. That and insulin were probably the first to go."

There were more cars on this stretch of highway than usual, but none clustered together, which made it easier to drive around them. I slowed to look inside a few. When I didn't see ash, I wondered, *where did they go? Why would they just up and leave?*

Miracle nudged Mindy aside, his tongue lolling out of the side of his mouth, crystal eyes taking in the road ahead of us. She stroked his black-and-white fur.

"Did you thank Miracle?" she said to me.

"Huh?"

"This good boy is the one who got me thinking something was wrong back there. I saw that creepy dude and went around back to the kitchen, thinking I'd get a knife or something. Crazy that some biscuit flour is just as good as a knife now, isn't it?"

I swallowed. "It's crazy."

The image of Mindy creeping up behind Sandman and dousing him with flour, knowing it was going to kill him, made my hands and feet ice cold.

"I just think of all that biscuit flour wasted," Dave said.

Mindy patted his arm. "We didn't have the other ingredients to make them anyway. At least it served a purpose."

Yes, it killed a deranged kid.

Pre-SHC, this is a thought that would have plagued me to no end. Confirmation that Mindy was a killer would have sent me running for the hills.

In this case, all she did was protect us. There was no rationalizing with Sandman. Maybe we'd come to the point where it was kill or be killed. As if the fear of going combustible wasn't enough.

A part of me appreciated Mindy's swift action. I smiled at her and she smiled back.

Wow. I hadn't had a woman smile at me in a long time. It felt good.

"We should stop and find more things like Motrin," I said. "I know we only brought that half a bottle from our medicine cabinet."

"Good idea," Mindy said. "I'm going to play with this fuzzy guy and try to wear him out."

Playing with Miracle involved letting him clamp his jaws

down on a wound-up dishtowel and engaging in a spirited tug of war with Mindy.

I spotted a truck stop and pulled over.

"Dave, you come with me." I opened the glove compartment and took out the two pistols we'd taken from the man who had broken into my apartment. I wondered what his body looked like now. It was a strange thought, but strange was the new norm. I still had to tell Dave about that night. It felt as if it had happened a lifetime ago. Dave would be horrified, but he'd find the dark humor in my lawn dart skills.

Dave immediately put his hands up. "Hey, man, you know I don't believe in guns."

"I didn't believe in spontaneous human combustion, but that's out the window now."

"Maybe we should leave one for Mindy. Just in case."

"She has her own. Remember?"

I saw what Mindy could do with flour. I could only imagine what she could accomplish with a gun. She looked over at us, her arm shaking from left to right as Miracle tried to get the dishtowel free. "Yeah, I'm good. Don't worry about me and Aja."

Dave and I stepped out to gunmetal skies. Chicago wasn't too far off, and I bet the city was one giant bonfire. I'd been to Chicago a few times for business. I loved how the city was never too crowded. You could walk or drive it without losing your mind. The music was great in the Windy City. But that deep-dish pizza sucked. And good riddance to hot dogs with a salad on top.

The glass door and windows to the mini-mart had been smashed long before our arrival. It looked as if someone had driven a car through the place. Everything was broken or scattered.

"Hello," I called out, the gun heavy as a sack of potatoes in my hand. Dave stayed at my back.

"I don't want you to shoot me by accident," he said.

Fair point.

There was a game room to the left, the consoles for Ms. Pac-

Man and Galaga dark and silent. In the lobby, there was a dormant food counter. When I turned to the dining area, my muscles locked up.

White tables and chairs filled the spacious dining room. Well, some were white. Most were scorched black and gray. Ash piles and rotting, stinking human extremities were everywhere. It looked as if there had been a mass extinction event. One person's sneeze had set off another's, and another's, until the place was ablaze.

Even worse than that were the rats.

The floor crawled with their furtive, brown bodies. They were feasting on the flesh of feet and hands and arms and half-legs.

I spun away, willing my gorge to stay right where it was.

"Oh Jesus. Jesus." Dave backpedaled from the dining room, not stopping until he hit into an ATM.

"Let's get the hell out of here," I whispered, terrified to alert the rats that fresh meat was here.

Now I noticed their chittering as they fought over the scraps. My flesh crawled and I ran faster than I had since sophomore year high school when I was on the track team.

Dave found bottles of Motrin, Advil, and Tylenol within the carnage of the mini-mart. I grabbed a few bags of pork rinds and beef jerky, along with some random cans of energy drinks and RC cola.

"I didn't know they made RC anymore," Dave said.

"For all I know, these cans are decades old. See anything else we need?"

We eyeballed the wreckage, heard the rats, and decided we had enough.

As we stepped outside and away from the rat buffet, we saw people outside the RV. They stood along the side of it, quietly staring at it as if it were the monolith that dropped from the skies in *2001: A Space Odyssey*.

"Shit," Dave muttered, hiding behind a support column

under the covered entrance. I took the one across from him. "What are they doing there?"

I secretly hoped Aja hadn't seen them and asked them to come along. It would be standing room only if we let them pile in. Plus, we'd probably get about three miles to the gallon.

They didn't look like they were in any rush to move on. If we waited long enough, maybe Mindy would burst out of the RV like Annie Oakley and mow them down.

I mentally kicked myself. That was a shitty way of thinking. Not everyone was going to be like Sandman. They could be perfectly normal, frightened folks, just like us.

Not able to fully trust Mindy's judgment, I knew I had to be the first to act.

"Stay right there," I whispered to Dave. "Just have my back... you know...in case something goes wrong."

Man, did I wish he had the gun.

I slipped my hand inside my pocket and rested my finger on the trigger guard. The worry about shooting my nuts off was outweighed by the case of nerves that made it difficult to put one foot in front of the other.

As I slowly approached the RV, not a single one of the seven people (I counted) turned my way. If hair and body type were an accurate way to tell who was loitering around, there were three men and four women.

I thought of pulling the gun out and putting some fear of lead into them but nixed it. What if they all had guns? Seven to one were terrible odds, especially when the man watching my back was only armed with bottles of pills.

I cleared my throat to get their attention.

No one so much as gave me a cursory glance.

"Excuse me."

One of the men finally turned around. He was bald and had deep-set, haunted eyes. He looked at me, but I wasn't sure he was seeing me, if that makes sense.

"Is there something I can help you with?" I said, trying to

imbue confidence in my voice that my body and mind didn't possess.

He cocked his head.

Now the others turned around. They all had that same faraway look.

"Help us?" a middle-aged woman with stringy brown hair said.

Oh boy. I didn't like the look of this group. It was obvious they were flying high on something.

"This thing wasn't here before," a portly man of around sixty said, pointing a stubby finger at our RV. "At least I don't think it was."

I tightened my grip on the gun. "No, you're right, it wasn't. We just wanted to make a quick pit stop, and now we'll be on our way. So if you don't mind."

I took a step toward them, hoping they might part like the Red Sea.

Instead, they looked at me as if I were a unicorn.

"It talks," a younger woman said. She was dressed in ripped-up jeans and an oversized shirt that hung off one shoulder.

It? I was an it? Maybe she *was* seeing a unicorn.

"Do you all mind if I get back inside my vehicle?" I asked.

A dark-skinned man with his hair tied up in pigtails ran his hands over his face. "Vehicle. Veee-hick-lllll. Whoa. Just fucking whoa."

The RV was surrounded by space cadets.

At that moment, I remembered a small article I'd read on the Internet when SHC first started taking hold. Sensing the end of the world, many people had decided to go on a drug fueled binge, gathering in small and large groups and ingesting copious quantities of hallucinogenics. From mushrooms to DMT and ayahuasca, the idea was to get so stoned you either didn't care that you were about to die, or you tripped so hard and so deep, you just might find the reason why SHC had descended on the world and know how to stop it.

At the time, I thought it didn't sound like a bad way to play out the string. Now, looking at the seven zombies milling around the RV, I was glad I'd stuck to the occasional whiskey.

"Do you mind letting me through?" I asked.

A man and woman looked to the sky. The portly guy turned and faced the RV again. None of them stepped away from the door.

"Come on, Dave," I called out.

He peeked out from behind the column.

"We'll just go in through the driver's side door," I said.

Dave hustled over, keeping his eyes on the stoners.

"Would you like some?" the first man who'd spoken said to us. He opened his hand to reveal a palm filled with pills. "We share everything."

"I'm sure you do," I said under my breath, imagining the group engaged in sloppy orgies that would have qualified as anti-porn. To him, I said, "No thanks. Drugs aren't our thing."

"Why not?" a woman with curly blond hair and wearing what I assume was a sheet piped up. "Everything's legal now."

Dave scrambled into the RV. A few seconds later, I saw him and Mindy at the windshield. "I'm a firm believer that just because it's legal, it doesn't make it right."

Why the hell was I engaging with them? I could have blown a raspberry their way and I don't think it would have fully registered.

As I moved to the open driver's side door, they shifted as a single unit to the front of the RV. Now I started to worry. Were they going to prevent me from driving a way and force us to join their druggie commune?

Not to mention, a breeze had started to kick up, throwing up dust from the ground. None of them had their nostrils protected. The last thing I needed was for them to set fire to the RV.

"Well, I have to get going," I said. "It would be great if you stepped away from my RV."

The woman with the unwashed brown hair smiled and said, "Oh, we're sorry. We're waiting for our ride, too."

I looked up and down the road. What the hell ride could they be waiting for?

"Yeah, well, have a safe trip."

As soon as I got behind the wheel, they shuffled away.

"What the hell was that all about?" Mindy asked.

"Just some people that make hippies look like corporate CEOs. I'm surprised Miracle didn't go nuts when they stood outside the RV."

"I guess the dog didn't sense any danger," Dave said, staring at the magnificent seven. "I don't blame them. They look like they don't have a care in the world. They might be the smartest people on the planet now."

"Definitely the highest," I said as I started the engine.

I rolled the window down and heard something approaching. I glanced at my side-view mirror and saw a blue minivan heading our way.

In fact, it was headed right at the RV at an alarming rate of speed.

"Shit. Hold on."

I slammed the RV into drive and hit the gas. Mindy and Dave fell over. Aja cried out from the back room.

Cutting the wheel hard to the right, I tried to get the RV out of the path of the incoming minivan. It adjusted for a terrifying moment, as if it meant to crash into us, but quickly got back on course.

That course was a beeline to the stoners.

"Get out of the way!" I shouted out the window.

The portly dude nodded and gave me a thumbs-up. "Maybe we'll see you again on the road."

I could have, should have, just pulled away.

But I didn't.

Because for some reason, I wanted to make sure the stoners were all right. Unlike Sandman, they weren't out to hurt anybody. They just wanted to ride into the sunset nice and numb.

I leaned on the horn to get their fuzzy attention, since the rocketing minivan didn't seem to cut through the psychedelic fog. I screamed at them to run. Dave and Mindy formed a chorus.

A few of them spun around, looked up, looked down, as if hearing spirit voices.

In the end, none of them registered their incoming death. The minivan made a terrific crunch as it plowed through them. The hood crumpled as bodies went flying. The windshield exploded and I watched the woman with the blond hair get swallowed into the void, violently colliding with the driver.

The minivan stopped when it hit into the back end of an eighteen-wheeler.

I watched it all without taking a breath. The amount of carnage the minivan had created in a nanosecond was beyond belief. Most of the stoners had been transformed into shattered bags of meat and bone.

We ran out of the RV to check on them, despite our eyes telling us they were beyond assistance.

The portly guy's face was inches from his own ass. Blood leaked out of every orifice. Mindy nearly tripped on a woman's severed head.

I jogged to the minivan. Smoke hissed from the crushed hood. Every inch of glass had blown out.

The woman who had gone through the windshield lay in a crumpled ball in the passenger seat well. She looked like a broken doll with limbs in all the wrong places.

"Ooohhh, man."

I nearly crapped myself.

The driver, an older dude sporting a red bandana and long, thin hair and a salt and pepper beard, turned to me with eyes so glassy I could see my reflection and said, "Did...did I just hit something?"

"Dave!"

He looked inside the minivan and gagged.

"We need to get him out of there," I said.

The driver's side was a crumpled mess. It was a miracle the guy hadn't been cut in half by the jutting metal.

"I got it," Dave said. He was big and doughy but he'd always been strong. He tugged on the door handle, grunting and cursing.

"How is he alive?" Mindy said when she joined the party.

"I don't know, and I don't know for how much longer."

It was impossible to tell if the blood that covered him was his own, the dead woman's or a combination of both.

The door gave way with a nails on a chalkboard screech. Wary of coming in contact with the dead woman, I gingerly reached across and undid his seat belt. He didn't protest or cry out as I hooked my hands under his armpits and dragged him out with Dave's help.

We laid him on his back. Dave checked him over, looking for signs of injury. He asked the guy if anything hurt, if he had any medical conditions and if he was on any medication.

"I think it's safe to say he's on loads of medication," I said.

"Sorry. Force of habit. I have to get re-certified for first aid and CPR every year for work."

"Have you seen my friends?" the guy asked, his eyes staring straight into the sky. "I said I'd pick them up."

We looked at the broken bodies and bloody asphalt.

"No external injuries that I can see," Dave said. "That doesn't mean he's not all busted up inside."

Mindy tried to remove his jacket, and a bunch of pills and little stickers came pouring out.

"Good thing for him," she said. "At least he won't be feeling any pain."

HONEY

The three of us carried the wounded driver into the RV and set him on the couch. He passed out along the way, although I thought he'd died. I imagined punctured lungs and spleens, shattered bones, and internal bleeding.

Mindy covered him with a blanket and Dave checked his pulse. Soon, the guy started snoring. Miracle came over and licked his face, but he didn't react. Mindy moved the husky away.

"Never know what this guy's sweating. Miracle could end up tripping balls."

We looked to one another for a moment and then burst out in nervous laughter.

"What's going on out there?" Aja called from the bedroom.

"I'll tell you in a second," I said.

Once we all caught our breath, Dave looked out the front window and said, "What the hell just happened? I mean, seriously."

"I don't think he's gonna know when he wakes up. But we should be prepared for him to be very upset," I said. "Until then, I'm getting us out of here and away from...all that."

By the time I got back behind the wheel, the birds were

already picking at the corpses. I steered clear of it all and merged back onto the highway. I'd gone about two miles before I was hit by a massive case of the shakes. Finding it difficult to handle the RV, I quickly pulled over.

Dave groaned. "Don't tell me we have to move cars already."

I angled out of the front of the RV and leaned against a wall. "I think my adrenaline wore off." I held up my fluttering hand. "Need to take a knee for a bit."

Mindy took my hands in hers. "Wow. They're so cold, too. Look, you just chill. I'll drive until you're ready."

Her hands felt so warm, so soft. "Thanks."

Just a couple of days ago, I would have put up some kind of protest. But Mindy had proven to be a good driver, and she had saved my life.

I sat at the dinette table. Dave put a glass in front of me. "Looks like you could use this." He found a bottle of bourbon we had tucked away in the compartment under my seat and poured three fingers worth. As he was putting the cap back on, he looked up front and said, "Oh shit, I'm sorry. Is this going to be a problem for you?"

Mindy turned around and waved him off.

"I can't smell it, and I'll be focusing on the road. No worries. Sam, you do you."

You do you. That's what that kid with the neck tattoo had said to me.

I had to hold the glass with two hands. Despite my shaking, I got it all down in two burning swallows. "Top me off."

Dave was a generous bartender. The second glass took more time.

"Hello?"

Crap, I forgot about Aja. The bourbon took a bullet train to my head, and I had to grip the table to steady myself.

"Whoa there," Dave said, reaching to help me.

"I'm good." I looked down at the bloody driver. "Well, better than him at least."

Naturally, Mindy took a sharp turn while I was walking, and

I smashed into the closed bathroom door. My shoulder was going to be sore after that.

Aja had three pillows propping up her back. When the RV rocked a bit, the pain registered sharply on her face.

"How's your back?" I was going to sit on the end of the bed but thought better of it. Better to sway with the RV and hope I didn't fall.

"Feels like I got kicked by a mountain goat."

I put a bottle of Motrin on the small shelf cut into the headboard. "Hopefully these help."

"What went on back there? It sounded like there was a car accident or something."

"Oh yeah, you could say that. We ran into a group of stoners. I mean, like floating on cloud eleven. One of their group plowed right into them as if they weren't there. If he was on whatever they were on, I'm sure he saw daffodils instead of people."

Aja popped the bottle and shook three pills into her palm. I handed her a bottle of water that had rolled down by her feet. "That sounds awful."

An image of the aftermath sent an extra tremble down my hands. "Be glad you didn't see it."

"Are they..."

"Dead? Yeah. Well, except the driver."

She shook her head. "The driver always survives."

"Well, not always. Look at James Dean. Anyway, we're not sure how hurt he is, but he's on the sofa right now. I assume he's sleeping since I don't think people snore like a buzz saw when they're unconscious from an injury."

"What I wouldn't give to be unconscious."

"Hold on."

I came back with a fresh glass and the bourbon and poured some out. "Here, this should do it."

She knocked it back like it was a shot and held the glass out for more. "Keep 'em coming until I can't feel."

I poured one for her and took a pull from the bottle.

We drank some more and talked a little bit, though it was stilted. Not like three years ago when Aja had minor surgery, and I took three days off from work to take care of her. She'd been in pain then, and I swore I felt it. So we watched movies and talked about vacations we were going to take, funny stuff we did when we were dating and the joy of not having in-laws. I don't think I'd ever loved her as much as I did during those three days when I was her protector.

"You zoning out on me?" she said, wiggling the glass.

"We keep this up, we're gonna have to knock over another liquor store."

Aja giggled and put her finger to her lips. "Shh. Mindy will hear. I don't want to be responsible for her going off the wagon."

"Honey, there are much bigger things than this bottle of booze that'll knock her off that wagon."

Aja cocked her head and gave an almost-grin. "Did you just call me honey?"

Did I? I was really feeling it.

"I don't think so."

"Yes, you did." She took a slow sip. "It was nice. You used to call me that all the time."

She was right, I did. When I first called her honey, she laughed and said I sounded like an old man or someone on a sitcom. But it grew on her, on us, and I used it often.

"Yeah, well, I'm clearly drunk."

Aja stretched in a way that I'm sure pre-bourbon would have had her screaming in agony. "I think I am, too. Thank God for booze. We're living like people in the old west. What happens when we need dental work?"

I nearly lost my footing when we ran over a pothole.

"I don't even want to think about that. I'm gonna go check on our sleeping DUI."

"Wait."

I stopped, my hand on the doorknob.

"I still love you. You know that, right?"

In a world where death was just a sneeze away, I should have taken advantage of the moment. Better to live in peace than simmering discord.

But then I thought back to months ago, and all the anger came bubbling up to my mouth.

"I know you *did*."

I quickly closed the door behind me, too much of a coward to see what damage, if any, my reply had done.

STONER GEECH

Our bloody, unconscious passenger slept all through the day and night.

My plan was for Mindy and I to take turns and just keep on driving, but the roads got worse with cars or very expensive urns, and at one point, Dave kept talking about getting ambushed as we pushed cars to the side of the road. It got so I was feeling as if we were being watched and a band of survivor crazies were ready to pounce.

We called it a day and hid in the tall grass behind a billboard. Mindy and Miracle slept with Aja. Dave and I crawled up to our bed. I checked on the guy all through the night, expecting him to be dead every time.

He didn't die.

In fact, he woke up while I was pouring myself a bowl of cereal at the crack of dawn.

"Hey, man, I'm starving," he rasped. He tried to lift his head but thought better of it.

I nearly dropped the bowl.

"You're talking."

"Yeah, and so are you. Got any Froot Loops?"

"Um, no. Besides, I don't think it's a good idea that you eat. Do you remember what happened?"

Were you supposed to avoid food with a concussion? I was no doctor, but I felt pretty confident that he'd at least suffered that. He looked like he was an extra in a zombie movie, caked in dry blood.

His head turned, and his eyes tried to focus on me. He squinted and said, "Do I know you?"

"Afraid not."

"Where the fuck am I? And why do I hurt so much."

I decided it was wise not to hit him with the horrid truth right away. Who knows what that would do to him?

"You were in a car accident. You're lucky we were there to get you out of the wreckage. You're even luckier to be alive."

"I was in a car accident? Sheesh. Feel like I was thrown down a long, rocky hill." He closed his eyes and winced when he clasped his hands over his chest.

"What's your name?" I asked.

"Me? My friends call me Geech. I don't let my enemies call me. Well, not that there are any left."

Geech. I'd bet if I got ahold of his birth certificate, I wouldn't see Geech scribbled on the first name line.

"Well, Geech, I'm Sam."

"You said we before."

He kept his eyes closed.

"Huh?"

"You said we were lucky to get me you out of the wreckage. You meet up with Daisy? Or was it Cheese Head?"

Cheese Head? His brain wasn't firing on all cylinders.

"I'm afraid I don't know Daisy or Cheese Head. We found you at a truck stop."

He popped up like a cadaver reanimated by a lightning strike.

"Wait. So where's Cheese Head?"

"I don't know."

But maybe I did know. I was about to tell him about the

people he'd turned to pulp when Dave literally jumped out of the sleeping berth. "Hey, he's awake. You feeling all right?"

Geech narrowed his eyes and took Dave in. Dave wore boxers with flying cheeseburgers on them and a Jersey Devils hockey jersey.

"No, I don't feel all right. What'd you do with Cheese Head?"

Dave looked at me. "Cheese Head?"

"His friend," I said.

"You think he was one of the stoners that he ran over?"

"Ran over?" Geech started trembling. "What do you mean ran over?"

I gave my forehead a good palm slap. "Look, it was clearly an accident."

Geech tried to get up but then sagged back onto the couch.

"Oh wow, he made it through the night." Now Mindy had joined the fun. "You must have been pretty baked."

I couldn't help noticing Mindy wore only a black bra and panties. I saw Dave's eyes practically leaping from his skull.

Mindy seemed unaware of her near nakedness. She turned to me and said, "How'd he take knowing he plowed into his gang of hippies?"

"Wait? What?" Geech's head swiveled between me, Dave and Mindy.

"He literally just woke up," I said. "I was trying to gauge how he was feeling." *Until you two dunderheads came along and freaked him out.*

"Where are my friends? I want to talk to them."

I sat next to Geech. He pulled his feet away from me as if I were a poisonous spider. "Look, Geech, let's first get some food and something to drink into you and then we can talk more."

"I'm not gonna let you poison me. I don't know what you're all talking about. What the hell did you do with my friends?" He struggled to his feet, his back to the wall. His eyes rolled up into his head for a moment, but then he snapped back to attention.

Mindy stood opposite him with her hands on her hips. "You

should be thanking us instead of accusing us. We're not the ones who got so stoned out of our gourds that we turned all of our friends into a blacktop stain."

"You're lying!" He pointed a shaking finger at her.

"You wish. Guess it's what happens when you check out and hide from your problems."

"Mindy," I said.

"What? He's going to know sooner or later. And I don't like be accused of things I didn't do." She narrowed her eyes at Geech. "Life sucks. We get it. Just man up."

Dave stepped between them. "Hey, that's not cool."

"Whatever."

Aja came stumbling out of the bedroom. "Oh my god." It was the first time she'd seen Geech and I had to admit, he was pretty ghastly looking. "How is he alive?"

"It's not his blood," I said.

Geech looked down at his crimson shirt and pants. With fumbling hands, he pulled the shirt over his head and undid his pants.

"Whoa, too much," Mindy said when he yanked down his underwear.

"I don't have any cuts," he said, mostly to himself. He was right, but he did have some wicked bruises, especially across his bony chest.

For some reason, he locked eyes with Aja and said, "I killed Cheese Head?" I'd never heard someone sound more piteous.

"I...I...I wish I could tell you," Aja said. She held on to the doorframe, bent slightly forward from the pain.

Tears spilled from his eyes. "Oh man, oh man, oh man, I just went back to check out that beer truck to see what I could get. I told them I'd be back in five, ten minutes tops. I don't remember the rest."

"If it'll give you any comfort, I don't think they felt a thing," Mindy said.

"Dude," I said to Mindy. She threw up her hands and went back into the bedroom.

Geech started blubbering, his body racked with great heaving sobs, snot bubbles forming and popping with disturbing regularity.

"You didn't do it on purpose," I said.

"But I did it! I murdered Cheese Head and Daisy and Wiggy and...and...and..."

Dave put his meaty hand gently on Geech's shoulder. "I wouldn't call it murder. You didn't mean to do it."

I tried to put myself in Geech's shoes. How would I feel if I'd been higher than the clouds for who knows how long, only to find out I'd laid waste to my oddly nicknamed friends? I think I'd be crying, just like Geech.

"You want something to drink?" I asked him, expecting him to ask if we had any liquor, the harder, the better.

"No, I don't deserve a drink. We wanted to go, but we wanted to do it on our own terms, you know? Until then, we were going to shrug off all of our anxiety and experience something greater."

He kept sniffing back the snot bubbles.

Geech rubbed his eyes and he gripped his knees, sniffling in earnest.

"We're just so sorry," Aja said.

The sniffling increased, bordering on some kind of nasal hyperventilation. His body suddenly went rigid and there was a wild look in his eye.

"Oh man. Thank you, Jesus."

Geech's head reared back, and his mouth opened in a wide O.

Dave backpedaled until his ass planted on the dinette table.

"Sam, get back," Aja shouted.

Geech sneezed before I could extricate myself from the couch. A wet curtain of snot hit me in the chest.

It was immediately followed by a muffled *whup*. I saw a whisper of flame curl up from the mass of gray hairs in the center of his chest. The acrid stench of burning hair was overwhelming.

Not for long, though.

It quickly took a back seat to the aroma of searing meat as the flame exploded from his trunk to his arms, neck, head and upper thighs.

Aja screamed.

Dave screamed.

Mindy came rushing out, yelling, "What the fuck?"

I stood there motionless, watching Geech burn.

Within the wriggling mass of flames, I saw his face.

And he was smiling.

The smoke alarm in the RV went off. Black, oily smoke was starting to coat the ceiling.

"We have to get him the hell out of here," Mindy said.

Dave leaped up to the sleeping berth and ripped the sheets off the bed. He tossed the blanket to me. "You get one leg, I'll get the other!"

I couldn't form words. A nod would have to do.

We wrapped the fabric around Geech's ankles. Through it all, the old stoner hadn't moved a muscle. I thought maybe he'd died until I heard him laughing. His cackling made every hair on my body stand on end.

Mindy threw the RV door opened and Dave and I dragged Geech out, his head thumping hard on the step, leaving behind a flaming print. We got him as far as ten feet from the RV before we had to drop him as the flames grew stronger and hotter. I was luckier than Dave.

When I let go of his blanket-covered ankle, all I had to do was slap my hand against my thigh to kill the tiny blue flames that had caught on the hairs on the back of my hand.

Geech's other ankle separated from his body. Dave was left holding a foot with one smoldering end. He screamed louder than a terrified deer, throwing the foot over the RV and running in the other direction.

I heard a concentrated whoosh and looked over to see Aja dousing the flames in the RV with the fire extinguisher. She put the ones out on the step and faced me.

"You all right?"

I was pretty sure my heart was about to give out. "I won't be. Ever again."

The smell of Geech was so deep in my nose, in my brain, I was positive I would be haunted by it in the afterlife.

"What about Dave?" she asked.

"He's just freaking out. He'll be okay, I think." Dave had slipped from view but I could hear him cursing in the distance.

Mindy stepped out of the RV, still in her underwear. Miracle stayed by her side. "Dude took wake and bake to a whole new level."

NEW RIDE

The one good thing about being in the mid-west was that there was no shortage of places to find a replacement RV. My first instinct was to keep what we had because the fire had mostly just scorched the leather sofa.

However, the gut-churning smell of burned Geech was too much to take.

We stopped at a place called RV Universe that looked like it had been raided by an entire population of RV enthusiasts. To my surprise, we found the exact same make and model as our trusty Ford.

"Easy swap," I said to Dave.

"We can get something bigger. Nicer," Mindy said, gesturing with her head at the mansion on wheels to our left. "I can handle it no problem."

I stood firm. "More room means the temptation to bring more people on board. Not again."

Mindy and Dave didn't argue. What they did do was help find the keys, gas it up and transfer everything we had.

Aja, on the other hand, had an issue with my choice. "You always were afraid of change. I guess you like sleeping with Dave."

I refused to let her get my goat. "Well, he has one thing going for him. He never cheated on me. So, yeah, I guess I do."

She pouted for the rest of the morning, slamming the bedroom door once we were all settled in.

"Maybe you should go talk to her," Mindy said. "She looks pretty pissed."

Aja's ire had been ratcheted up when I didn't tell her I loved her back. She'd made herself vulnerable and I hadn't taken the bait. She was butt hurt, both literally and figuratively. Now it was back to the offensive game.

The only problem was, I was tired of playing games. I just wanted to get to Consumption, take a breath and figure out the rest of my life.

"I don't think I'll make things any better," I said to Mindy.

"He'll just put the py to her ro," Dave said.

Mindy shook her head. "You'd think marriages would cut all the petty crap out and grow stronger at a time like this."

I busied myself checking mirrors and settling into the driver's seat. "Petty. Sure," I mumbled.

Dave, ever the tension buster, announced, "For road lunch, I'm making red beans and rice with fried Vienna sausages. Sounds good?"

Mindy sat beside me. "I'm starved. You could tell me you were putting Geech on a stick and I'd be like, hell yeah."

I drew in a sharp breath and started the RV.

"Too soon?" Mindy said.

"I can still smell him. So...yeah."

We made it a whole hour before the three of us had to go out and move cars and trucks around. By the time we were done, our pants were covered in gray ash. There was a point where that would have really bothered me. That point was long past.

I checked my map and realized we would soon take a decidedly more northern route, well away from the fictitious cabin in Wyoming we'd told Mindy about. I had no idea what the hell to do.

Earlier on, I was fine with considering that we just stop somewhere that seemed relatively safe and take off without her knowing.

Since then, she'd saved our lives and had proved herself to be pretty useful. But then again, there was an element of danger about her. There was a valid concern that she would turn on us at some point.

"What I wouldn't give for a baseball game, two hot dogs covered in relish, mustard, and onions, and the coldest beer west of the Mississippi," Mindy said, her feet resting on the dashboard.

"I'm more of a stadium sausage and peppers man," I said, pulling the visor down to cut the sun's glare. Much less smog in the skies on this stretch of road. I wished I could hug and kiss the blue skies and bright sun.

"Oh, sausage and peppers comes a few innings later. Well, after ice cream in one of those little plastic hats."

My stomach grumbled. Mindy's sounded off next.

"Hey, our bellies are talking," she said with a laugh. When they settled down, she asked, "Is it me?"

"Is what you?"

"You know. The tension between you and Aja."

I slowed down to steer around a flipped-over Dodge Caravan. "No, it's definitely not you."

Miracle barked behind us and Dave said, "No more rice and beans for you. You had enough." Miracle expressed his displeasure by farting loudly.

Mindy exhaled. "Good. I mean, not good that you're having issues. I just didn't want to be the one causing the friction. I've done enough of that in my life. It's weird. I was a fuck-up for a long time. Took me a while to get my head out of my ass. And look what happens when I do. The whole world goes tits up in the blink of an eye."

"More like the snort of a nose," I said.

She looked at me and smiled. "True. All those doomsday nut jobs never saw this one coming, did they?"

"They certainly did not."

She reached across and rested her hand on my thigh. "Time is short. We know that now more than ever. You two had to have loved each other once. Do you really want to go on like this?"

Her hand felt warm and my heart fluttered for a hot moment. She removed it quickly, but not before giving me a sensation I hadn't felt in a long time.

Oh boy.

I was falling for Mindy.

BRONCS AND BARBECUES

"Holy shit balls!" Mindy shouted.

The RV came to a screeching halt. Dave and I had been playing poker, using potato chips as poker chips. The cards and chips were swept off the table.

"Guys, you have to see this," she said, waving us to the front of the RV.

Dave looked down at the mess, watching Miracle gobble to chips. "Of course. I was winning."

"You would have lost eventually," I said.

I wasn't sure what to expect, but a lit rodeo sign would never have been one of the possibilities in my mind. The big neon sign showed a cowboy riding a bucking horse. It pointed to a parking area that was a quarter full of cars and horses. I saw people milling about the front entrance. Gray smoke billowed out from inside the stadium walls.

"What the hell is going on here?" I said, knowing my mouth was open wide enough to catch not just flies, but mid-sized birds.

"Must be Saturday night," Mindy said. When Dave and I looked at her, she added, "I lived in Montana for a year.

Saturday nights were rodeo nights. Man, those were fun. At least as much fun as you could have in Montana."

A car beeped behind us. I popped my head out the passenger window and saw an agitated man and woman idling in a Ram truck behind us. Both were wearing cowboy hats.

"We better keep going," I said.

Mindy turned the RV to the entrance. "No way am I passing this up."

The smell of smoky, tangy barbecue hung heavy in the air. Dave took a big whiff through his noseplugs and grew pale.

"We need to turn around and get out of this place."

Mindy gave him a sideways glance. "What? After all the nothing we've seen, this is like a lake in the middle of the desert."

"And probably just as fake," Dave said. "Don't forget, we're living during the actual end of the world. Who's to say what we're smelling isn't people? We could be driving right into some psycho cowboy cannibal cult."

Dave read a lot of dark graphic novels (mixed in with super-hero stuff, The Fantastic Four and The Flash being two of his favorites) and watched a ton of horror movies. Right now, all that entertainment was working against logic.

Although logic didn't dictate that there would be a rodeo at the end of the world.

"Maybe he's right," I said as the Ram passed by us, parking next to another huge truck. "Not the cannibal part. But there is a chance they won't be happy to see any outsiders. Big city idiots coming to small towns was never a good thing way before SHC."

When the man and woman in the RV ambled out, they looked at us and he tipped his tan-colored hat.

"I don't know, they look pretty cool to me," Mindy said. The man slipped his arm around his woman's waist, and they walked to the entrance. Both had on brown leather coats, jeans, and cowboy boots.

"That's exactly what they want us to think," Dave said.

"Then they'll turn on us, me especially because I have more bulk for their barbecue pit."

Mindy parked the RV.

"If you're so scared, you can stay here. I'm gonna check it out." She handed Dave the keys.

"Wait," I said. "You shouldn't go alone."

She raised an eyebrow. "Is that you volunteering to get out of this cramped mobile home and have some fun?"

"There's safety in numbers."

She looked over at the crowd filing into the rodeo. "Oh sure, two against them seems pretty safe to me. Just say you want to go to the rodeo."

Mindy was right. I did. When was the last time I'd done anything closely resembling entertainment that wasn't in my apartment?

Even if these people were cannibals, I hoped to see a good show before I was stuffed in the smoker.

"Dave, the guns are in the glove compartment. If anything goes wrong, take the RV and Aja and the dog and get the hell out of here."

"You can't be serious?" He looked to be on the verge of a major freakout.

Mindy opened the door, and we heard a band playing in the distance. I had never been a fan of country music, but at that moment, you could have tattooed Willie Nelson's face on my chest, and I'd be happy.

"Serious about what?"

We all turned to Aja who had come out of the bedroom, standing straighter than she had over the past few days. One hand gripped her side.

She then looked out the window and did an honest to God double-take. "I know I took, like five Motrin and a few sips of wine before, so I need to know if that's real."

"It is," I said.

"Smells so good."

"It does," Mindy said. "You want to come with us?"

Aja visibly sagged. "I don't think I'd make it halfway through the parking lot. Maybe if you can find a wheelchair or something and come get me."

"Sure thing," Mindy said, smiling.

I wasn't sure what the odds were of finding an abandoned wheelchair, but then again, we were at a rodeo in the middle of nowhere. Anything was possible.

"Dave will stay with you," I said.

"Why isn't he going?" she said as if he weren't right next to her.

"Explain your cowboy cannibal theory to her," I said. "We won't be gone long."

As Dave talked, I caught a vicious look from Aja as she watched Mindy and I head for the entrance. I could feel the heat of that stare slicing through my back as we walked.

"You ever been to a rodeo?" Mindy asked me.

"I'm from Jersey. Do monster truck shows at the Meadowlands count?"

"Almost, but not quite."

"Contrary to what Jon Bon Jovi has tried to make the world believe, guys from Jersey don't pretend we're anything close to cowboys."

We got in line with everyone else, most of them dressed in denim and looking as if SHC had never come to demolish civilization. As we passed through the turnstile, I reached into my pocket, expecting to have to pay to get in a force of habit.

No one gave us any funny looks and I didn't see any cowpokes chowing down on an outsider.

What I did see was a lot of smiling faces. And lights. And beer stands where the vendors pumped from kegs packed in buckets of ice. Burgers and steaks and onions sizzled on a long flattop grill. Folks lined up for beer and food without a single cent being exchanged.

An old Gretchen Wilson song blared from the overhead speakers.

"I think we died somewhere on the road," I said after

waiting on the short line to get a red Solo cup of cold beer and draining half of it in one sip. Mindy had gotten herself a bottle of water. "I mean, seriously. This can't be real, right?"

There must have been a crowd of two hundred, all of them roaring at the roping display happening in the dirt floor arena. Men and women rode horses, lassos whipping over their heads while chasing down young cows or bulls. I had no idea. Nothing in my New Jersey upbringing had prepared me for this.

Even the smell of hay and manure was this side of heaven.

Mindy nudged my ribs. "It's pretty amazing, isn't it? Gosh, I never thought I'd see this again."

Gosh? The rodeo had brought out a softer, kinder Mindy.

"Let's take a seat," she said, grabbing my hand and leading me down several rows.

I looked around. A few people had their nostrils plugged up, but not many. With all the dust in the air being kicked up by the livestock, I would have been so tense, you couldn't have driven a nail up my ass with a sledgehammer. These people didn't seem to care. They were simply there to enjoy the show and be around one another.

Mindy was enraptured by it all. The smell of steak and onions had my appetite in overdrive. "You want me to get you something to eat?"

"Yeah. Sure," she replied, not taking her eyes off the arena. It was bull riding time, and it was nothing like drunk girls riding mechanical bulls in bars with padding all around. I hurt all over just watching it.

I grabbed a steak for each of us with a side of onions, gravy, and baked potatoes. The smiling girl behind the counter said, "Enjoy. If you're still hungry, come on back for more."

I turned around and saw a makeshift kiosk where a heavyset man with a long gray beard was making biscuits in a cast-iron skillet over an open fire.

"You mind if I have a couple?" I asked him.

He used a spatula to drop a half dozen on my plate. "Have at it, son. Best biscuits you'll ever eat." He also handed me a plastic cup filled with what looked like fresh butter.

I reminded myself to save some for Dave. I hoped they'd let us take to-go food when we decided to leave.

Mindy tucked into her steak and made moaning noises that upped my internal temperature.

"You ever have a steak like this?"

I'd had steaks from some of the top steakhouses across the country, thanks to my job. I had to admit, none of them tasted half as good as this. It could have been the apocalypse talking, but I wasn't so sure.

Two couples behind us laughed and cheered and had a running conversation that would have bothered me in the past. Now, I couldn't get enough of their casual banter.

"What do you think?"

The way the light diffused around Mindy's windblown hair and highlighted her cheekbones, I had to take a moment to collect myself.

"I think I want to go to the rodeo every night."

I played my own words over in my head and was surprised to realize I meant it. Maybe Consumption wasn't the answer. Maybe this, whatever the hell town we were in, was the lone Eden left in America, if not the world.

Consumption was still a series of stories I'd read on the Internet. Here was proof that life could go on. Not just go on, but it was better. I didn't see anyone that didn't look happy as all get out. We came with hands full of gimme and mouths full of much obliged, and in return we got the best night of my life.

I hadn't meant to stay until the end, but we did.

When it was over, it was clear that people could remain and mingle for as long as they wanted. What else was there to do? For once, there were no time sucks like television, computers, and phones to plug into. Garth Brooks serenaded the lingering crowd.

And amazingly, despite the hay and dust and dirt, not a

single person went combustible. I didn't even see anyone *looking* like they wanted to sneeze.

But then I looked down at the arena and saw a horse let one out with a great shake of its head, its black mane flicking hard to the right.

"Did you see that?" I said to Mindy, pointing at the horse. "It didn't combust!" It reminded me of that terrifying moment with Miracle.

A woman dressed in a tracksuit with a Cubs baseball cap who had been walking by smiled and said, "Amazing, isn't it? I guess God prefers horses and other livestock. Never thought I'd be envious of a cow."

She broke into a high-pitched cackle as she walked away.

The horse sneezed again, and Mindy smiled. "I'll bet the person who would be able to figure that out is a mound of ashes by now."

She was most likely right. I wondered how many people were actually left in the world. And of those, how many would be of use in rebuilding society, if it even could be rebuilt. That line of thought just had me questioning why I was still around, so I switched tracks to rekindle my good mood.

"I hope there's some food left for Dave and Aja," I said, holding the two remaining biscuits and butter in my hand.

"I don't think that'll be a problem." Mindy ordered up some heaping plates and carried them out of the arena. Only a few cars and trucks had left the parking lot.

"That was amazing," I said. "If there was a gift shop, I would have bought myself a cowboy hat."

She smiled. "If there was a gift shop, they would have *given* you a cowboy hat."

"Maybe we should settle down here for the night. See what tomorrow brings."

"Sounds cool to me. I'm in no rush, unless you really need to get to Wyoming."

The white lie felt like a dozen soggy biscuits in my gut.

"No," I said. "No rush at all."

She bumped into me. "Good. I like it here."

"Me, too."

I was a jumble of emotions as we walked back to the RV. If Freud were to look inside my head, he might have jumped off the highest tree.

A few more were added to the mix when we got to the RV, and I saw Aja sitting in a folding chair next to a cowboy-looking dude the size of a linebacker. Her hand was on his knee and their eyes were locked on one another.

Dave stood in the open door of the RV, saw us, looked over at Aja and this stranger, and mouthed, *"I don't know what the hell is going on."*

HOWDY STRANGER

He said his name was Clint. Clint Rider.

I smelled some post-apocalypse fresh start syndrome. He'd more likely been born Ignacious Picklebottom than Clint Rider.

Though I had to admit, his physical persona fit the name, and vice-versa.

"I swear to God, my face was about an inch from the gravel," Aja said, her tongue a little thick, eyes this side of the surface of an icy pond. "I thought for sure I was going to break my nose. And all of a sudden, whoop, I was lifted right up. I was so dizzy, I thought I was gonna throw up."

Dave sat on the RV step, nursing a beer, while I found some small stumps that littered the parking lot and Mindy and I planted ourselves on them, taking in the newcomer. He could easily crush walnuts with his jaw and his five o'clock shadow looked permanent. His biceps pushed the limits of his blue denim shirt.

"I saw it in her face and for a moment there, I was ready to bail," Clint said, his smile revealing brilliantly white teeth. He must have raided a drugstore of all their whitening strips.

"I don't know how he did it," Aja said. She had a paper cup of wine, swinging it wildly as she talked, spilling some in the process. "I mean, I didn't even see him. It was like, like, Batman swooping in."

"I'm Batman," Clint said in a gravelly voice. "Seriously, I was just heading to the rodeo when I saw her start to take that fall. Luckily, I wasn't too far away."

"He just swooped right in."

I looked to Dave. "Where we you when all of this was taking place?"

He looked down at his feet and said softly, "Taking a shit."

Aja giggled.

I noticed Mindy was still holding the plates of food. She stared at Clint, too, as if she were mesmerized.

"We brought you back food," I said rather feebly. "They even had biscuits." I tossed a couple to Dave. His eyes lit up, but when he didn't dive into them, I could tell it was because he felt a kind of guilt, though I'm not sure why. It wasn't as if he'd invited Clint to come and make my wife all giddy and drunk and enraptured.

"I'll save it for later," Aja said.

My gut tensed. Back when we were dating, she rarely ate in front of me. She said it made her feel self-conscious, especially when she was around a man she was attracted to.

"You from around here?" I asked Clint, sounding more like a father interrogating his daughter's suitor than a husband.

Clint shook his head. "Nope. I'm from Texas. El Paso to be exact. My traveling home is that bad boy right there." He pointed to an expansive RV two rows back. It looked like it could comfortably fit a football team. "I stumbled on this place, same as you about a week ago. Can't say I have any pressing need to head out anytime soon." He picked up a stick and started drawing random circles in the dirt and rocks. "Besides, I think this is about as good as it gets now. I might just stay until...well, you know."

He looked like he was going to ask me a question, so I quickly cut in with, "What made you leave El Paso?"

"I don't know. Why not? Wasn't much left for me down

there. I lost my father and then my sister and her family. My friends, too."

Aja leaned closer to him with her sympathetic sad face. Even Mindy, having put the plates down, edged forward toward Clint just a little bit more.

Clint took a deep, steadying breath and added, "So I grabbed that monster and got on the road. I just wanted to get away, but the more I drove, the more I realized you can't run from your problems. Especially in this world now."

"You are so right," Aja said and patted his arm.

My blood started to boil. Why I was this mad was a mystery to me. I knew we were done as a couple months ago. And I had just had a dynamite time at a rodeo with Mindy who, I had to admit, I was developing feelings for.

I guess it was the fact that I was owed that time and those feelings for Mindy, after what Aja had done to me. I'd gotten all of two hours to bask in it before she one-upped me.

"They also say you can't put your arms around a memory," Dave chimed in. I worked hard to hold back my smile. I wanted to go over and hug the guy, especially when I could tell it irked Clint that he'd pissed on his pity party.

Clint slapped his knees and asked, "So, where are y'all headed to?"

Dave flicked a glance at me. Aja's eyes danced to me and then Mindy. I suddenly needed another one of those cold beers.

"I was thinking we'd stay here awhile and see how things go," I said, tapping my knee against Mindy's. It broke her out of her trance.

"Yeah. I mean, this place is pretty cool. It's like proof that civilization still exists," Mindy said. "Besides, you two have to see the rodeo tomorrow. Unless they only do it once a week."

"No, it's a nightly thing," Clint said. "At one point, they may ask you to run a concession for the night. This way everyone gets a chance to enjoy themselves."

"I call the biscuit bar," Dave said with a mouthful of biscuit.

Aja settled back into her chair without a trace of pain on her face. "I'll be good to go tomorrow night. You know why?" She paused, expecting to hear us all take guesses. When we didn't, she said, "Because Clint has painkillers! He's like an angel from above."

Boy, was she laying it on thick, making great pains to smile at Clint and shoot me a look from the corner of her eye to make sure I was properly upset.

"Nothing crazy. Just some muscle relaxants and a few other things I got from the pharmacy before there was nothing left. You never know what you'll need on the road."

The crickets around us started to get drowned out by the flittering bats above us. Clint stood and actually tipped his hat at Aja and Mindy. "It's late and I better head off to bed. I'll see you all tomorrow?"

"Heck yeah," Aja said, spilling some wine on the front of her shirt.

"G'night then." He ambled off to his mobile home, his gate just a tad bow-legged.

"He even looks good walking away," Aja said, her voice sounding very far away. I suspected the wine and pills were going to have her sleeping like the dead in short order.

I got up and grabbed Aja's plate of food, bringing it inside to wrap it up. Mindy followed me into the RV.

"That was rough," she said to me, low enough so she couldn't be heard outside. "But I guess I can't blame her. She looked pretty upset when we went to the rodeo. And you're still married and all."

I shoved the plate in the refrigerator. "It's way more than that. Trust me."

What I wanted to do was punch a hole in the wall. The only thing that kept me from doing it was knowing that would give Aja the satisfaction of knowing she'd gotten to me.

Unless this wasn't about pushing my buttons at all and she really felt something for Clint.

Scary thing was, I didn't know how I felt about it. One part of me was upset, kind of like an animal pissed that another had stepped into its marked territory, and the other part was relieved.

"If it makes you feel any better," Mindy said, handing me a beer while she got a water for herself, "I don't like him."

I chuckled. "It looked like you were hanging on his every word."

She gave a crooked smile. "That's what I wanted him to think. I was reading him. Don't forget, I come from the wrong side of the tracks. We're pretty good at sniffing out our own."

I took a drink and felt nervous about breathing my beer breath in her direction. "And?"

"Oh yeah, he's one of us all right. And by us, I mean me."

FRESH EGGS

I woke up to the smell of coffee and Dave's arm draped over my chest. I pushed his arm off and he didn't stir. When I looked down from our perch, I saw Aja in the kitchenette making coffee and what looked to be fresh eggs.

My head was a little sore from one too many beers. Aja had turned in—or passed out—right after Clint left. Dave and I brought some shitty beers outside the RV because I didn't want to drink them around Mindy, who stayed inside reading one of my Ray Bradbury books.

"Is that a real fried egg or am I hallucinating?" I asked, stepping down and scratching my head and various other places.

"Oh, it's real, all right." Aja pointed her spatula at a bowl of brown, broken shells.

"Where did you find fresh eggs?"

"Clint brought them over. There's a family that has a small farm just down the road. They barter eggs and milk and butter for different stuff."

My stomach grumbled loud enough to be heard in Hawaii. The egg in the pan looked and smelled so good, I started drooling.

"Suddenly, I'm starving." I went around Aja to get a plate.

She frowned at me. "You can make your own."

I was fine with that. I was well aware that we were past making breakfast in bed for one another.

"I'm bringing this to Clint."

His name was a tiny ballpeen hammer to my temples.

My anger pushed my hunger aside for a moment and I realized Aja was upright and not wincing in pain. "Guess your tailbone is feeling better."

"Much since the pills Clint gave me. He's pretty handy. Like a Boy Scout, but with much bigger arms."

I clenched my fists behind my back.

"For all you know, he's filling you with one of those date rape drugs. Take enough of those and you wouldn't feel a bull's horn goring your thigh."

She gave me a dismissive shake of her head. Her dreads were out of the usual band, falling over her shoulders and draped down her chest. It took me a moment to see that she'd also put on some makeup.

I sat and watched her slide the egg on a plate and cover it with foil.

"The stove is all yours," she said before she trotted out of the RV, closing the door harder than she needed to, as if to emphasize she had closed the door on our marriage.

"Joke's on you," I said to the empty space where she'd been. "That door was sealed shut months ago."

"Okay, if you're now talking to yourself, we need to reconsider giving you the keys to this rig." Mindy stepped out of the bedroom with Miracle at her side. Her hair was a tangled nest and she had pillow lines on the side of her face.

Miracle's tail wagged, at least until he saw me sitting there.

"I'm not crazy," I said, getting up and cracking an egg over the still-hot pan. "At least for the moment."

"Good. We have eggs?" She rubbed her stomach.

"Courtesy of Clint."

Her eyes darkened. "Oh. Where's Aja?"

"She made him eggs and is now in his RV, probably feeding them to him."

"I seriously doubt that. Aja doesn't seem like the feed your man type."

"She wasn't with me."

I wanted to make a sunny side up egg, but I'd messed it up, so I went with scrambled. "You want some?"

Mindy settled into a seat. "Yes, please. Do we have any hot sauce left?"

"That can't be a serious question," Dave said, his head and arms hanging over the end of the bed. "I pick up a bottle every time we stop for supplies. When the food supply comes down to canned stuff that makes you shiver, hot sauce can save the day. Sam, it's in the upper right cabinet."

I grabbed the bottle of hot sauce with a cartoon donkey on it. "Should I add more eggs to the pile for you?"

"Hell yeah. I wish I'd saved a biscuit from last night."

I added some canned mushrooms and green peppers, salt and pepper. The mound of scrambled eggs gave off mighty wisps of steam when I brought it to the table. We tucked in like soldiers. No words were exchanged. It was chow time and if you weren't careful, you might need to do a finger count when all was said and done.

Dave burped, and Mindy laughed while she let Miracle eat eggs from her palm.

Rubbing his belly, Dave said, "Well, at least Clint is good for something."

"I need to get some air," I said.

"You want to take Miracle for a walk?" Mindy said.

The husky made a low growl.

"He must understand English," I said. "I'll bet better than Dave."

As I grabbed some clothes and headed to the bathroom, Dave said, "Hey, I resemble that remark."

It didn't take long to freshen up, slap on some deodorant,

and change my shirt and underwear. When I walked out of the bathroom, Dave asked, "You want me to come with you?"

"I just slept next to you for seven hours. I'm good." I smiled to make sure he knew I was just having some fun...kinda. Sleeping with Dave had never been on my bucket list.

Mindy was putting on Miracle's leash. She looked at me as if she understood exactly what I was going to do. She patted Miracle's side and gave me a knowing nod.

The sun was out, and the birds were everywhere. We were far from the only RV that had spent the night in the parking lot. It was like a little RV town. I took in a deep breath and stretched and felt that should have been refreshing.

I looked over at Clint's mammoth RV just to make sure it wasn't rocking. The eggs suddenly expanded to four times their size in my stomach. I wanted to tell the birds to shut the fuck up.

What is wrong with you, I thought as I stomped on over to Clint's. *Why do you even care? If SHC hadn't happened, we'd be living separate lives by now, paying lawyers ridiculous fees to split up what little assets we have.*

I cared because I wanted to be the one to move on first. She'd broken us. I needed to be the one that picked up the pieces while she lived with the consequences of her actions. When I say lived with the consequences, I mean as miserably as possible.

Not cozying up to some model from a cowboy romance novel.

Dust kicked up as I made my way to his RV. I stopped for a moment, encased in a cloud of it that settled around my hips. Crap, I'd forgotten to plug up my nose in the bathroom.

Wait.

What if I scooped up a handful of that dirt and dust and blew it in Clint's stupid face?

One blow.

One sneeze.

Problem solved.

Except for the part where I had to live with myself for killing an innocent man. I may not like the guy, but he wasn't exactly Jeffrey Dahmer.

Although Mindy said he was this side of shady.

Still.

"Goddammit."

I took the last few steps and stood outside his door. I heard his deep bass, and then Aja's high-pitched laugh. I couldn't tell what they were saying, but the tone was all I needed.

Looking around first to make sure no one was watching, I pressed my ear against the cold steel of the RV. It didn't help. So why was I still plastered to it like the world's worst spy?

And what if I heard a moan?

What would I do?

I felt my neck and face get hot as I thought about my options. None of them were good.

I did have a pair of guns back in our RV.

Idiot, this pointless, my brain screamed at me. *If she wants Clint, let him have her.*

She's not his to take.

That's news to me.

I was so busy arguing with myself I didn't notice that Clint had opened the door. He and Aja stared at me with my ear against the RV. I saw the look of anger, disappointment, and something else I couldn't quite put my finger on Aja's face.

"Whatcha doing there, Sam?" Clint asked.

I straightened up, looked him in the eye for a long moment, and then turned and went back to my RV.

When you're busted being a sneak and can't think of what to say, retreat is always your best option.

PANIC AT THE RODEO

I spent the rest of the day away from the RV, exploring the area on foot. There were plenty of good-natured people around, sitting outside their own RVs or even tents, asking me if I wanted some food or to sit and have a drink.

Boy, did I want a drink.

I stopped back at the RV in the early afternoon. Dave and Mindy were playing fetch with Miracle.

"Where have you been?" Dave asked. "I was starting to get worried about you."

"Aja hasn't come back?" I asked.

"Nope. She's still over at Clint's," Mindy said. She had her hair tied up in a ponytail and wore a pair of Aja's shorts. The sun blazing in a cloudless sky had made it feel like late summer.

I wasn't in the mood to share my utter embarrassment and was both relieved and disturbed that Aja hadn't run over to make it public knowledge.

Miracle dropped the tennis ball, and it rolled to my feet. When the husky saw where it landed, it yipped once and bounded back into the RV.

"Deep down, he loves me," I said.

"Yeah, like I love swirlies," Dave said.

"You okay?" Mindy asked. "You look...pent up."

I wasn't sure how to take that. Was it concern or an offer?

"I'm fine. Hey, Dave, what do you say to some day drinking?"

"The same as always. Yes."

I looked to Mindy. "Crap, I'm sorry. I should be more sensitive."

"No, you should be yourself. Don't worry about it. You have the face of a man in need of a drink. I wish I could join you boys, but I think I'll take Miracle for a nice long walk." She whistled, and the husky came bounding out of the RV. She clipped the leash on his collar and headed off, giving us both a finger wave.

"Self-preservation," Dave said as we watched her go.

"What?"

"At least she's smart enough to realize she can't be around two dudes getting sloshed at lunchtime. I had an aunt like that. She'd just kind of wander off when the party got too hard."

Miracle ran in circles around Mindy, jumping and wagging his tail like crazy.

"Let's make our party to go," I said. "That way when Mindy gets back, she can just chill."

"Works for me. What's the poison du jour?"

"Surprise me."

We walked around the parking lot taking sips from a bottle of expensive tequila a client had given me for Christmas. I wondered if the guy was still alive, somewhere out there, and doubted it.

I felt the sun burning my face and the back of my neck and when the tequila started to make my head swim, I stopped, grabbing Dave by the arm. "Maybe we should get in the shade.
"

"What fer?" Dave's eyes were starting to go cross. "Although you are starting to look like a lobster."

"We can't all be Latinos, brother. But that's not the reason."

Dave took another shot from the bottle and tilted his head at me, the way someone would study an impressionist painting.

"What if we get overheated and then, you know, boom, we go combustible?"

"Is that a thing?"

The ground got all tilt-a-whirl for a moment. "I don't know. But it could be, right?"

Dave took it in and I could see he was deep in some kind of tequila-infused thought. "Shit, maybe."

We shuffled to a shady spot under a pair of oak trees. Two couples sat in folding chairs around a small fire. They had some impressive tents and were, like us, tipping back a few.

"You ready for the rodeo tonight?" one of the men asked. He hugged his woman with one arm and pointed at us with the other.

"Hell yeah," I said, or slurred. "Wouldn't miss it for anything."

"That's great tequila," the other woman said. She was drinking from a can of Natural Ice.

"You want some?" Dave said, holding the bottle out to her.

She hesitated and then the man next to her said, "Please don't tell me you're worried about germs. That's the least of our worries."

The people with her laughed and she took the bottle from Dave and knocked back one hell of a swallow. "I'll just assume you've had your cootie shot," she said to Dave with a sloppy smile.

"Circle, circle, dot, dot," Dave said. It sent us all into over-the-top, drunken laughter.

We introduced ourselves and sat for about a good number of hours drinking and talking about the rodeo. Even in my inebriated state, I found it odd that none of us brought up what we used to do, where we used to live, how we'd gotten here or any of the horrors we'd seen.

Then I realized this place was an oasis from SHC and the terror that lived deep within us every day. It was a big middle finger in the face of mankind's impending doom and a reminder that life could be simple and fun.

At one point I asked them, "None of you are cannibals, are you?"

Dave slapped my shoulder. "Really?"

The woman with the Natty Ice gave a chilling reply. "Not yet."

I couldn't tell whether or not she was serious. Which meant it was time to be on our way.

We said our goodbyes and stumbled our way to the RV. Mindy was sitting outside reading my book. She looked up at us and grinned. "Well, well, well. You've been very naughty boys."

Dave stared at his empty hand. "Did I leave the tequila back there or did we drink it all?"

"I don't know. Who cares? We should see if someone will lend us a cowboy hat for the rodeo."

"I think it would be better if you guys took a little pre-rodeo nap," Mindy said. She pulled two chairs closer to us and just about pushed us into them. "I'll keep watch over the Ponderosa."

I started to fall asleep, or more accurately, pass out, right away. Before I went completely under, I asked Mindy, "Is Aja here?"

The look of pity on her face would have hurt me if I hadn't been so numb.

I woke up to Dave shaking me by the shoulders. "Come on, buddy. Time to get our rodeo on."

I was still most definitely drunk, but even in that state, I realized I needed the distraction.

Mindy plopped a tan cowboy hat on Dave's head and a black Stetson on mine.

"Where'd you find these?" I asked.

"Guy over there was giving them away," she said, pointing to a yellow school bus that had been retrofitted into a mobile home. "Let's go, drunkies."

We filed into the rodeo with the crowd. I kept looking around for Aja and Clint, though I wasn't sure what I would do or how I would feel if and when I saw them together.

"First rule of business," Mindy said, "is for you two to eat." Dave peeled away as we waited for sizzling cheeseburgers and beans. He came back with two beers.

"I'm good," I said to him as I held his plate of food. It was hot enough to burn my hand.

"It's not like we have anywhere to go tomorrow," he said.

Mindy disappeared into the crowd after telling us, "I'll be right back. Meet you by the section we sat in last night."

I kicked Dave in the shin.

"Christ. What did you do that for?"

"Did you forget Mindy's a recovering alcoholic?"

"Dude, we're not the only ones who are drinking. Look around you. This is Bud country."

"I just think we should be a little more thoughtful."

As we walked to find some seats, Dave's face broke into a mischievous smile. "Holy crap, you like her!"

"What?"

We nodded at a pair of cowpokes as we squeezed past them to grab some seats.

"I get it. But it is kind of unfair. You're married. You've got Aja. I've got no one."

When we sat down, I looked around for Mindy and when I saw the coast was clear, I downed half my beer and tucked the rest under my seat. "I don't exactly have Aja. I'm not even sure I would want to have her."

"I hope it doesn't come to me being the last man on earth to find a woman."

"You're a prime catch," I said. "Not many nice guys left, you know."

He put his arm around me, and we got quite a few looks. "Aw, you love me."

Mindy seemed to pop up from nowhere right next to me. She had steak on a biscuit and what looked like a cup of juice. "Hard to find something to drink here that won't scramble your brain," she said lightly. "I miss anything?"

"Just some man-on-man love," Dave said.

When the rodeo started, Dave couldn't take his eyes off the feats of riding and roping. Mindy cheered them on.

I looked around for Aja.

And then I found her.

She sat close to Clint four sections over. They each had a beer, and he spoke close to her ear. A lot.

Fuck this.

I turned my attention to the rodeo, and my best friend and Mindy, stopping short of finishing my hidden beer.

But no matter how resolute I was not to give a rat's furry ass, I couldn't stop looking over at them.

Twice, I caught Aja looking at me. When our eyes met, I wasn't sure what to make of the expression on her face. Was she happy I was visibly upset? Or did I detect something else? Like she was nervous.

"This is freaking amazing," Dave said. "We are definitely staying around for a while." He polished off his burger and beans and beer and had gone up for another that was in a cup big enough to qualify as a fishbowl.

"You say that now," I said. "Wait until your hangover kicks in."

He waved me off and whooped it up.

"He's like a big, happy kid," Mindy said.

"Always has been."

A harsh wind swept through the arena, kicking up a whirl-wind of dust. I panicked for a moment and covered my face.

"I think you're good," Mindy said, putting her hand on my arm.

A few people around us, most of them with unprotected noses, rubbed at the grit in their eyes.

A trio of clowns tried to get the attention of a very angry and confused bull.

Another breeze ruffled my hair. Paper wrappers and napkins flip-flopped through the seated crowd. I looked up and saw a dark gray cloud the size of Delaware heading our way.

"Do they do rainouts at rodeos?" I asked Mindy.

"Who knows with this one? I have a feeling nothing stops them."

I heard the engine of Mother Nature seconds before she sent the winds of wrath hurtling our way. There was dust everywhere.

A man two rows ahead of us sneezed hard enough to send his trucker cap flying. Two terrifying seconds later, he went up like a bonfire. The man who sat next to him jumped from his seat and scrambled away.

I grabbed Mindy's hand. "We have to help him!"

Dave found my half a beer and ran down to dump it on his head. It did nothing. In fact, it only seemed to make the flames more intense.

Out of the corner of my eye, I saw another person burst into flame.

And another.

And another.

The wind howled and people sneezed and went combustible like a sick game of dominoes.

We, like everyone else, got up and ran.

Our hats were whisked off our heads by the damning wind.

I looked over to where Aja had been sitting. A woman, her body from the neck down engulfed in flame, tried to grab hold of her.

My heart stopped.

Clint kicked the woman in the chest with his cowboy boot, grabbed Aja and slung her over his shoulder as if he were Tarzan.

The crowd formed a huge dog pile as everyone tried to squeeze through the exits. The wind refused to let up, and people in the logjam combusted, setting fire to those closest to them.

"We're gonna die," Dave moaned. We were trapped, crushed between too many people to count.

I found it hard to disagree with him.

SAME 'OL, SAME 'OL

"Over there!" Mindy shouted above the frightened throng. I followed her gaze to the arena.

"What do you mean?" Dave was crushed against me. A pair of shrieking women had gotten between Mindy and me.

"Just follow me," she said.

I felt a sudden rush of heat ahead of me as someone only a few feet away went combustible.

"Watch out! Watch out!" Dave screamed.

The woman's hair next to Dave caught fire and her entire head became one big fireball. She must have had a hell of a lot of hairspray for it to combust that quickly.

As Dave pushed against me to get away from the burning woman, I felt something grab me by the collar. I turned to find Mindy trying to drag me against the tide. I didn't see how we could work our way through the packed crowd. It was three of us versus at least a hundred or more.

A tall man sporting a bolo tie slammed into Mindy. She quickly recovered and delivered a brutal elbow to his throat. He went down and disappeared. We moved forward, or backward according to how things were flowing, a couple of feet.

After that, Mindy went strictly for crotches, punching and kicking men and women with equal effect. All grabbed their groins and if they didn't drop, they at least spun away to let us through.

I attempted to do the same with a corpulent middle-aged man and missed. Our knees clacked together, and I almost slipped under the stampeding boots. Thankfully, Dave had formed an outer skeleton for me and kept me on my feet. Mindy threw a punch in the guy's ear that got him skedaddling out of the way.

It seemed like it took hours to break through, but in reality, it had to only be a minute or more.

In the stands, I counted seven human fires. In one of them, I could still see an arm resting on the seat's armrest, a beer still in its hand.

Now it smelled like a different kind of barbecue.

We looked around for any side exits and came up empty.

"We'll have to go out through the paddock area," Mindy said, running down the steps to the arena.

"What's a paddock?" I asked Dave as we tried to keep up with her.

"How the hell should I know? I'm not the rodeo whisperer."

We hopped over the wall and into the arena. I put my arm over my nose as an extra layer of protection because it was like jumping into a dust storm. My eyes stung as they were assaulted, tearing up and making it hard to find Mindy.

"Mindy!"

"Here!"

I saw her vague outline. Dave latched onto my belt loop.

"Almost there," Mindy said. "Just stay close."

She was right. I could just make out the faint outline of the swinging doors that let out the horses and cattle and bulls.

I gave a silent thanks for Mindy. Once again, she was saving my life and I wasn't ashamed to admit she was the stronger of the two of us. Make that three.

She grabbed hold of one of the gates and yanked it open.

Dave shouted something close to my ear that I took for a celebration.

And then the hammer of a very angry God hit my side and knocked me out cold.

"He's coming around."

I opened my eyes and closed them again. The brightness was too much to take.

"Hey, Sam, can you hear me?"

It was Dave.

Keeping my eyes shut, I replied, "Yes, which must mean I'm not in heaven."

"Haha. You got that right."

My face was enveloped in wet coolness. When I opened my eyes again, I saw Mindy holding a wet towel. "You took some shot back there. I think that makes you an official rodeo bad ass."

"Huh?"

I looked around and saw we were outside the RV. The clouds were gone and I could see a trillion stars. When I tried to get up, the pain in my side made me feel as if I'd been poleaxed.

"Whoa there, cowboy. You might want to take the whole sitting up thing in stages."

My eyes floated to my body. My shirt was gone.

"Where's my shirt?"

"We had to cut it off you to make sure you weren't bleeding or anything," Dave said.

"Bleeding? Bleeding from what?"

Mindy grinned. "You got run over by a bull, man. I'm not big on measuring stuff, but I'd swear you went ten feet into the air."

"And you were spinning," Dave added for good measure.

I groaned, happy I couldn't remember. I realized I was lying on a cot and asked, "Where did this come from?"

"How you feeling, Sam?" The baritone voice could only

belong to Clint. He tipped his hat at me. "When I saw you coming, I grabbed my spare cot and brought it right over. Didn't look like you were going to make it into the RV. Not many people get walloped by a bull like that and get to walk away."

I looked to Mindy. "I walked?"

"Not really. Dave and I carried you."

"I meant that as a figure of speech. See, he's gonna be fine," Clint said.

Aja stepped into view. Her eyes were locked on my ribs. I looked down and saw the extensive bruises that made me look like half a Smurf.

"You should give him one of your pills," Aja said, chewing on a nail.

"Already ahead of you," Clint said. He gave a pill to Mindy, who then gave it to me along with a bottle of water.

"Will it kill the pain?" I asked, sounding more miserable than I'd wanted.

"Most of it," Clint said.

Despite my disregard for the man, pain trumped all. I swallowed the pill and lay back.

"Give it ten or fifteen minutes," Clint said. "Then just ride the wave, buddy. Ride the wave."

While I tried to come up with some kind of snappy retort, Clint and Aja walked away, heading toward his RV. She took a backward glance and I thought I saw a flash of concern in her eyes.

Now that everything was coming into better focus, I saw people milling about, some of them with stunned looks on their faces. I heard a woman weeping somewhere in the darkness. Fires had been lit all around the parking lot.

"You guys are all right?" I asked Mindy and Dave.

"We're fine," Mindy said. "Just some bumps and bruises."

"Someone bashed my big toe and I'm almost too afraid to see what it looks like," Dave said.

Mindy patted his back. "Do you want me to do it for you?"

"Would you?"

"Don't do it," I said. "People who see his feet have not fared well. Why do you think he wears socks all the time?"

"Don't listen to him. He's a moron."

"Hey, I almost got killed by a bull. Show some respect." I started to laugh but the rippling pain put a stop to that. "By the way, thank you both. Were you in the Army or some kind of karate club?" I asked Mindy.

"Just the streets." She folded the wet washcloth and put it back on my forehead.

A gray-haired man with a handlebar mustache stopped by our RV. The buttons on his shirt were fighting the good fight not to pop off like champagne corks.

"You folks all right?" he asked.

My head swam for a moment. The pills were already taking effect.

"Yeah, we're good," Dave said.

"I got hit by a bull," I said, raising my hand as if I were back in Mrs. Melody's third-grade class.

The man looked shocked. "Did he really?"

Mindy and Dave shook their heads.

"Well, I guess that's better than, well, you know."

He made a salient point.

"I guess this is the end of the rodeo," Dave said.

The man turned his head away and spit tobacco juice onto the gravel. "The end? Not a chance."

"Even after what happened?"

He clasped a meaty hand on Dave's meaty shoulder. "Son, this isn't the first time that damn SHC has visited us, and it won't be the last. Now, we may have to cancel tomorrow night so we can clean things up, but it'll be back. When you think about it, what else is there to do? I know a lot of people who are here now won't be tomorrow, but I'm sure there will be others. And we'll be here to show them that you can burn us up but you can't beat us down. You all have a good night and I hope to see you again."

We watched him stop at the next camper to check on a family of five.

"Now those are some red state balls," Mindy said.

SEPARATION

As tempting as it was to stay and just rodeo ourselves until oblivion came, I didn't think I could ever shake those terrifying moments when people were going up in smoke around us, and I thought for sure we were next. The next morning, we took a vote, even Aja and Clint, and we all decided it was best to move along.

Hell, if this place existed, there could be others like it.

It gave me hope that Consumption wasn't just a bit of fake news or fantasy.

Unfortunately, I was in no shape to drive. Sitting up was beyond my current abilities. The flesh of my entire side looked like it belonged on an alien.

"Hope there's not internal bleeding," Dave said.

"Thanks for putting that worry in my head."

He hit his forehead with his fist. "I need to learn to use my inner voice. Sorry."

I was laid out on the couch with a pillow behind my head. "It's fine. Guess we just have to hope I'm not, seeing as there aren't any hospitals around to save my sorry ass."

Dave made breakfast and when it was over, Mindy said she'd take the wheel.

That's when Aja hustled out of the bedroom with a packed bag. Clint looked at her, then looked at me, and quietly excused himself from the RV.

"Where are you going?" I asked Aja.

"I'm going to ride with Clint. I made a copy of the directions, and we'll follow you."

I caught Dave and Mindy's worried faces as they too left the premises, taking the husky with them.

"Are you fucking kidding me?" I said.

Aja's lips thinned and her eyes narrowed. "No, I'm not. What do you care? It's not like you even love me anymore."

She let that hang between us for a few beats. A jolt of pain in my ribs paralyzed me.

"Admit it. If there had been no SHC, we would have been in divorce proceedings by now. You said it yourself. We're broken. There's no going back and fixing this. I see the way you look at me. I'm not blind or stupid."

"I'm not so sure about that."

She dropped her bag and threw up her hands. "See? You're only pissed now because someone else wants to take your toy away. Except you don't realize that you left the toy to be taken a long time ago."

Toys? She was comparing our marriage and its subsequent demolition to toys?

"Left the toy to be taken? Left the toy to be taken? Are you shitting me? I didn't start this. I'm the victim here. It's fitting this is happening at a goddamn rodeo because you've been riding on your high horse when you should have been the fucking clown months ago."

I couldn't tell if the tears that welled in her eyes were from anger or sadness. There was a time when even the ghost of a tear would send me into combat comfort mode. I never wanted to see Aja hurt.

"And maybe you're right," she said, flicking a tear away with her finger. "Which is all the more reason why I have to go."

"Yeah, well, enjoy your time with the dime store cowboy.

When he falls asleep, see if you can find his wallet. I'll bet my left nut you won't see the name Clint Rider on his license."

Aja picked up her bag. "Goodbye, Sam. If we make it to Consumption, I promise to leave you alone. Maybe without me around, you can stop feeling so sorry for yourself."

As she walked out the door, I lifted myself up, the pain nearly blacking me out, and shouted, "Go fuck yourself!"

Aja slammed the door.

Seconds later, it opened again.

"I knew you'd have to come back for the last word. You're so petty."

"It's only me," Dave said.

I felt myself deflate. "Oh."

"You all right?"

"Just freaking peachy. Did you hear any of that?"

Dave looked at his feet. "Everyone did. These walls are, like, super thin. Made me realize people can probably hear everything when I take a shit."

Normally, that would have made me laugh, forget what I was so angry about.

This wasn't normal. Nothing was. Nor would it ever be.

"She go to Clint's tour bus?" I asked.

"Yep."

I wanted to scream. I wanted to cry. I wanted to dance. Most of all, I wanted to be able to sit up without feeling like I was about to break into a million pieces.

"We should get going then," I said.

"You mean, without Aja?"

"They're going to follow us."

Picking at something on the doorway, Dave said, "Oh, okay. Yeah." Looking outside the RV, he said, "We're leaving."

He came inside and Mindy followed. She looked like she wanted to say something to me, but I turned away. I wasn't ready for consolations.

"We still going to your parent's place in Wyoming?" Mindy

asked as she scrambled into the driver's seat. "You know, all of us?"

I took a moment to stare at the ceiling. What I said next could possibly alienate two women from my life. But it had to be said.

"We're not going to Wyoming. There is no place in Wyoming. Shit, I don't even have parents."

Mindy turned around the face me. "Come again."

"My parents put me up for adoption when I was born. We left Jersey to go to this place in Canada called Consumption. It's up in the Northwest Territories. Before all communication crashed, I'd read posts that it was the one place in the world not affected by SHC."

"Consumption," she said, deadpan.

"A.k.a., the middle of nowhere. But maybe that's why it's so special. And maybe the stories were a lie and I'm wrong. I don't know. Won't know until we get there."

"So you lied to me all this time."

My stomach soured. I saw this tiny hole in the floor and willed myself to shrink and shrink until I could slip into it and disappear.

Mindy thrummed her nails on the steering wheel. "I get it."

I did my best to shift my body so I could look at her. "You do?"

She looked sad with her eyes all downcast and lips pulled tight. "You didn't know me. I threatened Aja to let me come along with you. Just tell me this. Do you feel like you know me now?"

The truth was, I didn't. She could be all the things I thought she was or none of them. All I knew was that she had a checkered past, had possibly killed several people (but then again, I was starting to feel that if you lived long enough in this broken world, you would have to take a life sooner or later), saved my bacon more than once and had moments when she was one of the most awesome people I'd ever met.

"I do," I said, biting down the white lie.

She started up the RV. "Good. Because we're stuck with each other, no matter what."

"Or until another Clint comes along."

She put the RV in drive, and we started moving.

"Fuck the Clints of this world," Mindy said.

I thought of Aja, and Clint, and fucking, and wanted to throw up.

LIBBY'S

"If we're heading to Canada, I think I need warmer clothes," Mindy said.

I felt the RV take a sharp turn and I had to hold on to the edge of the couch to keep from falling off. "Where are we going?"

"There's a big store called Libby's," Dave said. "You ever hear of Libby's?"

I couldn't say that I had. Then again, I'd never been to this part of the country before.

Mindy pulled the RV to a stop. "Hey, there's still some glass in the windows. That could be a good sign." She looked over at me. "You need anything?"

"I don't even know what would be in a Libby's."

"I'm hoping thick socks and sweatshirts at least," Mindy said.

"I need more Spam," Dave said. "Oh, and magazines."

"One without the pages stuck together?" I said.

"Ha ha, dick."

I reached my hand out and said, "Help me up."

"Dude, are you sure?"

"Yes. I want to see what's in Libby's. Sounds like a craft store but you never know."

When Dave pulled me off the couch, I immediately broke into a sweat. The pain went into warp drive and I had a hard time breathing.

"Maybe I can ask Clint for one of his pills," Dave said.

"I'd rather suck on your toes than take anything from Clint," I hissed through gritted teeth.

Dave and Mindy helped me out of the RV. Clint and Aja parked behind us and were standing next to his giant RV. Clint leaned awfully close to Aja. "Why'd we stop?" Clint asked. "We've only been on the road for an hour."

"Never pass up a chance for supplies," Mindy said, strolling through the empty window with Miracle by her side. I saw her slip one of the guns into her pocket before she left, so I wasn't worried for her safety. The safety of someone who might be hiding out in Libby's, yes.

"My place is pretty stocked," Clint said with cocky self-assuredness, "but you never know what you'll find. You coming?"

Aja shook her head. "That place looks creepy. I'm fine out here."

"Suit yourself. I'll be back right quick."

"You mind if I go, too?" Dave asked.

"That is why we're here. Go, find some canned meat," I said.

Dave lightly patted my back. "Maybe they'll have a heating pad or something."

The wind rolled over the parking lot. Aja and I stood opposite one another.

"You look terrible," she said. "You want one of those muscle relaxers?"

"Why is everyone trying to push Clint Fake Ass's pills on me?"

She held up her hands. "Hey, forget I said anything. You want to be in pain, be my guest."

I felt an argument coming on, like the interior of an oven while it was preheating.

Aja crossed her arms and looked away from me.

I tried to cross my arms, but the rippling agony in my ribs nearly knocked me out.

Then I thought, Aja doesn't give a crap about me. At least not the way a wife should care about her husband. That was made clear months ago. So why should I? She was now officially living with someone else. I thought back to all those fantasies I'd had of living my life as a free man back when she'd first cheated on me. I couldn't wait to get my life back, and to live it so hard and so well, Aja would feel like a turd on an hourly basis.

She twirled the end of one of her dreads, a little habit of hers that she did when she was either worried or deep in thought.

I wanted to say something but didn't know what. Words suddenly had very little meaning. Or was it too much meaning?

I shifted my feet and grunted, grabbing my side.

"Sam."

"Yeah."

Aja looked at me for a long moment.

"Dude, check this out!" Dave came waddling out of Libby's with reusable bags strung along his arms. "That place had everything. Well, a lot of everything at one time, but still. They even had a book section that was pretty much full. I grabbed every sci-fi book they had." He opened a bulging bag to show me the books. There was enough reading material in there to hold me for a few months.

Miracle barked behind us. Mindy carried several bags as well.

"Now I'm ready for Canada," she said. "Of course, the selection wasn't exactly straight from fashion week, but who really cares how we look anymore?"

Dave and Mindy brought the bags inside the RV and came out with gas cans. "I spotted some cars around back. We're gonna see if they have any gas," Dave said.

Miracle, now off his leash, ran to Aja. She bent down to pet him, but her eyes were on me.

"Good idea to make this pit stop," Clint said. "Can't have too many lighters and fire starters." He looked at me, then at Aja. The soles of his boots scraped against the asphalt as he turned to me. "You look like roadkill, Sam. Stay right there. I'll get you all fixed up."

Everyone left and now it was just Aja and I again. Miracle panted and barked, happy to see Aja. I was sure that hour apart felt like eternity plus an episode of *Keeping up with the Kardashians.*

I waited for her to say something.

In the end, I think she was waiting for me to break the silence.

Clint returned with a bottle of cold water and a handful of his goof pills. "Take two and settle in for a nice long nap. Should be feeling a little better when you wake up."

I stared at the pills in my palm. "Thanks, doctor."

Clint laughed. "We're all doctors now, Sam. You feel better. Come on, Aja."

He walked back to his trailer, stopping when he realized Aja wasn't at his heels.

"You should probably take one, too," he said to her. "I'm sure your back is feeling mighty stiff about now."

"I'm taking Miracle for a while," she said to me, not Clint. She and the dog walked past him and into the RV. Clint tipped his hat at me and followed them.

I gave him the finger. Or at least the space where he'd stood before closing the door.

BORDER CROSSING

As an American, I'd always thought Canadians were nicer, calmer, happier people. What did I have to base this on? Most of the great cast members of Saturday Night Live were from Canada, and they seemed awesome.

With that cheerier disposition, I also assumed that they had their shit together better than us. I didn't see a lot of stories about Canadian unrest in the news growing up.

All of my north of the border pre-conceived notions had led me to believe that crossing into Canada would be like the RV being whisked by a tornado and dropped into Oz. We'd go from the black-and-white ugliness of a country ravaged by SHC to a Technicolor dreamland of hope and a future that didn't end in self-immolation.

It had taken us a long while to get to North Dakota. When we weren't moving cars and trucks out of the way—and by we, I mean Dave, Clint, and Mindy—we were stopping for gas because Clint's airbus ate up fuel like it was M&M's. Over those few days, my ribs started to feel better, though my mood was pretty damn foul. Dave and Mindy mostly left me to myself and my misery.

I'd found that a glass of bourbon combined with one of

Clint's pills made the days go by in a nice haze. I read the books Dave had gotten from Libby's and mostly stayed in the upper berth, listening to Mindy and Dave talk or curse vehemently when they had to get out to remove another obstacle.

I was halfway through a paperback about a relationship drama with too many twists and turns for my addled brain to follow when Mindy banged on the ceiling.

"We're here."

Here? How did we get to Consumption so fast? I thought we were in North Dakota.

I looked around the sleeping area, at the books strewn about, the mostly empty bottle of bourbon and the last pill nestled beside my wallet. Had I spaced out that badly?

With just a little bit of effort, I slid down, landing between Mindy and Dave.

The border crossing loomed ahead of us.

It was a blackened shell, every entry point jammed with burned cars. It napalm had been dropped on the place.

"Well, shit," I said.

There wasn't a living soul to be seen. Though there were plenty of black birds feeding on things I preferred not to think about.

On the other side lay Saskatchewan, the entrance to Oz that had kept me going all this time.

Mindy thrummed her fingers on the steering wheel. "Maybe we just hoof it and look for another RV on the other side."

"And carry all our stuff?" Dave said.

"Without our phones telling us what to do, who knows how far we'd have to go before we found one," I said.

Mindy shut the RV off. "We should stay here for the night and try to figure out our next step. To be honest, I was starting to get a little cross-eyed." She patted Dave's arm. "Luckily our boy here can talk a blue streak. Thanks for keeping me awake."

Dave beamed. "I knew my irritating traits would come in handy someday."

I opened the door. "I need some fresh air."

"And a shower," Dave said.

I ignored him. I wasn't in the mood.

I stepped out and was buffeted by the wind. It was much colder in North Dakota. I contemplated going back inside for a jacket and decided to let the chill wake me out of my funk.

"Now what?"

I turned to see Aja approaching with Miracle. She'd apparently decided to keep the husky. I wasn't going to fight for custody, though Mindy and Dave griped a lot about the new arrangement.

"We'll figure something out," I said, unable to hide my irritation.

"You have a tank you can drive over this mess? Jesus."

"Just take it down a notch."

"Don't tell me what to do."

"Okay, can you *please* take it down a notch?"

I hadn't seen Aja in a couple of days, opting to stay in the sleeping berth instead of joining them for dinner outside. Absence, in this case, had made the heart grow angrier.

"Well, this is your plan. Fix it."

"Yes, I planned to have the border jammed with burned cars and trucks. Why don't you go inside and polish Clint's boots or dust off his hat or something."

Miracle barked at me. I was tempted to bark back at him.

"Real mature."

"Mature people are loyal," I snapped back.

"Go run off and tell that to Mindy."

"I will."

"Tell me what?"

Mindy had on a light jacket and Phillies baseball cap she'd grabbed from one of our stops in Pennsylvania. That already seemed like a lifetime ago.

"Nothing," I said, looking to Aja to see if she had the stones to press the matter with Mindy. Instead, she tugged on Miracle's leash and they went for a walk.

For the first time, I was proud of the husky when he lifted his leg and let out a hot, yellow stream onto Clint's front tire.

Clint popped out of the RV, shot a look of disgust at the dog, and walked over to us with his bowlegs. I had the feeling he faked the odd bend in his legs. All part of the cowboy ruse. Dave, Mindy, and I, in our lighter moments, joked about who Clint Rider really was. I gave him the name Sheldon McMinniver. Dave said he was actually a greeter at Walmart and Mindy added graphic details on his obsession with auto-erotic asphyxiation.

So it was no wonder we all tittered a bit when he stopped in front of us.

"Something funny?" he said in his exaggerated drawl.

"Not really," Dave said. "Just road cabin fever."

"Yeah, that's it," Mindy said, staring Clint in the eye, as if daring him to press her for the real reason for our mirth.

He pointed at the impasse. "Well, that doesn't look too promising."

"Nope," I said, popping my p.

"We can't even just roll them out of the way," Dave said. "And we sure as hell can't pull them." He turned to Clint. "Unless you have a winch or something in that monster."

Clint rubbed the back of his neck. "Can't say that I do."

"We could always wait and see if someone driving a stolen tow truck tries to cross," Mindy said.

All eyes turned to her.

"Just fucking with you," she said, her eyes twinkling in the afternoon light. "What would be the odds? I think we've already busted them with SHC."

Aja came back with a relieved Miracle. "So, what did you guys decide?"

"Nothing yet," Dave said. "I mean, it's pretty gnarly over there."

"Gnarly?" I said to him. "You grew up in Fort Lee, not Santa Monica."

Dave raised his chin and tugged on lapels that weren't

there. "Hey, it's the end of the world as we know it. I can be anything I want."

I noticed Mindy slide her disapproving gaze over to Clint. I wanted to give her a high five at the very least.

"Fantastic," Aja said. "I guess we have to find another place to cross."

I thought about that and said, "Then we have to find some new maps, because the one I have takes us here."

"Maybe we should have stayed at the rodeo," she said. "Instead, here we are, stuck in North freaking Dakota, chasing something you saw on the Internet. We must all be crazy."

No one said anything for what felt like a decade.

Finally, Mindy said, "From where I'm standing, if you're still alive, you're officially nuts."

Dave grinned, saw that Aja and Clint didn't agree, and looked to me. I gave him a quick nod.

I could tell Aja had woken up on the wrong side of the bed. Clint's bed, I assumed. She looked like she could spit nails.

"I should have just left you when...when everything went down."

The pain in my ribs took a distant back seat. "Did you forget I tried to get you to leave? But you said you needed time to find a place. So like an idiot, I let you stay. And then the world went to shit. You should thank me. If you left back then, you'd be fit to stuff in a pipe by now!"

"Oh, so you wish I was dead?"

I held out my arms. "There you go, making shit up when I speak perfect English."

"You're such a condescending asshole."

Clint took a half-step between us. "Now, maybe we should roll things back a bit."

We screamed at him simultaneously, "Shut up, Clint!"

Dave and Mindy shuffled until they were behind me. I wondered if that was supposed to be their way to figuratively let me know they had my back.

"This is ridiculous! You're ridiculous," Aja shouted.

"Don't get pissed at me just because you're scared and something isn't easy. I know it was waaaay too easy to do that shit on your phone. That's more your speed."

Miracle started growling at me. I hoped Aja had a tight hold on his leash.

"Maybe if you treated me nicer, that would have never happened."

"Treated you nicer? I did everything for you! Shit, I even spent my days off taking you to flea markets and candle stores and...and fucking Bed Bath and Beyond. What more did you want from me?"

Aja's upper lip curled. "I hate you."

It would have been so easy to take that low road. Instead, I countered with, "Trust me, I know."

To my utter shock, she took off her shoe and flung it at me. I ducked and it hit Dave in the chest.

"Ow. That hurt," he said, rubbing his chest.

She instantly softened. "Oh my god, I'm sorry. I didn't mean to hit you."

I could see that Clint was getting a quiet kick out of all this.

"That's right, Dave. I'm the one she wants, and likes, to hurt." I looked back at the burned-up mess at the border. "You want to get to Canada so you can start your new life? You got it!"

I stormed past Aja. Miracle nipped at my hand but missed. I bumped into Clint and ignored the sparks of agony in my ribs.

"What are you doing?" Mindy said.

"Yeah, buddy," Dave said.

I kept walking and yelled, "Taking care of the problem!"

Stomping up the steps into Clint's RV, I slammed the door behind me and settled into the swivel, leather pilot's chair. If I were in a better frame of mind, I would have taken a moment to take in the opulent splendor of the mobile mansion.

The idiot had left his keys in the ignition.

I fired the RV up and slammed it into drive.

Four shocked faces stared at me through the windshield.

I hit the gas and turned the wheel so I was on a head-on collision with the barrier between the good old and dead U.S. of A and Canada. Giving it as much as the RV could take, I pinned the accelerator, lashed the seat belt over my chest, gripped the wheel and plowed into what I hoped was the smallest pile of barbecued cars.

SUCCESS...IN A WAY

I'd never been in a car accident before. Not even as a passenger when I was in high school, and several of my friends drove like they had a hot date with the undertaker.

The brutality of the physical impact was something I was prepared for.

But the sound. It was like something I heard with my ears, but also with my soul.

Clint's shit kicker RV made for one hell of a battering ram. The first car I slammed, a Honda Civic I think, flipped up and went sideways, out of my view. I felt the resistance as I pushed the RV further, so I made sure to keep my foot mashed on the accelerator, even though it felt like my bones were about to escape the bonds of my flesh.

It sounded like concussion bombs going off as the RV made quick yet hazardous work of the impediment to our getting to Canada.

I didn't even realize I had broken completely through until I was about three hundred feet into Canuck Land. At one point, I had closed my eyes.

When I opened them, I saw a cloud of dust and debris in the side-view mirrors.

The front windshield of the RV was filled with a spider's web of cracks. I had no idea how it was still holding in place.

The engine shook violently, like a dog coming out of an unwanted bath, and gave up the ghost.

Everything went silent, save the ringing in my ears.

I unclipped the seat belt and knew right away that I had just wiped away any healing of my ribs. It hurt like a mother as I slid off the seat and walked with unsteady legs outside.

Clint's mobile mansion was toast. The entire front of it was as crumpled as tin foil ball. Steam and fluids of various colors poured from every direction.

The whole thing made me smile.

I took a deep breath of Canadian air and could swear that it smelled different. Cleaner. Healthier.

Feeling proud of myself, I turned to face the clatter of fast approaching footsteps.

"What the fuck did you do?" Aja wailed. That got Miracle howling as if there were a full moon.

"Really, what the fuck did you do?" Mindy said, though her tone and the twinkle in her eye made for an entirely different translation of the same question.

Clint ran past me to inspect the damage. He removed his cowboy hat and slapped it against his thigh. "I'll be dipped in shit. You killed my RV, Sam."

Dave brought up the rear, too breathless to speak.

Aja, however, could talk just fine. "Are you out of your mind? Christ, Sam, this is something only a crazy person would do."

Though my nerves jangled from the adrenaline rush, I felt calm inside.

"You said this was my problem. So, I fixed it."

"By destroying my home?" Clint said. He looked pretty pissed, which only made me happier. I was tired of his laconic attitude anyway.

"They say home is where you hang your hat," I replied, holding in an inappropriate burst of laughter.

"That's not funny," Aja said.

Mindy had to cover her face.

Dave recovered and grabbed me by my shoulders. "Are you all right? That was some wild movie stuntman shit right there."

"You're lucky you didn't kill yourself," Aja said. I couldn't tell if she meant that as a good or a bad thing. At that moment, I was riding an endorphin high as if I were back at the rodeo.

"Did you hit your head or anything?" Dave asked.

I shrugged. "I don't think so."

He squinted and fixed his eyes on the top of my head. "No, I think you did." When he reached out to touch my hairline, I felt the first trickle of hot wetness. "Crap, you're bleeding."

"Good," Clint said. "Serves him right. If this wasn't the apocalypse, I'd have your ass hauled off to jail."

Now Mindy and Aja were looking at me with worried faces. "I think we're gonna need a towel," Mindy said. "Head wounds get messy fast."

"I'll get one," Aja said, handing Miracle's leash to Dave. She rushed into the ruined RV and I heard her say, "Holy shit, everything is all over the place!"

"Here, I think you better sit down," Mindy said. Dave helped her set me on the ground.

I felt fine. Sure, maybe a piece of glass had dug itself into my head, but I didn't feel the least bit hurt.

"How many fingers am I holding up?" Dave said.

I stared at his raised middle finger. "Ha, funny. Fuck you, too."

He wiped the sweat from his upper lip and looked at Mindy. "Oh boy."

"Yeah, he's concussed. Where are we with that towel?" Mindy cried out.

Clint stood over me with his hands on his hips looking all kinds of smug. "That's a concussion with at least a dozen stitches. At least you can put Humpty Dumpty back together again. Unlike my darn home."

Mild-mannered Dave whirled around and said, "Can you

back the hell off, man? So what, your stupid bus is toast? It's not like it was really yours anyway. You'll just steal another one along the way."

Aja hurried over with a white towel. She pressed it to my head for a moment and pulled it back. It was now a crimson towel.

I felt Mindy's fingers carefully probing my scalp. "That's some flap of skin."

"Flap of skin?" I said. "I'm fine. I don't know why you're all getting so excited."

I tried to get up. Aja pinned me down.

"Don't move," she said.

"Please. I'm not a child."

"Listen to her," Dave said.

"I thought you were on my side," I said to him.

"I am. Which is why I'm telling you to do what Aja says."

I tried to get up again. Dave, Mindy and Aja grabbed parts of me.

"Sam, I'm serious," Aja said. Her eyes were big and wet and filled with concern. Or was it dread?

"Hold him," Mindy said. She rushed over to the dead RV and tugged on the bent bar holding the side-view mirror until it pulled off the side of the RV. She came back to me and tilted the mirror so I could see my head.

And the red, ragged triangle that wasn't part of my scalp before.

Dave shouted, "He's going down!"

That was the last I remember.

When I woke up, I was on the couch in the RV. It only took seconds for the stinging to make itself known on the top of my head.

"If going combustible doesn't kill you, this whole trip definitely will," Mindy said. She sat across from me flipping through a four-month-old *People* magazine.

I touched my head and felt something sharp and barbed. "What happened to my head?"

"I had to stitch you up. When you went all Maximum Overdrive with Clint's RV, your head hit the visor that must had flopped down from the impact. Considering what you did, you came away from it pretty lucky. Clint had a sewing kit, and I did my best."

I managed to sit up, though the interior of the RV swayed for a moment. "Do I dare look in the mirror?"

"Last time I showed you your head in a mirror, you passed out, so that's a hard no."

I looked around. "Where's Dave?"

"Out playing with Miracle. They're making up for lost time together."

"And Aja and the asshole?"

"Collecting what they can from his wreck." Mindy put the magazine down and walked over to me, checking her handiwork. "I do have some news for you, and I'm not sure how you're gonna take it."

"What? The world is dying and the baseball season has been canceled?"

She gave a halting smile. "First, I think what you did was pretty bad ass. You should have heard Clint scream when you took off in his RV. He sounded like a little girl." She laughed and I really wanted to join her, but the pain was too much. "As cool as that stunt was, it has led to Aja and Clint bunking with us."

I looked to the ceiling and then closed my eyes. "Guess I didn't see it through."

"Nope. Still doesn't take away from the pure beauty of it."

Miracle barked somewhere close by. I heard Dave trying to teach him to sit.

"You really liked it?"

"Of course. If another woman swept my husband off into his RV, I'd do the same." She paused and tapped her finger against her lips. "Scratch that, I'd probably do something worse. You're a cooler head than I am. But not by much now."

The sound of Clint talking to Aja as they approached the RV wafted through the open windows. Mindy looked out one of them and leaned down so we were face to face. She held my head in her hands and gently kissed me on the lips.

"It's the least you deserve for fucking with that phony cowboy."

My face felt hot, and my insides melted. The pain in my head and ribs was, for the moment, as gone as the future of mankind.

"Mindy...I..."

The door opened before I could finish.

"Remind me to get some air fresheners from my place," Clint said. He had a suitcase in one hand and one of those black lawn and leaf bags, filled with who knows what, in the other.

Aja flashed Clint an irritated look, or it could have just been my concussion.

"We'll take that back bedroom," Clint said. "Aja said she was using it before."

"Hold on a sec, Hoss," I said. My bubbling anger came as a hurried pulse along the sutures in my skull. "You don't just walk in here and tell us what to do."

He dropped the bags. The RV vibrated from the weight.

"How about I pretend you're not hurt and give you the ass whuppin' you deserve for that stunt you pulled."

"There are places in this world that will throw you in a hole in the ground for taking another man's wife. Consider your precious mobile penis compensator a very small price to pay."

Clint's right hand balled into a fist and his lips disappeared. I prepared myself as best I could. I hadn't had a fistfight since third grade. Mickey Gilligan had gotten the best of me that day, and I'd avoided fights ever since.

"Cut it out," Aja barked. "I'm not some possession you two can have a pissing match over."

Clint took a step back. A slow, stupid grin spread across his face.

"You're right. Guess our craft beer hipster here hasn't figured out you can't lose what you've already discarded. Maybe that smack on the noggin will have knocked some sense into him." He adjusted his hat and picked up his bags. "Now, let's get settled in."

As he ambled down the RV, Aja looked at me, then flashed her eyes at Mindy, before making a sharp turn on her heels and joining Clint. She slammed the door behind her.

"Oops," Mindy said with her hand over her mouth.

"Oops what?"

My mind was distracted for the moment. I actually considered grabbing one of the pistols and using it to scare the crap out of Clint. Now I knew why the Wild West was so wild. When there was little to no law and order around, and life expectancy was tenuous at best, anything went.

Just look at Clint's RV.

"I was playing around while you were out, putting on some makeup. I forgot I had lipstick on before."

I wiped my mouth and saw a red smear on the back of my hand.

OH, CANADA

I tried to sit up front in the passenger seat, but it was too uncomfortable, so I was back on the couch. I didn't get to see much of Canada when we first entered. We made a quick stop at a gas station and as much as I wanted to go out and forage for supplies, I couldn't get up. At least Dave found a road map. Then we were back on the road. I should have been excited that we'd made it this far.

Truth is, my mind was on other things.

I tried to read a book, but my eyes kept lifting off the page and settling on the closed bedroom door. Miracle was asleep with his head on his paws outside the door. I did a lot of rereading the same lines over and over again.

I flinched when Dave, who I hadn't realized was standing next to me, said, "You want me to knock on that door, maybe scare them a little?"

"First, thanks for the heart attack." The little jerk my body made did wonders for the pain level. I could feel my pulse beating at the top of my head. "I keep thinking, if I hear one moan, I'm going to lose my shit."

"With the shape you're in, you'd just end up hurting yourself more. But I can be your muscle."

That gave me my first smile of the day. "If you can find any, let me know."

"Oh, ha ha. Let's make fun of the chubby guy."

For a second, I thought he was serious. Then he lifted his shirt and caressed his distended belly. "Just remember, when we run out of food, I'll be the last man standing. Especially after I eat all your skinny asses."

"When there's no more Spam left in the world, Dave will devour the weak."

"Hell yeah. I'm here for a long time, not a good time."

I set my book aside and finally stopped staring at the door. Dave and I bullshitted about past exploits. The guy had a way of finding the lighter side of even the darkest moments. Right there and then, I realized how lucky I was to have him with me.

He looked over at Mindy who was humming to herself and then leaned in close, whispering, "She kissed you?"

I waved him off. "It was a pity kiss."

"I see the way she looks at you. She doesn't look at me that way."

"You're reading way too much into this. My Aunt Iris gave me more passionate kisses."

"Iris? The one with the mole in the center of her head that looked like a big old panic button?"

"The one and only. I've seen pictures of her when she was young. She was a hottie."

"Iris?"

"Iris."

"Stop trying to change the subject. What was it like? Any tongue?"

"I compared it to a kiss from my aunt. What makes you think there would be tongue? You're an animal."

"Goddammit!"

The RV came to a stop and Mindy jumped out of her seat. "Dave, you want to get Clint so we can move some cars?"

He jumped to his feet. "With pleasure."

He knocked hard on the door. Miracle sprang to his feet, tail immediately wagging. "Wake up, buttercup! We've got a jam to unclog."

Dave turned to look at me with a silly grin on his face and he gave us a thumbs-up.

"He is one goofy bastard," Mindy said.

"How did you know Goofy Bastard is his middle name?"

The door opened and Clint, filling the frame, swept his mop of hair back and set his hat on his head. He adjusted his belt and made a point of focusing his gaze on me, as if to say, *you know exactly what I was doing, pardner.*

I wanted to smash his face in.

"Is it a bad one?" Clint said.

"Nothing you two boys can't handle," Mindy replied, opening the fridge to get a can of Coke.

Dave and Miracle stepped out of the RV. Clint lingered for a moment and shook his head at me before joining them.

"What a turd burger," Mindy said.

"Feel free to run him over." My insides were wound up to tight, I felt ready to implode.

"Tempting. Tempting. But for now, we need him to move stuff. Like a human bulldozer."

We heard Clint shout something at Dave that didn't sound especially nice. Miracle barked. Mindy rolled her eyes. "I think I need to go out there and play peacemaker."

When she leaned over me, I thought she was going in for another kiss. I tilted my head up like a baby bird, hungry for what momma brought to the nest.

Instead, she handed me her can of Coke. "You can have some if you want."

And then she left. I felt like an idiot, but what else was new?

The air coming in from the door when she opened it was crisp. I shivered, though more from my stupidity than the weather.

"Aw, how nice. You're sharing cooties."

I hadn't seen Aja come out of the bedroom. I almost spilled the Coke.

"I'm sure you and the Lone Ranger are sharing a lot more," I shot back.

Aja clucked her tongue, something she did to annoy me, and said, "You don't know anything. You think you do, but you don't."

The pounding in my head ticked up a little bit.

"I'm not in the mood for your head games. Not when I have an actual fucking head *wound*."

For the briefest moment, I saw the mild contempt on her face break, replaced by genuine concern when she looked at my head. She worked hard to recover but I'd seen it.

"I'm surprised you're not running after Mindy, even with your head *wound*."

"And I'm surprised you're not hanging on to Clint's belt buckle."

We didn't say anything else after that. We just stared at one another in a kind of Mexican standoff. I knew she was looking for the same thing as me—the remnants of what we once had, what made us the couple everyone envied. Was there anything left? Or was this it? We'd fight until we got to Consumption and then part ways.

The funny thing about breakups is that they're never easy, especially when you've spent the better part of a decade together. It was the definition of the word, complicated. I never felt as if my emotions were on steady ground.

One second I wanted to be rid of Aja. The next, I wondered what it would be like to just be nice, to hold her.

God, I was messed in the head.

Dave came back and broke the stare down. "We're ready for action, Jackson. Who wants lunch?"

BROWNIES

We didn't make much progress that first day north of the border. Too many trucks in the way. Some started, others were dead as grunge music. Clint, Aja, and Dave had to get out to help Mindy negotiate her way through and around them.

It seemed like everyone had gathered in this slice of Saskatchewan and just gone combustible. The traffic heading to the United States far outnumbered those going into Canada. It made me doubt the stories about Consumption, but I kept my concern to myself.

At one point, Clint popped his head into the RV and said to Mindy, "How about I take the wheel for a spell, get this old tub moving?"

Mindy coldly replied, "You want to mansplain to me how to drive?"

He got back to signaling duty without another word.

"That's right, Brokeback," Mindy said, turning back to give me a wink. I had to admit, it kind of turned me on.

We stopped early, our roadblock removal team tired out and hungry. Dave started a fire on the side of the road and roasted up a packet of hot dogs he'd been saving for a special day. It would have been nice to have some buns, but you take what you can get when all the bakers had burned like an overdone bun.

The tension was thicker than Clint's skull as we sat around the fire, waiting for the hot dogs to be done. No one said a word. Side-eye abounded.

"Well, this is fun," Dave said. He handed the sticks he'd impaled the hot dogs on to Mindy. "Hold this for a second."

He jogged to the RV and came out a minute later holding a bottle of tequila.

"Now I know this would be more appropriate if we went south instead of north, but I figured we could add this to our shots." He pulled a small bottle of maple syrup out of his pocket. His other pocket contained four shot glasses.

"Don't mind if I do," Clint said, accepting an offered shot glass. Aja took one, but she didn't look happy.

I declined.

"What?" Dave was crestfallen.

"No booze tonight. I don't want to add a hangover to my list of ailments."

I looked over at Mindy, who was dressed in an overly large sweat jacket, roasting weenies over the fire. Her eyes met mine, and I knew she understood that I was skipping shot time for her. She gave an almost imperceptible nod and went back to concentrating on our dinner.

Dave poured out the shots of tequila and syrup and said, "To the magic of alcohol. May it give us the ability to tolerate one another on this, our first night as strangers in a strange land!"

"To the U.S. of A," Clint said. "And all it stands for."

Dave was puzzled but clinked shot glasses, nonetheless. The three of them downed their shots and Dave quickly poured another round.

"Here, let me help," I said to Mindy. She handed two sticks over. The skin on the franks was sizzling, just starting to blister. My stomach grumbled loud enough to be heard in Alaska.

Aja opened a bag of potato chips. They said they were sour

cream and onion flavored, but I thought they tasted like feet. Off-brand Canadian chips were not my chip of choice.

We all had a hot dog, including Miracle, and despite their terrible flavor, we devoured the chips. Dave, Clint, and Aja had enough shots to mellow out and start to talk as if they were deaf, laughing at things that weren't the least bit funny to a sober ear.

I saw Clint slide his arm around Aja and she moved away just a few inches.

Hmmm, what was that all about?

He tried again two shots later and that time she didn't move. They were all smiles, their eyes so glassy, I saw the distorted flames of the fire in them.

"You guys want brownies for dessert?" Mindy asked.

"Does the Pope shit in his hat?" Dave said. Aja and Clint seemed excited by the prospect. Or another shot. I wasn't sure.

"Come on, give me a hand," Mindy said to me. She had to help me out of my chair. We walked slowly to the RV.

"How are you going to make brownies without milk and eggs?" I asked her.

"I found of box of instant microwave brownies in Libby's. You pour it all in a cup and just add water."

I opened the door for her. "There was a time when that would have sounded fifty shades of nasty to me."

Now *her* stomach grumbled. "Apparently, now is not that time."

As soon we got in the RV, Mindy took off her jacket. She wore a tight t-shirt that said *Minnesota, Land of 1000 Lakes*. To my horror, she caught me looking at her chest.

"Oh, so you're a boob man."

I felt myself redden. "I was just reading your shirt."

Mindy looked down at it. "Not a lot of words there."

Crap. Had my eyes lingered that long? I tried to recover. "Look, I'm the last person to objectify a woman. I was just...I was just..."

"Looking at my chest," she said, and then she smiled. "It's

fine. I know all about the birds and the bees." She moved in closer to me. My throat went dry and my tongue swelled up. "I don't mind. You can look as long as you want."

"Mindy, I don't want you to get the wrong idea."

My knees felt as if they were going to buckle. She closed the gap between us. I could smell hot dogs and foot chips on her breath.

"That's funny, because I do."

She kissed me.

And not like my Aunt Iris.

I went from shocked to melted butter in an instant. My arms went around her, and we kissed deeply and forever.

When we finally came up for air, I said, "I shouldn't be doing this. I'm still married to Aja."

Mindy cupped my face in her hands. "You're right. You are. And I probably shouldn't be telling you this now, but she's not sleeping with Clint. I doubt he's even gotten to second base."

I had a hard time recalling what second base meant. It was difficult with all of my blood heading south.

"What? How do you know that?"

"A woman can tell. This is my way of telling you I understand your position, and you need to know everything that's going on before I kiss you again. Or you can walk away and I won't be mad. Well, maybe a little frustrated, but that's only because I'm human."

Aja wasn't sleeping with Clint. Was Mindy right?

It seemed a crazy thing to make up right as we were making out.

A fresh burst of laughter erupted outside. Aja's high giggle overrode Clint's horsey guffaw.

I cast my eyes back down at *Minnesota, Land of 1000 Lakes*, and then up into Mindy's eyes.

"Nothing wrong with being human," I said, pulling her so close we were basically one body.

The brownies took longer to make than expected.

TENSION

Mindy and I never went past kissing and a bit of groping. It had been a long time since I'd had any kind of release, and Lord knows, I wanted to get vertical between the sheets in the worst way. I was almost dizzy from it.

But aside from it not being a convenient place and time, a part of me wasn't ready. Mindy was the first woman I'd kissed in too many years to count. Jumping any further than that seemed out of my reach.

When we came back with steaming mugs of microwaved brownies (that were as terrible as you would imagine), Aja glanced in our direction and in an instant, I knew she knew. Far be it for a man to figure out the mystical powers of the fairer of our species. It only took her a second, that much I could tell. It wasn't as if we returned wearing goofy smiles or with our clothes on backward. I didn't even have lipstick on my face to give me away.

How do I know? Because I know Aja, and I saw her go from happily drunk to stone-cold sober in the blink of an eye. She also kept stealing odd looks at the both of us as we ate our brownies.

When we retired for the night, I worried, I mean wondered,

if Mindy was right about Aja and Clint and if our kiss had sent Aja and Clint's relationship, for lack of a better word, to the next level. The thought kept me up all night. That and Dave's drunk snores.

Unable to sleep, I was tempted to do two things during the night. Sneak over to the bedroom door and see if my fear was in fact a reality (though in all honesty, I was pretty sure Clint had a major case of whiskey dick, so nothing much would happen). Or step down and see if Mindy was awake as well so we could continue where we'd left off.

I opted to stay next to Dave.

Not my favorite decision ever, but a wise one for the moment.

I slept for about an hour, woke up around five and gave up trying to fall back to sleep. I dressed and went outside, walking a bit, trying to work out the pain that had me in a suplex. The fresh air was cold enough charge my brain and body.

There were no cars in either direction on the highway. Nothing but a pink sky and shushing wind.

The RV door opened just as I was coming back. I figured it was Aja and braced myself for impact.

"Hey Sam," Mindy said low so as not to wake anyone up.

"Hey."

"You didn't sleep either?"

I shrugged.

"Heard you tossing and turning." She tugged her sweat jacket around her, shivering. "Wow, this will wake you up. You're freaked out about last night, aren't you?"

I looked over her shoulder at the arc of sun just creeping over the horizon. "No. Maybe. No, I'm not freaked out. Man, I thought being awkward would just go away along with most everything else."

"This RV is the very definition of awkward," she said and then smiled, tucking a lock of hair behind her ear. "I bring the awkward. Always have. It's like my superpower."

She looked fragile, standing there shaking in the early

sunrise. Fragile was not something I thought I'd see in Mindy. I closed the distance between us and wrapped my arms around her.

"I'm sorry," I said.

She held me lightly, which I appreciated.

"Don't be. Sometimes, I'm sorry you all got stuck with me. Well, after I forced myself on you. Then other times, like last night..."

"Yeah, I get it. I'm glad you're with us. I wouldn't be here now if it weren't for you."

"How far until we get to Consumption? Do you really think SHC won't happen there?"

"Let's go inside, warm up and look over the map. And yes, I think it's exactly where we need to be."

Mindy made coffee while I spread a map we'd found at a Shell gas station out on the kitchenette table, along with the directions I'd written a lifetime ago. A few minutes later, Mindy slid beside me and handed me a steaming mug. I pointed on the map to where I thought we currently were.

"I think it may only be a full day's drive from here to Consumption. Kinda like when me and my buddies in college would drive from New York to Florida for spring break."

"Only with less wet t-shirt contests and weed," Mindy said.

I chuckled, remembering my two spring break sojourns. "Exactly."

"Don't you two look adorable."

Aja had come out of the bedroom, once again catching us unawares. It was amazing how good she was at that. Her hair was, in a word, askew, and the bags under her eyes were heavy. As she got closer, I could see she was still tripping on Clint's goof pills.

"Just trying to estimate how long it will be until we get to Consumption," I said, feeling like a little kid who had gotten caught stealing his father's porn stash. I hated myself for feeling that way. I'd done nothing wrong.

"How much longer?" she asked.

"Twenty hours, maybe a little more," I said.

I noticed Mindy kept her eyes on the map, the coffee mug cradled between her hands.

Aja pulled her dreads back and stretched her arms over her head until her shirt pulled up far enough to reveal the underside of her breasts. She looked me in the eye the entire time.

"Good. The sooner we're there, the better," Aja said. She took a bottle of water out of the refrigerator. "Then you can play house with Mindy all day and night. Betcha can't wait."

"Isn't it a little early for this crap?" I said, my blood instantly boiling. "Go back inside to your little cowpoke and let the adults figure out how to save us."

Aja laughed. "You're so adult. Just a few months ago, you were more concerned with Star Wars movies and visiting little shit breweries than being an actual man."

"Better than being glued to my phone and looking at dick pics."

The temperature in the RV plummeted.

Aja's face twisted into a sneer that I wouldn't have previously thought physically possible. Her hand reached blindly for something to throw at me. I wondered when we had become a couple in a comic strip from the fifties. Was a frying pan next?

Mindy surprised both of us when she said, "Aja, if you throw something and hit me, I'm going to spend the rest of my day making you regret it."

I could see the hamster wheel turning in Aja's head. She looked to Mindy, and then to me, and back to Mindy. Her hand flexed for a moment and then went back to her side.

"He has herpes," Aja said. "So, enjoy that."

She stormed back into the bedroom and slammed the door. I heard Clint say, "What did you do that for, darlin'?"

Mindy and I sat staring at the door for what felt like hours.

A century later, Mindy said, "You have herpes?"

"No."

"Not that it matters. Nothing much does anymore. What's a little herpes next to burning to death out of the blue?"

"You think it's safe to come down now?"

We looked up, and there was Dave hanging over the sleeping berth.

"I don't think I could say yes with any confidence," I said.

He came down anyway and poured himself a coffee. "I had crabs once."

THE BIG EMPTY

If I thought the roads were devoid of people in the U.S., driving north through Canada was like charting a vast wasteland of new territory. True, Canada had a tenth of our population, but damn.

I sat beside Mindy who drove without having to avoid a single abandoned car or truck. If we did see one, the paint charred, windows blown out, plastic melted, they were always pulled over to the side of the road. Canadians, apparently, were more considerate than Americans, even in the throes of a painful death.

We were making good time, but we were also running out of gas. We only had ten gallons in reserve in the storage bin. Gas stations were few and far between. Taking one of the random exits seemed like a crapshoot. Who knows how far we'd have to drive in some drinking water town to find a gas station?

"You know what I miss?" Dave said.

It wasn't quite noon, and he was on his second beer. There wasn't much else to do, especially for a guy who had spent so much of his pre-SHC time playing video games.

"What?" I said.

"Sneezing."

My hand went to my nose, touching the material I'd stuffed in my nostrils. I realized at that moment how many times I did that without thinking. It was like checking your phone before they became paperweights. Aja had been right. Tampons made excellent plugs and fit comfortably. However, we hadn't come across even a lone tampon the entire time on the road. I never thought I'd miss tampons. What man did?

"Why the heck do you miss sneezing?" Mindy said.

He shrugged. "I don't know. It was kind of a release. A mongo sneeze, you know, those big ones that cleared your nose, head, and mind, can feel as liberating as a good piss or shit, or even sex."

Mindy cringed. "You compare taking a shit to sex?"

"The act is different, but the end result is the same. You're getting the poison out, whether it's a vapor, gas, liquid or solid. We're all just factories for waste material. Now, I feel like I've got all kinds of stuff inside me that shouldn't be there." He took a drink. "You know, I had a dream last night about a killer sneezing fit and when I woke up, I was so sad I could have cried."

I desperately wanted to make fun of Dave, but I decided to be honest. "I had a dream about sneezing, too, just last week. I was so happy in it."

"You guys are nuts. I miss sneezing like I'd miss my period."

Clint came out from the back, his shirt tucked into his jeans so we could see his huge belt buckle. He even had his hat on. "You ladies talking about your monthly?"

"Your monthly?" Mindy said, disgust on her face. "How old are you, dude?"

He saw the beer in Dave's hand and said, "Morning drinking. Don't mind if I do." Clint grabbed a beer, popped the top, and took a long drink. "I kept expecting to get woken up to move cars to the point where I couldn't go back to sleep. We must be making good time."

As much as I didn't want to talk to Clint, I tried to be the better man. "We will until we run out of gas. Good thing we left your palace behind. It would be a roadside attraction by now."

Clint's eyes got beady and dark.

Okay, so I wasn't the complete better man.

I continued. "If we don't find gas soon, we're in trouble."

"How much trouble?" Dave and Clint asked simultaneously.

"Big time. If we break down and start walking looking for gas, it can make an Australian walkabout look like a trip to the corner store."

Mindy flashed a look of concern my way. I peeked over at the gas gauge. The needle was below a quarter of a tank. We could have saved some gas if we got rid of dead weight. I pictured Clint tumbling end over end as we watched him from the side-view mirror.

"If we break down, at least we have a place to live," Dave said.

"We'll freeze to death in here come winter," I said.

The beer kept Dave optimistic. "Freezing to death is like going to sleep. Better than burning."

"He does have a point," Mindy said.

My growing anxiety about the gas situation felt a little lighter. Maybe we were never actually meant to get to Consumption anyway. Maybe all of this was one last bit of adventure before joining the ash heap of humanity. I had to be grateful that we'd lasted this long, even if it was with Roy Rogers.

"We could get lucky and come across a car that has something left in the tank," I said.

We'd passed by signs for all kinds of animal crossings, trees, and deer grazing on the side of the road. Cars, like people, were in low supply.

"Why don't you read one of your books?" Mindy said to me. "You're making me nervous."

She'd caught me looking at the fuel gauge. Dave heard her and handed me the Orson Scott Card novel I'd been reading. For some reason, I'd been using part of a stick of beef jerky as a bookmark. All reason went out the door when you knew your own nose could spell your demise.

"Just pull over when the needle gets to the next bar so we can put what gas we have left in the tank," I said, diving into the world of Ender but having a hard time staying in it.

I was rereading the same page for the third time when Mindy pulled the RV over. I hoped to see a derelict car. Instead, I got tall weeds and vast nothing.

"Fill 'er up," Mindy said, trying to lighten the mood.

We all got out to stretch our legs, even Aja who looked dazed and hungover. Dave and I emptied the last two gas cans and screwed the tops back on.

"It's kind of scary," Dave said.

I clapped him on the shoulder. "We'll find something. I mean, people had to get gas somewhere up here."

"Unless we're where the people weren't," he replied in a faraway voice.

"We're on a major highway. They wouldn't build it if there was no one around to use it."

"Right. Yeah, you're right." He pulled a can of beer out of his pocket.

"You're drinking a lot lately," I said.

"Exactly. Some things are going according to plan."

The beer foamed from the top when he cracked it open.

Great. Dave had committed himself to alcoholism, with Clint in tow, and Aja was popping pills like they were Skittles. If and when we got to Consumption, would they even want us?

"Just try to take it easy," I said. "Booze, like gas, is in finite supply right now."

"But it won't be for long. Just like you said."

I prayed I wasn't giving him false hope.

We lingered about outside for a little bit, no one talking, and then hopped back inside. Mindy steered us back onto the road. I gave up trying to read. It seemed as if we were all glued to the fuel gauge.

I thought about running out of gas, running out of water,

running out of food. Of colder and colder nights, frostbite, hypothermia, starvation. All in a foreign country with nothing familiar to surround ourselves with as we breathed our last. It was dramatic, I know, but drama was our constant companion.

I felt someone come alongside my seat and was surprised it was Aja. She looked scared.

"How much longer do you think we've got?" she asked.

I thought about it. Ten gallons in an RV was the equivalent of a shot glass in a Honda. The needle had been making a steady march to E.

"I don't know."

"I need a drink," Clint said.

"Me, too," Dave said.

They went back for another beer.

I thought I'd been nervous before, but then teeny tiny snowflakes started pelting the windshield.

Now, my stomach felt as if it wanted to crawl out of my ass.

"Fucking wonderful," Mindy said. Her jaw was set, and her knuckles were white on the steering wheel.

I thought again of throwing Clint overboard. I'd better make sure I took the beer out of his hand, or Dave might jump out to get it.

Aja shivered and hugged herself. It wasn't from the temperature in the RV. We had the heat on low and it was still comfortable.

"I wish I died back at the apartment," Aja said.

"What?"

"You heard me. I could have gotten all this over with and I'd be free from worrying. But you had to drag me along and now I'm in Canada waiting for the inevitable."

Mindy kept her eyes on the road. I turned to Aja. "I didn't force you to come with me. It's not like I had to knock you at and put you over my freaking shoulder."

"Not physically, but that's what it felt like to me."

"Oh, bull crap. You were scared, just as much as I was. If you'd stayed behind, you wouldn't have just gone combustible.

You and I both know those people who were raiding the neighborhood would have done some pretty bad things to you before you sneezed."

"I would have made myself sneeze before they could touch me."

My nerves, riding a frayed edge, snapped. "Stop the car."

"It's not a car. It's an RV," Dave said.

Mindy slowed but didn't stop. "Why?"

"Just...stop...the...RV."

She hit the brakes, and we idled in the middle of the road.

"Go ahead," I said to Aja.

"What?" she said.

I got out of the RV and ripped open the side door. "Come on out and end it."

"You're an idiot."

"I'm an idiot? You just said you wished you were dead. Well, do it. Come on out, have a good sneeze and be done with it."

Dave came out with his hands up. "Whoa, Sam, I think you should take a breath."

"No. I think Aja needs to put up or shut up."

Aja stepped out of the RV. "That's what you want?"

"I'm just giving you a chance to *not have to worry* anymore. You're the one who brought it up."

"You'd love to see me burn, wouldn't you?"

I ground my teeth until it hurt. "If that was the case, I would have left your ass in Jersey! All I did was find a place that might save our lives and a way to get there. This whole trip has been about finding a future and putting this nightmare behind us. And all you can do is pop Clint's pills and say you wish you were dead. When did you become an ungrateful bitch?"

I never saw the slap coming. My head felt as if it had spun completely around.

"Don't you ever call me that!"

Spit flew from her mouth.

Mindy slipped between us, and Aja grabbed her arm.

"Stay out of this, you psycho!" Aja said.

Mindy bristled. "Who are you calling a psycho?"

Aja looked her up and down. "You. It's what we all think you are. A psycho addict who's probably killed more people than she can remember."

"What?"

"That's right. Your boyfriend thinks it, too."

I balled my fists. "I'm not her boyfriend. And that's a laugh coming from you. Too bad I don't have a black light to take into that bedroom."

Clint had been leaning against the RV, drinking his beer. "You're being impolite, Sam. And it's starting to make me mad."

"Go fuck a cow," I said to him with a dismissive wave of my hand.

"I've taken enough horse shit from you," Clint said. He removed his cowboy hat and tossed it in the RV. With two quick strides, he was within striking distance.

"Cut it out, guys," Dave said.

When Clint reared his fist back, he elbowed Dave in the mouth. Blood erupted from Dave's gums and splashed on Aja's face. Aja screamed. Dave wailed. Clint lowered his fist and looked confused.

"You hit me!" Dave said, cupping his bleeding mouth. "My tooth is loose!"

"Are you happy with yourself?" Mindy snapped. She dashed inside and came back with a hand towel, pressing it against Dave's mouth.

"I'm not happy," Clint said. "I hit the wrong man. I'm awfully sorry, Dave."

Dave had a tear in his eye. "Why don't you all get some perspective, man? What the hell is the point of fighting now? Who the hell cares? Why can't you all act like human beings? Not just human beings, but some of the last ones on earth? Maybe this is why the world got SHC. If this is as good as we can do after all this, we're not worth saving."

He walked away from us, despite Aja and Mindy imploring him to stay.

We looked to each other, no one saying a word. I could see in Mindy's eyes that she was hurt by what Aja had said. The side of my face throbbed. Clint pointed at me and then went back inside the RV.

"You know what, Sam?" Aja said. I could see she was about to cry.

I rubbed my face.

"Just forget it." She stomped into the RV and slammed the door.

The snowflakes got fatter and the wind colder.

It was just Mindy and me.

"You really think I'm some kind of psycho?"

"No. Not at all."

She stared at me long and hard enough to see into my soul. I don't think she liked what she saw there. Now she looked like she was on the verge of tears.

I was about to try to hug her when we heard Dave shouting, "I found it!"

He came out of the haze of snow, his head capped in white.

"Found what?" I asked.

"There's a sign for a Husky gas station just a little ways up the road. It says it's eight kilometers away. I have no idea what that means, but eight is a pretty small number."

We should have been happier driving to the Husky station, but the damage had been done.

A PAIR OF HUSKIES

The first thing Miracle did when we stopped at the Husky gas station was lift his leg and pee on one of the gas pumps.

"From one husky to another, right boy," I said.

Miracle glared at me, then saw Aja and went into tail-wagging mode.

The snow had stopped for the moment, but it was getting downright cold.

In all, the station had ten pumps and a good-sized store. The glass door had been broken, but it appeared as if someone had swept up the glass bits and thrown them away.

No one was on speaking terms at that moment, so we silently walked into the store and looked for anything that we could use. The shelves were pretty bare, but it hadn't been ransacked like the stations in America.

I thought, wow, the Canadians are even more polite when they scavenge for supplies.

I looked at the brands of canned foods left and they were all things I'd seen back home. Nothing screamed CANADA ONLY! We could have been standing in the middle of a mini-mart in Topeka, Kansas or Yonkers, New York for all we could tell. It was just another example of the homogenization of our world. I silently wept for the lack of unique identity.

We grabbed a few things but left most of it on the shelves. It had been a rule we'd adopted without talking it out. We weren't the only people left wandering in the proverbial desert. It was good karma not to horde everything and leave something for the next person or persons. Dave was the bag man, cans and packages of Ramen soup mix crinkling and clacking as he walked back to the RV with Miracle in tow.

Without electricity, there was no way to draw fuel from the pumps. And there were no cars left behind.

"Shit," Mindy said. "I'll bet there's enough gas down there to keep that RV running for a year."

"Maybe there's a pickaxe in the mini-mart," I said.

She shook her head. "Not funny. We really need that gas."

I almost asked Aja if she had YouTubed how to siphon gas out of a pump, but she barely looked my way.

Clint had his back to us and was taking a leak against the side of the store. The heavy splash of his beer-logged bladder was this side of off-putting.

"Guess he and Miracle have to fight over whose territorial mark is better," I joked.

Mindy wasn't laughing. I could see the hurt behind the frustration in her eyes.

There was no point in telling her I didn't think she was psycho. It would only make things worse. When women were mad at me, I always found it better to say less and avoid digging a bigger hole for myself.

"Hey," Clint called out as he zipped up and walked at the same time. "Looks like there's a delivery truck out back."

Everyone but Dave ran to the back of the station. Sure enough, a huge gas truck was parked, the passenger door open, what looked like mouse droppings all over the torn leather seat.

"Please don't be empty," I said.

Clint checked it out and my prayer was answered.

"Booyah!" Clint cried, pumping his fist. "Texas saves the day."

I shouted for Dave to come over, and the three of us, after some trial and error, found a way to extract the gas from the enormous tank. We filled all of our plastic gas cans and then filled some more that Mindy had found in the store.

Aja walked around with Miracle as we worked. It was better that way.

We filled the RV's tank and then filled those gas cans up before stowing them away.

"Let's hit the dusty," Mindy said, her hand on the driver's side door handle.

"I saw we wait here for a bit," I said.

"Why?" Dave asked. "We got what we needed and more. Consumption or bust, right?"

Ever since we'd crossed into Canada, I'd been feeling more and more like we were the last people on earth. It was depressing as hell, especially considering how terribly we were getting along. The sense of aloneness was also making me doubt everything I'd heard about Consumption. I wanted to wait at Husky for two reasons—to see if anyone else came by and lift my hopes that we weren't it, and to delay my potentially misguided dream of a better life in the Northwest Territory.

"We're getting close, but maybe there's someone out there lost and afraid. We could tell them about Consumption. Have them follow us."

"That's actually a cool idea," Dave said.

"I think it's stupid," Clint said. He had another beer in his hand. "But this is your rodeo. Hope it ends up better than the last."

Aja had nothing to say, though Miracle barked at me when he passed.

"It won't be long. I just want to see if anyone else stops here."

"You're the boss," Mindy said. "I have to pee." She disappeared behind the station.

Dave brought out two folding chairs and a jacket for each of us. I declined the beer he offered.

"Too bad we won't get to see a hockey game up here," he said. "That would have been a lot of fun. Best sport to see live, man."

I stared at the road, willing a car to appear.

What we did see was plenty of crows. At least that's what I thought they were. Could have been ravens. They were big and black and plentiful. That much I was sure of.

The wind picked up and my marrow had started to solidify. I said to myself that once my teeth started chattering, I would go inside with Aja, Clint and Miracle. Mindy had not reappeared from her pee break. I assumed she needed some time alone.

"Where the hell is everyone?" I said.

"I guess they're all dust in the wind by now," Dave said. He was drinking from a half-empty bottle of Basil Hayden whiskey now. I motioned for him to pass me the bottle.

"It can't be," I said, wincing from the heat of the whiskey. "I refuse to believe that the whole world has burned up, yet Clint still lives. It's not right."

"Clint's not such a bad guy."

I turned to Dave and he wilted.

"You're right. Perspective is everything," he said.

I checked the RV. It wasn't rocking, which was a good thing. Or was it? How could I move forward if I was still clinging to my past? A past that I'd wanted to forget when this whole trip started?

God, I was a mess.

"At least you have Mindy now," Dave said. "She can bring home the bacon, fry it up in a pan and then beat an intruder to death with that pan."

"Might be more humane than a lawn dart to the face." I took another swig of whiskey. The snow had started up again and I knew the temperature was dipping, but now I felt all warm inside.

Dave took the bottle from me. "You're thinking we're going to find more of this when we get to Consumption, aren't you?"

"Shit, I hope not. Back when we lived in the apartment, Aja and I used to talk about moving to someplace remote in like Maine or Nebraska. Just go off the grid and start a new life. Buy one of those tiny houses. Actually, two tiny houses so we had one for all our stuff. The city was just so cramped and we knew there was a better way to live out there if we had the guts to just do it." Miracle barked inside the RV and I heard his paws scratching at the door. "Now everywhere is Nebraska or Maine, and it feels so...so..."

"Lonely."

"Yeah. Lonely."

"But you still have me."

"For better or for worse."

We bumped fists.

Miracle would not stop pawing the door.

"Will one of you let the dog out?" I shouted.

Clint and Aja apparently had better things to do.

"Christ." I got up, had to wait a moment until the spins dissipated, and tore the door open. Miracle bounded out of the RV, clipping me in the side as he galloped to the Husky mini-mart. "I wonder what's got him all riled up."

Dave craned his neck to watch the dog run. "I don't know. Maybe he smells a cat."

I thought of the hell that would rain down on us if Miracle just kept on running and never came back. Mindy and Aja would be very upset. Unnaturally so, considering all of the humans they had lost recently. That's why Miracle was so important to them.

The husky went inside Husky and barked his head off.

"I'll get his leash," Dave said.

"Good idea."

Dave was about to open the RV door when we heard the revving of a motorcycle.

And then there was another.

We looked around, searching for where the noise was coming from. The snow, sensing we needed clear visibility, swirled harder and thicker. I waved my hand around my face to clear the snow away.

A woman screamed.

Scratch that.

Mindy screamed.

KIDNAPPED

Clint and Aja poured out of the RV.

"What's going on?" Clint said.

"Was that Mindy?" Aja said.

I ran toward the mini-mart. The sound of the motorcycles grew louder. Miracle's barks and growls were dampened by the heavy atmosphere. With each pounding step, my ribs sent shockwaves through my body but I ignored it.

Mindy's scream had been solitary. If there hadn't been motorcycles around, I would have assumed she'd fallen and hurt herself.

This was something else.

My heart raced, and I wished my legs could pump just as fast.

I heard the others behind me, calling out for Mindy.

I just made it to the first set of gas pumps when a pair of motorcycles blazed from out behind the mini-mart. The snow prevented me from making out the faces of the people riding them. I could see they weren't wearing helmets, and they had long, black hair.

What stopped me dead in my tracks was seeing Mindy slouched over the back of one of the motorcycles. I could tell it was her because I knew her camouflage pants anywhere. She was clearly unconscious or worse.

The guy riding the bike with Mindy strapped to it noticed me and took a hard right turn to avoid me. He almost wiped out on the slick surface.

Almost but not close enough.

He—or she, it was hard to tell with the hair—hit the throttle and made a beeline for the highway.

I spun around and waved my arms.

"Get back to the RV!"

Miracle came bounding out of the mini-mart, running past me until Dave was able to grab him by his collar.

Aja nearly collided with me. "What? Why?"

"They have Mindy!"

"Who?"

"I don't know!"

We got back to the RV quickly, but by the time I jumped behind the wheel, we could no longer hear the deep hum of the motorcycles. I gunned the RV to life and nearly tipped it over, trying to turn onto the entrance ramp to the highway.

"Why would someone take Mindy?" Clint said from somewhere behind me.

"How the hell should I know? Just keep an eye out for those motorcycles."

I powered the windows down so we could hear the bikes. The wipers worked hard to keep the windshield clear, but the noise they made irritated the hell out of me. We didn't need anything gumming up the works.

The interior of the RV was absolutely freezing. Snow started to coat everything. Miracle started howling. It made the hairs on the back of my neck stand up.

I heard a sharp clack-clack and looked in my rearview mirror to find Clint pumping a shotgun I didn't know he had. The rhinestone cowboy might just come in handy for once. Whoever had taken Mindy wasn't a friendly. I just hoped we could gain some ground on the motorcycles, knowing that an RV was not exactly built for speed.

I notice Aja wasn't complaining about the shotgun.

"You see anything?" I asked Dave. He leaned forward in his seat until his nose was almost touching the windshield.

"This freaking snow isn't helping."

I looked left and right, searching for any turnoffs. When one did eventually appear, I'd have to make a decision to see if the motorcycles had left the highway or not. It was a decision that could cost Mindy her life. Despite all we'd been through, I wasn't sure if I was equipped to make such a choice.

"They looked like Indians to me," Clint said, dipping deep into his drawl. I was surprised he hadn't called them Injuns.

"They call them indigenous up here, or First Nations," Dave said. "I read it in this guidebook I grabbed from a gas station outside Saskatchewan."

"I don't give a coyote's asshole what you call them. Any person who snatches a defenseless woman for no reason deserves what this shotgun can give them."

Now, I wouldn't exactly describe Mindy as a defenseless woman, though even she had obviously been unable to stop her captors. They must have been lying in wait the entire time we were stocking up on gas and supplies. Without any CMPs around to help, her rescue was in our hands.

No, in *my* hands, since I was the one behind the wheel.

I felt like I was going to be sick.

Dave bounces in his seat. "Wait. Look! You can see the tire marks."

Enough snow had fallen so we could see twin marks in the snow where the motorcycles had been.

Finally, the snow was working for the good guys!

The RV's motor started making noises it never had before, and I realized I had taken her to a speed that made the mobile home as uneasy as we all felt. I felt I could let up on the gas a little bit because we had a trail of breadcrumbs to follow, but not much. If the snow kept getting worse, that trail would disappear under a layer of evil white powder in no time.

We drove for miles and miles, and it looked like we were gaining ground judging by the freshness of the tracks. I kept waiting for Aja to say something, like blaming me for getting them into this mess. She stayed between Dave and I, eyes on the road. She was no fan of Mindy, but Mindy had become part of our dysfunctional family. None of us knew where this road would lead us, but somewhere along the way on this crazy road trip, it had become us against the apocalypse.

I noticed Clint taking belts from a bottle of vodka. It made me nervous.

Suddenly Dave hollered, "Stop!"

I mashed both my feet on the brake, and the RV fishtailed dangerously. Everything in the RV flew off shelves and flat surfaces. Aja cried, "Oh!" and went skidding along the floor. Clint hit the deck, and the shotgun blew a hole in the roof. The report was deafening. My ears started ringing immediately. Dave gave a decidedly lady-like shout and cringed in his seat.

When I finally got the RV under control, I turned to Dave and said, "What did you see?"

He pointed out the side window. "They went down that road."

Sure enough, the tracks had veered off the highway and down a narrow road that I would have missed if not for Dave and the snow.

I backed the RV up and got us off the highway.

The road, if that's what you could call it, did its best to chew up our tires and suspension. We bounced around like jumping beans.

Clint said, "Shit. The roof is toast."

"I don't care. Just be ready."

I could see where the motorcycles had zigged and zagged, crossing each other's path. We passed by a leaning one-room house made up of what looked to be particle board. There was an outhouse out back.

We were definitely not in New Jersey anymore.

More equally decrepit houses lined the road. They looked cold and dead, like the world itself.

A little voice inside my head told me we were getting close. It was only a matter of time.

"Get the guns," I said to Dave.

He opened the glove compartment and took out the pistols.

Hanging desperately onto the wheel as it kept trying to jerk out of my hands, I said to Aja, "When we find them, stay in here with Miracle."

"Okay," she said.

Again, I'd been expecting something different from her. This was more like the old Aja who trusted me, which seemed strange since we were ready for a shootout to save the woman who I'd made out with.

We saw a barn that was in need of some Amish love and several houses that were nothing but burned-out shells.

"What the hell is this place?" I said, gritting my teeth to prevent myself from biting my tongue.

"I think it's a reservation," Aja said.

"This looks like a leftover from the Dust Bowl. They can't expect people to live like this."

"Yeah, well, not everyone gets a casino," Clint said.

I wanted to tell him what an asshole he was, but part of me knew he was right. The world was a fucking mess long before SHC. It dawned on me that the planet might have conspired against the organisms that had cocked it all up. Deep in the belly of that Icelandic volcano, Mother Nature had been busy creating the spore that would spare the planet from the onslaught of humanity.

The tracks veered off the so-called road and down a long driveway. At the end, there were three houses made of whatever scrap parts were available. A smoking chimney stuck out of the one in the middle.

Both motorcycles were parked outside.

I stopped the RV.

"We ready for this?" I said, keeping the engine going in case we needed to make a fast getaway.

Dave handed me a gun. "No, but do we have a choice?"

There was always a choice.

But here we were, in the center of a reservation that I couldn't tell had been ravaged by SHC or had always been a shit hole.

Mindy was in the middle house.

It was time to go get her.

RESCUE PARTY

Miracle sensed that Mindy was near, because the husky just about lost his mind. Aja had to wrap her arms around him to settle him down.

"Aja, get in the driver's seat."

"Okay, but why?"

"Because if things don't go our way, you need to get the hell out of here."

"I'm not leaving you."

"If I'm dead, you have my permission."

I looked to Clint and Dave. "How should we do this?"

"I say we bust their door down and go in guns blazing."

"That only works in spaghetti westerns," Dave said. "And you're not Italian. If they haven't seen the RV or heard Miracle, I say we creep up and take a look inside, find out what we're up against."

"And then we blast our way in," Clint said. He was slurring his words, and I was pretty damn sure he would blast us before the people who had taken Mindy. Look what he'd done to the RV!

"I think maybe you should hang back," I said, even though I'd love to put him in the line of fire.

I opened the door and the cold wind hit us in the chest and rocked the RV.

"Fuck, it's cold," Dave complained.

I couldn't feel a thing. I was too busy worrying about a million possibilities, almost all of them ending badly.

I never said I was an optimist.

Dave and I crept up the slight hill in a crouch. I kept expecting shots to ring out and for the bee sting of a bullet in my shoulder. The houses on the side were ruins. The only thing living in there was possibly rats hunkered down for the storm.

We stopped below the window at the front of the house or, better yet, shack. I motioned for Dave to keep an eye on the door.

Very slowly, I lifted my head up until my eyes were even with the bottom corner of the window. I looked inside.

My heart thundered.

Mindy was sprawled out on a ratty couch. Flames blazed in the fireplace.

Sitting around what looked to be a homemade table were three people, two men and one woman. They all appeared to be somewhere in their thirties. All had long, jet-black hair. They were drinking out of coffee mugs and talking. Definitely indigenous or First Nations or whatever Dave had said was the appropriate term in Canada.

I held up three fingers to Dave.

He mouthed, "Do you see Mindy?"

I nodded.

Clint may have been right. The best thing to do would be to kick the door in and take them by surprise. There was a chance we could grab Mindy and be back on the road before they realized what the hell had happened.

The cowboy was beside the RV, his rifle pointed at the house. Or maybe us. I couldn't be sure.

I crawled over to Dave, my hands getting cold in the snow. Whispering close to his ear, I said, "That door looks pretty weak."

"This whole place looks like a big fart will take it down."

"I'm going to try the handle. If it's locked, I'll kick it in. You follow me and keep your eyes and gun to the left where the people are sitting. I'll grab Mindy, and we'll run like hell to the RV."

"And hope Clint doesn't shoot us."

We eyed Clint in the short distance.

"We'll hope no one shoots us." I clapped him on the shoulder. "Put the fear of Dave into them."

"There is no such thing as the fear of Dave."

"Then just pretend you're playing Grand Theft Auto or Call of Duty."

Dave nodded. "Call of Duty. Right."

I took a few deep breaths to calm myself. "Here goes."

I snuck around to the door and put my hand on the ice-cold knob. I tightened my grip and gave it a slow, gentle turn so as not to alarm Mindy's captors.

It turned with ease.

Guess no one locked their doors around here.

Of course, from what I'd seen of Canada, why bother? The people in this shack were the only reason to lock a door.

Dave got up and stood on the other side of the door.

I offered a prayer to anyone who would listen, expecting my words to fall upon a universe of deaf ears.

I turned the knob and swung the door open.

The people at the table stopped their conversation, and three heads swiveled my way.

As I ran toward Mindy on the couch, Dave barreled in, shouting at the top of his lungs. "Don't move, motherfuckers! I'll blow your goddamn heads off and skull fuck your remains!"

The ridiculousness coming out of his mouth almost made me stop.

I scooped Mindy up and pulled her to my chest. Her eyes struggled to open, and she mumbled something I couldn't quite get.

"Hey, man, we don't want no trouble," the oldest guy of the three of them said with his hands raised.

"Yeah? You should have thought of that before you kidnapped our friend, assholes!" Dave said, spittle flying from his mouth. I'd never even imagined this side lived within the big guy. This could have been proof that video games were truly bad for people. Or good, in this case.

I headed for the door. Dave kept his gun on the alarmed trio.

Eddies of snow swirled through the door. I tried to calculate how long it would take to run to the RV. I also pictured myself slipping in the snow and botching the entire rescue.

"Who are you people?" the woman asked.

"We're none of your fucking business, that's who we are," Dave spat. The way the gun trembled in his hand, I wasn't sure they were buying what his mouth was selling.

"Why are you taking that woman? Did she do something to you, too?" the younger of the men said.

I stopped at the door's threshold.

I should have been running, but my curiosity got the better of me. "What do you mean by that?"

The woman parted her hair that had been covering the side of her face, revealing a purpling, swollen eye, bruised cheek and split lip. "She did this to me."

Dave's head bounced between me and the First Nations kidnappers.

None of them had gone for any weapons. Their expressions were ones of bewilderment.

Now, I suspected mine was, too.

"She did that to you?" I said. "Where?"

"At the Husky station. We went there for supplies and came across that woman. When she saw me, she attacked me. I didn't do nothing to her. But she was crazy. When she saw my brothers, she jumped back and slipped and hit her head. Knocked herself right out. We couldn't just leave her there in the snow."

My head spun. What the hell?

"Why did you run from us at the station, then?"

The older brother leaned forward in his chair and squinted at us. "That was you? Hey, we've learned not to trust anybody. Was she with you?"

"Yes!" I said louder than I'd intended, only because I was on such shaky ground. My arms were beginning to tire from holding Mindy as well. "Didn't you see us at the station?"

The younger brother took a sip from his mug and said, "We came from a back way. All we saw was this White woman who got very violent, very quickly."

Dave lowered his weapon. "Oh man, I'm sorry. I...we didn't know. And that does sound like Mindy."

"Do you mind?" I said. When no one protested, I set Mindy back down on the couch and felt the back of her head. She had one heck of a knot protruding from her skull. "So, you weren't kidnapping her?"

"No," the wounded sister said. "We figured the best thing to do was take her back here until she recovered. Though my brothers were prepared to defend me if she attacked me again."

I wiped the sweat from my forehead despite the cold. "Yeah, that's understandable. Like my friend said, I'm sorry if we freaked you out. We thought we were walking into an entirely different situation."

Their weary gazes spoke volumes. It was if we were just another couple of fools in a long line of racists who assumed Native Americas, or in their case, First Nations, were not to be trusted and always up to no good. I wanted to plead our case but decided it wasn't worth it.

"Unnnggghhh," Mindy moaned.

I crouched beside her and touched the side of her face. "Mindy? It's me, Sam."

Her eyes opened and found mine. "Sam?" She tried to lift her head, but her eyes snapped closed again. "Oh, why does my head hurt so bad?"

"It sounds like you fell and cracked it pretty good."

She opened one eye and shifted her gaze from me to the siblings. "Where the hell am I?"

That was a good question.

I turned to the siblings. "I'm Sam, and the woman who attacked you is Mindy. That's Dave, my best friend."

"Hey," Dave said.

The older brother spoke for all of them. "I'm Chadwick, this is my brother, Henry, and my sister, Rose. I'll get something for her head."

Chadwick got a towel out of a drawer and went outside. He came back in with the towel full of balled-up snow. He gave it to me so I could apply it to the back of Mindy's head.

"Feel any better?" I asked her.

"A little. I thought they were going to jump us."

"Why did you think such a thing?" asked Rose. Her face looked to be in more need of the cold towel than Mindy's head.

"I...I don't know. It's just that you were hiding out back and..."

Again, we got that look from Chadwick, Henry, and Rose. I felt about half a foot tall.

"I can't say this enough. We're so sorry. And thank you for taking care of our friend, even after what she did to you, Rose. That was very kind of you."

Rose gave a slight nod.

"Are there any more of you?" I asked.

Henry shook his head. "We're all that's left on the rez."

"You're the first people we've seen since we got to Canada," I said. "And there weren't all that many in the U.S. either, except for one place."

For the first time, I noticed that none of them had plugged their noses. If they went around like that all the time, it was a major miracle even they were still around.

"You're from America?" Chadwick said. "Where are you headed?"

"To a town called Consumption," Dave said. "You ever hear of it?"

I thought I detected an odd look pass between the siblings.

I was going to ask them more about Consumption.

Unfortunately, Clint ran into the shack.

He let his shotgun do the talking.

SHIT STORM

The first shot sent Chadwick spinning down to the ground, clutching his arm. Clint's second shot went wide of Rose and reduced a hanging wood carving above the refrigerator to splinters.

I dove on top of Mindy to protect her from unfriendly fire.

"Please don't shoot!" Henry said, backing up until he almost fell into the sink.

Clint spun and turned his shotgun on the defenseless guy.

"Clint, stop!" I shouted, though it was hard for me to hear even my own voice at that point.

A split second before Clint pulled the trigger and irrigated dozens of holes in Henry's chest, Dave dropped his shoulder and barreled into Clint's side. The shotgun went off, but once again, peppered the ceiling and thankfully, not Henry.

Dave kept on driving Clint until they were both on the floor.

"What in the fuck are you doing?" Clint grumbled.

"You idiot!" I screamed. "They weren't doing anything wrong. Why did you shoot at them?"

Clint adjusted his cowboy hat and looked utterly perplexed. "You'd been in here a long time. I just thought..."

The shooting had fully roused Mindy. Her gaze was still a little dazed, but she was with it enough to say to me, "Hey, he had a thought. First time for everything."

"Chadwick!" Rose rushed to her brother.

"Just stay here," I said to Mindy, joining Rose and Henry.

Chadwick's face had gone pale as a bedsheet. Blood seeped from between his fingers where he was holding his upper arm.

"We need some water and clean towels," I said.

"There is no running water anymore," Henry said. He caught his sister's eye. "I'll get a shirt and some snow from outside."

"Okay," she said breathlessly.

I didn't know what to do or say. I turned to my left and saw Dave beside me, looking down at Chadwick.

"You're gonna be all right," Dave said.

"You a doctor?" Chadwick said between his gritted teeth.

"No, I'm afraid not."

"Then forgive me if I don't exactly believe you."

Rose said, "I need to take your hand away so I can see the damage."

Chadwick loosened his grip on his arm. His shirtsleeve was in tatters. All I saw was blood and shreds of fabric.

"Hold on," Rose said.

She got up and rummaged through some drawers, coming back with a pair of rusty scissors. She cut the sleeve, and I had to look away.

His upper arm was dotted with black holes, and each hole was an erupting volcano of blood. When she touched his arm, the bleeding intensified.

"It's not too bad," Rose said. I wanted to ask her what she was seeing, because I had an entirely different impression. "Looks like birdshot. I'll just need to dig them out."

"Dig them out?" Dave said, his face a mask of pure horror.

Rose pointed at me. "Take any knife from that drawer and use some matches to heat up the point."

I did as I was told, finding the knife and then a box of wooden matches on the windowsill. My clumsy fingers spilled half a dozen matches onto the floor. I grabbed three more and struck them along the side of the box. With a nice flame going, I waved it along the sharp, pointed tip of the knife. I knew exactly what Rose had intended to do. It was like when my foster mother Anna used to heat up a sewing needle before digging yet another splinter out of my foot. She insisted I always wear shoes in the house after the fourth time because I was a natural born splinter magnet.

When the first three matches sputtered out, I lit three more and got the knife good and hot.

"Here you go."

Rose didn't waste time. Nor did she prepare her brother or tell him to hold his breath or put a belt in his mouth.

Chadwick's flesh sizzled on contact.

I could smell it, and it made me woozy.

Dave backed away to make room for Henry who had returned with a damp shirt. It was a Shania Twain world tour concert tee.

While Rose and Henry worked on Chadwick, I stood over Clint who, for some reason, seemed content to stay on the floor.

"He'll need antibiotics. You must have some in your little stash. And some painkillers."

I noticed Clint avoided looking over at the impromptu operation going on in the kitchen.

"It's not like I have an unlimited supply," Clint said.

"You just shot that man for no goddamn reason. Get him some pills or I swear to God, I'll shoot you myself!"

Clint's eyes flicked to his shotgun. Dave, in a rare display of catlike reflexes, snatched the gun away.

Clint shook his head and said, "Fine. Be right back."

To make sure this entire escapade was fubared, we heard the RV's engine rev and gravel crunch as it backed away.

"Shit. Aja," I said, running out the door.

I ran in the snow, waving my arms, screaming Aja's name as

she backed the RV out of the drive. She must have assumed we were all done for and decided to make a fast getaway.

"Stop!" I shouted.

I couldn't see her because of the snow, and I assumed she couldn't see me, either.

Clint came chugging past me. As much as I hated to admit it, he was our best chance to catch her. I was the walking wounded and Dave ran like a crippled bear.

I looked back at the parked motorcycles and wondered if Rose would lend me one to catch up with Aja.

Then I thought of Chadwick leaking blood and figured that was too big of an ask.

Clint pulled further and further away from me, much like the RV. Aja had it on the road leading out of the rez now and was seconds away from leaving us in the dust.

Clint waved his cowboy hat over his head while he pleaded with her to stop.

The RV stopped for a moment, I assumed so Aja could put it in drive.

An alarming ache in my ribs drastically slowed my legs.

There must have been a little jet pack in Clint's boots because he somehow made it to the front of the RV.

Unfortunately for him, Aja must not have noticed because she ran right into him. Clint did a chest bump with the RV's front grille. He flew backward so hard and fast he'd come out of his boots.

At least he got the RV to stop.

Aja exploded out of the RV. "Oh my god, oh my god, oh my god!"

Clint was on his back, lights out, snow rapidly covering his body.

I stumbled on, not sure if I was happy or wigged out. On the happy side, would I be content with Clint just being wounded, or would I need more?

Aja fell to her knees and brushed snow off his face. His

trusty cowboy hat was nowhere to be seen. A trickle of blood crept out from the corner of his mouth.

"Is he alive?" I asked.

She took hold of his hand and felt the side of his neck. "I...I think so."

"Why were you leaving?"

She turned on me. "That's what you told me to do! I waited a long time, and then I heard the gunshots."

"*Now* you listen to me."

Aja started to cry, and even if you hooked me up to a lie detector test, I'd swear those tears weren't about smashing into Clint.

We heard footsteps and saw Dave huffing and puffing his way to us. I spied a slowly staggering figure behind him and assumed it was Mindy.

"Holy crap, what happened?" Dave said, a great cloud of vapor pouring from his mouth.

"Aja hit him," I said.

"I didn't see him!"

"Is he dead?"

"Aja doesn't think so."

"He's not dead, you morons. Help me get him in the RV."

Mindy finally made the party. "Whoa, who killed Clint?"

"Aja says he's not dead," Dave told her.

"Dave!" Aja shouted. "Help me."

I grabbed Clint's leg and the three of us crab-walked him into the RV. Mindy stayed a few steps behind us, holding the back of her head as if she were trying to prevent her brains from escaping.

Miracle got very excited when we all came inside and at one point, jumped up and landed his paws on Clint's chest. I had to work hard to hold in a laugh. Clint moaned a little, proving Aja right. I made a mental note to give Miracle a treat later.

Mindy pulled her hand away from her head and showed me her red palm.

"Okay, let's get you down, too," I said.

"I'm fine. Head wounds aren't as ugly as they look."

"Even so, just pop a squat."

She sat at the kitchenette and I gave her a bottle of water and some paper towels. I also went out and filled up one of my clean t-shirts with snow. "Put that on your head."

Once I knew Mindy was going to be okay, I checked on Clint. Someone had unbuttoned his shirt and exposed his black and blue chest.

Dave said, "Better than getting shot...I guess."

Clint's head rolled back and forth on the pillow. Aja whispered over and over again how sorry she was.

"Can I get him anything?" I asked.

"We should ice his chest," Aja said.

There went another t-shirt. She took it from me and gently touched it to his chest. Clint winced and said, "Cold, man. Cold."

"He'll live," I said, not to be flip, but to reassure Aja. I could tell she was right on the edge. If Clint had died, she'd destroy herself by her own guilt. I didn't think she would exactly mourn the loss of a great love. At least I hoped that would be the case.

"Clint shot a man at the shack," I told Aja. She looked horrified. "He got his shoulder pretty bad. We need to get him some antibiotics and painkillers."

"Christ. Hold on." Aja opened a cabinet and pulled out a huge plastic bag full of pill bottles. She rummaged around until she came up with a couple of bottles. She then put a palmful of pills into an empty amber bottle. "I hope this is enough."

I looked inside it and screwed the cap on. "Looks like it will be."

As we left Aja to administer to Clint, Dave whispered, "Now that's karma."

"Too soon."

I looked up at the snow coming through the holes in the roof. "We're gonna have to fill those in."

"I think there's some epoxy in the toolbox," Dave said.

Miracle had his head on Mindy's lap. She ruffled his fur, keeping the shirt of ice on her head.

My body ached all over. All I wanted to do was lie down and sleep for a few days. My nerves were frayed from the chase and gunshots and blood.

"I better check on Chadwick," I said.

"I'll go with you," Mindy said.

"No, you stay here with Miracle."

"I'm not some wallflower."

"Trust me, that we all know. But even you can tell by that golf ball on the back of your head that you need to chill."

Mindy laughed.

"What's so funny?"

"I'm actually freezing right now. Chill is all I can do."

"I got it." Dave turned the engine back on and cranked the heat.

Mindy kept laughing. I worried about that knot on her skull. We'd have to keep an eye on her.

Dave and I trudged through the snow to the shack. I knocked on the door.

"Go away," Rose said.

"We just wanted to make sure your brother was okay," I said into the door.

"Don't pretend to care now," Henry said.

"I..."

"Leave us alone!" Rose shouted.

Dave grabbed my shoulder. "Come on, man."

"I just need to know he'll be fine."

"Dude, a White guy dressed like a frigging cowboy just busted into their house on the rez and shot an Indian, just to put this in historical perspective. They don't want to see us, and I don't blame them. Let's just leave them be and not cause them anymore harm."

He was right.

"I'm leaving some antibiotics and painkillers for you," I said, settling the bottle within the snow. "We're so, so sorry."

Silence was our answer.

"Let's get off the rez and find a place to ride out this snow-storm," I said. When Dave saw me limping, he put an arm around me and helped me the rest of the way. "We're a hot mess. The people of Consumption will take one look at us and tell us to hit the road."

Dave opened the RV door. "Maybe the road is where we belong at this point."

SNOW DAY

The little snowstorm that could turn into a full-on blizzard sometime around nine that night. I'd found a spot off the highway behind a jumble of boulders that looked as if they'd been dropped from the sky by those ancient aliens I used to see so much about on the History Channel.

Mindy had fallen right back to sleep, and I wasn't sure that was a good thing considering her head injury. I covered her with a blanket and kept a close eye on her.

Dave and I were talking about what he was going to make for dinner—something with canned hash—when we heard Clint cry out. I know it's not good karma to wish pain on someone, but karma be damned.

"He lives!" Dave said with an exaggerated Bela Lugosi accent.

Aja came bustling out of the bedroom. She looked exhausted. She went straight to the refrigerator and got a bottle of coconut water. Clint got to moaning and groaning.

"Well, that has to be some kind of relief," I said to Aja. "See, you didn't kill him."

"I have to give him something for the pain." She closed the

fridge door and leaned against the counter. For a moment, I thought she was going to cry.

"You look like you're about to fall. Give Clint some of his loopy meds and come back out here. He'll be asleep anyway."

"Come out here and do what? Play checkers with you guys?"

I wanted to crack wise, but I'd only seen her look this wiped out and on the verge of collapse once before. It had been the night her friend Gia had passed away from a short battle with brain cancer. Aja had been there at the hospital when Gia died and spent hours with her family afterward. When she came home, she was a shambling wreck.

I hated seeing her that way then, and I hated it now.

"Just give me, like, ten minutes and come back here," I said.

She went back into the bedroom and I wasn't sure if she was going to return. Regardless, I went up to mine and Dave's sleeping berth and ripped off the sheets. There was a clean pair in the cabinet, and I put them on.

Dave got to work on dinner.

By the time Aja came back, there was food on the table set aside for her. It was some kind of hash and quinoa thing that smelled better once he doused it with hot sauce.

I put my hands on her shoulders and guided her to a seat, expecting her to tell me to get off of her any second. She didn't.

"Now, eat, drink this all down," I said as I poured her a vodka soda, "and go up there and sleep."

Mindy started snoring at that moment, perking Miracle's ears up.

"I have a perfectly good bed," she said without any of the vitriol she'd embraced lately.

"You do, and there's a wounded, mumbling cowboy in it who I guarantee will keep you up all night."

She stuck her fork in the food, poked around a bit and looked at me. "Why are you suddenly being so nice?"

I was asking myself that same question. "Because you're exhausted and hurting, and you need to rest."

A gust of wind rocked the RV.

"And until we find a lawyer, and if SHC has and silver linings, they're all filling that great ashtray in the sky, you're still my wife. There were a couple of things in our vows that I'm beholden to."

I saw her eyes flick to Mindy, but they didn't linger.

"Fine." She filled her fork. "And thank you."

Dave and I brought our bowls to the front seats so Aja could have some peace and quiet. We watched the snow come down and the sky grow dark. I heard Aja put her bowl and glass in the sink and go up into the berth.

"That was really nice of you," Dave whispered.

"Or just being a human being."

"Nah, it's more than that."

"Just shut up."

"Shutting up."

For the next few hours, we played cards and watched the storm get worse and worse. I grew tired of flicking the windshield wipers on from time to time and just let it all pile up. We didn't need to see it to know how things were outside. Hearing it was more than enough.

"How much does it snow up here?" Dave asked as he beat me in rummy for the fifth time in a row.

"I don't know. A lot, I assume."

"You think enough to cover the RV?"

"What? Like up to the roof?"

"Yeah."

Truth was, I had no idea. It hadn't even occurred to me until Dave brought it up.

Dave shuffled the cards and said, "I saw this movie where this man and woman were snowed in in their car for a long time. It didn't end too well for the guy."

"It never does," I said.

We played one more round and slept in the driver and passenger seats with blankets pulled up to our necks. I kept getting woken up by the howling winds. The RV shuddered and Miracle whined until Dave had the husky sleep on his lap. It looked awkward and uncomfortable, but somehow it set them both at ease and they slept for the rest of the night.

I was up with the sun and turned on the wipers. They didn't move.

Aja was still asleep, as was Mindy. I didn't even hear Clint, so I assumed Aja must have really dosed him.

I could hear the winds and the tapping of snow hitting the RV. I kept my blanket wrapped around me and opened the side door. An icy finger of wind went up my legs and into my boxers. Shrinkage had nothing on the physical change that overcame my nether region.

All I saw out there was snow. And lots of it.

Poking my head outside, I saw the snow was past the midway point on the tires.

Could Dave be right?

All I knew was that getting out of our little spot was not going to be easy if the snow didn't let off soon.

"Close the door."

Mindy was sitting up, rubbing her eyes.

"Sorry." I slammed it shut without thinking. Miracle started barking. Aja said, "What's going on down there?"

"Sorry," I said again, trying to regain some of my lost body heat.

Aja climbed down from the berth. Sometime during the night, she'd changed into my hokey three-wolf moon t-shirt that was extra long, which had made it an ideal sleep shirt. "I have to pee."

Once she was in the bathroom, I asked Mindy how she felt.

"A little better. I think the lump's gone down."

I felt the back of her head and couldn't be sure if it had or not.

"The good news is that you have all day to rest up. Snow's pretty bad. We're not going back on the road any time soon."

I didn't like hearing myself say it, but that was the stone-cold truth. Consumption wasn't far away, and I could almost taste it. Unfortunately, it would have to wait.

I also remembered Henry's face when I had mentioned Consumption and disliked Clint even more. What was Henry going to tell us?

"Are you serious?"

"As a head wound." I smiled.

Mindy smiled back.

She stretched her arms. "That's fine by me. I'm starving."

"The cook is asleep, but I can pour a mean bowl of cereal."

Miracle nudged Mindy's arm so she would pet him.

"That would be great. I hope we have some cheerios left."

Mindy reached across the table for my hand. The bathroom door opened, and I pulled my hand back.

"Great. My turn," I said quickly to cover my tracks. Aja had an arched eyebrow, suspicious of me. I couldn't look at Mindy, who was either hurt, mad or confused. Most likely all three.

After faking going to the bathroom, I busied myself with making breakfast by adding water to powdered milk and pouring out some cereal. Aja did not check on Clint, and I wasn't sure what to make of that.

My stressing that she was still my wife had done something to both of us. I was sure of it. What exactly, was the million-dollar question.

We ate in uncomfortable silence. I wished the dog would bite me, just to break the tension.

Miracle had no regard for my feelings.

At least something hadn't changed.

LOCKDOWN IS NOT BETTER THE SECOND TIME AROUND

Living in New Jersey had not prepared me for a Canadian snowstorm. It went on for two days and the snow piled so high, I had to put all my weight into the door to open it.

Clint's bruising looked awful. But his breathing was clear, and it didn't appear that he'd broken any ribs.

God looks after children, drunks, and butthead cowboys.

The atmosphere in the RV was a shade below pleasant. It suddenly seemed smaller than before, like that garbage pit with the closing walls in Star Wars. Aja, Mindy, and I all seemed to want to say something to each other, but without the others around to hear it, and that wasn't happening any time soon.

So the pressure grew between us while Dave and Miracle spent a lot of time in the front of the RV. Aja slept in the upper berth again because Clint tossed and whined like a baby with a full diaper. At least until we shoved some pills down his throat.

While he was asleep, I searched for all the guns in the RV and hid them where Clint hopefully couldn't find them. Aja, Mindy and Dave watched me do it and didn't say a word. At least we could all agree on one thing.

"Do we have a shovel?" Aja asked the next day. She was playing solitaire on the kitchen counter.

"Pretty sure we don't," I said.

"We better find a way to make one, because without it, we're not going anywhere."

"I can look in the outer compartments."

"You'll need to do some digging to get to them. I can help you."

"Thanks."

When I turned to go up to the berth and find a pair of gloves, I caught Mindy's eye before she quickly turned away. She was not happy.

"I'll help, too," Dave said.

Once we'd all put on warmer clothes, we dared to open the door and stepped into snow that went past our hips. Miracle had been going out to relieve himself several times a day, leaving a narrow depression. He leaped into the snow, happy to be in his element.

The snow had mostly stopped, though the wind was brutal as ever. I wondered if we'd driven through some wormhole and ended up in the North Pole.

I closed the door before we froze Mindy.

When we exhaled, the steam was thick enough to cover our faces as if we were blurred for our protection in a TV interview.

"Here we are," Dave said. "The OG trio."

"More like the Three Stooges," Aja said. When she smiled, I almost fell back into the snow.

I said, "All righty, let's see if we can find anything to excavate us from this mess."

We used our hands to pull snow away from the side of the RV. Miracle barked and came to join us, his muzzle covered in frost. It took longer than expected because certain layers had frozen over. Dave and I bashed the ice with our fists and Aja got to digging.

An hour later, I was gassed and couldn't feel my fingers or toes. We'd packed heavy winter clothes, knowing we were driving to northern Canada, but the wind and ice and snow laughed at our puny attempts to keep warm.

Aja's teeth chattered, and she'd removed her gloves to blow on her hands. "I forgot how much I hate the cold."

Dave pointed at me, smiling. "Hey, you look just like Santa!"

I had no idea what he was talking about, until I looked down at my beard, which had been acting as a snow catcher. I batted a good deal of the snow off my whiskers.

When I tried to put the key in the lock to one of the outdoor compartments, it went nowhere.

"Lock is frozen. I need a lighter."

"I'll get it," Aja said before Dave. She trudged into the RV and was in there a long time. I was sure she'd found the lighter right away and was just warming up.

"This is kinda nice," Dave said.

"What? Freezing our asses off?"

"It's not that cold."

"That's because you have a layer of Spam keeping you warm."

"Ha ha. No, I mean the three of us working together with no friction."

A harsh breeze nearly knocked us into the snow. I had to admit, he was right.

"Say that again if Aja isn't back out here in a few minutes."

I flexed my fingers to make sure I still had some feeling, and my knuckles hadn't turned to ice. Dave made a snowball and got Miracle to chase it. The husky set off for the snowball and disappeared into the snow.

The RV door swung open and Aja brought me the lighter.

"Sorry it took so long."

Her teeth were no longer clacking together. "It's fine. You warm up some?"

"Some."

I sparked the flame and held it to the lock for a good minute. When I tried the key again, it slipped right in. Dave had to help me open the door because the hinges had turned to stone. We looked around, tried another compartment, and the closest thing to a shovel was the lid to our small barbecue grill. It would have to do.

But not now.

The sun was already starting to run away, its ass probably chilled by this damn weather.

We went back inside and stripped off our outer clothes by the door so we didn't track snow everywhere. Dave had to hold on to Miracle's collar to whisk the snow from his coat.

"Any luck?" Mindy asked. I'd expected her to be cross, but she sounded genuinely concerned.

"A little," I said. "The barbecue lid will do in a pinch."

"Cool. I made hot chocolate for you all."

"Have I told you yet that I love you?" Dave said.

At the word love, Mindy made it a point to look at me. I could feel the heat rise to my face.

"No, but it's always nice to hear someone say it."

That one hurt me. I could feel Aja's eyes at my back while I untied my boots.

Back when our marriage was good, Aja used to ask me if I would ever cheat on her. I always told her the same thing. "Not a chance. I've spent too much time, money, and energy on you, and there's nothing left for anyone else. Besides, I can't think of anything more exhausting and terrifying than a love triangle. I'd rather have bees inserted in my ass than go through all that."

Where were those bees now?

It wasn't like I had cheated. We weren't on a Ross and Rachel break. Our marriage had gone combustible, and we were still together because of our circumstance. After the crap I had endured, I was more than allowed to kiss Mindy. To feel something for her.

Yet I had reminded Aja that she was still my wife.

I was right. Love triangles were as bad as I'd thought. I contemplated pulling a Jack Torrance and just sitting down in the snow until I became a popsicle.

"I have to check on Clint," Aja said. She sounded tired and, I'm not sure, disappointed?

Dave went straight for the hot chocolate. Miracle shook himself dry and sent what snow and water remained in his fur everywhere.

"Miracle!" Mindy shouted, holding her hands in front of her face.

I took a sip of the hot chocolate. It burned my lips and tongue and esophagus. I didn't care. I needed warmth in my core, STAT. I poured a cup for Mindy and sat next to her.

"Thanks for this," I said.

"You have icicles in your eyebrows." She went to pluck them out, then seemed to think better of it.

Dave slipped into the bathroom.

I took a deep breath. "Look, Mindy..."

She put her hand on mine. It felt so wonderfully warm. "Don't say anything. Please."

"It's just..."

"It's just the end of the world and we're doing our best to ride it out."

I wanted to pull her into my arms. I wanted to kiss her.

But I also wanted to do the same with Aja.

And that made me an asshole.

I did as she asked and kept my mouth shut. We drank hot chocolate and didn't move our hands, at least until Dave came out of the bathroom.

"You guys want to play Monopoly?" he asked. The Monopoly game had been something Aja had found at one of our raiding stops. We'd yet to crack it open. It was fitting that we played a game that could go on forever while we waited for the right moment to plow our way back onto the highway. For all I knew, we were here for good, and our heat and water would run out and we'd be the first people in a world ravaged by fire to be consumed by ice.

"Sure, why not?" Mindy said with a note of resignation.

I had just bought my first house on Atlantic when we heard a commotion in the bedroom. And not the 'getting busy' kind.

Clint's voice was raised and Aja was trying to calm him down.

Dave stopped shaking the dice. We looked over at the bedroom door.

That's when I heard Clint say, "Don't touch me, you black bitch!"

I saw red. And then things went black.

I came to with Dave and Mindy pulling me off of Clint. My fist throbbed, and Clint's nose was bent sideways. Aja was in tears, pressed against the wall.

The good news was Clint was no longer talking.

SAVED

"You didn't have to do that," Aja said without much conviction.

We sat around the dinette. Mindy and Dave nursed hot chocolates. Aja and I had gone for the harder stuff.

Clint's broken nose whistled as he breathed loud enough to be heard through the closed door.

Dave had made a tightly packed snowball so I could ice down my knuckles. Water dripped onto the table.

"I beg to differ," I said.

"He's right," Dave said.

"My father was a racist pig, and I wish I'd done the same to him," Mindy said.

Aja twirled her glass of vodka in her hands, staring into the clear fluid. "He's not racist."

I felt my anger start to rise. "Oh, sure, all non-racists call women black bitches." I wanted to go in there and punch him again. Aja had dropped more pills into his mouth and when he was out, tried to reset his nose. It still looked like a warped potato to me.

"That wasn't him talking," Aja said. "It was the medication."

"More like truth serum," Dave said. He got up to check on Miracle who had fallen asleep in the driver's seat.

I said, "If it were up to me, I would just leave his ass in the snow. Let nature take care of him."

"We can't do that," Aja said.

"Why not? Look, there aren't many people left in this world. With the few that we have, do we really want that baggage to survive?"

When Aja and I had first started dating, we'd lost a couple of friends who'd said they just didn't see us fitting together. That was dumb ass code for a White man shouldn't be with a Black woman. We were happy to shut them out of our lives. When we got married, we'd said we were happy that neither of us had any family. Fewer people to disappoint us.

Aja knocked back the rest of her drink and leaned back in her seat. "We can't kill him."

"Did I say kill him? That's up to fate and nature."

She squeezed my thigh under the table and turned my face to her. "Please. Let's not talk about that anymore."

My body was still humming, and I wanted to talk a whole lot more about it.

Aja looked so frail at that moment I forced myself to take it down ten notches.

"You're not going back there with him."

Here comes the fight, I thought. Aja was going to remind me I was in no position to tell her what to do. And poor Mindy would be in the middle of it all.

"Where will I sleep, then?" she said instead.

"In the bedroom. We'll swap him out here. Why should he get the most comfortable bed in the house?"

"And what about me?" Mindy asked.

"You can have the sleeping berth. Dave and I survived the front seats." Sure, she'd shared the bedroom with Aja before, but this was after.

"We don't have to do all that," Aja said.

I stood up to help make my point. "We do and we will. It's either that or Dave and I chuck him out the door."

Aja deflated. "Okay."

"Okay?"

"Yeah."

"How about you, Mindy?"

"Works for me. The sleeping berth is about the only place I haven't slept in so far." Man, she was a trooper. I just hoped she wasn't harboring an atom bomb's worth of resentment and would try to Lorena Bobbitt me while I slept.

I nodded and folded my arms. "Good. Dave, help me get broken Billy the Racist Dope over to the couch."

"You bet."

It took some time wrangling Clint's dead weight. Aja and Mindy made the beds with semi-fresh sheets. Where was a laundromat when you needed one? Every time I looked at Clint's crooked nose, I grinned.

When it was all done, we were exhausted. There were way too many high-running emotions for such a cramped space. To conserve energy, we shut the lights out early and settled in. Miracle had followed Aja to the bedroom. I heard Mindy settling in above us, while Clint's tin whistle tooted away.

Dave took three quick shots of scotch and fell right to sleep.

Traces of adrenaline kept me awake. I felt like I was a kid again, overtired and anxious. I read a Terry Brooks fantasy novel by flashlight, every now and then looking at the packed snow on the windshield, wondering if we'd ever get out. If there was something beyond the veil, so to speak, there must be one hell of a party going on. And here we were, stuck in an RV in Canada with a bigoted jerk, waiting to freeze to death.

After an hour or so, I started to doze off, imagining I heard the tiptap of little elves digging their way to us.

What felt like just moments later, I was being shaken awake by an overexcited Dave.

"What the heck is wrong with you? I just fell asleep."

"It's eight in the morning, dude. You slept like a corpse. Look!"

He pointed at the windshield.

At the clear windshield.

"Where's the snow?"

"It rained most of the night. We must have gotten caught in some southerly wind flow or something. I was already outside. I think we can get the hell out of here today."

"No way."

I opened my door and looked at the ground. The rain had washed a good number of layers of snow and ice away. The sun was out, and the air was filled with the sound of crackling ice.

Excited, I woke Mindy up so she could see.

"Yeah, baby!" she shouted into the mild wind.

I then went back to the bedroom and went in without knocking. Aja was curled up on her side. Miracle was next to her. The husky spun his head to me and gave a low growl.

"I come bearing good news, you stupid dog."

Aja stirred. She turned, opened her eyes and pushed her dreads from her face. "What's going on?"

I opened the blinds on the window. She cringed when the sun hit her face, but once she could see, it was all smiles. Before I knew it, she was out of bed and hugging me.

I didn't know what to do. It had been months since we'd last had close contact like this.

Hugging her back seemed right.

"Do you think we can get back on the road?" she asked.

"Looks like it. And I checked the map last night. If the road is passable, we can be in Consumption in five or six hours."

We realized then that we were hugging. The disengagement was more awkward than the hug.

"Right," I said. "I'm going to go outside with Dave and dig a little more around the tires, and then we'll get going."

"I'll make breakfast."

"Cool. Cool. Well, yeah, this was a nice way to start the day, right?"

"Totally."

I left before I got to sounding even stupider. I was smoother with girls I didn't know when I was thirteen.

Dave and I put on coats and boots and got to digging. Physical labor was the chicken soup my soul needed.

ON THE ROAD AGAIN

To say the roads were treacherous was like saying SHC was a wee bit hazardous to your health. It took some jostling to get the RV out of the rut of ice and snow. The highway was a gleaming sheet of ice under the sun's morning glare. I had a hard time seeing until Mindy found a pair of sunglasses in one of the consoles. The frames were huge and round, and I felt a little like Elton John, but at least I could see the road.

This was one case where the whittling down of mankind by SHC was a plus. If there were any other cars on the road, coming or going, we probably would have hit them.

"Fish tail," Dave said from his perch between the front seats.

I calmly adjusted the wheel to straighten the big bus out. "You don't have to say it every single time."

"I've got nothing else to do."

Mindy sat in the passenger seat with my crude directions and a map. Aja was terrible with maps. I'd learned that when we went to Maine in an area where our GPS was rendered useless. The rental house came with directions that had been emailed to me. Aja as navigator got us lost for the better part of an hour. I realized we had made a wrong turn when I saw we had entered New Hampshire.

Clint whimpered on the couch as the RV did its dance. He was coming to after we'd decided no more pain meds. We wanted all hands on deck when we arrived in Consumption. The walking wounded were going to step out of the RV on our own two feet.

On a side note, I wanted him to hurt, just a little. Apparently, Aja did, too, because she didn't fight me on the painkiller ban.

Black bitch, my ass.

I felt the back of the RV start to veer and turned the wheel into it.

"Boy, this is fun," I said.

"I can tell by those vanilla ice cream knuckles," Mindy said. "How about I take over?"

"What about your head?"

"Still screwed on right. Sorta. I'm fine. I've driven in worse."

"Were you one of those ice road truckers?" Dave asked, genuinely curious.

"No, but I drove trucks...sometimes on ice. Just stop nice and slow and we'll switch."

I wasn't going to argue. I'd gotten pretty good behind the wheel of the RV, but driving in these conditions was too steep a learning curve.

We got out and met at the front of the RV. The wind was gone and the sun felt like it came straight from heaven onto my face. It should have been a quick changing of the guard. Instead, we both stopped, just inches apart from one another.

I wanted to hug her as much as I wanted to run away.

"I'm sorry you got dragged into my drama," I said.

"All of life is a drama. Especially now." She put her hair in a ponytail and pulled it through the back of her baseball cap. "I gave it a shot. There was a time I wouldn't have even tried, drowning my feelings in booze. So, in a way, it felt good."

"Look, I don't know what's going to happen with Aja and me."

Mindy gave a half-smile. "I do. I saw that look in your eyes when Clint said what he said to her. Whatever happened between you can't completely wash away what you have. She's your wife. I'm just a hitchhiker. You don't have to feel guilty about having feelings for your wife."

It felt like someone was closing their fist around my heart.

"You're not just a hitchhiker. You're a part of us now."

"I'll be the nosy neighbor next door who drops in at inopportune times."

We laughed, steam rolling out of our mouths and noses.

Dave honked the horn. I gave him the finger.

"If it means anything, you're the best thing that's happened to us on this trip," I said. "We wouldn't be here without you. I owe you more than I can say."

She poked me in the chest. "I'll hold you to that. But first, let's see if Consumption is all it's cracked up to be."

When I got back into the RV, I caught Aja's eye. She was at the dinette, reading one of my books. I couldn't remember the last time she'd shown any interest in my love of science fiction. A copy of Childhood's End by Arthur C. Clarke was in her hands. I flashed her a smile to tell her everything was all right and not to read anything nefarious into my little powwow with Mindy.

Aja smiled back and put the book down. "Good. Now I feel like we won't slide off the road."

"Your lack of confidence wounds me," I said as Mindy put the RV in drive.

"Ow, man, why does my nose hurt?" Clint said.

Aja didn't run to his side.

"Just sit back and shut up," I said to him.

"What's his deal?" Clint asked Aja in his nasally tone.

"You don't know?" Aja said.

He yelped when he touched his nose. "I think my nose is broken."

"Oh, it's bad," Dave said.

"I don't remember it being broken in the accident."

"That's because it wasn't," I said. "I did it."

He tried to sit up, but his body wouldn't let him. "Why in the hell would you do that?"

I didn't want to repeat what he'd called Aja. She didn't need to hear those words ever again. A potential silver lining of SHC was putting an end to racist assholes. Hopefully, Clint was the disgusting exception.

"Let's just say you earned it."

"What, for shooting an Indian?"

"First Nation, dude," Dave said. "You really are a freaking caveman."

Clint looked around, searching for an ally. When he found none, he closed his eyes and asked for something to kill the pain.

I said, "Suck it up, buttercup. We'll be in Consumption in a few hours. I want you ambulatory so you can get off my RV. And you might want to change your stance on indigenous people, because from what I had learned, this place could be your Little Big Horn if you're not careful with your mouth."

Clint mumbled something about me and asked Aja to give him a break.

She kept reading the book.

Mindy proved to be a much better driver on the treacherous roads, but to be fair, they got clearer as the day went on. At one point, Dave had started drinking beer and eating pork rinds.

"Let me have some of that," Aja said. She took the can from him and tipped it back and then filled her mouth with pork rinds. It was like looking at our life from well before SHC.

I wanted a beer myself, but it was probably not the best thing to do sitting right across from Mindy.

"Where are my painkillers?" Clint cried out.

"Where they need to be," I replied, spotting a road sign and checking the map. We were starting to make decent time and my heart beat a little faster with each passing mile.

"They're mine. Give them to me."

"Fat chance."

"Aja, please."

She put the book down. "Sam was right. If you start popping those pills, you'll be dead weight by the time we get to Consumption. That's not going to happen."

"Come on, baby, just one. One won't knock me out."

Aja glowered at our resident cowboy. "Don't call me baby."

"I didn't mean nothin' by it."

I watched with pride as she picked the book back up and disappeared behind it. Case closed.

Clint struggled to get up. "I'll just get them myself."

Mindy jerked the wheel hard. Clint fell back onto the sofa and slammed his shoulder into the RV wall.

"Sorry. There was a squirrel on the road," Mindy said, flashing a knowing grin my way.

Clint massaged his shoulder. "A squirrel. Right."

It did the trick because he resigned himself to staying on the sofa.

"You think we'll be there before nightfall?" Dave asked.

"At this rate, definitely."

Would there be anyone at Consumption? We'd seen only three living people since we'd gotten into Canada. My doubts were larger than Saturn's rings.

"We need to fuel up," Mindy said.

She stopped the RV, and Dave and I emptied three gas cans into the tank.

"I just want to thank you, man," Dave said.

"Thank me for what?"

"For taking me. For saving my ass. I'm pretty sure I'd be dead by now if it wasn't for you...and Aja."

I punched him in the shoulder. "You're my best friend. No way was I leaving you behind."

Icicles on the wheel wells dripped by his feet. More of those big ass black birds circled overhead. I bet they were hoping one of us would drop dead so they could settle in for a nice meal. Or was that just the city in me being paranoid?

"You wanted to leave Aja behind, back when this started. But you didn't because you're a good guy. Not the likeliest of heroes, mind you, but a damn good guy."

I emptied my can and screwed the top back on. "Are you getting soft on me now?"

He patted his belly. "I've always been soft. Now, I'm soft and grateful."

"Yeah, well, just don't try to kiss me."

"Not a chance. You're too much of a bearded otter. I prefer twinks."

We laughed until we were doubled over.

It was strange how many touching moments I was having outside the RV. I wondered if I should call Aja out next and find out just what the heck was going on with us.

Back inside, I looked at the map again. "If I'm right, we only have thirty more miles to go."

Mindy hit the gas. "Then let's chew them up. I think we all need to spread our wings a little more."

Those last thirty miles weren't easy, simply because we had to jump off the highway just as we saw signs for Yellow Knife. I wondered if maybe we'd find people still alive in the city. We'd been in the RV for what felt like years. What would a detour really cost us?

But now my blood rushed in my ears, and I felt as nervous as I'd been when I'd asked MaryBeth Michels to our junior prom. My palms were sweaty and a few times, I got the spins from my over-excitement.

Having to concentrate on the map and guide Mindy down roads without signs or signs covered in snow kept me from totally losing my cool. You could feel the anticipation in the RV. Even Clint had stopped his griping. Aja had set the book aside and kneeled by Dave in the space between the two front seats with Miracle on her lap.

The trees on the side of the road got taller and closer until it felt as if we were driving into an enchanted forest. I worried that we had made a wrong turn when the paved road gave way to loose rocks and packed dirt. It kept on narrowing until the side-view mirrors brushed against leafless limbs.

"You could get lost out here forever," Dave said.

Aja slapped his arm.

My eyes flicked from the map to the road and back again.

"You sure this is the right way?" Mindy asked. The front of the RV dipped into a pothole that was more sinkhole. I didn't exhale until the rear made it through without an axle snapping like a toothpick.

"I'm not sure of anything at the moment. But this looks right on the map, and this is clearly some kind of road."

If I'd steered us wrong, I couldn't even find a place to turn the RV around. We were hemmed in by nature. Mindy would have to drive in reverse the whole way, which was no easy feat, even for her.

I wanted a beer in the worst way, but even Dave had stopped drinking. When I set the map on my lap, it fluttered because my hands were shaking.

We could be so close.

Or we could be inching further and further away.

"I keep waiting for a moose to stop us. Or Smokey Bear," Dave said.

"Or a great big bear," Aja said.

This looked like prime bear country. I wondered if the metal of the RV was thick enough to keep a hungry grizzly out, or if it would look like a can of tuna and the bear had the claws to open her right up.

I shook the thought away.

Concentrate on getting us to Consumption.

Sweat trickled down the side of Mindy's face.

"You want me to take over?" I asked.

"No. I'm fine."

She didn't take her eyes off the so-called road. The automatic headlights switched on and I craned my neck to look up.

There was blue sky up there, peeking between the heavy, dead branches. But we saw less and less as the trees multiplied.

"This doesn't feel right," Aja said, mostly to herself, but loud enough for me to catch it. I reached back and took her hand.

"Hopefully that means we're right on target. Place is so hard to get to, even SHC can't find it."

Her smile died quickly and I gave her hand a squeeze.

Rocks popped under the tires, setting my nerves on fire. What if we got a flat out here? There was barely room to make a tire change. *If* we could change a tire on a fully loaded RV. I was pretty sure AAA wasn't manning the phones.

"Are we getting close?" Mindy asked.

I felt like tossing the maps out of the window. "Honestly, I have no idea. Let's keep going for a little while longer and see."

"Way to get us lost," Clint jeered.

"I could always punch you in the nose again," I said. "And I guarantee it will hurt more the second time."

Clint chuckled. "You come on and do that, Mr. Hipster. It won't change the fact that you can't find your little Shangri La."

Shangri La? I would settle for Detroit as long as I didn't have to worry about sneezing into oblivion.

"Clint, shut the fuck up," Aja said.

"You happy now?" Clint said. "You even turned my lady against me."

I started to get out of my seat. Dave pushed me back.

"He's not worth it," Aja said.

"Dude, he's just a broke back moron," Dave said.

I didn't care. I wanted to strangle the bastard.

Miracle yipped as I tried to squeeze past Aja and Dave.

The RV came to a sudden stop, and I went backward instead. My ass thumped against the dashboard and the back of my head whacked the windshield.

"What the hell?"

Mindy pointed out the window. "I think that's it."

I turned around and saw a break in the trees. The road

wound down a steep hill. Down in the bowl of a valley, there was a definite town bordering a tremendous lake. It had to be Dark Lake, and it looked like it lived up to its name. The water looked black as midnight.

From our vantage point, it would have looked like any one of a thousand dead or abandoned towns.

Except this one had curlicues of smoke that wasn't just random, but pouring out of chimneys.

I took it all in and wanted to drop to my knees and weep.

We'd found Consumption.

WELCOME TO CONSUMPTION, POPULATION, WELL, WHATEVER

There were no signs announcing that we had indeed found the almost mythical Consumption, but I knew we had finally arrived.

First, I spotted what appeared to be a recently cleared area filled with cars, trucks, and RVs similar to ours. They had been packed together not so they could pull in and out, but as a place to store them for a long period of time. It would take a dozen or more valets to rescue any vehicles within the center of the mass.

On the rim of Dark Lake, I saw more tendrils of smoke and assumed they came from chimneys poking out of cabins hidden within the trees. There were people down there. Lots of them. And so far, it was all controlled smoke, no combustible fire.

"Holy shit, we did it!" Dave said. He popped up and walked down the RV.

Mindy gripped the wheel and had a smile two feet wide. "I can't believe it."

Aja wrapped her arms around my neck. I felt wetness on my cheek and saw she was crying. "I'm sorry I doubted you."

"It's all right. I doubted myself plenty of times, and I'm not apologizing to myself."

We jumped when we heard a loud pop.

Dave thrust a bottle of champagne out to us. "If this doesn't call for a celebration, nothing does."

I took a quick glance at Mindy. She nodded, and I grabbed the bottle and tipped it back. "It's warm."

"I couldn't keep it in the fridge because you'd all see my surprise."

Aja took the bottle and sipped large. After wiping her mouth with the back of her hand, she gave the bottle to Dave. He gulped it down and looked at reclining Clint. "You may be an asshole, but here."

Clint hesitated as if we had somehow designed this moment to trap him and poison his drink, even though we were all drinking from the same bottle.

"Oh, hell, maybe it'll cut the pain." He took a long drink. Dave grabbed the bottle back.

"You know what? Fuck it," Mindy said. "A sip won't kill me."

"You sure?" Dave asked.

"Just give me the bottle."

Mindy took a tiny drink and rubbed her nose. "I forgot how fizzy it gets when it's hot. You all ready to say hello to the people of Consumption?"

She gave me the bottle. "I've got nothing else on my calendar."

There wasn't much in the bottle but five people's backwash, so I stuck it in a side pocket on the door. The RV jounced and jostled all the way down to the town proper.

It took me several minutes to realize Aja and I were holding hands. It felt good. It felt right. And when I looked at Mindy, I didn't feel entirely guilty.

As we got closer, Miracle started getting antsy. He let out a few howls that set my hackles to rising.

"Can you shut that mutt up? It's giving me a headache," Clint griped.

Seeing the real Clint the past couple of days made me want to chuck him in the icy lake. I didn't because I figured the locals would do it sooner or later when he said or did the wrong thing. It was only a matter of time.

The jammed parking lot was on the edge of town. There was no fence penning it all in. Just a big field dotted with tree stumps and dirty cars and trucks. As we drove by it, I looked to see if anyone was living in the visible RVs. Much like the highways of Canada, the RVs were empty. The license plates were from all over Canada and the United States. There must have been a few hundred in total, which meant the vast majority of people had thought stories about Consumption were just another bit of fake news. If they really thought this was the one safe haven from SHC, there would have been tens of thousands, if not ten times that.

"Wonder where the visitor's center is," Mindy said with a nervous laugh.

I suspected that anyone living in Consumption would have seen us coming from a country mile. It seemed odd that there was no one out and about to greet the interlopers.

"What should we do?" Aja said. "Drive up to the nearest house and knock on the door?"

"I can think of worse ideas. And they must be used to it by now."

After the lot, we drove by a long building made of corrugated metal. It turned out to be some sort of storage shed for boats of all sizes, wrapped up for the cold season, which I assumed was about nine months out of the year.

"Aw, crap," Dave said.

"What?" I asked.

"Miracle peed. When's the last time we let him out?"

"I don't know. It's a moot point now."

"Unless he has to poop."

Dave grabbed a roll of paper towels and got on his hands and knees. Clint patted Miracle's head. "That's right. You show them who the real master is."

Dave stopped mopping up pee. "You know, I thought you

were all right at first, despite making that dick move on Aja. Man, was I wrong."

"If it wasn't for you people, I'd still have my RV and probably be at the rodeo right now."

"We didn't put a gun to your head."

"Nope. Just a nice set of boobs."

This time I did get up, stomped over to Clint and flicked his nose. He reacted as if I'd hit him with a cattle prod. "Now shut up."

"How about this one?" Mindy said.

She pulled up in front of a weathered one-story house. There was a rusted four-by-four in the driveway, along with a snowmobile. The most encouraging thing about it was the light on in the bay window.

Feeling proud for making Clint squirm, I said, "Mindy, keep the motor running. Aja, Dave, and I will see if anyone's home."

"Why do you want me to keep the motor running?"

"Just in case."

I didn't think I needed to voice any specifics. With the way things had gone, we needed to be prepared for anything.

"Should we bring the guns?" Aja asked.

I thought about it for a moment. We were coming to this town for salvation. How would they react if they found out we came packing heat?

Mindy was at the ready and had easy access to our firepower if needed.

"No, I think it's better if we leave them here."

"You're the boss."

We put on heavy coats. Miracle waited by the door.

"No, baby, we can take you out later," Aja said.

Miracle started whining. When he wouldn't move out of the way, Aja had to take him by the collar and put him in the bedroom. He started scratching at the door like an angry cat.

Dave opened the RV door. The wind coming off the lake was like a knife made of ice cored from deep in the Antarctic.

Clint shivered. "It's colder than a witch's tit. Go on and close the damn door."

I left it open a little longer, hoping his nuts would freeze. Aja had to tug on my arm to get me to join her and Dave.

"Let's hope Consumption is happy to meet the rainbow coalition," I said.

The gray paint on the house was cracked and peeling. Three wooden steps led to the front door. They creaked loud enough to worry us that they were going to snap. Dave and Aja stepped off them.

"You knock," Aja said.

I did and I didn't want to be the one. Seeing as I was the only one at the door, and this had been my idea, it made sense that I made first contact. Taking a deep breath, I rapped on the door twice.

The wind screamed for a moment, but no one answered the door.

I knocked again.

Dave and Aja stamped their feet.

"Maybe they're out getting more firewood," Dave said.

"Or fell in the fireplace and that smoke is them," Aja said.

"Not funny."

I looked to see if there was a bell anywhere. No dice.

"We could try that one," Dave said as he pointed to a brick house about fifty yards away.

This was not the reception I was expecting. Could be the townsfolk of Consumption were sick of people descending on their town.

"You see anyone looking out their windows?" I asked.

"Only Mindy," Aja said.

"Screw it. Let's try the brick house."

"Said the big, bad wolf," Dave added.

I turned around and the door suddenly opened. I was so surprised, I nearly fell down the stairs.

A woman stood in the doorway. She had long, flowing,

raven hair and was wrapped in a blanket. The bottom half of her face was hidden behind a leathery mask.

She took one look at me and turned her head and called out, "We have another one!"

NORTHERN HOSPITALITY

A bear of a man joined the woman at the door. He also wore a leather mask.

"Is...is this Consumption?" I managed to croak. The way they glared at me made me uneasy. I had a hard time reading their dark, deep-set eyes.

The man spoke. "Where you from?"

"Um, New Jersey?"

"You don't sound so sure."

"No. Yes, I'm sure. Lived there all my life."

"Where did you hear about us?"

For a moment, I was confused. Was he talking about him and his woman, or the town? I looked back to Aja and Dave for help. If anything, they seemed to have taken a few steps backward.

The town. They had to be talking about the town, stupid!

"I, uh, I read about Consumption on the Internet. Back when there was an Internet. That's my wife, Aja, and my friend Dave. We left Jersey and made the drive up here because we heard that SHC doesn't happen here."

The couple stared at me for a long time without saying a word. I was beginning to feel that we weren't wanted. A small town like this taking on an influx of frightened survivors would put a strain on things. We could just be the straws that broke the camel's back.

Finally, the woman said, "Yes, this is Consumption."

I waited for more. Or they waited for more from me. I was on some shaky ground here.

"Is it true?" I asked.

"Do you see any fires?" the man replied. His voice sounded odd. Not having much experience with indigenous accents from northern Canada, I didn't ponder it.

I looked around, seeing mostly trees and feeling the cold breeze coming off Dark Lake. "No. No, I don't."

"Then what do you think?"

Again with the silent stare down. If this was what life was going to be like in Consumption, I thought getting back on the road might be our best bet.

"Okay. So..."

When the couple burst into raucous laughter, I actually flinched. The bottoms of their masks flapped because they were laughing so hard.

"I'm sorry, we just wanted to have a little fun with you," the man said. "Not much else to do up here lately except greet the newcomers."

My heart dropped and rose again. I put my hand on my chest. I willed myself to smile. "Wow, you really had me going there."

"Come in, all of you," the woman said. "You must be hungry."

"I'm always hungry," Dave said. He and Aja joined me on the top step.

"We have two other people with us. One of them is a little banged up, but do you mind if I bring the other? Her name is Mindy," I said.

"Sure," the man said. He held out his hand. "My name is Fred. This is my wife, Wilma. Welcome to Consumption."

I paused for just a beat. Fred and Wilma? Were they still messing with me?

Fred must have seen the confusion on my face and said, "Our last name isn't Flintstone. We've heard just about every joke you can dream up."

"I'll get Mindy," Dave said as Aja and I walked into Fred and Wilma's home. A fire blazed in the fireplace and the furniture looked sturdy enough to survive a nuclear bomb. A homemade quilt rested on the couch. I smelled something good cooking in the oven.

I'd gone from wanting to run away to feeling right at home.

"You're the first people who have come by in four days," Wilma said, motioning for us to take a seat on the couch. "We were beginning to worry that there weren't any people left."

Aja took my hand when we sat. "It's a valid concern. We've only seen three people since we got to Canada."

"Only three?" Fred said, setting his bulk into what was probably his favorite chair.

"Yep." I didn't feel the need to mention that Clint had shot one of them.

We talked for a minute with Fred and there was a knock on the door. Dave and Mindy came in and introductions were made.

"You're just in time," Wilma said. "Dinner is ready. Who likes raccoon?"

None of us said a word.

Fred and Wilma broke up again. "I'm kidding. It's chicken," Wilma said, setting a plump, golden brown chicken on a cutting board. "Boy, we can have a lot of fun with you. Is everyone from New Jersey like this?"

Aja made a nervous laugh. "Yeah, pretty much."

"Let's eat," Fred said. "Get to know each other. Wilma and I are veterans at this, since we're the first house folks come to when they arrive."

We gathered around a table that easily sat eight. Fred carved the bird and Wilma doled out plates piled with stuffing, mashed potatoes, and green beans. My stomach jumped for joy and everyone heard it. Meat that didn't come from a can was a delicacy I didn't think I'd ever experience again.

"Is your friend hurt bad?" Wilma asked. "We can have the doctor take a look at him."

"He'll live," I said. "He's more of a stray than a friend."

"I'll make sure to fix him up a plate."

"Thank you," Aja said. "That's very nice of you."

Mindy and Dave sat across from Aja and me, while Fred and Wilma took the opposing heads of the table. Pretty much all manners and conversation stopped once we started digging into the delicious meal. I'd never tasted anything so good. This was nothing like a chicken you got in a supermarket. I didn't chew so much as inhale my dinner.

It wasn't until most of us were done that Mindy said, "Your masks. Do you wear them because you think SHC is contagious, or does it keep you from going combustible?"

Fred looked at her quizzically. It dawned on me that they had kept their leather masks on all during dinner, their forks disappearing under them as Fred and Wilma ate.

"What does going combustible mean?" Fred asked.

"Oh, sorry. It means going up in flames," Mindy said.

"Interesting. Well, you could say it's a little of both. We're very cautious here, which is why I suspect we've fared so well." He pointed at Mindy's stuffed nose. "I see you have your own version of protection. What's that you have in there?"

Mindy tapped the orange foam plugs in her nostrils. "These were meant to be earplugs for swimming. They do a great job of keeping the sneezes at bay."

Aja chuckled. "When this whole thing started, and we realized sneezing set off SHC, we used tampons. But those disappeared pretty quick."

Wilma shook her head. "Oh my, that must have been some sight to see. Well, you make do with what you can."

Dave and I helped Wilma clear the table, and slices of freshly baked blueberry pie were set out for dessert.

"I swear we've gone to heaven," Dave said. "You're an amazing cook, Wilma."

"Thank you. I have a lot of experience. More so since SHC came to be."

Aja's hand rested on my leg while we ate the pie. I inched closer to her until our thighs touched.

"How many people have made it here?" Aja asked with a dollop of blueberry at the corner of her mouth.

Fred swallowed a bit and cocked his head. "Oh, less than a thousand."

"That's a lot of people for a small town," I said. "We saw all the cars outside. Where do you manage to fit everyone?"

"There's more to Consumption than you can see. Our forest is home to many cabins. Even more so on the other side of the lake. When the first refugees came here, they helped us build even more. Now, it's getting too cold to build, but with the way things are slowing down, I don't think there will be a need."

"It must be putting a strain on your resources."

"It's why we tell everyone to eat up and enjoy their welcome meal. It's going to be a long winter, but we'll get by. Good thing for us that no one trusts what they see on TV and the web. If they did, we'd have broken weeks ago."

"We've been getting by with Mr. Spam over here," Mindy said, tapping Dave's arm. "He can do a lot with the stuff, but it doesn't compare to a real chicken."

"Any of you hunt before? I don't suspect there's a lot of hunting in New Jersey."

Mindy raised her hand. "I'm from Pennsylvania and I used to hunt with my cousins all the time."

"Good. I'll let my friend Barney know. We can put you on hunting detail."

"You have a friend named Barney?" Aja said.

Fred hit the table with his fist and let out a belly laugh. "Nah. Our hunt leader is an old guy named Chuck. He takes some getting used to. Just make sure to stay upwind of him."

I promised myself that if he mentioned having a dog named Dino, I'd beat him to the punchline.

"We have a cowboy in the RV who might have shot a prairie dog or two," I said.

"When he's feeling better, we can give him a trial run."

I wiped my mouth with a cloth napkin. My stomach was wonderfully bloated. I was in desperate need of a nap.

"How about an after-dinner drink?" Fred said.

"That sounds great," Dave said.

Fred went to a cabinet and took out a bottle filled with clear liquid. He poured a little bit into a glass for each of us. Mindy didn't refuse. I hoped that sip of champagne hadn't set her back.

"Welcome to our town," Fred said, raising his glass. "We look forward to getting to know you better."

We clinked glasses and downed the alcohol. The stuff was liquid SHC. I thought it was going to burn a hole right through my esophagus. "Wow," I said as my eyes watered.

"I make it myself," Fred said with a note of pride. "Best shine in Canada."

Dave and Aja looked to be in pain. Mindy took it like it was Kool-Aid. She tipped her glass toward Fred and he poured her some more.

"Two is the max, young lady. Any more than that, and you'll wish you'd gone...what did you call it...combustible?"

Mindy swallowed the second shot with ease. "I haven't had a drink in a dog's age. I'm sure two is all I need."

Wilma pulled the curtain over the sink aside. Sometime during our meal, day had turned to night. "Looks like we'll have to wait until tomorrow to get you all settled in. Hope you don't mind one more night in your RV."

"Not at all," I said. "We're just thrilled to be here. It didn't look like that would happen quite a few times. Plus, I wasn't entirely sure the stories were true."

"We are as advertised," Fred said as he got up from the table. "I'll come knocking in the morning. Wilma will fix you up a nice breakfast, and I think we can put you all in the cabin on the west end of the lake. Sound good?"

"Sounds amazing," Dave said. He shook Fred's hand. "Thank you for everything. Meeting you, seeing this town, it gives me hope for the first time in a long time."

"There'll be hard work ahead, but nothing young folks like you can't handle. As long as we all work together, we can lick this thing."

I was ready to vote for Fred for president. He saw us to the door, and we thanked him and Wilma over and over.

I looked across at the RV and thought I'd be glad to be out of it, but in a lot of ways, I'd miss it, too. That little motor home had taken us across the country and all the way up to Canada. I wondered if I could ask Fred if we could keep it by the cabin, instead of jamming it into the big lot.

A large husky padded by us, not even bothering to give us a quick glance.

"Looks like Miracle will have company," I said.

"Maybe huskies are immune," Aja said.

"I gotta take a grumpy," Dave said.

"For the love of God, do it outside," I said. "Spare us on our last night all cooped up."

"Roger that." He ducked into the RV and came out with a roll of toilet paper. "I'll lay good money that toilet paper is scarce around here. Wonder what we'll use when it's all gone."

"That's why we have two hands," Mindy said. She took an awkward step and nearly went down. "One for wipin' and the other for washin' the wipin' hand."

Aja's nose crinkled. I didn't like the sound of it, either, but she was probably right. Or we could use leaves. I'd burn that bridge when I got to it.

Clint was dead asleep. Aja put his plate of food in the fridge. His snores rattled the RV's walls.

"I'll turn him on his side," Mindy said. She gave him a half-roll, and the snoring quieted.

I found an amber pill bottle on the floor. "Looks like he found his stash."

"Good," Aja said. "I like him better when he can't talk."

Mindy fed some chicken to Miracle. I noticed she also had a can of beer in her hand.

"Hey, Mindy, do you think that's a good idea?"

"Our puppy needs a good meal, too."

"No, not the dog." I eyed the beer.

"Fuck it. I can start all over tomorrow. We just found the only place possibly in the world where we have a chance of dying of old age. I'm celebrating. Sobriety can hold off for a day."

I'd had friends in AA and NA, and I'd learned to keep out of their struggle. If they needed me, they would come to me. I didn't have enough experience with addiction to lecture Mindy on what she should and shouldn't do.

Aja and I sat at the dinette table. That moonshine was still boring a hole in my stomach. It was like the acid blood from one of those monsters in the *Alien* movies.

"Do we have any antacids?" I asked.

"I'm sure Clint has some in his bag. I'll go check."

Dave came back inside. "Good call, buddy. I think I just lost five pounds."

"Please, spare us."

"You want a beer?" Mindy asked.

A shadow of concern fell over Dave's face. He looked to me. I shrugged. "Um, sure. Guess a nightcap can't hurt."

She tossed him a beer. When he popped it open, foam jetted out of the top, much of it landing on a sleeping Clint. We were laughing when Aja came out with a couple of chalky pills in her hand. "What's so funny?"

I pointed at the beer soaking into his shirt. Aja giggled while I chomped on the tablets.

We all talked for a bit and Mindy thanked me for getting us all here. Somewhere between telling her she didn't have to thank me and listening to Dave recount the time he and I went to Atlantic City for a bachelor party, the food and stress and relief sucked me down into a deep, wonderful sleep.

CONSUMPTION BY TWILIGHT

I woke up, looked around, and saw that, for the first time, I was in the bedroom. Aja lay curled on her side next to me.

Correction. I was woken up by Dave. He smelled like the floor of a brewery.

"You up?" he whispered.

"What do you think?"

"You passed out before. I had to carry you in here."

I rubbed my eyes and stretched. "I think it was a food coma. Did you come in here just to shoot the shit? Because I'd rather go back to sleep."

"No, dude. Come with me and check this out."

I was still in the clothes I'd worn the day before. I really wanted to tell Dave to leave me alone, but I wasn't in the mood to argue. We'd accomplished our mission, and the time for that crap was over. Even Aja and I were getting along.

I followed him out of the bedroom. Miracle stood still as a statue, looking at the door. Clint snored like a buzzsaw. So did Mindy from the upper berth.

"So, what's so important that you had to wake me up?"

"I was sleeping in the driver's seat when I thought I heard something."

Oh boy. Was he still drunk?

"And?"

"And then I thought I saw something."

"Did you actually see or hear anything?"

"Maybe."

"Please don't tell me it was a bigfoot."

Dave shook his head. "That's crazy. No, I think it was people."

I wanted to wring his neck. "We're in a town, and people live in the town. Nothing crazy about that."

"I'm not stupid. The thing is, they were running around. It looked like they were hiding around the RV."

I ran my fingers through my scalp, scratching at phantom itches. "Maybe they were just curious. We are new in town."

"You saw that lot. We're just one of hundreds of others. What's the big deal?"

"That's my question. Can I go back to sleep now?"

"Just, just come outside and check things out with me."

"It's freezing out there. It'll wake me up so much, I won't be able to sleep again."

Dave picked my coat off the floor. "Please. Humor me." I knew there was no arguing with him. He would just wear me down.

I reluctantly shrugged into my coat. "After today, you're going on the wagon with Mindy."

"That's cool by me. We should bring Miracle, too."

"Sure. The more the merrier." I hoped he heard the sarcasm in my voice.

Dave went to the front of the RV and grabbed one of the guns and stuffed it in his pocket.

"Why are you bringing a gun?"

"Why are people hiding outside?"

"To make sure the crazy Puerto Rican doesn't shoot them. Come on, man. Leave that here. You'll just end up shooting yourself if you get spooked. Or worse, me."

Mindy mumbled something in her sleep.

"Too bad Mindy had her setback tonight," Dave said. "I'd feel safer with her."

"You wake me up and now you insult me. Thanks, pal."

"Don't mention it." He clipped the leash on Miracle's collar. As soon as he opened the door, Miracle took off. Dave tried to get a grip on the leash, but he ended up being dragged outside and falling to his knees. The leash slipped out of his hand, and Miracle went barking into the night.

I stood on the top step of the RV giving him a round of golf applause. "Brilliant. Now that was worth being woken up."

The knees of Dave's jeans were soaked and filthy. He didn't even bother trying to wipe them off.

I was about to tell him that Aja and Mindy were going to kill him for losing the husky when we heard something snap in the dark to our right. Both our heads spun in the direction of the noise.

"That could be one of them," Dave said close to my ear.

"Or some of the local wildlife that won't be happy to see us is more likely."

"Let's check it out."

"If you say so."

We crept around the RV. I prayed we weren't about to cross paths with an angry moose. I'd once heard that they were worse than a bear. I didn't want to find out.

We turned the corner and found...nothing.

"Look." Dave pointed at our feet. The moon was nearly full and gave us plenty of light to see by. There was a hodgepodge of footprints in the mud.

"And?"

"Someone was here."

"Yeah, lots of people. Those footprints don't necessarily mean they were made just now. Half of them are probably ours."

I saw the lights on in a few houses across Dark Lake. The way the light flickered, I knew it had to be candlelight.

"Can we please go back inside? I'm freezing my sack off out here."

Dave looked around, squinting into the darkness. After a while, he said, "Fine. You think Miracle will be smart enough to come back?"

"Just fry up some Spam, and he'll come running. Come on."

As I turned to head back into the RV, I bumped chests with someone hard enough to knock the wind out of my sails. We both hit the deck.

There was a clank of metal.

I turned my head and saw a knife on the ground. Not just a knife. It was a blade big enough to saw a horse in half.

"Holy shit. Holy shit," Dave said, helping me up.

The man on the ground was middle-aged, with salt and pepper hair.

But that wasn't what had gotten Dave's attention.

His mask had slipped off his face.

Where his nose had been was a grisly chasm. I just knew vile fluids lurked in there.

He jumped to his feet and pulled his mask down. He didn't bother going for his knife. The man turned to run, but Dave wrapped him in a bear hug. He kicked at Dave's shins. I grabbed him by the collar of his coat.

"What were you planning to do with that knife?"

"Let me go."

Dave squeezed harder and the man let out a heavy puff of air.

"What's going on here?"

"I don't have to tell you nothing."

"I kinda think you do."

All of a sudden, he stopped struggling. His gaze was fixed on something over my shoulder.

Dave's eyes went wide.

I spun around.

We were surrounded. A dozen men, all wearing masks, crept out of the shadows.

"You want to stay?" the man said.

"What?"

"Do you want to stay?"

I didn't know what to say.

"Because if you do, we have to make sure you're not a liability to our town."

With that, the men lowered their masks.

None of them had noses.

I clenched my ass cheeks to make sure I didn't crap myself.

"Now, you can join us, or you can feed us," the man said.

Dave dropped him and backed into me. "What the fuck, man?"

The man adjusted his mask. "You can have a good life here. But there are rules. And something very important that needs to be taken care of first. Or you can help us get through the winter."

The circle of men took a step toward us.

"You're not suggesting that..." I couldn't bring myself to say it.

"I ain't suggesting anything. I'm *telling* you."

Moonlight glinted off the blades brandished by the other men.

Holy Jesus, they were going to cut our noses off!

Dave shouted, "Back off, weirdos!"

He had the gun in his hand, swinging it around so each of them had it pointed at their head for a moment. It would have been threatening if his hand didn't shake as if he were standing in the middle of a packed jumping castle.

"You're not gonna shoot anyone, boy," a noseless man with flowing gray hair said. He thankfully raised his mask, which was a sign for the others to do as well.

"Keep thinking that," Dave said.

I felt defenseless and useless. I had no weapon unless you counted a bladder that screamed for release.

"So, what's it gonna be?" The carving gang took another step forward.

"Wait!" I held up my hands. "Look, we'll just get back in our RV and leave right now."

"That wasn't one of your options. Either way, you came, and you're gonna help us."

I swallowed hard and balled my fists. Not that I thought I could punch my way out of this. Not a chance. Knives trumped fists every time.

They came closer.

Dave cocked the hammer back on the pistol.

I know I couldn't see their mouths, but I had a gut feeling they smiled at that.

Tugging Dave's arm, I backed up, my left hand feeling out for the cold steel of the RV. If we could just get inside before these lunatics jumped us. Even though my nose could be the cause of my demise, I was in no mind to part with it.

The man Dave had temporarily caught made a whistling sound and cocked his head. "Get 'em!"

Two men large enough to qualify for their own zip codes darted forward. The gun slipped out of Dave's hand. It went off the second it hit the ground. A man standing in the background grabbed his leg and fell.

It was a good shot, but at the wrong person.

One of the mountain men barreled into me. He grabbed my shoulder and threw me against the RV with an iron arm bar.

Dave yelped and was pinned against the RV just inches away from me.

"You don't have to do this!" I shouted. "You don't have to do this!"

I may as well have been speaking another language. The man's coal-black eyes stared into me, and through me, as he brought up his blade. I tried to pry his arm off my chest and neck. It was like attempting to move a freight train off a track.

It may not have been manly, but I screamed at a pitch that was just above a dog whistle.

The man hoisted me up until my feet didn't touch the

ground. The tip of the knife was as cold as well water where it touched the skin on the side of my nose.

This is it, I thought. This madman is going to slice my nose right off my face and I'm going to feel every horrid moment of pain. And if I survive the shock and blood loss, I'll have to look at that noseless face in the mirror every day. For the first time since SHC started, I wished for a sneeze.

"You made your decision yet?" the man said from somewhere to my right. "One slice or many?"

Bile clawed up from my belly.

"Why can't you just let us go?"

"Because I said so. And because I don't like your attitude, I'll make the decision for you. Finish them."

MAYHEM

I couldn't remember the last time I'd been to church, but suddenly, I could recall all my prayers. I rolled them off, one by one, in my head.

Scrunching my eyes closed, I waited for the inevitable.

That's when I heard the growling.

There was a commotion behind the man who was about to butcher me. He turned his head, and the weight lifted from my chest. My feet hit the ground. The man flailed in a ragged circle.

Miracle had latched onto his crotch. In his pain and panic, the man had forgotten he had a hefty blade in his hand.

Then he stopped and calmly looked down at the snarling husky.

"Miracle, let him go!"

The man swung the knife down, aiming for Miracle's head.

A shot rang out and the man's head exploded in a crimson mist.

I looked over and saw Clint leaning out of the window. Smoke billowed from the barrel of the rifle in his hands.

The next shot caught the man holding Dave in the side. He folded into himself, and Dave skipped away.

"Get in, get in!" Clint shouted.

I grabbed Miracle by the collar and headed for the door. Mindy and Aja stood in the doorway, each with a gun. I pushed Miracle in first, and then Dave. I leaped into the RV and Mindy slammed the door.

Dave and I lay on the floor, trying to catch our breath.

"What the hell went on out there?" Mindy said.

Miracle licked my face. I patted the dog, my savior, and got to my feet. "The masks...no noses...wanted to cut ours off...or use us for...for food."

Aja crushed me in an embrace. "Are you serious?"

"Unfortunately...yes."

"Are they out of their minds?" Mindy said. I could smell the booze seeping from her pores.

Dave was up and said, "Pretty much. I've heard of biting off your nose to spite your face, but this is ridiculous."

"They're gone," Clint announced. "Took off like scared little jackrabbits."

I had a feeling they wouldn't be gone long. It's not as if they would be worried about us going to any authority. Five happy meals had landed in their laps, and they weren't going to let it just drive off into the sunset.

"We have to get out of here...now," I said, scrambling to get into the driver's seat.

Aja followed close behind. "Why did they want to cut your noses off?"

"I think they believe it keeps them from sneezing."

"Idiots," Mindy said. "Looks like Canadians are just as dumb as Americans. Wonder where they got that load of shit from. I was in AA with a guy who had lost his nose from snorting heroin. He used to sneeze all right, and it was disaster. His hanky looked like a Jackson Pollock painting every time."

I fumbled for the keys. "Well, it's what they believe. Oh, and if we don't want our noses cut off, they're going to eat us."

"Oh, Jesus," Aja said, plopping into the passenger seat.

"Don't sit there," I said. "You're too exposed. Clint, you mind coming up here?"

"On it."

"Aja, you and Mindy just stay away from any windows."

Aja nodded. There were tears in her eyes.

"No way am I hiding away like some damsel in distress," Mindy said. Her words had a slight slur. She racked the shotgun and positioned herself by the side window. If she was still drunk, I didn't think we could count on her crack-shot skills.

Aja went to the dinette area. I keyed the ignition and tapped the gas pedal.

"Dave, you keep an eye on the back window in the bedroom."

"Yeah."

"Take one of my guns," Clint said, motioning with his head to the dinette table where there were a couple of handguns. "And try not to drop it."

"If you hadn't just saved my life, I'd say something you wouldn't like."

Clint smiled. "We all know you love me."

I put the RV in drive, scanning the darkness. I kept waiting for someone to jump out. The tricky part now was making the U-turn to get us pointed to the road out of Consumption.

The RV's shocks took a hell of a hit as I plowed over a rise on the side of the road and took out a mailbox.

My hands were numb, making it difficult to put the RV in reverse. I hit the gas too hard and backed the RV into a tree. Dave yelled, "Dude!"

I got it in drive, spun the wheel, and barely kept to the road.

It sounded like rocks were being thrown at the RV. Aja cried out in pain. I spun around and saw her gripping her upper arm.

"What happened?"

She pulled her hand away, and it was covered with blood. "I think I've been shot!"

A bullet came through the windshield. Clint and I were peppered with pebbles of safety glass. I ducked, which made it impossible to drive, but I tried anyway.

"You motherfuckers!" Mindy screeched. She used the butt of

the shotgun to blow out the window and started shooting. Clint fired randomly out our non-existent windshield. Between the two guns, I felt I was rapidly going deaf.

I dared to poke my head up, hoping that our return fire would give us a small window to make a getaway.

I was wrong.

It sounded like the Fourth of July out there.

The wheel spun out of my hands and the RV veered into a ditch.

"What happened?" Dave called out.

"I don't know!" The engine sputtered but didn't die. I tried to excavate us from the ditch, but it only seemed to make things worse.

Clint opened his door and leaned outside. "Tires are blown out. Well, shit."

His skin was waxen in the moonlight and covered in sweat. He was hurting big time, but even he knew it was all hands on deck if we were going to get out of this alive.

The shooting outside had stopped.

Why?

As if reading my mind, Clint said, "Well, they did what they wanted to do. They crippled us. Now that can come get us without filling us with too much lead that'll just ruin the meat."

I was as revolted as I was angry.

Keeping low, I crawled over to Aja. "Let me see."

"I'm fine."

"Just let me see."

Her flesh was scorched a bit and when I wiped away the blood with my sleeve, I saw a perfectly straight line. The bullet had grazed her, thank God. I wrapped a dishtowel around it.

"I need you to stay on the floor in case they start shooting again."

"Not a chance." Aja scooped one of the handguns off the table.

It didn't seem the time or place to argue with her.

"Clint, Dave, you see anyone?"

"Nope," Clint said.

"I do. The gray-haired guy from before. He's walking real slow toward us. Wait, he's not alone. There are a couple of others, but they're keeping to the side of the road."

"Do they have guns?" I asked.

"Um, no. Just those knives. Oh, and the gray-haired dude also has a machete."

"We could just pick them off."

Clint tried to wiggle out of the front of the RV. His mind was set, but his body was fighting him. "You two will just end up shooting some trees."

Mindy opened one of the kitchen drawers and tossed things aside. When she found the pepper, she smiled and stuffed it in her pocket. "Time to show them the error in their ways."

"Do not go out there," I said.

"Watch. This'll be fun."

There was a maniacal gleam in her eyes that at that moment I knew didn't come from the moonshine. She was truly happy to go out into certain death and take on the three men approaching the RV. I didn't know whether to be scared for her or the men.

Mindy slipped out of the window.

"What the hell does she think she's doing?" Aja said.

"Let's just watch her back and try not to shoot her," I said.

I peered out of the broken side window and watched Mindy walk toward the men like she didn't have a care in the world. When they were half a dozen feet apart from one another, she stopped.

"You can count me in," she said.

The men gathered together and stared at her.

"I didn't come all this way just to end up on your dinner table. I came here to live and if you have the answer to SHC, I'm game."

I couldn't believe what I was seeing and hearing. Mindy was, in every sense of the word, certifiable.

"What about the others?"

She shrugged. "I don't really care. I'm here to take care of me. So, do we do it here or somewhere else?"

The men leaned close to one another and conferred with whispers. Then gray hair said, "You can come with us, but if you try anything, we'll cut you down. You hear?"

"Yeah, I hear."

"John will take you to my cabin."

The man on gray hair's right reached out for Mindy's arm. She let him take her, and he roughly pulled her to him. I saw her put her hand in her pocket. Like lightning, she lifted the guy's mask and tossed pepper in his face. He dropped his knife and swatted at his face.

Gray hair and the other man spun toward Mindy with their blades ready to do some dirty work.

But Mindy was faster.

She managed to get pepper under their masks and dropped and rolled, just missing getting sliced as they lashed out with their knives.

The first man stopped flailing, reared back and sneezed. A fountain of goop fell out from under his mask.

The flames started at his neck and raced up his head. He started running, looking for all the world like a matchstick in motion.

Seconds later, the fire took the rest of him.

His buddies looked on in horror.

"You guys really are morons," Mindy said just before she sprinted back to the RV. I helped pull her in through the window.

Gray hair sneezed next. His ankles flared up, and the fire danced up his legs and torso. He batted the flames as best he could, but that only set his hands and arms on fire. His screams ripped through the night and he fell face forward.

The last one took off for the trees, but not before he let out a whopper of a sneeze. We watched the mobile bonfire zigzag through the trees, lighting them up as he brushed past them.

A bullet pinged off the RV. We all ducked, waiting for it to ricochet throughout the interior.

Clint fired some shots at random.

Things got very quiet after that. All we heard was the crackling of the fire as it consumed more trees.

I couldn't help feeling that the townspeople of Consumption were gathering somewhere out there so they could make a final push and make us pay for what Mindy had done. Not to say I wasn't grateful for her actions. Those guys more than deserved it.

"What do you think's going on out there?" Dave said.

"Y'all remember the Alamo?" Clint said.

"Not funny," I said.

"Wasn't meant to be."

The forest fire reflected in Mindy's eyes. "I say we light the whole town up. I mean, if this is the best the universe can do, saving these psycho asshats from the end of the world, we need to correct some mistakes."

"I just want to get the hell out of here," Dave said.

"Well, it's not going to happen with this RV," I said. "She's toast."

"How's your arm," Mindy asked Aja.

"It burns, but it could be a lot worse."

We waited some more in the dark and quiet. Eventually, all heads turned to me.

"What?"

Aja took my hand. "Honey, I think we all know we're not getting out of this. The odds are overwhelmingly against us. The question is, do we wait here and let them kill us, or do we go out in a blaze of glory?"

"You can't ask me to decide how we die."

"I'm with you no matter what," Aja said.

"Me, too," Dave said.

"I choose blaze of glory," Mindy said. "But I'm with you."

"I still have plenty of bullets," Clint said.

Tom Petty once sang that the waiting was the hardest part. I never knew how right he was until that moment.

"I say blaze of glory."

There were no fist bumps or shouts of joy. We were, after all, choosing a kind of suicide. Although Mindy looked pleased.

"So, how do we go about this?"

"Hey," Dave said. "Someone's coming."

We scooted to the back window.

Fred and Wilma slowly approached the RV with their hands up.

"It's a trap," Clint said.

"Hard to argue against that," Dave said.

I agreed. I also knew that the couple wasn't alone. Out where we couldn't see were plenty of other Consumptionites. So much for taking it to them.

"I'm going to go out there and talk to them."

"Are you crazy? No way," Aja said, gripping my arm.

"If they wanted us dead, we'd be dead by now. Right?"

No one disagreed with me.

"You all stay in here and watch my back."

"I'm going with you," Dave and Aja said at the same time.

"Not a chance in hell. I'll feel better knowing you're in here. And I need all the mental strength I can get."

"Take the shotgun with you," Clint said.

I waved him off.

I took a few deep, shuddering breaths and put my hand on the door handle. "I'll be back before you know it."

Aja smiled at me with trembling lips. Dave looked terrified.

I opened the door and stepped outside where Fred and Wilma waited for me.

MEET THE FLINTSTONES

"Hello, Sam," Fred said.

"Seems kind of late for pleasantries," I replied, shocked that my voice wasn't quivering.

He put his hands on his hips and shook his head. "I guess you're right." He gazed at the two burning bodies behind me. "You do that to Gus and Phil?"

"Yes, but only because they were coming to kill us."

My knees felt like rubber. I'd never been so scared in my entire life. I could feel Aja, Dave, Mindy, and Clint watching me from the RV. I had no idea where this conversation was going, but I'd committed to finding out.

"Fair. Fair," Fred said.

"You must have known that a person can still sneeze without a nose," I said. "So why disfigure everyone?"

"We're very aware that you can still sneeze," Wilma said. "But we've learned it happens a lot less without your nose. We don't know why. Ever since we started doing it, things have been good. Oh, we have a few people go up every now and then, but not many."

I felt my testicles tighten up, knowing what I was going to

say next. "And all the people who've come here? How many have agreed to your little plastic surgery?"

Fred looked over at the lot of cars. "A few."

"And the rest, you eat?"

Fred and Wilma looked uncomfortable, choosing to let my question hang in the air.

"We traveled all this way to find a group of cannibals who think they can stave off SHC by altering their faces. Excuse me for saying, fuck you! If this is all that's left of humanity, SHC did the planet a favor."

Fred made an odd tsking sound behind his mask. "You privileged White people only want to do what it takes as long as it's easy."

I narrowed my eyes at him. "This privileged White person survived when millions didn't. And I didn't do it the easy way. So you can take your racist bullcrap and shove it so deep up your ass, you choke on it."

Wilma said, "We came here to tell you that you can go."

"Very convenient when you've destroyed our mode of transportation."

Fred swept a hand at the lot of cars. "Take your pick."

I stared at them a moment, trying to decide what the catch could be. "Why are you doing this now?"

"Because you're dangerous people," Fred said. "Bad luck. Keeping you here any longer will bring worse things upon our town."

"Well, you're right about that." I thought about what would happen if we set Mindy loose.

"Just go," Wilma said. "And don't ever come back."

Like we would ever consider such a thing?

"It's not like there's anyone to tell," Fred said.

I didn't trust them. I had no reason to. But this could be our only chance to escape this hell.

"One last question," I said.

"Sure."

"How many people are actually living here?"

Fred tucked his thumbs under his belt. "That's for us to know and you to never find out."

That's when I knew the population of Consumption was far less than any of us could have imagined. In fact, I'd bet there were more dead bodies waiting to be served up for dinner than townies.

And Fred said *we* were dangerous.

"If we go now, I need you to back off."

"It's cold out here. Wilma and I have better things to do. Just don't take long. The keys are in all of the vehicles."

Glass broke behind the husband and wife. A ball of flame erupted, revealing several men dodging to get out of the way. Shots rang out and one of the men dropped to the ground.

More glass broke and fire was everywhere. I turned around and saw Mindy, Aja, and Dave hurling Molotov cocktails in every direction.

"Best way to get back on the wagon is to dispose of the temptation!" Mindy said when she caught my eye.

When the Molotov cocktails exploded, Clint took people down the second they were exposed. He may have been an asshole, but he was like Wild Bill Hickok with that rifle.

I looked back at Fred and Wilma.

Wilma had a gun in her hand, and it was pointed at me.

I backed away, tripped and fell on my back.

A red dot bloomed on her forehead. Her eyes rolled up and she collapsed.

Fred looked at me with murderous fury in his eyes. A second later, he had no eyes.

Bullets zipped through the air, coming and going from every direction.

"Get in here!" Aja shouted.

I crawled on my belly to the RV faster than if I'd run. Dave and Aja pulled me inside.

Mindy slapped a gun in my hand. "You did say blaze of glory."

She crammed a canvas bag full of my books. She then doused it with lighter fluid. "Just keep shooting."

With that, she jumped out of the RV, lit the bag and went running toward Fred and Wilma's house, hurtling over their bodies. Aja, Dave, and I joined Clint, pulling our triggers as fast as we could. Mindy got to the porch, kicked the door open and tossed the bag inside. She dropped out of sight. I saw flames flickering inside the house.

"Mindy's down!" Clint shouted.

No!

"We can't leave her out there," Dave said.

I agreed, but I couldn't see what else we could do. It was a war zone out there and we were lacking in the Kevlar vest department.

"Hold your fire," Clint said.

The RV took on more bullets. A mirror shattered and glass fell in Aja's hair.

Clint put a finger to his lips. He then started wailing, "Christ almighty! Oh, Jesus, talk to me, Sam! Aja! Dave! I'll kill those bastards for what they did to you!"

He looked out the window.

"Here they come. Aja, where'd you put the gas cans?"

"By the sofa."

I looked at Aja. "When did you get the gas cans?"

"Right when Mindy threw the first Molotov cocktail."

"You could have gotten yourself killed."

I realized instantly how dumb that sounded.

Keeping his voice low, Clint said, "We got nine, no, ten little." He turned to Dave. "First Nations approaching. Who has the best arm?"

Aja and Dave turned to me. It was true, I had pitched in high school.

"When I say now, you throw that gas can right at them, okay?"

I went over and got the gas can. It was the metal one we'd

picked up somewhere in Illinois. It held five gallons of gas and it was filed to the brim.

We held our breath and waited.

Clint held up a finger.

He sliced the air with that finger and said, "Now!"

I opened the door and tossed the gas can as hard as I could. It landed right at the feet of the men and women.

Clint fired and the gas can exploded. Gas and fire went everywhere, setting all but two of them ablaze.

I heard a crazed screech and watched as Mindy ran from Fred and Wilma's burning house. She had the shotgun and used it to fill the two survivors with buckshot. That wasn't enough, because she tossed pepper in their faces and stood over them as they sneezed, just barely getting away from the burst of flame.

She walked casually to the RV.

"Get down," I told her.

She ignored me.

"I think we're good. For now," she said. Her right thigh was bleeding. Her jeans were shredded with holes. She saw me looking at her leg. "Yeah, I gotta put some pressure on that. Plenty of time to inspect the damage later. Did he say the keys are in those cars?"

"Yeah."

"Good. Maybe you can help Clint get out of the RV while I grab that Jeep over there."

I felt like I was in a daze. When I went back inside, I said to Clint, "Mindy wants you."

"I figured. Time to finish the job. Give me a hand, will ya?"

It took us fifteen minutes to load Clint into the Jeep, along with the spare ammo and five more Molotov cocktails.

"We should be back by dawn," Mindy said.

"What are you planning on doing?"

"Making Consumption, like everything else, a thing of the past. We can't let anyone else fall into their trap," Clint said, and for a moment, I admired the guy.

They drove off. I watched the Jeep until the red rear lights faded from view. Then we heard a gunshot. And a new fire broke out.

It went on like that for hours.

Dave, Aja and I took that time to find another RV. This one was slightly larger, and I considered how much gas it would consume. We didn't want to waste all night moving cars around to get to the optimal RV.

We parked it next to our old RV and got busy transferring all of our stuff. By the time we were done, we were beyond exhausted.

Black Lake had changed color, reflecting the orange fires that had broken out all along its rim. Mindy and Clint had both gone off the deep end and were doing what was left of the world a favor. I found my old morality lacking in light of this new era in humanity.

Dave fell asleep sitting in a folding chair as we waited for Clint and Mindy to return.

I got the first aid kit and treated Aja's wound. It had already stopped bleeding.

Even though it was cold, I sat in the grass and looked out over the lake. Aja lay on my lap and I wrapped my arms around her. We didn't speak for a long, long while.

As the sky started to turn pink, I said to her, "Why did you do it?"

She positioned herself so our noses practically touched. "Because I thought you'd fallen out of love with me."

"What? That's crazy."

"No, it's not. I think you forget how much you were working. All those long nights at the office. You missed our anniversary."

"I did?"

"Yes. You did. I'd made this amazing dinner, and you called and said you had to work late. Honestly, I thought you might be having an affair. I got scared. And I was lonely. It was only ever talking. And it was stupid. I'm so sorry. Things just got out of hand and...and..."

I shushed her by kissing her lips. When I pulled away, we were both crying.

"Why didn't you tell me all of this?"

She wiped the tears with her sleeve. "Why didn't you ask me?"

I kissed her again and held her tight.

"We're a real couple of idiots," I said.

"Yep. It's why we belong together."

True to their word, Clint and Mindy came back at dawn looking utterly bushed. I didn't know whether to be frightened of them or proud. We settled for tired head nods and woke up Dave so we could all crash in the RV.

"Pretty sure we got them all," Mindy said. "Along with where they kept the bodies. Be very glad you didn't see that."

We couldn't have kept guard or driven away if we tried. Aja slept in my arms and all was quiet in our new RV.

ALL'S WELL...
SIX MONTHS LATER

"Come on. Are you ready yet?"

I knocked on the door and heard rustling inside.

"Perfection takes time. I'll be there in a minute."

I cracked a beer and looked around our double wide. Everything was in order. I had a stack of books by my reading chair and Aja had her easel, paints, and canvasses next to it. This was smaller than our apartment in New Jersey, but we felt like king and queen of our castle.

The smell of barbecue wafted through the open window.

There was a knock on our door.

I opened it and startled Dave. "You know how it is."

Dave cracked a smile. "Tell me about it. Laurel is doing something with her hair that's taking forever."

His double wide was right next to ours, on the western edge of the rodeo parking lot. He'd met Laurel, a total Kentucky babe, not long after we returned to the one true spot of humanity after the disaster in Consumption. They'd been inseparable ever since, which was good, considering she was carrying his baby.

"How about a beer?" I said.

"How about that's a question that never needs to be asked?"

I tossed him a semi-cold PBR, and we touched cans. We

were both wearing cowboy hats and boots that made my feet cramp, but it was a necessity on rodeo night. I didn't want to look like a tourist.

"How's this?"

Aja appeared dressed in denim with white fringes on her sleeves. She had a white cowboy hat that barely contained the bulk of her dreads.

"You look beautiful," I said, truly meaning it.

"If you told this sister that she'd be playing cowgirl a year ago, I would have told you to stop smoking crack."

"There's a lot of things that would not have made sense a year ago," Dave said.

"True, that," Aja said. "Now where's my beer?"

I got her a PBR, and we went outside. The sun was out with just a few thin clouds in a bluer-than-blue sky. Cars pulled into the lot. We got a kick out of watching the expressions of the first-timers.

Miracle came bounding out of the woods that bordered the parking lot. He'd grown a lot and liked to spend his days running around. He came to me, and I gave him a good petting. No one who lived around us told us to put him on a leash. Miracle was a people lover and great with kids. He was our dog, but if you asked the folks living out here, they would say he was everyone's dog.

"Sorry it took so long," Laurel said. She was starting to show, and Dave rushed to help her down the stairs. "This guy. He treats me like I'm made of glass."

"You have the future of humanity in there," he said, rubbing her stomach.

"And God help us all," I said.

Laurel wasn't the only person who was pregnant. Almost three-quarters of the childbearing women in our makeshift rodeo town were pregnant.

It was a very good thing, because the world needed babies, especially now that we hadn't seen someone go combustible in months. Maybe those spores had worn themselves out. No one was sure. We weren't ready to take the plugs out of our noses yet.

Yet.

Aja and I had talked about starting our own family. It was definitely on the table. We just needed to know this was going to be a safe world for our boy or girl. Time would tell.

"You all ready?" I said.

The couples linked arms, and we walked to the front gate. Tomorrow, we'd be the ones working inside. Everyone took turns, gladly. The day after, Dave and I would go out hunting for supplies while Aja and Laurel worked on the huge garden behind the stables.

Once inside, we went straight for the pulled pork stand.

"I have four specials set aside just for you."

Mindy beamed at us, pulling out four sandwiches wrapped in tinfoil.

"Thanks, Mindy," I said.

"Don't mention it."

Mindy lived in an RV on the other side of the lot. We'd been through hell together and would always be friends. But we realized some separation was best. We'd seen her very dark side, and she knew that we knew what she could do when push came to shove. It was always there—would probably always be there. No matter, she was a part of us.

"I saw I'm going on the run with you tomorrow," Mindy said.

"Yep. Keep an eye out for..."

"Books. Yeah, I know. I'll come by and sit with you later."

We took our seats. A family of four sat beside us, taking the rodeo in with mute fascination. They looked like they'd been on the road a long while and were in desperate need of a good time.

"Welcome to the rodeo at the end of the world!"

The announcer's voice boomed through the overhead speakers.

That announcer was Clint. He'd wanted to try his hand at

roping and riding, but his body hadn't healed well enough for the rough stuff. So, twice a week, he manned the mic up in the observation booth.

Unlike Mindy, Clint would never be a part of us, but he was a part of our history. We were all cordial when we saw one another, and he had come over for a drink a few times. Our trip to Canada had changed him, for sure. And that was a good thing. I don't know if he remembered what he called Aja. He hadn't apologized, and we'd just let it go.

I slipped my arm around Aja and looked over at Dave and Laurel, so happy to have found one another.

"I love you, babe," I said to Aja.

She tilted her head up and kissed me, which wasn't easy because we were both wearing cowboy hats.

"I love you, too."

We settled back and watched the rodeo with our friends, appreciative of this very special place, this very special moment, gifted to us.

A LOOK AT

WE ARE ALWAYS WATCHING

They See Everything. They Know Everything. And They Never Stop Watching...

When West Ridley's family is forced to abandon New York for a crumbling Pennsylvania farmhouse, he expects misery—but nothing could prepare him for the horrors lurking within its walls. His father's worsening illness, his mother's exhaustion, and his grandfather's drunken ramblings paint a bleak picture of their new reality. But it's the eerie warnings and shadowed figures that truly unnerve him.

The words "WE SEE YOU" scrawled on his ceiling are just the beginning. Something sinister roams the halls at night, whispering through the silence, watching from the darkness. Grandpa Abraham swears the house is haunted. But the truth is far worse than restless spirits—because in this house, secrets are buried deep, and the Guardians will do anything to keep them hidden.

As the Ridleys unravel the mysteries of their new home, one thing becomes chillingly clear: escape is impossible. No matter where they go, the watchers remain.

AVAILABLE NOW

ABOUT THE AUTHOR

Hunter Shea is a lifelong horror hound and writer of over thirty books of monstrous mayhem, ghostly frights and newfound terrors. Some of his bestselling books include the critically acclaimed *Creature, They Rise,* and *The Montauk Monster*, the nostalgic *Money Back Guaranteed* series, and *Jessica Backman's Death in the Afterlife* trilogy. His books have been found in the International Cryptozoology Museum and his face on the Discovery Channel where he talks about, well, monsters.

He can be heard and seen on his two long-running podcasts, "Final Guys and Monster Men", both informed and humorous explorations of the best – and worst – movies, books, and interviews with some of the hottest writers, directors and producers in modern horror, tales of true life hauntings, UFOs and more.

He's a father, husband, cat owner (aren't all horror writers?), pizza and beer lover, battle-scarred Mets fan, and leader of Hunter's Hellions, the greatest gaggle of lunatics on the planet. He lived with the ghost of a young boy for 25 years, was part of a mass UFO sighting in the 80s, and is still waiting for Bigfoot to show up in his yard.

www.huntershea.com